PRAY
FOR US
SINNERS

ALSO BY PATRICK TAYLOR

Only Wounded
Pray for Us Sinners
Now and in the Hour of Our Death

An Irish Country Doctor
An Irish Country Village
An Irish Country Christmas
An Irish Country Girl
An Irish Country Courtship
A Dublin Student Doctor
An Irish Country Wedding
Fingal O'Reilly, Irish Doctor
The Wily O'Reilly: Irish Country Stories
"Home Is the Sailor" (e-original)

PRAY
FOR US
SINNERS

PATRICK TAYLOR

A TOM DOHERTY ASSOCIATES BOOK  NEW YORK

PRAY FOR US SINNERS

Copyright © 2000 by Ballybucklebo Stories Corp.

Previously published by Insomniac Press in 2000.

A Forge Book
Published by Tom Doherty Associates, LLC
175 Fifth Avenue
New York, NY 10010

www.tor-forge.com

Forge® is a registered trademark of Tom Doherty Associates, LLC.

The Library of Congress has cataloged the hardcover edition as follows:

Taylor, Patrick, 1941–
    Pray for us sinners / Patrick Taylor.—1st ed.
        p. cm.
    "A Tom Doherty Associates Book."
    ISBN 978-0-7653-3518-0 (hardcover)
    ISBN 978-1-4668-2142-2 (e-book)
1. Irish Republican Army—Fiction. 2. Political violence—Northern Ireland—
History—20th century—Fiction. 3. Ordnance disposal units—Great Britain—Fiction.
4. British—Northern Ireland—Fiction. 5. Northern Ireland—History—1969–1994—
Fiction. I. Title.
    PR9199.3.T36 P7 2013
    813'.54—dc23

                                                                    2013006315

ISBN 978-0-7653-3521-0 (trade paperback)

Forge books may be purchased for educational, business, or promotional use. For information on bulk purchases, please contact Macmillan Corporate and Premium Sales
Department at 1-800-221-7945, extension 5442, or write specialmarkets@macmillan.com.

First Forge Edition: June 2013
First Trade Paperback Edition: June 2014

Printed in the United States of America

0 9 8 7 6 5 4 3 2 1

To all those who strive for peace in Ireland

ACKNOWLEDGMENTS

This book, which is my first novel, was nurtured by some very special people who helped me bring it to its first publication:

Carolyn Bateman
Janet Irving
Nick Bantock
Salman Nensi
Adrienne Weiss

Since the publication of the Irish Country series some remarkable others have been instrumental in the reissue of *Pray for Us Sinners*:

Tom Doherty
Natalia Aponte
Paul Stevens
Alexis Saarela
Jamie Broadhurst
Fleur Matthewson

To you all I tender my most sincere thanks.

PRAY
FOR US
SINNERS

ONE

"Bugger it."

Lieutenant Richardson raised his head above the top of a low wall. Droplets trickling down his Plexiglas visor distorted his view: narrow, red-brick terrace houses, two boarded up; black stains above the sashes where fires had raged after a riot; a green, white, and gold tricolour hanging limply from a distant upper-storey window, proclaiming the Republican sympathies of the neighbourhood. The deserted neighbourhood.

The citizens had been cleared out because, at the far end of the street, to Richardson's left, an ordinary-looking blue van was parked. Ordinary-looking, and potentially deadly as a grumbling volcano. He could see rust streaks showing through the blue paint. The bomb-disposal robot, known as the wheelbarrow, stood stolidly beside the van.

The voice of the sergeant ammunition technician came over the headphones, tinny, distorted. "It's the wheelbarrow, sir. Sodding thing's stuck."

"Hang on, Sergeant." Lieutenant Marcus Richardson, ammunition technical officer, 321 Explosive Ordnance Disposal Company, Royal Army Ordnance Corps, started to sweat despite the chill drizzle that misted his helmet's visor and darkened the fabric of his massive EOD "heavy" suit. His chest armour rose in a hollow arc in front of his mouth and was reinforced by a thicker pad over his lower abdomen and genitals. Behind, a wide tail hung down below the backs of his knees. He crouched, bulky as the Michelin Man.

"What seems to be the trouble, Sergeant?" As Lieutenant Richardson spoke calmly into the built-in microphone, he peered at the wheelbarrow. He could make out its caterpillar tracks and the hydraulic rams that drove its articulated arm. The dark green of the cylinders contrasted sharply with the silver of the pistons. Nothing moved. At the end of the arm, the lock-busting gun dangled over the van's roof, lifeless as a corpse on a gibbet. The angled arm and pig stick reminded him of a vulture, waiting silently.

"Dunno, sir. The bloody thing won't respond to command signals. The jack-in-the-box is on the fritz, too. No picture. The transmitter's at it again."

Damnation. Without the closed-circuit TV system—"the jack-in-the-box"—he might as well be blind. This was the second time this week that the thing had malfunctioned. If Sergeant Crowley, fifteen years with the unit, couldn't sort out the problem, no one could—certainly not a twenty-six-year-old lieutenant on his first tour in Northern Ireland. A lieutenant who, as ATO in charge of an inoperative robot, would have to go in, find the bomb, and render it harmless.

"You sure, Sergeant?"

"Sorry, sir. Dead as a bloody dodo."

Marcus felt the familiar tingle of anticipation. His friends at Sandhurst had thought him crazy choosing the Ordnance Corps. He'd never bothered to explain why. He was an Ulsterman, a Protestant Ulsterman, and if the other officer-cadets wanted to think that by going into bomb disposal he was fighting some kind of holy war against the Provisional IRA, that was fine by him. Marcus Richardson, living proof of the Sandhurst motto "Serve to Lead." He grinned.

And yet there was some truth in the supposition. As far as he was concerned, no one who had grown up in Ulster and had any feeling for the place could fail to hate what the Republican hard men had done in the last five years. But the truth was—and he knew it—his real interest was unexploded bombs. Like the one in the blue van.

"Right, Sergeant. Pull the men back." Marcus turned and waited as the other members of the team climbed into the modified Mercedes-Benz they used for transport in urban areas. He caught a glimpse of the unit's Felix the Cat sticker on the driver's door. Felix the cartoon cat, impervious to all explosions, was the good-luck charm of the EOD company and so well known in the Security Forces that his name was the team's radio call sign.

Ammunition technical officers were not as invincible as Felix, Marcus told himself, but he was unconcerned. All his life he'd needed to face danger and had found opportunities racing sailing dinghies, playing rugby football, boxing. Challenging himself, pushing himself.

"Oookay," he whispered to himself. The Mercedes was gone, safely round the corner. He was on his own. He turned and sat, encumbered by the body armour, back to the wall. So much for the marvels of technology. The inoperative wheelbarrow was as much use as a heap of scrap metal. He was going to have to deal with the device with his bare hands because no armoured gloves allowed the necessary sensitivity of touch.

His hands were chilled. He rubbed them together to restore the circulation. What would it be this time? The Provisional IRA, at that time, favoured a homemade mixture of amyl nitrate fertilizer and sump oil for making car bombs. It was fairly stable stuff. Might be dynamite. Not too bad, unless it was poor quality and had sweated nitroglycerine.

He kept on rubbing his hands. Numb fingers would be no help finding and removing the detonator. Mercury tilt switches were tricky. The slightest movement would make the liquid metal run the length of the glass tube and complete the circuit. Then it was stand in line for wings, angels, for the use of. Two. He grimaced. Timers were worse, particularly if you failed to beat the clock. He took comfort from the thought that, if there was a timer, it would probably have been set some time ahead. The van had been stopped by a routine patrol and its three occupants arrested. A piece of good luck for the army. It wasn't likely that this street had been the target, and Provo bomb-transportation squads had enough sense to give themselves time to deliver their devices and make their getaway.

"How's it going, sir?" The tinny voice again.

"Bugger off, Sergeant. I need to concentrate."

"Sorry, sir."

Marcus checked his equipment. Simple stuff. A couple of screwdrivers, nonconducting pliers, wire cutters, insulating tape. He taped the tools to the cuffs of the EOD suit and hauled himself to his knees, forcing the stiff Kevlar leggings—strapped on behind like wicketkeeper's pads—to bend. Finally, he pivoted to face the wall.

He raised his head, protected in its futuristic carapace, above the concrete coping stones. He noticed soft moss growing where the mortar between had cracked. He could see the rows of stunted terrace houses, their slate roofs glistening in what was now a steady downpour. Belfast in February—not quite April in Paris.

The rusty blue van and the wheelbarrow waited for him, silent partners in their own *danse macabre*. He would have to cover fifty yards of empty street, already well inside the four hundred metres that an ATO was meant to stay back. Whatever genius had come up with that recommendation had never been in Belfast's warren of slums.

Marcus hoped that the security cordon had done a thorough job clearing the surrounding area—the Provos often posted a marksman. Bomb-disposal units were vulnerable to sniper attacks—indeed, Headquarters believed that using car bombs as bait had become a new Provisional IRA tactic. Two-step operation, the CO had called it. Blow up a bunch of civilians and then snipe at the troops when they move in.

Yes, you had to be daft to do this. Utterly bloody daft. Here he was, risking life and limb from gunfire, if not the bomb itself—like poor old Alan Cowan, who had lost both arms and been blinded when trying to neutralize a similar device.

Marcus ran his tongue over dry lips, listened to the faint, rapid hammering of his bloodstream, and held both hands in front of his visor, fingers splayed. Steady as a pair of rocks. Unprotected, very soft rocks.

He pushed himself back from the wall, feeling the bricks rough and damp beneath his palms. The screwdriver taped to his left cuff caught on a piece of masonry and, stripped from its securing band, clattered to the pavement. He froze.

Unexpected noises were always troubling. Very troubling. Craning to see over his chinpiece, he dipped his head beneath the top of the wall.

The blinding intensity of the light was followed immediately by the roar of the explosion. The shock wave shattered the wall and bowled Marcus over onto the pavement, where he lay on his back like a stranded beetle while soft rain and hard bricks fell on his chest. The thumping of masonry against armour gave counterpoint to the chime and tinkle of glass tumbling from shattered windows.

He had just enough time to mutter "shit" before a concrete coping stone slammed into his helmet and turned out the lights.

TWO

"High explosive. TNT. 1 pound net. Dangerous." Dangerous, for Christ's sake. Trust the Brits to state the obvious. Davy McCutcheon stacked the blocks, aligned the two on the top tier with the two beneath, and reached for a roll of insulating tape.

That morning he'd gone with his friend Jimmy Ferguson to collect the trinitrotoluene from the 2nd Battalion, Provisional IRA, explosives dump in a safe house in the Falls Road district of Belfast. The blocks were the right size to conceal in wrapping paper that had originally covered pounds of butter. Davy had snugged his packages in a basket with the rest of his groceries and walked past two British patrols on the way home to his terrace house on Conway Street.

The soldiers hadn't bothered him. He was used to troops on the streets of Belfast. The buggers had been there since 1969, with their patrols and their Saracens and their sangars—fortified observation posts.

Davy had more to worry about than squaddies clumping about in their great boots, clutching their self-loading rifles. The four pieces of TNT had been the last in the cache, and there'd been no bloody detonators. He'd had to send Jimmy off to find another source. Where the hell was Jimmy, anyway?

Davy wound three turns of tape round the middle of the charges. Damn it, he'd forgotten the scissors. He exhaled through his moustache, set the roll aside, rose, and limped to a dresser.

He glanced at a framed photograph hanging beside the hutch. A woman, midthirties, smiling in the sun, dark hair tossed by the wind. He smiled. *Aye, Fiona girl,* he thought, *you're as lovely now as when that snap was taken on Tyrella Strand.* She'd not be home until tonight, and he'd have the job finished by then, which was just as well. Fiona did not approve of his involvement with the Provos. She hadn't said so for a while, but he knew.

He opened a drawer. Where the hell were the bloody scissors? He grunted as he found them, picked them out, slammed the drawer, and stood, frowning at another faded snap on the wall. A man and woman posing stiffly in their Sunday suits.

He'd inherited Ma's eyes, though he couldn't see the blue of them in the old black-and-white. He wished he could remember her better. Remember more than her eyes. Remember more than the day Da had come home grim-faced to tell a six-year-old Davy that Ma had run off with a bus conductor and she'd never be coming home anymore.

He'd kept that picture because it was the only one of Da. Davy had been able to see how lost Da had been without her. He'd tried to be both mother and father, and he'd given Davy more than the sharp McCutcheon nose, heavy-boned height, broad shoulders, and powerful hands. He'd given Davy "the Cause" to believe in. "The Cause." The reunification of Northern Ireland with the other twenty-six counties and the banishment of the British after eight hundred years of occupation.

Davy rubbed the web of his hand over his moustache. It was grey now, like his thinning hair. He'd had dark hair in 1952, when Da had enrolled him in the IRA as a lad of sixteen. No mucking about in the Fianna Éireann, the boys' unit. He and his friend Jimmy Ferguson had gone straight in to join the men. Men who had fought with Michael Collins against the English in the Tan War of 1920. Men who had assassinated Collins in August 1922, at Béal na Bláth in County Cork, after he had signed the bloody treaty that let England keep the six counties of Ulster. Men whom young Davy had worshipped as heroes.

A brave while ago, Davy thought, as he moved to the table, sat, and sliced through the tape. He bent to the work he'd done many times before. How many? He'd lost count. He snipped the last piece of tape and admired his handiwork. Four pounds of TNT neatly prepared. It was his job. His job for the Cause.

The Cause in the early days had been all he'd lived for. It was like having the family he had never known. The lads met clandestinely to train at night in the remote Antrim Hills. The senior men indoctrinated the recruits with tales of heroes and rebels, the litany of Ireland's glorious failures as her sons had tried to throw off the invaders' yoke.

Faith in their forefathers was all very well—he'd believed Da, believed that one day Ireland would be free, drunk it all in as a novitiate priest takes his Communion wine, swallowing with it his faith in the life everlasting—but back then the IRA had known it would take more than faith to remove the British. So Davy learned to drill, to use the old Lee-Enfield .303 bolt-action rifles, Webley revolvers, and Thompson guns. Like cowboys and Indians for grown-ups. And he'd learned to make bombs. For the Cause.

When his training was over there had been an induction ceremony. The new recruits had been called to attention: "*Paraid, aire!*" Davy, the tallest, stood on the right of the front rank. They raised their hands and repeated the IRA declaration—the organization had abandoned oaths in the twenties because the Catholic Church objected to oath-bound secret societies. "I, David O'Flahertie McCutcheon, promise that I will promote the objects of the *Óglaigh na hÉirann* to the best of my knowledge and ability and that I will obey all orders and regulations issued to me by the army authorities and by my superior officers."

Davy was still "obeying all orders." He rubbed his left thigh, the ache there, the reminder.

"Damn your pride, Da," he said to the photograph. Davy thought of the months he'd spent in 1957, lying cold and lousy in a dugout in the Sperrin Mountains. One of his own bombs had detonated prematurely. Its blast had done for Davy's left thigh, killed four other men—and Da. Davy'd lain there helpless, nursed by Jimmy Ferguson until his shattered leg had healed.

Davy mumbled as he stared at his dead father's photograph. "It wasn't cowboys and Indians after that. Not for me."

He turned back to his work. The TNT would be no bloody use until he'd built the timer. He lifted a piece of insulated wire and stripped four inches of the plastic covering away. The copper shone where the scissors' blade had scratched. He bound the metal filaments around one jaw of a wooden clothes peg and repeated the operation with a second piece of wire, wrapping it round the other jaw. The two bare pieces of metal would touch when the peg closed. He produced a packet of cigarettes and took one out. He'd have liked to have one, but—he looked at the TNT and smiled.

Davy bored a hole below the filter, threaded a piece of fine string through the hole, and bound the cigarette to the legs of the clothes peg.

The tension forced the jaws apart. When lit, the cigarette would smoulder at a speed of one inch every seven minutes. It would take fifteen minutes for the string to be burnt through and the jaws to snap shut, completing the circuit. Simple but effective. At least it would be when Jimmy Ferguson arrived.

Davy tied the final knot and glanced through the window. Rain fell, splashing off the pane and making grubby streaks in the patina of industrial soot that clung to the glass. He looked at his watch. Jimmy was nearly an hour late. Had something happened to him? Christ, Davy had enough to worry about without having to be concerned about Jim Ferguson.

Sometimes Davy worried whether he still believed in the Cause. Killing soldiers was all right, but too many civilians had died for Davy's liking. They didn't attack civilians back in the fifties. Davy still wondered why his commanders called that campaign off in 1962. That was when he'd quit the IRA, what was now called the Official IRA. And he'd kept out until 1970.

When the riots started in Belfast in 1969, the remnants of the old IRA had been useless. Made no attempt to protect the Catholic ghettoes from the Protestant mobs. The folks who lived on the Falls said IRA stood for "I Ran Away." Davy hadn't even bothered to reenlist, not until a splinter group formed in 1970—a group that promised to go after the Brits, a group that called itself the Provisional IRA. They were the hardest of the hard men and they were not going to let anything stand in the way of their goal: Brits out and a united Ireland. And that was what Davy was after, had always been after.

Freedom, he thought, was a long time coming, and was union with the Republic any closer? He nodded, reassuring himself. Aye, it was, and he believed all right, *had* to believe, that Ireland would be free. He owed it to Da and he owed it to himself to struggle on, until one day— one day soon—the British would be gone.

Davy heard the knock, rose, and limped to the front door.

"Where the fuck have you been?" Davy spat his words.

"I'm sorry, Davy." Jimmy Ferguson's thin weasel's head twitched sharply to one side.

"Come in." Davy stumped back to the kitchen, leaving Jimmy to close the door and follow.

Davy sat, watching Ferguson shrug out of his wet raincoat and drape it over the back of a chair.

"Look, Davy"—Jimmy's chin twitched forward and to one side—"I'm sorry. The fucking Falls is crawling with Brits. I'd to take the long way round."

Davy grunted. He hated the way his friend shot his jaw.

"Don't be mad, Davy."

"Sit down."

Jimmy sat. He reached into an inside pocket of his raincoat. "I got them. Here." He handed over a wooden box.

"Jesus, Jimmy, don't tell me you let a few Brits scare you."

Jimmy's jaw twitched again. "Come on, Davy. You know bloody well three of the First Battalion lads was lifted in that van two days ago." He pushed the box closer to Davy. "I couldn't have brought these if the peelers got me."

"You think someone touted?"

Jimmy kept his gaze on the tabletop.

"Jimmy, who the hell's going to grass on us? Only Second Battalion command knows about us."

Davy could hear the scuffling of Jimmy's feet on the kitchen floor. He'd no time for Jimmy's worries. "Christ Almighty, the CO's closer than fleas on a dog. What did he promise us when we joined up?"

Jimmy shot his jaw.

"Jimmy, what did Sean Conlon say?"

"That he'd keep me and you out of the regular units. We'd just have to make bombs and deliver them to safe houses."

"Right. Sure you know we never get to meet the other men in the battalion. Who the hell could grass on us, Jim?"

Jimmy looked up. "Nobody, I suppose."

"You suppose? Jimmy, you and me's a cell. Like your man Che Guevara's lot." Davy saw Jimmy's lower lip trembling. Davy leaned forward and, like a lover in a candlelit restaurant, laid one palm over the smaller man's hand. "We're safe as houses." Davy's blue eyes held Jimmy's pale ones.

"I suppose you're right."

"Aye. Now. What's in here?" Davy lifted the box and opened the lid. He smiled. "You done good."

Jimmy laughed, a high-pitched hee-hee. "I had to go away the hell up to Ardoyne, so I had, and get them from one of First Battalion's lads."

Davy took a thin copper cylinder from the box. "Number sixes?"

"Aye, and I've tested them on my galvanometer. They're all dead-on."

"Great." Davy pulled the TNT toward him. He slipped the cap into the cap well in the end of one of the blocks. "Just the job." He removed the cap. "I'll need to wire the circuit." He untwisted the lead wires that came from the end of the cap.

Jimmy watched. "It's a bugger about the three lads in the van."

"Aye." Davy joined one wire from the cap to one from the clothes peg. He used a Western Union pigtail splice.

"Still," Jimmy babbled on, "the timer worked, and the paper said the blast got another army bomb-disposal man. That's two more of the buggers. Some Brit called Cowan got took out a few weeks back."

Davy finished connecting three double-A batteries to the lead from the other side of the timer. "Good. Them's our proper targets, Jim. Soldiers and policemen."

Jimmy narrowed his eyes. "Bothers you, doesn't it, Davy, hitting civilians?"

"Aye. I don't like it. Not one bit." He busied himself covering the bare end of the cap's other lead wire with a piece of insulating tape. "That's her now. The Active Service boys can finish wiring the detonator."

Jimmy said, "Four pounds'll make a hell of a bang. I wonder what it's for this time?"

"What the eye doesn't see, the heart doesn't grieve over. If it's not the Security Forces, I don't want to know." Davy rose, closed the lid of the blasting-cap box. "I'll hang on to these," he said, as he carried the box to a cupboard and opened the door. He removed a bag of cat food and buried the box among the pellets. "It'll be all right in McCusker's grub 'til I get back."

"Do you want me to come with you?" Jimmy asked, eyes averted.

"Not at all. It's not too far to the drop."

"Thanks, Davy."

"Never worry," Davy said as he reached for a small sack of spuds he wanted to use to camouflage the devices. "Away on home to the missus. I'll take a wander past the nice British soldier lads that's here to protect us poor Catholics."

THREE

The "nice British soldier lads" Davy was avoiding were men of 39 Infantry Brigade, which had Belfast as its tactical area of responsibility. The troops were headquartered at Thiepval Barracks on the outskirts of Lisburn.

A small, dapper man, forty-four, clean-shaven, the whites of his eyes yellowed from too much quinacrine, sat in a cramped office in one of the Thiepval's old red-brick buildings. He was worried—very worried— and as he always did when preoccupied, he toyed with a heavy signet ring. He examined the crest, a winged dagger beneath which the motto read, "Who Dares Wins." It was the badge of 22 Regiment of the Special Air Service. The SAS.

He'd fought with them in Malaya as an intelligence and counter-insurgency officer. He'd done a second tour in Indonesia, and there, despite the quinacrine, he had contracted malaria.

In 1967 he'd been invalided out of the army, the only life he had ever wanted. He spent the intervening years living with his widowed sister Emily in the village of Bourn, outside Cambridge. Now he had a second chance, but if he didn't produce soon that chance would be gone.

Major John Smith ran his hands over his khaki pants. God, but it was good to be back in uniform. He knew very well he would not have been, but for that phone call last month from Sir Charles Featherstone, Permanent Under-Secretary to the Northern Ireland Office.

Major Smith closed his eyes and recalled the interview in Whitehall with Sir Charles, the promise—and the threat.

Sir Charles had not risen from his desk.

"Have a seat, Smith."

He sat down. Why did he feel like a fourth-former summoned to the headmaster's study? John Smith studied the man behind the desk.

Sir Charles Featherstone was in his early sixties, thick grey hair swept straight back, bushed at the temples. His nose was sharp and stood stiffly between deep-set blue eyes. His neck was wattled above his starched white collar. His Guards tie showed above the waistcoat of his pinstriped suit. He spoke. "I'll come straight to the point, Smith."

"Sir."

"I got your name from Frank Kitson. You met him in Malaya, I believe."

"Brigadier Kitson? Yes, sir."

"He says you can be trusted." Sir Charles cocked his head to one side. "Would you like to come back in?"

John Smith looked directly into Sir Charles's eyes. "Very much, sir. Very much indeed."

"You'd not mind working in Ulster?"

"No, sir."

Sir Charles steepled his fingers. "I need a man I can rely on. An operative working for me and no one else."

John Smith sensed that he should remain silent.

"The intelligence situation's a shambles over there. Do you know how many units are operating?"

"No, sir."

"Neither do we. Not completely. MI6 have pulled out. MI5—'BOX,' as they call themselves, because their address is a post office box—are still there. The Royal Ulster Constabulary have two departments. C is the ordinary criminal investigation bunch. E is their special branch, antiterrorist. And the civilian organizations are child's play compared to the military."

Sir Charles cracked his knuckles. "Thirty-nine Brigade ran a mob called the Military Reconnaissance Force. Your old chum Kitson's idea. Total flop. We packed them up this year. Replaced them with 14 Intelligence Company.

"As if all that wasn't bad enough, every regular army unit's intelligence officer fancies himself to be Le Carré's Smiley and runs his own agents. There might even be some of your old mob, the SAS, on the ground—not officially, of course."

Sir Charles harrumphed. "The Royal Ulster Constabulary won't talk to the army. The army mistrusts the RUC. Even in the army, the daft buggers don't talk to each other. It's a bloody shambles."

Sir Charles scowled. John Smith saw the look and felt his muscles tighten as the civil servant continued. "And the Provos have begun to mount operations that could only have worked with the benefit of top-grade inside information. There's a mole somewhere in our organization, in Thirty-nine Brigade's tactical area of operations. Your job will be to find him—and gut him."

"Yes, sir." John Smith sat rigidly at attention.

"Remember, Smith, you'll be working for me. No one else."

"Will I be working completely alone, sir?"

"No. The CO of Fourteen Intelligence, Harry Swanson, has been briefed about you. He's a Yorkshireman. Calls a spade a bloody shovel. He'll provide you with logistic backup, documents, access to files."

"Sir."

"There's another chappie who'll be able to help you. He's sound as a bell. Completely familiar with the local situation. Ulsterman. Catholic. Name's Eric Gillespie. Detective Superintendent in the special branch. Give you the local colour." Sir Charles's smile was a puckered rictus. "I'm told it's predominantly orange and green."

Smith mentally filed the name. "I thought the army didn't trust the RUC, sir."

"Quite right. Neither do I. They're the only ones who can mingle with the hoi polloi. Lots of chances to pass on information. The bloke you're after might very well be a copper."

"But, Sir Charles, if there could be a leak in the police, why use their people?"

Sir Charles grimaced. "You'll need one local contact. It's like a foreign country over there. Gillespie's been screened, he's a closemouthed bugger, and the previous chief constable, Sir Graham Shillington, is an old friend of mine. He vouched for Gillespie. He's one of their best operatives. Trust him, to a point, but don't tell him what you're really after. He may be on our side, but he *is* still RUC, and he's a Catholic."

Smith heard the distaste in Sir Charles's voice as he continued: "And so's the new chief constable—chap called Jamie Flanagan. If he found out through Gillespie that you suspected the coppers—what do our American cousins say?—the shit would hit the fan."

"What do I tell him I'm supposed to be doing, sir?"

Sir Charles laughed. "You're just another independent intelligence operative. After PIRA names, ammo dumps, the usual stuff."

"Oh."

"Now get over to NI. They're expecting you at Lisburn Headquarters. The brigadier's been told to leave you alone to get on with your job. You'll have access to all the files." He opened a drawer and produced two envelopes. "My minister's written this." He handed one to Smith. "It instructs the powers that be over there to 'render all assistance.'"

John Smith rose and accepted the letter, tucking it unopened into his inside jacket pocket.

Sir Charles's blue eyes fixed on Smith. "Take all the time you need over there—within reason. Report directly to me." He held out the other envelope. "Your commission's in here, Major."

Major Smith accepted the buff envelope. Major Smith. He'd hardly dared hope for so much. He heard Sir Charles say, "Pull this off and you'll have the deepest gratitude of Her Majesty's Government. Shouldn't be surprised if I couldn't find a half-colonel's job for you. Of course, if you don't . . ."

Major Smith looked through his window at the razor-wire fence surrounding Thiepval. Pull this off? He was no closer to finding the Provos' inside man than he had been when he'd arrived here a month ago. How much longer would Sir Charles wait?

There was a way to try to find the leak. It would be risky and depended on identifying the right man for the job. The major'd considered the possibility for the last two weeks, working with a reluctant Harry Swanson of 14 Intel. Harry had not wrapped up his opinion. Putting a British officer on the street to infiltrate the upper echelons of the PIRA would be hazardous in the extreme. Having registered his protest, Swanson had started running background checks.

The ringing phone interrupted the major's train of thought. He lifted the receiver. "Hello?"

"John?"

"Yes, Harry?"

"Can you come over to Palace Barracks in Holywood the day after tomorrow, the sixth? I think I've found the chap you're looking for."

"What?" Major Smith's fingers tightened round the receiver. "Who?"

FOUR

At 8:14 A.M., as weak sunlight struggled through the lattices of the coal cranes on the banks of the Lagan and glinted from heaps of anthracite piled on the pier, a nondescript-looking man left from a Ford Prefect parked on Queen's Quay. He carried a small suitcase.

He dodged through the traffic and crossed the road to the entrance of the Belfast and County Down Railway station. A throng of commuters spilled from the portals. The man jostled his way through the crowd into the concourse. Before him a diesel locomotive stood at one platform, its engine leaking greasy exhaust fumes. He glanced up to the overhead clock. 8:17. The next commuter train would arrive at the other platform in fifteen minutes.

He looked to his right. The porter's trolley was where he had been told to expect it, parked beside a glass-fronted news kiosk. The kiosk was close to the gate where the passengers would be funneled to hand over their tickets to the ticket collector. There was no sign of the porter whose job it had been to leave the loaded trolley where it stood. The man smiled. The porter was a sensible lad. Very sensible.

He slipped his case among the heap of luggage on the trolley, bent, opened the leather lid, straightened, and lit a smoke. He touched the lit cigarette to another bound to a clothes peg inside the case, closed the lid, shoved the case farther onto the trolley, and walked away.

The ticket collector lounged, back turned to his gate, staring along the track.

At 8:35, as the last of the disembarking passengers queued at the ticket gate and those who had been allowed through hurried past the kiosk, the smouldering tobacco burnt through the string, and the words

"High explosive. TNT. 1 pound net. Dangerous" vanished in an inferno of incandescent gas.

The ticket collector was impaled on the broken cast-iron railings of his gate. He died before the jagged metal ripped into his chest. A woman was thrown ten feet to slam into a child pushing a toy pram. The girl's arm was snapped by the force of the collision. She screamed for her mother, who struggled to stand, trying to ignore the grating agony in her three crushed ribs.

The blast shattered the kiosk's panes and hurled glass shards while torn pieces of magazines and comics—*Tit-Bits* and *Woman's Own*, *Beano* and *Dandy*—fluttered in the smoke-filled air like demented confetti.

And through the acrid fumes, the shrieks and curses, pleas and groans joined in a lamentation for a province torn by hatred and sectarian war.

The Ford Prefect crossed the Upper Falls Road. Its passenger grunted, "Let me off here." Carrying no suitcase this time, he walked easily, making his way to a street corner.

Another man leaned against a wall. He carried his right shoulder higher than his left, and the left lens of his National Health Service granny glasses had been replaced by an opaque leather disc. He barely nodded as the pedestrian passed, rubbed his finger under his nose, and strolled on.

Brendan McGuinness smiled. The mission he had planned had gone off smoothly. He poked a finger under his leather patch and scratched the eye socket.

McGuinness turned and opened a front door. He let himself into a dingy hall. He shrugged. Four pounds of TNT was small beans. One of Sean Conlon's men's efforts. Sean was fiercely protective of his men. McGuinness, commanding officer of 1st Battalion, had little time for Conlon and his 2nd Battalion volunteers. The man had a soft spot. That hadn't mattered yet, as long as they could work together smoothly on brigade staff, Sean as adjutant and Brendan as information officer. This morning's job showed how they could cooperate. First Battalion had needed a bomb delivered to a safe house, and Sean had readily agreed to have his 2nd Battalion bomb makers provide it.

McGuinness entered a scruffy kitchen. He ignored the pile of pots and a grease-encrusted frying pan lying in a pool of scummy water in the kitchen sink.

It was one thing for Sean Conlon to help out with little things, but had he the stomach for something really big? He'd better have.

McGuinness's job as Brigade IO was to sift incoming information and use it to ensure the security of the Provo volunteers, as well as to advise on the targets that, when hit, would do the most damage to the British. His old sources were working well but hadn't been used to plan today's raid. This morning's attack had been little more than a diversion. Random violence on a small scale kept the Security Forces on the hop and could not compromise his most precious intelligence asset.

His eye socket itched, and he poked his finger in to scratch. He might have only one good eye, but his ears were everywhere in Belfast and, after the move out of these cruddy quarters in a couple of weeks, he'd have one more listening device. One that neither Sean nor even the Officer Commanding the Belfast Brigade would be privy to.

It would need to be tested. It would take a week or two to have the system set up, but once it was working the Belfast Provos could truly inflict major damage on the Brits. And when the PIRA began to go for major targets, ones that would carry serious risks to attack—like the one his prime source had suggested as a real possibility—then they'd see what Sean Conlon was made of.

FIVE

"You'll be leaving this evening, Lieutenant Richardson." The young nurse smoothed the corner of the sheet. "Now take these." She handed him two painkillers.

He popped the pills in his mouth and washed them down with a mouthful of water.

"Good." She took the glass.

Marcus wished he could hear her more clearly, but the ringing in his ears refused to go away. He felt so bloody useless, stiff and bruised and stuck in hospital. At least no bones were broken. Nothing smashed up inside. But it had been a near thing on Saturday. Too bloody near. It had given him pause for thought. He shuddered but said, "Thank you."

She smiled, showing small white teeth. She had great eyes, green and feline. He wondered what she'd look like in civvies—or, better still, out of them. She must have noticed his look. Pink spread from beneath her white starched collar. "Now settle down," she said, but the smile remained. "The ambulance will be here soon."

Her name tag said J. LOUGHRIDGE. She hadn't been on duty when he'd regained consciousness yesterday. They'd told him he'd been out for twenty-four hours. The blast had been on Saturday, so this must be Tuesday.

He tried to give her his best smile, but the split in his lower lip stung. "Ouch!" He dabbed at his mouth with the tips of the fingers of his right hand. "What's the J for?"

"None of your business." She turned to leave, then paused and looked at him, the smile returning. "If you must know, it's Jennifer."

He lay watching the play of the late afternoon sunlight streaming through the window behind his bed, the rays brightening the sway of the curtains where she had passed. Jennifer. Jennifer Loughridge. An Antrim girl by her accent. He had a vivid image of the way her eyes had shone when they'd reflected the light as she turned. He'd seen the same green fire in an emerald, deep and lustrous.

He might be able to play the wounded hero with Nurse Loughridge. It had been too long since he'd enjoyed the company of a woman. He really would have to try to get Nurse Loughridge's phone number.

He was not given the chance. The door opened, a Royal Army Medical Corps corporal appeared, helped Marcus into a wheelchair, and trundled him to where an RAMC ambulance waited. The inside was spartan and smelled of disinfectant. He heard the engine start, and the vehicle lurched as it was driven away. Marcus settled back on the stretcher, assuming he was being taken back to Thiepval, where his unit was stationed.

The trip was taking much longer than it should. He sat up, swung his legs to the floor, and, bracing himself against the swaying of the vehicle, peered out the small window in one rear door. They were not on the M1 motorway, the shortest route to Lisburn. He could see the gantries of Harland and Wolff's shipyard, the great yellow bulk of the Goliath crane over the dry dock and the Cave Hill behind. This was the Bangor to Belfast road.

The vehicle made a right turn and stopped. Marcus heard the driver speaking. The ambulance moved forward. They had passed two sentry posts flanking gates in a high fence of Dannert wire. There was only one army base on the Bangor to Belfast Road. Palace Barracks, outside Holywood. Now why the hell had the driver brought him here? Marcus did not know how fast Harry Swanson had moved to effect this transfer.

The doors were opened and the orderly helped Marcus into the chair and pushed him toward the front door of a small, red-brick, semi-detached house, one of a row of identical semis that in times of peace had been married quarters.

The orderly opened the door. Marcus had had enough of wheelchairs. He stood, ignoring the look of horror on the man's face. "At ease, Corporal," he said and stepped into a narrow hall. He ignored the NCO's expostulations but followed his instructions to go upstairs. By the time Marcus had come into a bedroom he was happy enough to climb into the bed.

He tried to ask why he was here, but the corporal brushed the question aside with a regulation "Sorry, sir, dunno," tucked Marcus in, and left the room.

The chintz curtains were drawn and the room was beginning to darken. It must be six or seven o'clock. He hadn't realized how tired he was. The aftereffects of the blast, he supposed. He might as well have a zizz and wait until he awoke to wonder about what he was doing here.

SIX

Marcus was not pleased. No one had come near him since yesterday morning. And the corporal who'd brought Marcus here had told him he was not to leave the house. It was bloody well about time . . .

Someone opened the front door. Marcus swiveled in his chair. A short man stood in the kitchen. His tweed suit could not disguise his military bearing, and his sallow cheeks and yellow sclera suggested that he had seen service in the tropics.

The stranger's voice was clipped, English public school. "Major Smith. Brigade HQ." He did not offer to shake hands.

"Sir." Marcus rose.

The major moved to the table. "Feeling better?" The question sounded like an order.

"Yes, sir." Marcus trotted out the Ordnance Corps' one-liner—"Shaken but Not Stirred"—as he looked at the major's eyes. A line from the song "Mr. Bojangles" came to mind—he had the eyes of age.

"MO says you'll need a few weeks to recover."

"Yes, sir." That was fine by Marcus.

The major sat, steepled his fingers, and began tapping the tips rapidly together. "Sit down, boy."

Marcus sat.

The major raised an eyebrow. "Mind if I ask you a few questions?"

"No, sir. Not if I can ask you why I'm here."

"Later, laddie. Now let's see if I've got this right: born in Bangor; Protestant; father a professor of agriculture, presently on sabbatical at Texas A&M in America, mother with him; no brothers or sisters. You finished your B.Sc. on an army scholarship, Sandhurst, RAOC, blues for rugby and sailing, half blue for boxing, out of the country for the last five years"—he paused. "So far so good?"

"Yes, sir."

"How do you think we're doing in this nasty little war here?" The major's eyes were hard as obsidian.

Marcus pointed at the bruise on his left cheek. "Someone makes pretty effective bombs."

"True. That's where you can help. We'd like to know who that 'someone' is."

This was moving too quickly. What was the major suggesting? The man's eyes reminded Marcus of a python he had once seen in the Belfast zoo.

The major said, quickly and in a very matter-of-fact voice, "You know a lot about explosives. You can mix with any crowd of locals and speak 'Northern Ireland.'" The small man's Oxbridge speech slipped and the last two words came out harsh and grating, a fair imitation of the accent of the Falls—"Norn Irn."

Marcus felt slightly ashamed. He was embarrassed by his brogue and had adopted a veneer of vocal gentility. The army called it the chameleon effect.

"Oh yes," said the major. He reached into the inside pocket of his jacket and chucked a piece of paper onto the table. "You might like to read this press release."

Marcus took the paper. "Lieutenant Marcus Richardson, RAOC, died last night of injuries—"

"What?" Marcus heard his own voice over the buzzing inside his head. His words were shrill. "What?"

"Deepest condolences, old boy. Your father seems to have taken the news like a man. I gather your mother was a bit upset. She'll be over for the funeral in a couple of days. Army expense, naturally. Seems your old man can't make it."

"What the hell is going on?" There was an edge to Marcus's voice. He remembered how surprised he had been when his father refused to go to Grandfather's funeral.

The major coughed. Politely. "I'll put that down to shock—this time."

"Shit."

"That's 'shit, sir.'" The major's eyes slitted.

Marcus controlled himself—just—as his training reasserted itself.

The major softened his approach. "Look, I need your help. It's bloody nearly impossible to find out what's happening on the street. Someone like you could fit in."

"Fit in, sir?"

"It just seemed that if you were dead, you'd be less likely to be recognized by someone who knew you when you were still, if you'll forgive the pun, living in Ulster."

It was too much for Marcus to digest. Undercover work, Dad not coming to bury his only son.

The major interrupted his thoughts. "If you resurfaced on the street in Belfast you could keep your eyes and ears open, pick up a few odds and ends."

"I don't know anything about intelligence work."

"Neither do some of the charlies who are out there at the moment. That's part of our problem." The major smiled. "We'd soon teach you, though."

SEVEN

The garage was attached to a white stucco-covered house. It was dark in the garage, and there was the smell of mouse droppings. A man worked by the light of a pencil torch gripped in his teeth. He sat beside a Volkswagen, his head bent over a flat metal box. He ignored the four sticks of dynamite nestled inside the container, the mercury tilt switch, the batteries and the tangle of wires.

He concentrated on the face of a kitchen timer, the kind that rings. This one wouldn't. The bell had been removed by one of Brendan McGuinness's armourers. A metal plate, wired to the batteries inside the box, had been fixed at the zero mark at the top of the dial. A second piece of tin, connected to the detonator, had been screwed to the arm that marked elapsed time. It would strike the plate at zero when the desired number of hours had elapsed.

The man shone the thin beam on his wrist. His watch said 4:11. He redirected the light to the timer and twisted the timing arm to 5:00. He could hardly hear the faint ticking. The circuit would be quite safe until five hours had passed; then, with the plates touching, it would be armed. Still, nothing would happen, not until the mercury in the tilt switch was disturbed and the liquid metal touched both ends of the glass tube.

Inside the stuccoed house, Bertie Dunne sat up in bed. He was racked with a fit of coughing. He felt like shit. He'd been hot as hell when he'd gone to bed and for the last hour had shivered and sweated. He was getting the flu. His wife stirred beside him.

"You all right, Bertie?"

"Aye." He'd not let some stupid infection get in the way of his plans for tomorrow.

"You're burning up."

"I'm rightly."

"You are not." She switched on the light. "Look at you. Your face is red as a beetroot."

"I'm all right, woman." He watched her get out of bed. "Where are you off to?"

"I'm for getting you some Panadol, so I am."

Bertie coughed. "Would you get me a hanky while you're at it?"

"Aye."

He watched her go, saw the light go on in the landing.

The man in the garage froze when the upstairs lights of the house shone in through his window. He had just finished fixing the magnets on the metal tin to the chassis of the Volkswagen. He switched off his torch and peered out. No lights on downstairs. Someone was probably taking a piss. He hoped that Mr. Bertie-fucking-Dunne's prostate was acting up. Serve the Orange cunt right.

Dunne was a tough bastard, usually moved about only in his own Loyalist neighbourhood, rarely traveled without several bodyguards, had a track record of reprisal killings of Catholics, and was a prime target on Brendan McGuinness's list.

The lights went out. Only the one in the back of the house—the man guessed it was probably the bedroom—stayed on. He relit his torch and examined the concrete floor. There were scuffs in the dust where he had slid under the car. He shone the beam around the walls, careful not to let it shine through the window. He found what he was looking for, lifted a broom, and with a few careless strokes covered the evidence of his movements.

He replaced the broom, doused his light, and let himself out the side door. He glanced up. The upstairs window was still lit. Piss on you and your prostate, Dunne, he thought as he slipped into the shadows, heading for the car that was waiting for him at the end of the road.

.   .   .

Bertie Dunne pulled the bedclothes round him. The Panadol had better work. He had to meet tomorrow morning with two other senior Ulster Volunteer Force men. Their Protestant paramilitary group had big plans for a couple of Fenian bastards from Ardoyne. If the Security Forces couldn't get the Republican shites off the streets, the UVF could. Permanently.

"Better now, dear?" his wife asked.

"Aye. Thanks. Put out the light." He heard her sniff. There was no fooling Jeannie. She knew he was feeling lousy. The light went off.

"We'll see how you are in the morning," she said. "If you're no better, you're not going out."

"I am so."

"Don't be stupid. You'll kill yourself."

He was worse in the morning. She took his temperature, tutting as she read the thermometer. "A hundred and three. You're for staying in bed."

"What time is it?"

"After eight."

"Look. Call you Willie Mills. Tell him I'm sick."

"Never mind Willie. I'm calling the doctor."

"Jesus, would you call them both?"

"All right."

His head felt like someone was using a rivet gun on it. He rolled over. Maybe Willie would see to the Fenians. He heard her in the hall below.

"Thank you, Doctor. I'll nip round and pick up the prescription." Jeannie Dunne hung up. The kitchen clock said nine. As she shrugged into her raincoat, she called upstairs. "I'm just going out for a wee minute."

She opened the garage doors. Normally she would have walked—it wasn't far—but not in this downpour. She'd take the Volkswagen.

To stop terrorists throwing petrol bombs from speeding cars, the Security Forces had built huge speed bumps in front of police stations. As Jeannie's car climbed over the mound of solid tarmac, the mercury flowed. The detonator fired. The blast from four sticks of dynamite vapourized the metal box and melted a four-foot hole in the speed bump. The force smashed through the front axle and hurled the Volkswagen onto its roof.

Jeannie Dunne lost both legs and needed sixteen plastic procedures to give her something that resembled a face.

EIGHT

The split on Marcus Richardson's lip had almost healed and his bruises were fading. His hearing had cleared yesterday, and for that he was thankful. Life had been confusing enough since the major had dropped his bombshell two days ago, without the added complication of feeling as though his head was full of bees.

Still, a few aches and pains were a lot better than being the real subject of the major's press release. That had been a hell of a thing to do, to tell a man he was dead.

At first, Marcus had reacted with disbelief, anger, and sullen hostility. And not all of his anger was directed at the major. To hell with Dad's stiff upper lip, his dislike of funerals. The man only had one son. Could he not have bent enough to come and see him given a decent burial? It was, Marcus realized, an opportunity not given to many, to see how one's nearest and dearest would react to the news of one's demise. Dad's response had been predictable, but still it stung.

Marcus had been given no chance to dwell on his hurt. Major Smith had continued to expound on the security situation, obviously unconcerned about Marcus's feelings.

It seemed that the British were lagging badly on the intelligence front. Major Smith had explained that indeed the increased army presence in the Republican neighbourhoods was inhibiting the terrorists' ability to function, to move about freely. He had described how static observation posts and electronic surveillance devices helped, but although the Royal Ulster Constabulary had their touts, the RUC were unwilling to share their informers' intelligence with the army. "And," he had said, emphasizing the point, "the best information always comes from HUMINT. Human intelligence. Men and women on the street." He'd paused and frowned. "That's the problem."

He had explained how the Republican ghettoes were tribal and any strangers were suspect, especially if they didn't talk like the locals. That was where Marcus's ability to speak Norn Irn would be priceless.

Not even allowing the younger man to ask any questions, Smith ploughed on: "You've been out of the country for five years and you're an explosives expert. They can always use experts. Some of their blokes are good, but some are a bit ham-fisted. Do you know forty-four of them have scored 'own goals' since 1969?"

Marcus had shuddered. Enemy or not, he'd felt a professional sympathy for anyone who had blown himself up.

The major continued. "It can get quite absurd. A few years back, the Provos' own quartermaster general—bloke called Jack McCabe—took himself out. He tried to move ammonium nitrate explosives with a metal shovel on a concrete floor.

"Imagine how interesting your expertise would be to the Provos."

Marcus's curiosity had been piqued, but he still had not been particularly interested until the major outlined the specific nature of the task.

His job would be to identify the Provos' 2nd Battalion bomber and his superior officers. The major had hinted that it was probably one of the 2nd Battalion man's devices that had nearly killed Marcus.

It was then that he sat up and began to pay closer attention. In the days since the explosion, Marcus had understood that with the right precautions, bomb disposal was not as dangerous as it might appear. What had happened to Al Cowan seemed careless, like the kind of thing that could happen to anyone who took a corner too fast in a sports car. But being blown up and lucky to escape, despite strict adherence to procedure, cast the whole issue in a different light. Marcus had begun to wonder if there might be an honourable way out of bomb disposal. The major was offering one—at least in the short term.

"I'll not wrap it up," the major had said. "It'll be dangerous. The Provos don't run Sunday schools."

It had dawned on Marcus that what he was being asked to do would be risky, but the clincher came when the major pulled out a silver cigarette case. Marcus immediately noticed the crest and the motto, "Who Dares Wins."

"Are you SAS, sir?" He'd seen the wistful look on the major's face.

"Not anymore." He'd shaken his head as if to shoo away a bothersome fly, looked Marcus straight in the eye, and said, "But you could be. Do exactly what I tell you, find the bomber and his bosses, and I'll put in a recommendation that you be accepted for one of their assessment courses."

Christ! Now that was a goal to shoot for. The Special Air Service Regiment, four Sabre squadrons, the elite of the British army. It was an opportunity offered to very few. And he could not ever be criticized for leaving the RAOC to join the SAS.

Except, of course, there was an intermediate step. He would have to find the bomber, and before he could do that he would have a lot to learn. A hell of a lot.

Major Smith had explained that Marcus would be confined to these quarters for the duration of his training. He wanted as few people as possible to be aware that Lieutenant Richardson was still alive.

The schooling itself would be a three-step operation.

Marcus would need to change his appearance, and to that end he had been told to let his hair grow and to cultivate a droopy moustache. Any curious stranger with a military haircut appearing in the Catholic slums of Belfast might just as well shoot himself in the head and save the Provos the bother.

A new wardrobe had been provided. Jeans; serge trousers; coarse, collarless shirts; V-necked sweaters; cheap windcheaters; socks; and pairs of scuffed leather shoes. All the clothing fit: thirty-six-inch inside-leg trousers with a thirty-two-inch waist, size 16 collars, size 11 shoes. There were items that had come from Canada—T-shirts and a red jacket, large size, with a prancing horse and the words CALGARY STAMPEDERS on the back. He guessed it was for supporters of some kind of sports team. Haircuts and clothes were the easy part—anyone could play at fancy dress.

In two weeks a captain would be coming over from SAS Headquarters at Stirling Lines to give Marcus a crash course in intelligence and counter-insurgency. He was looking forward to meeting the SAS chap, who, with a bit of luck, might be a brother officer in the not-too-distant future.

The toughest part was going to be mastering the cover story. Marcus would be impersonating a real man. A man from his own hometown,

Bangor. A man with a lower-class background who had emigrated to Canada and worked in the oil fields of Alberta—with explosives. The explosives part would be easy. Royal Army Ordnance Corps officers were taught how to disassemble bombs and naturally had to understand how such devices were constructed.

But Marcus would also have to possess a thorough working knowledge of Canadian customs and the geography and recent history of events in Alberta—particularly the northern town of Fort McMurray and the city of Calgary, where the chap spent his leaves from the oil wells.

And Marcus would have to be word perfect in the details of his double's past life—his likes and dislikes, his family and friends. The bits about family and friends would be simple memory work, but Marcus wondered about embracing his double's tastes. His own life had been privileged, and he recognized that he had little idea how the working class—the *Catholic* working class—went about their daily lives.

Marcus knew nothing about Catholicism. Middle-class Ulster Protestants ignored the other faith, laughed the ethnic jokes about the thick paddies and might aver—with the same patronizing tolerance that some white Americans showed blacks—that some of their best friends were Catholics. They were not particularly keen, however, on any suggestion that their daughter might marry one.

He had been surprised to find that he felt a vague sense of unease when he realized that he must learn enough of the Roman liturgy to pass as an adherent. It was a price he would have to pay, and not a very high price at that.

Major Smith would live in the other half of the semi for the duration of the training. It would be his job to drill Marcus in his cover story, over and over again, until, as a good linguist thinks and even dreams in foreign languages, he would think and react as a different person.

Major Smith had given Marcus a large green binder. In it were all the details of the life of the man Marcus Richardson was to become. A working man, a Catholic man, a man called Mike Roberts.

NINE

There had been no word from Sean Conlon and no requests for more devices in the four days since Davy had built his last bomb. He was grateful for the respite. Fiona would be home soon, expecting him to have made his choice. He sat, head bowed, at the kitchen table. He did not want to believe she meant what she had said last night, and yet, knowing her as he did, he must. He'd gnawed at his options—black or white—as a terrier worries a rat, certain of what he must do, yet hating himself for it. He loved her so much.

He'd met her six years earlier, before the Troubles, when she soared into his universe like a bright comet from another galaxy. They'd met by chance. Davy had been walking along the Lagan Embankment and she'd come the other way. As they passed, she stumbled and he grabbed her arm. She laughed and thanked him. Her laugh touched Davy. He blurted out that his name was Davy McCutcheon and asked the stranger with the raven hair, the black almond eyes, and the laugh warm as hot chocolate if she'd like a cup of tea. To his amazement Fiona Kavanagh said yes, she'd love one.

Love one. Over cups of tea, he had fallen in love for the first time in his thirty-eight years; his days with the IRA had left little time for women. Fallen in love? He'd plummeted with the desperation of a sixteen-year-old. And his love had been returned. Until now. Because of politics.

He had thought in the early days that she believed in the Republican cause as strongly as he did. She'd been one of the first members of the Northern Ireland Civil Rights Association. Until she'd explained, he hadn't understood that NICRA's agenda was less one of union with the Republic than fairness for all in Ulster—one man, one vote—and an end to discrimination against Catholics. "The IRA want reunion at any cost. We want peace and justice, but we refuse to pay a price in blood," Fiona had told him.

Perhaps her temperance was because she was better educated than him. She had a teacher's certificate from Stranmillis College and taught at the primary school on Ross Street, just round the corner.

After he met Fiona, Davy redoubled his efforts to find work. As usual, it was a fruitless search. His shame, when he had admitted to Fiona that he had no trade, was that of a priest in the confessional who had broken his vows of celibacy. She had merely shrugged.

By that time he had told her how he'd spent his younger days, what had happened to Da. She'd been horrified to hear about his father, but as for the rest? He wasn't sure that she entirely approved, but she had understood, and had never criticized him for his past or his lack of skills.

That was Fiona Kavanagh. A strong woman who thought for herself and, when her mind was made up, was as hard to shift as the Mourne Mountains. He'd first found that out about six weeks after they had met, when, stumbling over the words, he asked her to marry him. She laughed, a throaty sound, melodious as the mouth music of the Hebrides. She said they were as good as married, and now that he'd asked, she'd move in with him, but—but they wouldn't need the dreary mumblings of some priest. She said something about "bourgeois conventions." He hadn't been quite sure what she meant, but he never raised the subject of marriage again.

She'd come to Conway Street, bringing her possessions and her ginger kitten, McCusker. He was a big tomcat now, curled up asleep under the table.

When had it all started to go wrong? Davy McCutcheon knew the answer: when he joined the Provos. She'd not said much at first, grudgingly accepting his explanation that the PIRA's job was to defend the Catholic ghettoes.

When Ó Brádaigh and MacStiofáin and the rest of Army Council had decided that the Provos could go on the offensive, she began to wonder aloud how Davy could work with "a bunch of unprincipled killers."

It had come to a head the night of the Abercorn bombing, March 4, 1972. Nearly two years ago. The Provos had left a bomb under a table in the popular restaurant in the Cornmarket in central Belfast. Two patrons were killed and more than 100 wounded.

She'd been sitting with him in the little front parlour when she put down the *Telegraph*, looked straight at him, and said, "Davy, I wish you'd get out."

He shook his head. "I can't. Not now."

"Why not, Davy?"

"Because I've gone too far to turn back. I owe it to my da. I owe it to myself. Anyway, we're going to win. We have to win."

"By killing innocent people? Look at this, for God's sake." She tried to hand him the newspaper.

"No." He turned to her, held her shoulders in his big hands. "By beating the British army." Her eyes were black in the dim light, black and soft as ripe damsons, and yet he'd seen a hardness there. A hardness he had never seen before.

She'd hesitated, then said, "I don't think I can go on living with you, Davy. Not unless you leave the Provos."

"What?" She might as well have slapped his face.

"I mean it."

"Jesus, Fiona."

They talked for hours, and she went back on her threat, told him she loved him too much. And he held her, kissed her, and caressed her until her breathing had quickened and she'd thrust herself against him. On the sofa. The pair of them like kids in the backseat of a car.

She didn't mention leaving again and made no open criticism of his PIRA work, and Davy had buried the once-spoken threat, almost forgotten it.

Until last night.

Davy leaned back in his chair. He stared at the photograph of Fiona laughing on a beach. She was thirty-four when the snap had been taken. Before the Troubles. Before the first streaks of silver had appeared in her shiny black hair. Och, Fiona.

Everything from last night was in his head, jumbled like the tinsel in a kaleidoscope, but making clear patterns—patterns he did not wish to stare at.

She'd been very quiet after supper. Hadn't wanted to talk about what her kids had done in class, the daily activities she called her "infants' efforts."

Finally, he asked her, "What's up, love?"

She paused for a long time, then said, "Did you read about the bomb in the station, on Tuesday?"

"No." He shrugged. She should know that he hardly ever read the papers. He didn't want to know.

"The ticket man was killed."

"I'm sorry." He didn't know what else to say.

"Was it one of yours?"

"Dunno." It could have been. He saw the pleading in her eyes. "I don't think so."

"Doesn't matter." He'd never heard such a defeated tone in her voice.

He fidgeted. "Do you mind if I've a smoke?" She tolerated his habit. He usually went out into the yard, but something told him not to leave her this time.

"Go ahead."

He took his time selecting a Woodbine, lighting up. He looked at her through the smoke. She was shaking her head slowly, the dark wings of her hair moving, framing her face. He could not meet her gaze as she said, "Two of his daughters are in my class."

He rose and leaned across the table, reaching out his hand to comfort her. To touch her swaying hair. But she moved away from him.

"I don't know what their mother was thinking. She sent them to school today."

He could see the film of moisture before her eyes.

"The younger one, Deirdre, asked me, 'Why, miss?'" She flicked the back of one hand across her left eye, inhaled, and stared into his being. "What do you say to a little girl, Davy?"

He looked away.

"What do you say? He died for Ireland? He's with the angels? It was an accident?"

The cigarette shook between his fingers.

"It was no accident, Davy, and you know it."

"I'm sorry."

"Sorry? Sorry? For God's sake, is that all? You never see what your bombs do. You're like those pilots in the Second World War. High above the carnage, conscience clean."

Davy slumped back into his chair. She was right. He hadn't seen. Didn't want to see. He'd seen enough the day Da died.

She stood. "Do you remember what I said after the Abercorn?"

Davy clasped his big hands like a supplicant altar boy, bowed his head, and waited.

"Davy, I love you."

He looked up, a tiny smile beginning, but it was banished when she said, "Two years ago I asked you to get out. Now I'm telling you."

"Fiona . . ."

"You choose, Davy. The Provos or me."

"But . . ."

"No buts, Davy." She stepped back. "I'm going out."

"I'll come with you."

"No, thank you." The ice in her words chilled him like the touch of a corpse's hand, and he could do nothing but stand and watch as she left.

She hadn't come home until the small hours. He'd pretended to be asleep, not knowing what to say. He'd lain beside her until the morning, his eyes wide, his mind churning like a cement mixer with a slipped clutch. He hadn't moved when she rose, dressed, and left, pausing only to look down on him and whisper, "I love you, Davy McCutcheon."

He'd spent the day bleary-eyed, heart-sore, waiting, doing little things about the house—vacuuming, dusting, mending the broken latch on the gate to the yard, anything to occupy his mind. But school would be over now, and she would be coming home.

Davy heard her key in the lock, the door opening, and her footsteps in the hall. He rose. She stood in the doorway, a pile of exercise books under one arm, her raincoat and head scarf soaked. He made no move to go to her.

"Well?" she asked.

He shook his head. "I can't."

"All right." She set the books on the table, turned, and left.

Davy stood, hands dangling by his sides. He loved her, loved her more than the life in his body, but . . .

But Da had died for Ireland, as hundreds of others had; many more had sacrificed their freedom, their homes, their loved ones. He, Davy McCutcheon, had made the Provo Declaration. He had given his boyhood and young manhood to the grey, grim "Cause," and now he must give up the only lovely thing he had ever owned, he thought. He had no choice. He knew he'd never had a choice, never since the days Da had spun his stories of Kathleen ni Houlihan. Ireland was in Davy's soul like Jesus Christ in the heart of a Carmelite nun.

He heard her footsteps on the stair. Owned? He had never owned Fiona Kavanagh, he corrected himself. She had given herself, and now he had returned the gift he cherished above all. For the Cause.

TEN

As Marcus Richardson had known in theory and discovered nine days earlier in practice, a motor vehicle loaded with explosives is a powerful weapon. The concept was the brainchild of Seamus Twomey, a bookmaker who had been involved in the IRA's Operation Harvest. He, like Davy, had quit in the early sixties but returned to offer his services in 1969. He had been one of the group that had met to consider splitting from the Official IRA and founding the Provisionals, and he became one of the Provos' leaders when the schism occurred.

In 1970 Twomey was adjutant of the Belfast Brigade, Provisional IRA—the post now held by Sean Conlon—and second in command to Billy McKee. He rose to become Officer Commanding. In March 1973 Twomey moved to Provisional IRA General Headquarters in Dublin.

Twomey's gift to the PIRA, the car bomb, had allowed them to score a number of successes, but sometimes the Provos miscalculated. On July 31, 1972, three car bombs were placed in the main street of the village of Claudy. The Provos had intended to limit the number of casualties by telephoning a warning. The telephone booth they'd counted on using had been vandalized. No warning was given and the village was devastated. Nine people were killed at once and two died later.

The Security Forces countered by making it illegal to park an automobile within town limits unless someone remained in the vehicle. They reasoned that, while the Provos may have been fanatics, they were not a bunch of kamikaze pilots. But even such measures did not prevent devices being ferried by car for delivery into the heart of Belfast.

On the night of Monday, November 6, 1972, the army erected an eight-foot-high wire fence with forty-one gates around the centre of the city. No vehicles were permitted to pass except in emergencies.

Behind the fence, the department stores—Robinson and Cleavers, the Athletic Stores, and Brands and Norman's—and such smaller businesses as travel agents, jewelers, bookstores, tobacconists', cafés, and restaurants, cowered.

This Monday morning, as he did every day, a blind man had come to sit on a folding stool outside Robinson and Cleavers, cloth cap on the pavement before him. With a fiddler's bow he drew sweet, melancholy tunes from a saw grasped between his knees. The shoppers and the businessmen, students and labourers, nurses, and all whose lawful pursuits took them to the city core strode by him, hiding in their own thoughts, all pretending that there was no danger, all wishing fervently to get away from Belfast. A few—a very few—dropped coins in the saw player's cap as they hurried by. None lingered to listen.

And over all, behind the barricade, the green-domed City Hall towered silently, brooding like the commander of the besieged garrison of a veldt town in the Boer War who wondered not if, but when, the next assault would come.

A young, fair-haired woman, smartly dressed in a cashmere sweater and plaid miniskirt beneath a lightweight, reversible raincoat, waited until one of the RUC constables at a gate in the fence finished rummaging through her handbag. There was nothing inside to raise anyone's suspicions. A wallet, dark glasses, several tissues, some elastic bands, powder, mascara, keys, loose change, a rosary, a Saint Christopher medallion, and a lipstick. Max Factor's "Coral Pink."

Nothing out of the ordinary at all, and yet, as Moira Ryan waited, she could feel the moisture in her armpits, on the palms of her hands. But Brendan had said it would be all right. And Moira trusted Brendan McGuinness.

"Carry on, miss." The policeman returned her bag and watched her hurry through, staring at the swell of her breasts under her mackintosh, wishing he'd been allowed to body search her.

Brendan McGuinness waited in the back of a windowless Morris Eight van. He'd driven it from Belfast to a deserted airfield near Kirkistown, on the Ards Peninsula in County Down. He shifted on the rough seat, wondering for a moment how the girl was getting on. She should be through the security fence by now. Another small operation, like the attempt on the life of that UVF bastard, Bertie Dunne, but one that would give the Brits something else to think about. He had to keep the bastards on the hop. The more of them that were preoccupied with ensuring the everyday safety of the civilian population, the fewer resources they would have to interfere with the major coup he had been planning—planning with only one other man privy to his thoughts—since McGuinness had got word of the opportunity to strike a devastating blow.

But he needed more detailed information about the target.

Where the hell was his contact? He should have been here twenty minutes ago. Brendan McGuinness rapped his fist against the paneling of the van's side. He heard another car coming closer. He slipped a hand into his jacket pocket, taking reassurance from the Smith and Wesson automatic beneath his fingers.

The engine stopped. He heard a door slam, footsteps on the concrete surface of the old runway, and a knocking on the van's back door. McGuinness bent forward to open the door.

He saw a short, heavy-set man, hair trimmed in a crew cut. He could not make out the man's features as he climbed in and shut the door.

"I've got it," he said.

Brendan forgot his irritation at the man's tardiness. "All of it?"

"Pretty much."

"Tell me."

Moira Ryan passed the saw player, pausing to drop a tenpence coin into his cap, hearing his "thank you, madam." She wondered how a blind man would know she was a woman. He must have heard the click of her high heels.

She joined the line of shoppers outside Robinson and Cleavers and waited her turn to be searched again—this time by a private security guard—entered the store, and made her way to the women's clothing department. A shop assistant helped her take off her beige raincoat, admired her cashmere sweater, and gave advice about this spring's fashions. It took her twenty minutes to pick out four dresses she wanted to try on.

The assistant showed her to a changing room, apologized because there were so many other patrons this morning, told the young woman to take her time.

Moira let herself into the cubicle, carrying the dresses and her raincoat over one arm. After closing the door, she hung the dresses on a peg on the chipboard wall and turned her raincoat inside out. When she slipped the coat on, the outside was dark green.

She twisted her long hair into a knot on the top of her head and secured it with elastic bands from her now-open handbag. Her hair was soon covered by a head scarf. The tissues were next. She stuffed them into a pocket of one of the dresses, a pretty paisley-patterned one, hanging on the hook.

Moira hesitated as she removed the dark glasses and the Max Factor "Coral Pink" lipstick. She took a deep breath, twisted the base of the lipstick, listened until she heard a crunching noise, and slipped it into the nest of tissues. Then she put on the sunglasses and let herself out of the cubicle.

The assistant was at the far side of the department, serving another customer. As Moira passed, she saw the shopgirl glance in her direction, hesitate, and shake her head, clearly not recognizing the short-haired woman in the green coat and sunglasses.

Twenty-five minutes had elapsed from the time she entered the store to the moment she left and joined the crowds on the street outside.

The same twenty-five minutes had brought a satisfied smile to Brendan McGuinness's one-eyed face. He had heard even more than he had hoped for when he had said, "Tell me."

"You'll like this," the squat man said.

"Get on with it."

"Right. First, the technical stuff is just about set. One of our people with the GPO has finished his job at the Brits' end."

"Good."

"The equipment for your end'll be ready when you move to your new quarters."

McGuinness nodded. "I'll look after that. The move's next Sunday."

"Fair enough."

"What about the other operation?"

"I don't know the dates yet, but one of them's coming, just like I told you last week."

"Look. We can't mount an attack if we don't know the time and place." McGuinness let an edge of irritation creep in.

The man opposite did not seem to be bothered. "Hold your horses, I'll look after that. My lot'll be handling the security, so they will. As soon as I hear, you'll hear, all right?"

"Are you sure?"

"Of course I'm not fucking well sure. Are you sure the sun'll come up tomorrow? But the British are having their general election on the twenty-eighth. Both Ted Heath and Harold Wilson have said Northern Ireland will be a priority if their party gets in."

"That doesn't mean either one'll come here." The news about the new surveillance equipment was good, but this uncertainty was not what McGuinness wanted to hear.

"Jesus Christ! Do you think that's the sort of thing an English politician would be yelling from the rooftops?"

"No."

"Didn't I just tell you my mob are to be in charge of security for a prime minister's visit? The boss had me in yesterday and told me to start planning for it. My men are running round like bees on a hot brick. Do you think he'd waste our time like that if it wasn't going to happen?"

"No."

"So, stop getting your knickers in a twist. It's money in the bank one of them will come, and I'll give you the word the minute I hear. You start thinking about how to take him out."

It was then that a slow smile of grim satisfaction split Brendan McGuinness's face from ear to ear.

"Now," said the man, crouching as he rose, "I'm away the fuck out of here. I'll be in touch."

Brendan nodded, his mind already focused on how he would arrange to have a British prime minister killed. And it didn't matter to him, not one bit, if the bugger was Conservative or Labour.

He sat back against the wall of the van, barely hearing the slam of its back door. He'd need to give his agent a while to get clear, but he'd not waste the time. There was planning to do.

It was unlikely the PIRA could get a sniper close enough, he thought.

It would have to be some kind of explosive device. He prayed the consignment of the new Czech plastique, Semtex, would get through on time.

What Moira Ryan had left behind in the pocket of a paisley-patterned dress was much more primitive than Semtex. It was a variant of the Durex bomb, invented in Derry in 1970. Sulfuric acid, sealed in a vial of candle wax, was placed inside a condom—usually a Durex condom, hence the name. The sheath was placed inside a container full of sodium chlorate, a common weed killer. When the device was squeezed, the acid was released, and it ate slowly through the latex, giving the bomber time to escape before it ignited the chlorate.

Devout Catholic members of the PIRA refused to use these devices because condoms were proscribed by the Church. Moira had had no such scruples, and in her device the candle wax had been replaced with a small glass ampoule. Twisting the base of the lipstick advanced a screw that crushed the glass.

She was safely at home when the latex gave way. A sheet of flame set fire to the tissues, and in seconds the four dresses were ablaze with greedy tongues licking at the dressing-room walls.

A startled shopper noticed tendrils of smoke escaping from beneath the changing-room door. She screamed and pointed.

The shop assistant ran to the door and opened it. Flames roared out like dragon's breath, roasting her alive.

Outside, the blind man caressed the notes of "The Town I Love So Well" from his saw, but the tune was smothered by the hoarse shouts of the shoppers pouring from the store's front doors and the "nee-naw, nee-naw" of emergency vehicles passing through gates in the eight-foot-high fence.

ELEVEN

Marcus had been here in this semi for a week and a day. He sat in an armchair, wearing jeans and an American T-shirt, and stared at a blown-up photograph of rhododendrons on the wall—garish blooms frozen in time.

His funeral had been four days ago. Major Smith had attended, full of condolences as the army honour guard lowered a ballasted coffin. It must have been very hard on Mum, traveling by herself. He wondered if she would be back in Texas by now.

He'd had time to stifle his disappointment that his father did not attend. Sometimes Marcus wondered what kind of a man his grandfather had been—must have been pretty bloody Victorian to have raised a son who could bury his feelings so deeply he deliberately avoided events that might call for some outward show. Grandpa Richardson had died before Marcus was old enough to really know him, but maybe that was why Dad was such a perfectionist, such a hard man to please, had been for as long as Marcus could remember.

Like the day Dad had wanted a six-year-old Marcus to walk on the old seawall beside Billy Caulfield's rowboat jetty in Bangor. The scene played in Marcus's mind, clear as if it were yesterday.

They'd been out together fishing. When they came ashore, Daddy said that rowing was hot work and asked if Marcus would like an ice cream.

"Yes, please."

"You'll have to earn it." Daddy stopped in front of a low sandstone wall. "Let's see you walk on the wall."

Marcus swallowed. He knew the big boys walked on the coping

stones, but it was an awfully long way down to the rocks below. "On there?"

"Come on. Up." Daddy wrapped his arms round Marcus and hoisted him. "It'll be easy if you don't look down."

Marcus peered over the edge. Below—miles below it seemed—waves broke over the jagged shore.

"Marcus, come on. Don't be a sissy." His father's voice was taking on the tone he always used when he found some error in Marcus's homework, when he'd say, "If there's an easy way and a hard way, you'll find the hard way."

Marcus stared at his feet. The wall seemed only inches thick, and the rocks . . .

"Are you going to walk?"

"I can't . . ."

"Hold my hand."

"No. I want down."

"Take my hand."

"No, Daddy. I'm scared."

A clock on the living-room wall made a whirring noise, bringing Marcus back to the present, yet he could still hear his own words—"No, Daddy. I'm scared"—could still remember his tears as Daddy lifted him off the wall and strode off for home. No ice cream. Stupid bloody wall. He'd even gone back on his own—three days later—scrambled up, and, heart in mouth, walked. He'd never told anyone, but he'd done it.

When he had grown old enough, he played rugby, just like his father, and found to his delight that he enjoyed his ability to ignore the possibility of being hurt. He played well enough to represent his university, but not well enough to be picked for the provincial side, never mind Ireland. His father had been capped twice.

When the time had come to choose an army specialty, that disregard for danger led him to bomb disposal. He'd tested himself again and not found himself wanting for courage—until his brush with death. Now, with a bit of luck, he would be able to move on to the SAS with no loss of face. That bit of luck would come if he worked hard enough at his new assignment. He was working as hard as he could under the tutelage of Major Smith and when he was left alone to digest the information about Canada and the oil industry, the Catholic Mass. He'd even learned the Catholic kids' doggerel version of the Hail Mary: "Holy

Mary, Mother of God, serve us all a piece of cod." The childish substitution was certainly more comforting to chant than the line that belonged in its place: "Pray for us sinners, now and at the hour of our death."

Notes were strewn on the table, along with the green folder. Mike Roberts's folder. He hadn't mastered every detail, but he was getting there. It helped that Major Smith refused to call Marcus anything but Mike or Roberts. It was a funny feeling, having two men living in the same body, having to stifle one and encourage the other. Perhaps this is how schizophrenics feel, Mike thought.

He looked at his watch. 0855. Major Smith would be here at 0900. Exactly. Marcus glanced back at the Timex he'd been given to wear. Mike Roberts would have a cheap watch, but Marcus missed his Rolex. It had been a present from Dad when Marcus finished his seven-month course at the Kineton School of Ammunition. Dad attended that passing-out ceremony. He handed over the watch with a gruff "well done," and Marcus glowed.

"Where are you, Roberts?" The major called from the hall.

Marcus checked his Timex. 0900. Exactly. "In here, sir."

The major sat in his usual armchair. "Getting a handle on the bandits?" He pointed at the opened briefing notes. "Good. You've only got three weeks until your finals."

"Finals, sir?" It sounded like an examination.

"And if you don't want to end up like some of the Freds, you'd better pass."

"Freds, sir?"

"Drop the 'sir.' Name's John."

The invitation to dispense with military formality was a concession. "Thank you. Go on, John."

The major lit a cigarette. "Thought I'd give you an idea of what you'll be up against—and how not to do it. Right. Freds. That was a right regal cock-up. The Freds were the special detachment of the Military Reconnaissance Force."

He stood and walked to the mantel, leaning against it like one of Marcus's old lecturers. "The Provisional IRA are a suspicious bunch. We couldn't even send uniformed patrols into their parts of the city for quite some time. The buggers set up no-go areas. Our lot backed off. The Military Reconnaissance Force, MRF, was formed in 1971. There were forty regular soldiers in plain clothes who looked for PIRA men on their own turf." The major looked wistful. "Brave lads. If any one of them was rumbled, he was on his own."

"Those soldiers were the Freds?"

The major shook his head. "No, they were the MRF. The Freds were the special detachment of the MRF. Clear?"

"Not really."

"Look." The major held out his left hand. "MRF. Plainclothes regulars." He held out his right hand. Ash fell from his cigarette onto the carpet, and he rubbed it in with the toe of an immaculately polished black shoe. "Keeps the moths out." He looked back to his outstretched right hand. "Special detachment. Ten ex-Provos, working for us. Para captain was in charge." He made a derisory sound. "Freds."

"How on earth were Irish terrorists persuaded . . . ?"

The major's grin was feral. "Gave them the choice of working for us or going down for some very long, very, very hard time." He drew on his smoke. "They worked bloody well, too, until the silly buggers in charge got ambitious."

"You've lost me again, John."

"The Freds were billeted in these semis. Their handler lived next door in the other half. Tight security. We let them out in armoured personnel carriers with an intelligence crew. The Provo, 'Fred,' would look through the slits. When he spotted one of his mates, the soldier-photographer took a couple of quick candids. After a patrol, Fred would put names to faces. Worked like a charm, and we took quite a few unpleasant characters out of circulation"—he shook his head, as a father might when a small child has done something particularly foolish—"until some stupid sod thought that the Freds might do even better if we let them go home and mingle with their old comrades."

Marcus handed the major an ashtray.

He tapped the ash. "The information officer of D Company, Second Battalion of the Provos, began to suspect a chappie called Seamus Wright." He gave a small, exasperated snort. "Why his handlers let him go and live back on Leeson Street with his wife, I'll never know. I'd rather not think about his interrogation." The major's smile held no sympathy. "I believe it lasted for five days."

"Jesus." Marcus tried to shut out the mental pictures.

"Wright implicated Kevin McKee, and to save their skins the pair of them became double agents—for a while."

"What happened?"

"They're not working for either side anymore."

Marcus felt the hairs on the backs of his arms rise.

"Good thing, too. Before their friends, um, dispensed with the services of Wright and McKee, the bastards had created havoc."

"How?"

"By feeding us duff information. Wright and McKee identified Provos as members of the Official IRA, in whom the intelligence services had little interest, and Officials as Provos." The major hunted through a file, produced a photograph, and said, "Here's a good example."

Marcus looked at the picture. Two middle-aged men stood on a street corner. The taller, a heavy-set man, had thinning grey hair and a moustache. The other had a face like a fox. "Who are these two?"

"A couple of has-beens. That's Davy McCutcheon on the left. He was with the old IRA back in the fifties, along with his mate Jimmy Ferguson. They're both over the hill. Not much interest to us." He grunted. "When Seamus Wright was playing at double agents, he tried to persuade us that those two were Provos along with another bunch of old Officials. We didn't fall for that one."

The major took a cigarette from the silver case. Marcus noted the SAS crest. He smiled at the thought of Major Smith's promise. The major inhaled. "It got pretty nasty at the end. Wright and McKee blew the MRF's cover. On second October two years ago, the Provos took out three MRF operations. Two and Three Battalions, PIRA, hit a house on College Square East and a massage parlour at 397 Antrim Road."

"A massage parlour?"

"Hidden mikes pick up quite a lot."

Marcus stifled a laugh at the image of a terrorist, clad in nothing but his balaclava, ArmaLite rifle in one hand, a weapon of an entirely different kind in the other.

The major did not smile. "I'm glad you find it amusing."

"Sorry, sir."

"It's John."

"Sorry, John."

"Not as sorry as the driver of the Four Square Laundry van. His job was to collect dirty clothes from the Republican ghettoes and rush them to a forensic laboratory before having them washed and returned to their owners. Amazing what the forensic wallahs can find. Traces of explosives, burnt powder, lead from bullets, blood." He paused. "An action squad from One Battalion raked the van with automatic fire. Killed the driver of the van, Sapper Ted Stuart. Nice young lad, I'm told." He crushed out his cigarette. "Lance Corporal Sarah Jane Warke was lucky to escape with her life."

"Sounds a bit dodgy to me," Marcus said.

"It's that, all right." The major looked him directly in the eye. "I'll not lie to you. It's bloody dangerous. But we're in a bind. MRF's pretty well gone. The information I just gave you is hush-hush, by the way."

Marcus was flattered by the confidence.

The major lowered his voice. "We've got to find a way in. Without intelligence, you're blind." The major's jaundiced eyes narrowed. "We have to beat those Provo bastards. You will be a great help, you know."

Marcus warmed to the praise.

"Keep up your studies, Mike."

It still felt funny to be called by another man's name.

"Right." The major stood and moved to the door. "That's enough from me for one day. Back to your books. Captain Warnock's coming over from Stirling Lines next week. Give you a crash course in fieldcraft and surveillance."

TWELVE

It was a hell of way to spend Saint Valentine's Day, alone in a cramped kitchen. A week now since Fiona had gone, and Davy missed her sorely. He ached to see her, but he knew that she had made up her mind and would not budge unless he did as she had asked.

Jimmy had been round on Saturday. He always came on Saturdays, had done for years. He'd tried to plead with Davy to do what she wanted, even hinted that he was thinking about quitting himself. He had a son and daughter in Canada. Both of them had been suggesting for years that Jimmy and his wife should emigrate and join one of them.

Davy had known Jimmy's kids since they were wee. Fergus and Siobhan had been like the children he'd never had. Never would have now. Fiona had said that as long as he was a Provo she'd bear him none.

A ginger tomcat appeared on the window ledge, jumped on soundproof paws to the linoleum floor, sat, surveyed Davy, and began to wash. Davy watched as the animal hoisted one hind leg behind a tattered ear and began to lick its arse. It looked as though the cat was playing a cello.

"Home, are you, McCusker? Do you miss her, too?"

Fiona had left the tom behind. Davy remembered laughing when she told him the animal had been named for Bobby Greer's pet on the BBC radio serial *The McCooeys*. The fictitious Greer's cat had a taste for "soup with peas in."

He rose from where he sat at the table, leaving the remains of his supper, glad of the animal's company. He bent and scratched McCusker's head. "It's all right for you. You can come and go as you please."

The cat stopped washing and pushed his head against Davy's hand. "Do you think maybe we should enroll a few cats?"

McCusker looked at Davy with pansy eyes.

Davy ignored him, his sense of frustration growing as he thought about how heavily the Security Forces patrolled the streets now. Sixteen—for Christ's sake, sixteen—sangars, fortified observation posts, armed and defended twenty-four hours a day, had been thrown up in Catholic neighbourhoods. The Brits had conducted a house-by-house census to try to identify the likely haunts of the Provos and their supporters, and the soldiers carried photo-identification cards, "bingo cards," of known Provo volunteers to help them spot their prey.

He silently thanked Sean Conlon for persuading Billy McKee and the rest of the Belfast Brigade staff that some of the experienced specialists, the bomb makers and armourers, should be kept isolated from the rest of the volunteers. Sean had been right. McKee hadn't been so lucky. He and Frank Card had been arrested in April 1971.

McCusker made a soft mew.

Davy picked the cat up, tickling him under the chin. "The bloody Brits are the cats just now, McCusker, and us scuttling about like a bunch of mice."

McCusker bit Davy's finger.

"Hungry?" Davy tucked the cat under one arm, lifted a small plastic bowl from beside the dresser; took two steps, one short on his bad leg, one long; opened a cupboard; and pulled out a bag of dried cat food. He put the animal on the floor and poured a few brown balls into the bowl. Only ten days ago he'd stashed the blasting caps in a bag like this. They were safe now in his hidey-hole in the room next door. He wondered when the hell he was ever going to use them.

McCusker stood on his hind legs, front claws needling well up on Davy's thigh.

"Take your hurry in your hand," Davy said as he placed the bowl on the floor. McCusker crunched the dry pellets with audible ferocity. Davy stood for a moment watching. He was fond of old McCusker and now he was all she had left him, except for the memories.

Davy looked through the window. Gloom slid over the rooftops of the city, gloom shrouded in factory haze and drizzle. The undersides of low clouds, just visible in the gap between the terrace houses, reflected the wan glow of neon streetlights.

Ah, bugger the Security Forces. He'd sat here feeling sorry for himself for a week. It was time to stir himself, go and have a jar and a bit of company.

The clock on the wall said 6:10. He'd have to wait. Although Army Council frowned on drinking, they bent their own rules in the face of reality. Volunteers were only to avoid pubs before 7 P.M.

Davy went back to the table, sat, and pushed the dirty plates away. Fiona wouldn't have let him get away with that. Feeling guilty, he rose, carried them to the sink, and started to scrub off the congealed fat.

McCusker looked up at the sound of the dishes clanking. He stopped and sat alert, ears pricked, whiskers pointing forward. Davy was sure that cats could pick up messages through their whiskers from other galaxies. As silently as he had entered the room, McCusker left through the still-open window.

Davy called "enjoy yourself" after the departing tail. He wished Mc-Cusker well on his nocturnal pursuits, but feared for the mice that skulked in the shadows.

The image of cowering mice lingered as he took his Dexter raincoat and duncher from a peg on the door and let himself out.

Davy moved slowly through the narrow backstreets and alleyways. The Falls had suffered badly in the early days of the rioting, when Protestant mobs torched houses and pubs with homemade Molotov cocktails.

He turned a corner where his usual pub, the Arkle Bar, used to stand, its fallen masonry and blackened beams mute reminders of the ferocity of Loyalist hatred that burned like the petrol they used to torch the building.

The wind blew drizzle into his face, chilling him. He turned into a back alley, rutted and muddy. His leg ached. He stopped to massage his thigh, bending his head to the rain, failing to pay attention to his surroundings.

"Evening, sir."

Davy stiffened then straightened up slowly. A British soldier in a mottled Denison camouflage smock and combat helmet—so he wasn't a Para, they wore different helmets—blocked the end of the alley. Where the hell had he come from?

"Dirty night, sir." Glaswegian by the burr.

"Right enough," said Davy.

"On your way home, sir?"

"Aye." Jesus, the obvious next question was "Where do you live?" It would be difficult to explain why he was heading in the wrong direction.

The soldier lowered his weapon, the raindrops coursing along the dark metal barrel. "You're lucky, sir. Me and my mates are stuck out here for a fair few hours yet." He pointed out into the street beyond.

The rest of the squad would be out there, crouched in doorways, quartering the road. "Aye," said Davy, thinking, *and you want me to say thank you, don't you, you skitter?* "It's a good thing you are; we could use a bit of peace and quiet." He was relieved to see the young man smile. "I'll be getting on, then."

"Right, sir. Safe home." The soldier stood aside, letting Davy walk past the rest of the detail, meeting no one's eyes, keeping his head down. Despite the pain in his thigh, he managed to disguise his usually rolling gait. He'd not give the bastards anything to remember him by.

He did not look back until he had crossed the road and walked into the shadows of another side street. He stopped, leaned against a wall, and rubbed his thigh, hard, with the heel of his hand. Jesus, but it ached. Still, only a wee way to go. He continued, past a small tobacconist's, mesh-wire-grilled windows, spilling a tiny pool of lighted comfort into the dark. Just round one more corner and three houses along. The door was shut. He rapped on the peeling-painted wood with his knuckles.

The door opened and a white-haired man peered out. He sneezed, sniffed, and wiped his nose on the back of his sleeve. "How's about you, Davy? Come on in."

The small living room of the house had been made into a bar. Men in collarless shirts and V-necked pullovers sat at tables or lounged against the walls. The air was blue with tobacco haze and smelled of unwashed undervests.

He forced his way to the bar, exchanging greetings with the men he passed, men who had known him in the old days, men who had no idea that Davy was now an active Provo.

"How's about you?" The barman leaned over and shook Davy's hand.

"Rightly. Gimme a half-un."

The barman handed Davy a glass of whiskey. Davy paid and found a chair at a table close to the bar. Acknowledging the beery greetings of the other occupants with a nod, he sat, lit a Woodbine, and sipped his whiskey, grateful for its warm, peaty taste. He tried to ignore the whining about the injustices of being a Catholic in Ulster. If the Provos hadn't taken him in, he might have become just like the rest of these deadbeats. Jesus.

He finished his drink and was wondering about having another when he saw a man stand at the table opposite. The lad was about twenty—jeans, shirt, a woolen scarf loose round his neck. He was unshaven, his eyes unfocused, and he swayed slightly. He tilted his head back and opened his mouth.

The notes were pure and sweet, the words sad and lovelorn. He sounded like a young John McCormack.

The winter it is past and the summer's come at last,
The birds they do sing on every tree,
Their little hearts are glad,
But mine is very sad,
For my true love is far away from me.

The final line of the verse hurt. God, it hurt. Davy could see her, black hair, chuckling eyes. He mouthed the words of the chorus: "So straight I will repair to the Curragh of Kildare, and it's there I'll find tidings of my dear," as the hum of conversation died.

Despite the ache for her, Davy let himself be soothed by the music, lulled by the words. While the other men pounded out their approval, he rose and bought another whiskey, a double. The boy started to sing "The Legion of the Rearguard." Davy turned his back to the bar. In the far corner three men were waving fingers in the air in time with the music. Two held two fingers aloft, the other a single digit. So the first two were locals from the 2nd Battalion and the lad with the one finger up was a visitor from 1st. He'd be down from the Upper Falls or Andersonstown or Ballymurphy. Their area of operations covered Lisburn and the surrounding countryside, too.

Davy searched his memory. First Battalion's CO was that shit Brendan McGuinness. One of the stop-at-nothing boys. The kill-women-and-children rebels. Davy spat, found an empty bit of wall to lean against, and listened to the words.

Eager and ready to defend you for love of you they die.
Proud march the soldiers of the rearguard.

Soldiers, he thought. Right, not murderers. Och, to hell with it. The song went on. As long as the youngster was going to perform, Davy would sit here, listening, enjoying, remembering—and wishing that Sean would get in touch. If Davy could no longer be a lover, at least he could be a soldier. But when would the call come?

THIRTEEN

Angus McKenzie, the Glaswegian private who had stopped Davy Mc-Cutcheon on his way to the pub, hefted his SLR. Up ahead, the sergeant ordered a halt. McKenzie squatted on the pavement. He was sick of Belfast. He'd not had a job in Glasgow since he'd left school, and the recruiting poster had seemed attractive: a grinning squaddie in a swimsuit, arm round a stunning bird, blue water, palm trees. "Join the Army and see the world," it said. He spat. "See the world?" And he'd got fucking Belfast. Still, his regiment was on roulade, only here for six months, and those six months would be up at the end of this week. Two more days, then back to their depot in Scotland. Couldn't come soon enough.

As last man in the file he could see the rest of the squad, hunkered like him. He took off his caubeen and ran his fingers through his hair. He wished they were allowed to wear steel helmets, but some brasshatted bastard had decided that helmets were seen as threatening by the civilian population. And self-loading rifles weren't?

He heard the sergeant yell, "All right. Move yourselves."

He crammed his caubeen back on his head, careless of the beret's bright red hackle, then stood and trudged along the Belfast street. He paid little attention to the lout leaning against a house on the corner, blowing his nose into a large white handkerchief.

It had been a short flight from Belfast's Aldergrove Airport to Heathrow. The major paid the cabby, went through the building's front doors, and took the lift to Sir Charles's fourth-floor office.

"Come in, Major. Have a seat."

Major Smith sat. "Thank you for seeing me, Sir Charles."

"Tea?"

"No thank you, sir. I'd better get on with my report."

"Are you getting close?"

"Not yet, sir." Major Smith saw Sir Charles's eyebrows move closer to each other as furrows appeared on the man's forehead. "But I'm making progress. I've a pretty good idea where our man's not, where to concentrate now, and how to do it."

"Tell me."

"Well, sir, Harry Swanson's been most helpful, even if he wasn't too happy about my suspecting any of his Fourteen Intelligence people and insisting we clear them first."

Sir Charles smiled. "He'll survive. Some of Swanson's mob come from the Republic of Ireland or the Catholic slums of Belfast."

"Yes, sir. We concentrated on Thirty-nine Brigade. You said the mole was working in their tactical area."

"Quite right."

Major Smith pulled a file from his briefcase. He stood, placed it on the desk, opened the file, and bent over. "Here's the chain of command of a Fourteen Intelligence company detachment seconded to the Second Paras. Field-intelligence NCOs, Intelligence subaltern. Staff captain, Intelligence." The column was marred by a cross-check. "All these men are utterly reliable."

"Good Lord, and you've done this for all of Swanson's command?"

"Just the ones with Thirty-nine Brigade, sir."

"You've been hard at it, Major."

Major Smith permitted himself a brief smile. "Gillespie, the RUC man, has been most helpful. A bit suspicious at first. You were right, sir, about the police not trusting the other intelligence services. He's an amazing repository of all kinds of information about the PIRA."

Sir Charles smiled. "And you've given him no reason to suspect what you're really after?"

"None, sir, and that's been all to the good. I'm pretty sure now the man we want is somewhere in the RUC Special Branch."

"Go on."

. . .

The dicker stuffed the handkerchief back into his pocket and ambled along the street in the opposite direction as the British squad approached the corner.

In an upstairs room, six houses from the corner, a man dressed in overalls pulled on a pair of rubber gloves. He'd seen the hanky signal and knew the soldiers were on their way.

The gloves felt tight, but Brendan McGuinness had been insistent. Wear the overalls and gloves. Do the job. Dump the outer garments. They would absorb any traces of powder. There'd be none on him if he was unlucky enough to be picked up. Leave at once and give the weapon to a dicker who would be waiting inside the back hall. He would return it to the battalion quartermaster.

The man picked up a rifle and steadied it on the window ledge. Eight British soldiers approached, four on either side of the narrow street. He sighted, just below the red hackle on the caubeen of the last man in the nearest file.

Sir Charles listened patiently as the major handed over another file and said, "These are the last twenty Provo attacks on the army. As far as I can puzzle it out, the PIRA would have needed some kind of inside gen to mount them." He paused. "Can your people find out, quietly, which RUC E Branch officers might have had any knowledge of our troops' movements prior to each of these attacks? I didn't think you'd want me to ask Gillespie, sir."

"Quite." Sir Charles hesitated. "I'll have a word with Sir Graham Shillington. He's retired now as RUC chief constable. He's an old friend and can keep his mouth shut." He grunted. "My minister would go berserk if I were to be responsible for upsetting our relations with the RUC. Mind you, it'll take Sir Graham a few days."

"I could use a few days. I'm putting a man on the street."

One of Sir Charles's eyebrows rose. "Isn't that a bit risky?"

Major Smith nodded, not betraying at all to Sir Charles exactly how risky it was going to be for Roberts, né Richardson, when he made contact with the Provos.

. . .

The sergeant turned away from McKenzie's corpse and threw up. He'd seen men killed before, but never one who had been shot in the head. He'd not known that brains look like porridge.

FOURTEEN

Marcus had worked since Sunday with the SAS captain, Captain Rupert Warnock. Warnock had introduced himself and asked if he was speaking to Mike Roberts, the chap who was going to go into the Republican areas of Belfast.

Warnock had clearly been well briefed, and Marcus, after two weeks of thinking of himself as Mike, had no trouble answering to the name. He wondered what Mr. Hyde would have done if someone had addressed him as Dr. Jekyll.

Warnock had come straight to the point. "We've not much time. My job is to give you enough know-how to fit in locally, not compromise yourself, perhaps give you a chance to pick up some useful stuff while you're there and have a fighting chance of getting out of any tight corners." He poked Marcus in the midriff and remarked, "Getting a bit flabby."

He instituted a brutal regime of calisthenics. The burpees and sit-ups and push-ups were getting easier after four days.

Warnock spent two days briefing Marcus on techniques for striking up acquaintances in bars, how to ask leading questions without seeming to do so, and how to read a face. It seemed that when a subject important to the listener was broached, or if a man was lying, his pupils contracted. And there was the "Pinocchio effect"—liars invariably touched their noses with a finger, presumably to see if it had grown. The two role-played until Marcus was sick and tired of being a friendly stranger in a pub.

Yesterday he'd started learning the words and tunes of a dozen Republican songs, like "The Men Behind the Wire," "Four Green Fields," and "The Broad Black Brimmer." Warnock assured Marcus that anyone purporting to be of Ulster extraction and with Republican sentiments would have a repertoire of such ditties. They were tuneful, but not a patch on Mozart.

Today Warnock was to give Marcus a rundown on the Provisional IRA.

They sat together at the table, a table overflowing with maps of Alberta, Belfast, Calgary; a Roman Catholic Breviary; books about football in Alberta, Canada—he now knew what his Stampeders windcheater was about—photographs of suspected Provos; and notes. Notes from the major, notes from Captain Warnock, and, somewhere under the heap, the green folder containing what Marcus now thought of as "The Life and Times of Mike Roberts."

The SAS captain explained to Marcus how the Provisional IRA could trace its roots back to the United Irishmen of the eighteenth century. Led by Wolfe Tone and Henry Joy McCracken, they had risen to expel the English and been thrashed. An American anti-British group, the Fenian Brotherhood, had flourished in the States among refugees from the potato famines of the 1840s.

In 1916, at Eastertide, followers of Patrick Pearse, Joseph Plunkett, and Éamonn Ceannt had rebelled while England was enmeshed in the meat grinder of First World War. The men who captured the General Post Office in Dublin styled themselves the Irish Republican Army. They found little popular support, and England reacted to the threat on her western flank with ruthless efficiency. The rebels were defeated, and their leaders—all but Eamon de Valera, who could claim American citizenship—were executed. England had secured her flanks, but Ireland had a fresh crop of martyrs whose example would raise fresh men to carry the banner of the IRA.

And the world moved on. The First World War ended. Ireland was partitioned. The twenty-six southern counties, predominantly Catholic, became the Irish Republic; the northeastern six counties, mainly Protestant, remained a part of the United Kingdom. World War Two staggered to its bloody conclusion. Vietnam came and went. Russians and Americans circled the earth and raced to be the first nation to put a man on the moon. England shed her empire in India, in Africa, in the islands of the Pacific and the Caribbean. And still the six counties of Northern Ireland clung resolutely to mother England's skirts like a terrified two-year-old.

Committed Republicans still hewed to the Irish Republican Army. They tried and failed to unite Ireland by force. In the midsixties, the remnants of the IRA, bypassed by history, were reduced to meeting at sentimental gatherings of the National Graves Association, which cared for the resting places of old Republican heroes, or the Republican Welfare Association, which offered what assistance it could to dependents of those who had suffered for the Cause. By 1969, the year Ulster went up in flames, there were fewer than sixty men in Belfast who regarded themselves as members of the IRA.

When the remaining IRA men tried to assume their old role as protectors of the Catholics, they had neither the manpower nor the weapons to succeed. In May 1969, when Ruairí Ó Brádaigh asked how much material the Belfast IRA possessed, he was informed: "a pistol, a machine gun, and some ammunition."

The old IRA had failed its constituency, but in its ranks were men who believed that the organization could be rebuilt and could, in time, move to the offensive against the British. The dreams of the men who had been executed after the failed Easter Rising, the martyrs of 1916, could be fulfilled with one more big push. A few days before Christmas 1969, a small group met and agreed to abandon the ways of the old IRA. They elected a Provisional Executive of twelve, who in turn selected a Provisional Army Council. These men, Seán MacStiofáin, chief of staff; Ruairí Ó Brádaigh, Dáithi Ó'Connaill, Leo Martin, Patrick Mulcahey, and Joe Cahill were the leaders of the Provisional Irish Republican Army. The Provos.

Until 1970 an uneasy harmony prevailed between the new men and those who had stayed with the old guard, the Official IRA, but at the end of April 1970 a group of Provisionals fired thirteen times at a group of Officials in Andersonstown. All of the shots missed, but in March 1971 Charlie Hughes, Provo commander of D Company in the Lower Falls, was shot dead by an Official. His death sobered the hotheads of both factions and brought the sides together to try, unsuccessfully, to bury their differences. The internecine struggle ended in April 1972, when the Officials had had enough and withdrew from the struggle, leaving the Provos, the toughest of the hard men, to continue the campaign.

Marcus was fascinated by Warnock's encyclopedic knowledge. "I never paid much attention to Irish history," he said.

Captain Warnock shrugged. "You'd better know who Wolfe Tone was if you're going to pass as a Republican. Here," he handed over a slim paperback. "It's all in here."

"Thanks."

"And you'll need to understand who the individuals are you might run into." Warnock stood. "Being in the Provos is a family business. Eighty percent of the volunteers have at least one other family member in the organization."

"Really?"

"Umm. That chap Gerry Adams. Three of his brothers have been or are in."

"I see."

"The volunteers are all working-class." Warnock grinned. "I suppose it is more fun to be a Provo than an unemployed greyhound walker. Gives a man stature in his community."

"Right," said Marcus. "And a bit of cash."

"Not really. A Provo volunteer only gets twenty pounds a week and he can't have that if he signs on for unemployment benefits. I doubt if many are in it for the money."

"Then why—"

"Some of the younger ones are in it for kicks. They don't usually last very long. Some are there for revenge. It's a tightly knit community, and it's damn near impossible to live on the Falls or in Derry without having had a relative or a friend killed, wounded, or imprisoned. A lot of that sort pack it up after a while, too."

Marcus nodded.

"The really hard men—the ones in for the long haul—are the idealists. You know the type. Dreams of Celtic Twilight, sings 'A Nation Once Again,' knows the names of the sixteen martyrs of nineteen sixteen better than his own address, and remembers the potato famine better than his last hot meal. They tend to be the Fifties Men."

"Sorry?"

"Fifties Men. The Provos date blokes by when they got involved. There're none of the men of nineteen sixteen left, but there are still a few Forties Men, and a lot of the early senior Provos were Fifties Men left over from their Operation Harvest. They call the recent crop Sixtyniners." He scowled. "I suspect our children will be dealing with the Two Thousanders."

Marcus laughed.

Warnock did not. "You have to understand how bloody suspicious they are, particularly of strangers. Now we do know that a number of men with Republican backgrounds who had been living abroad have come back to join up. But if you're going to persuade the bold boyos you've come back from Canada, you'd better be damn well word perfect in your story."

Marcus glanced at the pile of books.

"Because if you're not, the Provos don't take chances."

"I'm sorry. I don't understand."

Warnock's grin was chilling. "Let's just say if you blow your cover, you'll never have to worry about passing the examinations for promotion to captain."

FIFTEEN

McCusker lay on the floor beneath the table, paws tucked under him like a sphinx with amputated front legs. He's a loaf of cat, Davy thought. Wolfed his supper and now he's going to have a snooze. Davy sat and picked up the newspaper, known as "The Pink" because the Saturday-evening sporting edition of the *Belfast Telegraph* was printed on paper that colour. Linfield had lost to Glentoran, 2–0. Coleraine had won. Mind you, beating Glenavon this season wasn't hard.

The ginger tom opened his eyes and pricked his ears at the sound of hammering at the front door.

"Do you reckon that's Jimmy, McCusker?" Davy put down "The Pink" and looked at the clock. Six. "He's a bit early." Davy rose and limped to the door. Jimmy'd said he'd pop round for a bit of a blether. Davy opened the door.

Jimmy stood there rubbing his hands, cupping them and blowing into the hollow. "Bloody freezing, so it is."

"Aye," said Davy, pleased to see his friend. It was two and a half weeks now since Fiona had gone. Fifteen lonely days. He followed Jimmy back to the kitchen.

"Turn on the fire, for God's sake." Jimmy bent and flipped the switch of a two-bar electric heater. As the element glowed cherry-red he squatted and held his hands to the heat. "That's better," he said over his shoulder. "Cosy enough." His smile was wry. "It must have been bloody parky for them Brits over in Cupar Way."

"What Brits?"

McCusker sat up, disturbed by the urgency in Davy's voice.

Jimmy stood. "The lads found another of them secret hidey-holes last night. Four soldiers in the attic of a deserted house, infrared sniper scopes, cameras and all. They fucked off as soon as they knew they'd been rumbled. The fellow that lived next door heard noises, like. He took a wee dander over. He was poking about on the top floor when the trapdoor opened and a big soldier jumped on him. Your man near shit himself." Jimmy laughed his high-pitched hee-hee. "Can't be much fun for them soldiers, stuck for days in places like that. No heat, no WC nor nothing. The fellow that found them took a look in the attic. He said the smell would have put you out."

Davy noticed that his friend's jaw had not twitched once. And Jimmy was laughing, even if it sounded a bit forced. That was a better sign. Maybe the last few weeks of enforced idleness had been good for him. Davy himself had found the boredom hard to take. Wars weren't won by men sitting around on their arses.

Davy waved Jimmy to a chair. He'd not let Jimmy see the concern. "You'll be asking them round for a cup of tea and a piece next."

Jimmy sat, picked his nose, and hee-hee'd. "What've you been up to, anyway?" Jimmy kept shifting in his seat.

Davy shrugged and said, "Minding my own business." The less he moved about, the less he was likely to be noticed, but staying cooped up all day could arouse the suspicions of the watchers, too. "I've been to see Celtic play a couple of times, picked up my dole, had a few jars, read a bit." Tried not to think about her, he thought. Tried and failed.

"Whenever the missus would give me peace, I done a fair bit of reading myself." Jimmy cocked his thin head to one side. "Did you ever hear 'September 1913'?"

Davy never ceased to be amazed that Jimmy, child of the slums like himself, had an abiding passion for the works of William Butler Yeats. Aye, he'd heard the bloody thing a thousand times, but if Jimmy wanted to recite Davy had nothing better to do than listen Jimmy's harsh voice softened.

Davy let his friend carry on until he finished with,

Romantic Ireland's dead and gone,
It's with O'Leary in the grave.

. . .

Jimmy seemed to take his pleasure in the cadences, the rhymes. Davy heard the words. He rocked slightly, thinking, *Aye, but you're wrong, Mr. Yeats. Romantic Ireland's not dead and gone. She's still worth fighting for.* As he fought and his dead father had fought.

Davy's Ulster wasn't just the mean streets of the Falls or the grimy Lagan, flowing past the docks and the Queen's Island's shipyards to Belfast Lough. It was the white beaches of Antrim, the bustle of Smithfield Market, the purple, brooding Mourne Mountains, where the silence was only broken by the chuckling of the Shimna River.

By God, he did know what he was fighting for, and for whom. The people: poets and platers, singers and bobbin shifters, drunks and scholars, whores and wives. The Ulster people, humorous, warm—and absolutely, utterly unforgiving of a wrong. He wondered why, for all the injustices, past and present, he could not find it in his heart to hate the English. He simply wanted them gone.

Jimmy was saying something.

"Are you in there, Davy?" He leaned across the table. "That's a powerful poem, so it is."

"Right enough." Davy had no desire to tell Jimmy what he had been thinking. "You're a grand man for your Yeats, Jim. But you didn't pop in just to do your party piece."

Jimmy's jaw twitched. "Not at all. Like, ah, it's been a brave while since we've had a job. Three weeks since that ATO got killed. Do you think they've forgot us?"

"I'd doubt it, Jim. I reckon Sean's keeping the pair of us hid. For a special job, maybe. It's not as if just because we're not working the war's stopped."

"Aye. There's been plenty of action. Just about every night."

Davy's lip curled. "Soft targets. Shops. Pubs. It's time we hit the fucking peelers or the army again."

"They took out a Scottish soldier on Wednesday." Jimmy looked down at his boots and back to Davy. "Still, it's been nice and quiet for us, like."

"What are you trying to say, Jim?"

"D'you ever think about getting out, Davy?"

"Not at all. You getting cold feet?" Stupid question. He knew bloody well that Jim was, and in truth so had Davy. She'd come back to him if he did.

"Me? No way. Just wondered. I'd a letter from Siobhan. She says Canada's a great place." Davy heard the wistfulness in his friend's voice.

"Jimmy, I don't know as much Yeats as you, but you once told me one of your Mr. Yeats's poems, 'Remorse for Intemperate Speech.'"

Jimmy said, "Aye, he wrote that, in 1931. Twenty-eighth of August."

"All about great hatreds and fanatic hearts?"

"I know every word." Jimmy frowned. "But sure, Davy, you don't hate, do you?"

"Not at all. But I want the Brits gone." Davy knew he could very well need Jimmy's help soon. He wasn't going to get out of it. Davy sought for words of encouragement. "Your Siobhan says Canada's a great place?"

"Aye."

"So's Ireland. And it's going to be a better place. You and me's going to help see to that. Aren't we, Jim?"

"Oh, aye. Right enough."

"Good. Sean'll send for us soon. I just know it'll be a big one, but nothing we can't handle." Before Davy could say anything more, he heard a noise like a miniature cement mixer coming from under the table. "Ah, shit." He dropped onto his hands and knees. McCusker had sicked up a mess of half-digested cat food. He crouched, staring at Davy. Davy stood. "Bloody cat's been sick. Serve him right. That'll teach him to bite off more than he can chew."

SIXTEEN

A short, thick-set man sat by himself at a table in a dark corner of the public bar of the Elbow Room on Dublin Road, toying with a glass of sherry. He kept in the shadows, his coat collar turned up and the lower part of his face obscured by a woolen scarf. A bowler hat covered his closely cropped hair. A large Samsonite briefcase lay on the tabletop, hiding him further. Another businessman, dropping in for a quick one on his way home.

He seemed not to be paying any attention to his surroundings. He was, in fact, watching a skinny youth sitting at the bar clutching a glass of stout in one hand and a cigarette in the other. The man in the bowler hat recognized the youth as Cathal Fogarty, a volunteer with C Company, 1st Battalion, PIRA.

A packet of twenty Gallagher's Green cigarettes lay on the counter. Cathal dragged on a fag, hacking as the smoke burnt his throat but brought him no comfort from his worries. He glanced at the fingers holding the cigarette, nicotine-yellow from the bitten nails to the second knuckle. His gaze, never still, darted about the room.

It was practically deserted. Not many people came into this bar at six o'clock on a Tuesday night, and a pissing wet one at that. Cathal could just make out the shape of a figure at a table in the corner, head made to look ridiculously large by the outline of his bowler.

Cathal had never been here before. He usually hung about up in Andersonstown—1st Provo Battalion territory. He was here because he had been ordered to be. When he was told to jump, he did.

He'd come early. The man he was to meet wouldn't be here for another ten minutes. Cathal just wished the bugger would get a move on.

He wanted to get it over with, collect his money, and get back to the safety of Andersonstown. He was going to piss off tomorrow and go to his sister's in Fivemiletown. Belfast was getting too bloody hot.

The spring that closed the swinging front door twanged, and Cathal turned to watch a man shake himself like a wet spaniel, pull off a sodden cloth cap to reveal a shock of ginger hair, and make his way to the bar. Cathal's hand was clammy on the glass as he stared into his drink, studiously ignoring the newcomer.

Cathal stubbed out his cigarette. A familiar voice—too bloody familiar—ordered a Younger's Tartan. Cathal waited, picking at a tag of skin by his thumbnail, staring at the oaken tuns mounted in the wall behind the bar, reminders of the days when Guinness came in wooden, not aluminium, barrels. He heard the barman say, "Here y'are," the chink of glass against marble, and the metallic sounds of coins. He felt the pressure at his shoulder.

The bloke with the ginger hair stood there. He gave no sign that he knew Cathal Fogarty as he said, "Have you a match?"

"Aye." Cathal rummaged in his pocket for the box of Swan Vestas. "Here."

"Ta." The stranger pulled out a packet of Greens, removed a cigarette, and set the packet on the counter beside Cathal's. He lit his smoke, returned the matches, picked up a cigarette packet, and returned to his drink.

Cathal waited. His breathing was slower now that the transfer had been made. "Rusty Crust" would have the information he wanted in what had been Cathal's packet of fags and—Cathal pocketed the other smokes—he would be a hundred quid better off with no one any the wiser.

No one except a man in a bowler hat sitting in a dark corner, finishing his sherry.

The ginger-haired man, Detective Sergeant Samuel Dunlop, E Branch RUC, left the Elbow Room, walked up Dublin Road to Amelia Street, and got into a parked Ford Consul. The waiting driver pulled away from the curb.

Not until he was safely back behind the high wire anti-bomb fencing of the Springfield Road police station did Sam Dunlop open the packet

of Gallagher's Greens. The note was there, stuffed between four cigarettes. Fogarty had made out well on this transaction—not only had he
collected a hundred pounds, but there had been *ten* unsmoked fags in
Sergeant Dunlop's packet.

Fogarty'd been brought in by the CID blokes on a breaking-and-
entering charge six months earlier. He agreed to pass information in
return for having the charges dropped, and he'd been a useful source so
far. He was the one who'd given the tip about the van bomb that killed
the poor sod of an ATO, Richardson. Dunlop had been sure, though, to
make it seem that the arrest of the van's occupants had been the result
of a routine stop-and-search mission. Reliable informers were hard to
come by.

The sergeant read Fogarty's note by the glare of the arc lights surrounding the barracks. He whistled. The words, written in a jerky hand,
said, "Explosives and weapons dump at 12 Slieveban Drive."

He looked at his watch. Seven. Dunlop went into the building and
headed straight for the inspector's office. It would only take an hour to
arrange the RUC detail and the protecting troop escort, half an hour
to Slieveban Drive in Andersonstown. By 9:30 the PIRA would be short
of more supplies and, with a bit of luck, some personnel.

Brendan McGuinness's face was puce as he slammed the telephone receiver down. "Fuck it! Fuck it! Fuck . . . it!"

Sean Conlon sat watching the information officer's rage. Turlough
was in bed, and Sean saw no reason to disturb the man. It was after
midnight. He and Brendan had been putting the finishing touches on
the plan for the attack that was to be launched the next night.

"I don't fucking well believe it." Brendan's fist pounded on the shining tabletop.

Sean said nothing.

"The Brits took out Slieveban Drive about three hours ago."

"So you've lost First Battalion's ammo dump?"

"Five hundred pounds of explosives, detonators, Cordtex, sixteen
ArmaLites, two RPG-7s, five thousand rounds of 7.62-millimeter ball
cartridge"—he paused—"and three explosives men. The buggers were
building the mine for tomorrow night."

"Pity about your men."

"Never mind the fucking men." Brendan paced away from Sean, swung back, and snarled, "There's no way now we can set up the attack for tomorrow night."

"So? There'll be other chances."

"You think I don't know that? For God's sake, it was the first time we could give the survelllance equipment a decent field trial."

"I thought you had it working."

"Christ, Sean. Routine stuff. Routine stuff's coming in loud and clear, but it's not the same as when the buggers are after a real target. They could use some kind of code. I have to know."

"There'll be a way to set up the kind of mission you need."

"How? Your quartermaster's out of explosives. That was our last lot until the next shipment comes in from Dublin, and I've no more munitions men."

"We've stockpiled weapons here."

"Jesus. Guns and a few grenades? Do you fancy taking on armoured Land Rovers with nothing else?"

Sean shook his head. "No. But it's a start."

"Shit. I've got to get hold of my action squad and my inside man. Tell them the whole thing's off."

"Can you?"

"The lads is easy, but I can't talk to him. I'm not due to see him for a few days, but I can get him a message."

"Do it."

Brendan strode to the phone and dialed. "Hello, Billy? Tell the boys to tuck their heads in. Aye, it's off. And leave a note in the usual place. Say, 'No party tonight.' Aye. 'No party tonight.'" He hung up. "He'll get that when he checks the dead-letter drop."

"Good, because it's still a good plan, and we don't want your source to get a reputation for giving false alarms."

"True."

"Can we hold off for a week or two?"

"Have we a choice?"

"No. It'll take a wee while to organize, but I've a man who could make a land mine out of his granny's knickers and a piece of string."

Brendan nodded. "Go on."

"Let me get hold of him, get him on the job, and that'll give you time to get in touch with your fellow."

"If your bloke can do what you say, it could work."

"Aye. You can test your fancy gear, see if you can hear the Brits in action, and we'll take out a few more of their troops."

McGuinness thought for a moment. The British General Election was in two days, on the twenty-eighth. Another week or two wasn't so important. The British PM would be unlikely to visit Ulster for at least a month, probably longer. Sean was right. "Sounds good. We'll talk to Turlough about it in the morning. Who is your man, by the way?"

"Davy. Davy McCutcheon."

SEVENTEEN

Captain Warnock had left ten days ago. Warnock and his "Let's just say if you blow your cover, you'll never have to worry about passing the examinations for promotion to captain." Today was to be a different kind of examination—the finals the major had mentioned at the start of Marcus's training. Marcus rose early, impatient, wanting to get on with it.

He finished shaving, running the razor over the strip of skin that stretched from his lower lip, round the centre of his chin, and down over his throat. He looked in the mirror. The split in his lip had healed, leaving a pale, thin scar. The bruises had turned from black to a yellowy greenish-purple, like the skin round the vent of a pheasant hung for too long. His new moustache was an expanded Pancho Villa—full over the upper lip, narrower at the corners of the mouth, and widening again as it ran down his chin and in underneath. He frowned when he discovered some grey hairs among the black.

The acne was an irritant. He lifted the dark, oily fringe from his forehead and peered at the angry red pustules. A military haircut would stick out like a sore thumb, but after four weeks—and he had been ready for a trim before all of this—he was starting to look like John Lennon in his Maharishi phase.

"*Ohm mane padme ohm,*" he intoned solemnly. The smile in his hazel eyes, reflected in the glass, gave the lie to his gloomy voice. He didn't mind the length of his hair. He just wished that this Mike Roberts character was a man of more fastidious habits.

Marcus Richardson spoke to his reflection: "Mike Roberts, you're a right heap of shit, so y'are." His accent was thick County Down. Norn Irn.

It had taken time to work into his new persona—Mike Roberts, the man in the green ring binder—but it had been fun. No, he corrected himself, a wee lad from Bangor would never talk about "fun." It was powerful *craic*, so it was—so far. This finals business? He wondered if it could be any worse than the "render safe procedure" he'd had to take at Longmoor before graduating. They'd given him a real sod of a parcel bomb to deal with.

He buttoned his shirt and trotted down the stairs. He looked at the briefing materials strewn around the small living room, a far cry from the tidy heaps that John had left on the first day. So much to have learned in so short a time.

In the kitchen an electric clock hanging crookedly on the beige-painted wall made a wheezing noise. It always did that just before the hour, and the noise irritated him. Five to eight. John wouldn't be here for another two hours. Marcus hadn't had anything to eat yet, and eating would help to pass the time. Until finals.

He sat at the kitchen counter, spreading butter on the cut surface of a triangular piece of soda bread. A wee cup of tea in his hand and a bit of soda farl and butter. That's what Mike would fancy. He'd like the soda bread fried with bacon and eggs. Mike was a grand man for the pan.

Mike Roberts. Same initials, and Mike sounded like Marc, the diminutive used by his friends. Convenient that the real Mike Roberts from Bangor was on a rig somewhere away to hell and gone, north of a place called Fort McMurray, Alberta. Marc and Mike. Initials, birthplace, and familiarity with explosives. That was where any true similarities stopped.

The rest of Roberts's background was very different from Marcus's. Roberts was a Catholic, but Marcus felt uncomfortable reciting the phrases of the Mass. Roberts's tastes, according to the briefing notes, were coarse: fish and chips, which he probably chewed with his mouth open; beer; soccer; betting on the horses; dances at Caproni's in Bangor on a Saturday night. He'd left school at sixteen.

Roberts was not the sort of man a British army officer would meet socially. Which posed the question, How had the major known about him? Marcus had asked, a couple of weeks ago, but the major had deflected the question with a dismissive, "Don't worry about it. You'll just have to trust me." The funny thing was, once he overcame his initial anger and a feeling of being used, Marcus had come to trust John

Smith. He looked forward to their daily sessions and enjoyed the man's company.

Smith was straight as a die. Not one bit hesitant about giving a tongue-lashing if a task had not been completed to his satisfaction. Marcus thought of his father. He was a perfectionist, too. One thing about the major, though, he was generous with his praise for a job well done.

John had said last night that if Mike passed this final test, he would be told the exact nature of his mission and, within a couple of days, would be in action. It was about time. He just hoped that all of this was going to be worth it.

It certainly would be if John kept his promise, once this was over, to arrange for Marcus's acceptance on a Special Air Service Regiment aptitude course. He knew how tough the SAS selection process was but was confident he could pass. He'd have to. If he didn't, he'd be back in the bomb-disposal business, and he was quite sure now that he could live without that particular job.

He knew even at the time he'd chosen bomb disposal that he'd been unsure of his reasons. Proving to himself that he could conquer his fears was all very well, but not at the price of having his head blown off. He'd been lucky he'd not been closer to the blue van with the bomb.

"Morning, Mike."

"Morning, John." Marcus looked up from his reading as the major stood aside to let a stranger precede him into the living room. The man wore cavalry twill trousers, a striped shirt, and an old khaki battledress blouse. He was short, compact, and slouched. He needed a shave and his brown hair was cut in an unfashionable crew cut. His head was wet. He must not have been wearing a hat. Marcus tried to guess the man's age. Forty? Forty-five?

His thin lips were set at twenty past eight. The stranger folded his arms and examined Marcus, looking at him as a butcher might look at prime beef before deciding precisely where to cut.

The major lit a cigarette. "Pity neither you nor the real Roberts smoke. It's a handy way to meet people in pubs—cadge a fag, offer one."

Marcus smiled. "I tried one once. Bloody near thew up." He could tell by his nod that the major approved of the use of Belfast vernacular: "thew" for "threw."

The major said, "Now, Mike, when you're on the street trying to find out anything you think might be useful, the opposition will be finding out about you. Newcomers always get the once-over." He paused. "We think there's a fair chance they might try to recruit you into the Provos. An explosives expert, just back from Canada, unknown to the Security Forces, would be too good to miss. But your cover story has to fool them completely." He raised one eyebrow. "Some of those chaps might appear a bit dense, but they're not stupid, and if they do suspect, you'll find yourself in very deep difficulties."

The other man grunted. "Aye, and you'd not like that." His Belfast accent was so thick as to be almost incomprehensible. "We don't like touts, so we don't."

"We?" Marcus played the eye-contact-dominance game.

The major explained. "My friend Fred here was with the Provos."

The man continued to stare.

Marcus looked away.

The major drew on his cigarette. "If they do go after you, boy, it won't be name, rank, and serial number and cite the Geneva Convention. You'll have to be able to persuade some very hard men that you really are who you claim to be, or—"

"If they don't think you're dangerous," Fred snarled, "you'll get a six-pack—bullets in the elbows, knees, and ankles." He pointed one index finger at his own temple. The fingernails were bitten to the quick. "If they decide you're a bad fucker," he snapped his thumb forward, "head job." He gave no inflection to the matter-of-fact remark.

"So," said the major, crushing out his cigarette, rising, and walking round the table to stand behind Marcus, "Fred here is going to interrogate you. He's the IO of Second Battalion."

Marcus took a deep breath. He must now become Mike Roberts, in name and in character.

Fred moved his chair closer. "Do you know why you're here?"

"Aye. Your other fellow," Mike nodded his head back to where the major stood, "said you wanted to ask me a few questions."

"Does that not bother you?"

"Not at all. Fire away." He lounged in the chair. No reason for an innocent man to be tense.

"Name?"

"Mike Roberts."

"How long have you lived in Belfast?"

"Three weeks."

"Where were you before that?"

"Canada. I worked on the oil rigs. Money was terrific, so it was."

"Where were you from before Canada?"

"Bangor."

Fred picked up a file. "Says here you grew up in Four Victoria Road. That's up by Ward Park?"

Mike laughed. "Not at all. It's at the start of Seacliff Road, just across from Billy Caulfield's rowboats. There's a sandstone-capped seawall. Turn left, past Barry's Amusements, the Palladium, High Street, Luchi's, The Boulevard."

"Roberts. When I want a conducted tour I'll ask. Just answer the fucking questions." There was a sibilant tone in Fred's voice. "Mother's name?"

"Jean. She was killed when I was wee." He let his voice hold a tinge of sorrow. Not difficult when he thought of his real mother, who believed him dead.

Fred rammed his bristly head forward and spat, "How long have you been working for the Brits?"

Mike jerked backward. "What?" Don't get rattled, he told himself. "Away off and feel your head."

"Say the first two lines of the Hail Mary."

"Hail Mary, full of Grace, the Lord is with Thee; Blessed art Thou amongst women, and blessed is the Fruit of Thy womb, Jesus." Mike crossed himself.

"What killed Jane?"

"Tarzan, for all I know. Who the fuck's Jane?"

"Your mother."

"I already told you her name was Jean. Jean. Are you deaf or stupid?"

Fred's eyes narrowed. Spittle flecked his lips as he shouted, "Don't you call me stupid, you wee shite." He leaned forward and stabbed Mike's chest with a rigid index finger. "Do you know what kind of trouble you're in?"

Mike began to rise. He remembered what Captain Warnock had said, not to be afraid to show anger to an interrogator, as an innocent man certainly would. "Shit. I don't have to take"—he felt hands force him back into the chair and a voice from behind saying, "But you do, son."

He squirmed but couldn't turn. The pressure of the grip on his collarbones was painful. He was surprised by the major's strength.

Fred calmed down as suddenly as he had exploded. "I'll ask you again. How long have you been working for the Brits?"

"I'm not." He let his feigned cockiness evaporate. "Honest to God. I'm not."

Fred looked in the file. "Where've you been for the last nine years?"

"Canada. My da took me and my two brothers out there—"

"Mrs. Kildare, number 6, Victoria Road, says you were a great lad for a song when you were wee. Says you knew every word of 'The Cruise of the Calabar.'"

Mike said nothing.

"Give us a verse or two."

"Ah, come on . . ."

"Now!"

Mike coughed, cast his mind back to the pages of the students' songbook, and sang,

Come all you dry land sailors and listen to my song.
It's only a hundred verses so I won't detain you long.
It's about the adventures of this . . .

The punch rocked his head back. The scar on his lower lip burst, filling his mouth with the coppery taste of blood. Fred stood over him, file open in one hand, accusatory finger pointing. "You, you miserable cunt, you're not Mike Roberts. You're Lieutenant Marcus Richardson, Royal Army Ordnance Corps."

The stinging blow had momentarily scrambled his mind, but he mumbled past the pain of his split lip. "I'm not. I'm not." He felt his eyes filling. "I'm Michael Roberts from Bangor. A good Catholic, from Bangor. For fuck's sake, I'm on your side. Honest to God."

The man called Fred had left.

"Sorry about that, but it was necessary." The major leaned across the table from where he was sitting and took back his bloodstained handkerchief. "Stopped?"

"I've had worse boxing."

"Of course." The major glanced at the red blotches on the white linen before stuffing it into the pocket of his Donegal tweed sports jacket. "Must say I thought you did rather well."

Marcus managed a small smile. "Dead-on."

His smile was returned. "Good. I'd have been disappointed if you'd said, 'Thank you.'" The smile faded. "Of course, the real thing would be considerably worse, but play your cards right and it won't come to that. The story—and by the way you do seem to have learnt it well—will hold up. You'd the right amount of insolence, and there's nothing wrong with showing fear."

Marcus said nothing. He had not been acting at the end. He had been terrified when the ex-Provo erupted.

"Fred's not the bloke's real name, and he's not a Provo." The major looked embarrassed. "RUC Special Branch, actually. Very solid chap."

Marcus felt the stiffness in his jaw. "I noticed."

"What? Oh. Quite." The major smiled. "Quite. Well done." He pulled an envelope from the inside of his jacket. "Some final details." He put the buff packet on the table, his jaundiced gaze firmly locked on Marcus's eyes. "We've been through most of this before, but you'd better refresh your memory and look carefully at the new stuff. You're going in on Friday."

"Friday?" The dryness in his mouth, not the split lip, made speaking a tad difficult. "That's the day after tomorrow."

The major held out his hand. "I'm proud of you."

Marcus took the hand. "Thanks, John."

"Have a bit of rest today and tomorrow." The major picked up the envelope. "Take a look at this. Your new address is in here. Number Ten Robina Street, New Lodge. A bed-sitter's been rented in your name." He opened the envelope and removed two typed sheets of paper and some black-and-white photographs.

Marcus began to reach for them but was forestalled when the major said, "Patience, laddie. Look at these first." He handed over the typescript. "Please read this very carefully. It gives you the details of what you've to look for, how you're to report, and"—he hesitated briefly—"how to get to hell out if you think you've been spotted." He lit a cigarette. "Take your time."

Marcus began to read. It was clear from the first page that he was not being asked to be James Bond and single-handedly overthrow the entire Provisional IRA. He was to move into his flat, get to know the neighbourhood, frequent the betting shops and pubs, and spend some of the money he'd purportedly made in Canada. He was to try to become accepted by the locals and keep an eye out for any of the men whose photographs he had been studying for the last four weeks. If he met any of them, he was to make a special effort to strike up a conversation. Flaunt his Republican sympathies and boast that he had become an explosives expert while working in the Alberta oil patch, had heard other Irishmen had come back from overseas to fight for the Cause, and thought that he should, too. Sooner or later, if all went well, he would be approached.

"Seems simple enough."

"Read on."

The second page was more specific. Once approached, he was to go along with his recruiters, even to the lengths of making the Provisional IRA declaration of allegiance. His mission was to identify the bomb maker or makers of 2nd Provo Battalion and as many of their battalion or brigade officers as possible. The more senior Provos he could make contact with, the better.

"So you want the officers?"

"We do."

"Right." Marcus returned to the instructions. Reporting was to be kept to a minimum. If something were to be passed back, he was to make an appointment to see a Dr. Kennedy, whose surgery was on the Antrim Road. The major would have someone there to take the report. That method should be used infrequently and only when he had something of real importance. A telephone number was given for emergencies only. Marcus recognized that it did not have the Belfast 0232 prefix. He started to ask where the phone was located but realized that if he was meant to have the information, it would have been given.

The final paragraph was headed "If Compromised." His experience with the man called Fred was fresh in Marcus's mind. "I don't fancy the sound of this 'If Compromised' bit."

"Shouldn't worry, old boy. You're going to be damn good at this." The major's smile was open, honest.

Marcus took comfort from his friend's obvious confidence and trust.

Major Smith stubbed out his cigarette. "If the one in a million does happen, the procedure's simple. It's all in there." He nodded at the typed pages. "Head for the nearest army observation post or patrol, RUC officers, or barracks and give them the password."

Marcus consulted the page. "Whigmaleerie"

The major laughed. "Right. What is a whigmaleerie, by the way?"

"A whatchamacallit. A thingamabob."

"Mmm. Whigmaleerie." He handed Marcus two photographs. "Here's a few more. These two just came in last night. This chap," he indicated a young man with a set of whiskers not unlike the ones Marcus had grown, "we think is quartermaster for D Company of the Second Battalion. This is Frank Fitzsimmons, First Battalion. He'll not be around by the weekend. We're onto him."

Marcus saw the major's expression. He looked like a man who had found something disgusting on the sole of his shoe as he said, "You know 'Fitz' is old Norman-Irish for 'bastard son'? He's well named." The major picked up the remaining pictures. "Have a good look at these brave boyos." His upper lip curled and his voice was venomous. "These sods were involved in the M62 bombing last month. These are older pictures, but we'd like to know if these men have resurfaced in Belfast. We really do want to have a word with them."

Marcus heard the anger. He shared it. On February 4, nine soldiers, a woman, and two children had been killed when a bomb exploded on a bus from the army camp at Catterick. "I'll keep a special eye out for them."

"Good lad." The major stood. "Get your gear together and get rid of anything that would connect you with us. I'll pick you up at nineteen hundred on Friday."

Marcus stood quickly. It was really happening. He had a clear idea of what was expected of him, and obviously John had confidence that "Mike" would perform well. That was important. The major was not the kind of man that Marcus would let down. He picked up the photographs, anxious to commit the faces to memory.

The major said, "Silly of me. I nearly forgot." He produced a small camera from his jacket pocket. "Just need a couple of candids. Stand over there by the wall."

Marcus moved away from the table.

"Not in front of those bloody rhododendrons."

"Right."

The series of flashes blinded him. He wondered what the pictures were for.

"We'll airbrush out that split in your lip." The major put a hand on Marcus's shoulder. "Sorry that the interrogation was so tough."

Marcus adopted Mike's character, shrugged, and said, "Sure thon fella couldn't have knocked the skin off a rice pudding."

The major did not smile. "He's done a lot more than that. And the lads he was imitating? So have they."

"No sweat."

The major turned as he reached the door. "I know you'll do well, Marcus."

Mike looked over his shoulder to see who the major was addressing. "Who's this Marcus fellow?"

"Well done, Mike."

"I seen *The Great Escape*. Gordon Jackson's pretending to be French and a German says, 'Good luck' in English. Stupid bugger Jackson answers in English. That trick has whiskers."

The major chuckled and then asked, "What's the last line of the Hail Mary?"

And Marcus answered, "Holy Mary Mother of God, pray for us sinners, now and at the hour of our death."

EIGHTEEN

Davy had been ordered to 15B Myrtlefield Park at two in the afternoon on Thursday. He rang the bell and waited. The front door opened.

"Come on in, Davy. Good to see you." It was the commanding officer of the 2nd Battalion.

"Sean Conlon?" Davy stepped forward and clasped the man's hand. "Sean—what the hell are you doing here?"

"Will you come in, man."

Davy was hustled into a ground-floor flat. He heard the door close behind him. The room was beautifully furnished, high-ceilinged, spacious, and well lit by a bay window. This was very grand. He snatched off his cap.

"Here. Give us your coat. Sit down. How are you, Davy?"

"Well enough."

Davy took one of the chairs surrounding a mahogany dining table. He kept his hands in his lap, worried that his sweat might mar the polish.

"Make yourself at home." Sean sat at the other side of the table. The broad grin on his open face could not disguise the dark circles under his blue eyes.

"Jesus," said Davy. "This is very swank."

"Aye. Not the sort of place for the likes of us."

Davy nodded.

"We hope the Brits think that way, too."

"What?" Davy stiffened. "What Brits?"

"The ones that keep searching houses in the Falls and Ardoyne and the Pound Loney and all the other places where they go hunting for us. Do you think they'd break into houses where the rich people live?"

"Right enough." Davy smiled at his mental image of an irate company director, standing beside a door with a shattered lock, giving a British squaddie the bollocking of his life. "Right enough. They'd never come to a place like this. It's a dead brilliant idea, Sean, so it is."

Sean Conlon's smile faded. God, thought Davy, the man looks tired. Thirty-five and he looks fifty. "How long have you been living here?"

"Not long enough. Did you hear what happened last week?"

"What?"

"The fucking soldiers cleaned out First Battalion's dump and their explosives men."

"Shit." Davy hawked, but could not bring himself to spit on the plush carpet.

"Aye. Shit, but do you know what?"

"What?"

"We're going to hit back. We've a job for you. The buggers that raided the supply dump."

"Good. What do you need?"

"A land mine."

"No sweat. What'll the quartermaster have for me? Gelignite? TNT?"

Sean shook his head. "That's the problem, Davy. There's a shipment due from Dublin, but it's not in yet. We've nothing left since the raid on First Battalion's folks. Last night's attack on the Grand Central Hotel was a five-hundred pounder. It cleared out Second Battalion's reserves."

Davy grunted. "More civilians."

"Come on, Davy. The Brits were using it as an army HQ for the Royal Horse Artillery."

"I'm glad it wasn't one of mine." He paused. "You're out of explosives?"

"Aye."

"No problem. Be like the old days. You'd be amazed what can be made with stuff that's just lying about. What's the target?"

"Army Land Rovers."

"Pipe bomb'll do it. I'd need to go out with the action squad to set it." Davy wondered why the CO had a worried look on his face.

"Would you go out?"

Davy's grin broadened. "Aye, certainly. It's been a brave while since I had a close-up whack at the shites." His grin faded and he peered at Sean. "You said army, didn't you?"

"Aye."

"That's all right then. I'd not want to go after civilians."

"I know how you feel, but the pair of us have to do what Army Council says, and they reckon that part of our job's to make this province ungovernable."

"I suppose railway ticket collectors are part of the government." Davy hardly considered his words. Unbidden, his mind had turned to Fiona.

"What?"

"My last one took out a ticket man. His kids were in Fiona's class. She took such a scunner she left me."

"Jesus, Davy. I'm sorry."

Davy heard the concern in Sean's voice.

"Aye. Well. We'll say no more. When do you want the mine?"

"Do you think she'll come back?"

"I said, 'When do you want the mine?'"

"Friday, two weeks. Unless the stuff comes in from Dublin before. We'll let you know. If it does, you'll not need to cook up something in your kitchen."

"I'd still need a bit of time, and I'd have to know what explosives I'd be using if you do get the new stuff in."

Sean lowered his voice and Davy wondered why. If there was anyone else here, they would not have to be kept in the dark. "We should be getting some of the usual stuff, but if it all works out this time we'll be getting our first consignment of Semtex."

Davy whistled. Semtex. He'd read about the stuff in a badly translated Czech manual but had never worked with it. Hadn't the first clue how to. "Semtex? That's pretty powerful stuff, so it is."

"It is, and we'd only use it for important targets. Even if it comes in, we'll not be sending you any for this one."

Davy was not sure whether to be relieved that he would not be asked to work with the new plastique or annoyed that his next mission was not considered important. He scowled.

"Come on, Davy, I didn't mean it that way."

"Aye. Well."

"Look. I can't give you the details, but this raid on the army Rovers is important. It's the first step in something really big that we're planning."

"Oh?"

Sean smiled. "Davy, even if I wanted to tell you, I couldn't. Sometimes our Brigade IO plays his cards very close. He's told me there's a big one coming, but I don't know the details myself."

"Sean, I believe you."

"I know." Sean rose. "Davy, get this one out of the way and I promise you'll get your chance with the Semtex."

Davy stood and took Sean's outstretched hand. "Don't bother your head about this one."

"I won't. And I meant it about the Semtex. You'll get it for the big one."

"I know," said Davy, flattered at Sean's automatic confidence in his munition man's expertise—and already wondering where in the name of Jesus Christ Almighty was he going to find out how to work with the stuff.

Sean Conlon watched through the bay window as big Davy limped down Myrtlefield Park toward the Lisburn Road. Sound man, Davy McCutcheon. One of the old guard. They'd fought together for four years now. Just like Davy to want to be reassured that he would be attacking the military. And he would be, when an army patrol was decoyed out to a remote country lane. A mined country lane.

When McCutcheon went out this time, the action squad would be 1st Battalion men. They wouldn't know Davy, and he was to keep it that way. Sean wanted to keep his best armourer's identity secret, even from his own volunteers. Good munitions experts were hard to find and, as far as Sean was concerned, should be protected from any chance an informer might give them away. He heard the door open and turned. He greeted two men. "Brendan. Turlough."

"Sean." Brendan McGuinness crossed the room and stood, left shoulder higher than his right, facing Conlon. "So? Can the old bugger do it?"

Sean nodded.

McGuinness raised one dark eyebrow. He had heavy brows that met over the bridge of his nose. "Sure?"

"Of course I'm fucking sure."

McGuinness grunted. "I'd rather have used one of my own men, but we've no other choice."

Turlough Galvin spoke softly. "Sean?"

Sean saw the fleeting look of ill-concealed contempt on McGuinness's foxy face. *You don't like Turlough Galvin, do you, Brendan? You reckoned you'd succeed Ivor Bell as Brigade CO, not Galvin. He's a better man than you, Brendan.* Sean spoke directly to Galvin. "Davy's experienced, he's reliable, he takes pride in his work, and"—he put just enough sting in his words—"you seem to have been a bit careless with your armourers, Brendan."

McGuinness bridled. "Nothing careless about it. Someone grassed."

Galvin snapped, "Who?"

McGuinness smiled. "Cathal Fogarty. I got the word from my man last night. We're looking for Cathal."

"Cathal? Jesus," Galvin said. "Find him."

"We will." McGuinness said. "We will."

"Do that." Galvin's tone brooked no discussion.

"I said I will," said McGuinness. "Come on, we've a raid to plan." He turned to Sean. "When'll McCutcheon be ready?"

"I told him the twenty-second."

McGuinness smiled. "Good. That gives my man time to set it up. Once he's fed the Brits the information about an arms dump, he'll let us know when they'll send out the patrol."

"And you'll be able to monitor their conversations?" Turlough Galvin asked.

McGuinness frowned. "I hope so. I've been buggering about with the stuff for the last week. It's too good. Sometimes it takes a while to sort through everything that comes in." His frown lifted. "But it's clear as a bell. Hear every word."

"Good," said Turlough Galvin. "Keep at it."

McGuinness looked at Galvin. "Turlough, how much longer will it be until the lads out in Libya are up to speed?"

"Hard to say. Gadhafi's lot can be pretty disorganized."

"Fucking A-rabs."

Sean said quietly, "Those 'A-rabs' have given us millions, arms, Semtex, and they're training our new explosives experts. Watch who you're calling names, McGuinness."

Turlough Galvin snapped, "That's enough."

McGuinness bowed his head. "All right, Turlough." He smiled, showing uneven teeth. Teeth that had a slight green discolouration. "We'll see how McCutcheon does." The smile fled. "But as soon as the boys get back from Libya, McCutcheon's expendable."

NINETEEN

Rhododendrons. The major was sick of rhododendrons. The bloody things leered out of that god-awful print next door and lurked in an identical picture waiting for him when he returned here to his half of the semi.

He lit a cigarette. He'd be out of these quarters tonight. It would take half an hour to drive Richardson to New Lodge, and then the major could head over to army HQ at Thiepval. He'd be glad to be back home in an officers' mess and to have Richardson in play.

The doorbell rang. Smith opened the door to a corporal standing at attention. "Delivery, sir." The corporal handed over an envelope.

"Thank you, Corporal."

"Sir." The NCO about-turned and marched away, his ammunition boots crashing on the tarmac.

The major closed the door and returned to the living room. He glanced in the envelope before throwing it on the table. Canadian passport and Alberta driver's licence, both in the name of Michael Roberts.

He was assailed by a fit of coughing. Bloody cigarettes. The medical officer had told him to stop smoking, spouting some rubbish about lung cancer. His malarial spleen was more likely to get him. It was the size of a rugby football and fragile as a jellyfish. The Malays used to murder people with a gadget like a knobby crucifix called a larang. If they belted a chap below his left ribs with the larang, his malarial spleen went pop.

He stood up and stepped to the window, looking across the Bangor to Belfast Road and over the marshes of the shores of Belfast Lough. To his left, in the distance, the Goliath crane loomed over the dry dock of the Harland and Wolff shipyards. To his right he could see the high perimeter fence and the sentry posts at the gateway, posts manned by armed soldiers. God, it was good to be back in the army.

He ran his fingers along the windowsill, inspecting them for dust. His fingertips were filthy. He hated dust and felt that since he had left the army, his life had been turning to dust. He pursed his lips. Today any idea of patriotism, Queen, and country was passé, but, damn it, being a soldier was all he'd ever wanted.

He walked to the kitchen, turned on the tap, waited for the plumbing to disgorge a thin stream of rusty water, washed and dried his hands on a towel. He folded the towel in threes before hanging it back on the rail, neither end overlapping the other. He looked at his watch. Harry Swanson should be here soon, and not long afterward they would collect Richardson and drop him in New Lodge. Then—what had Holmes said to Watson?—"The game's afoot."

He went back into the dining room. A fly-tying vise was mounted on the edge of the table, the half-finished body of a Royal Coachman held in its jaws. He sat and admired his handiwork. He could certainly finish it, and a few more, before it was time to go. That was the difficulty with fly-fishing. As often as not, when the fish had taken the lure, it made a run for freedom, and the fly was gone forever.

And he had to think of lures now. He pinched the bridge of his nose between a forefinger and thumb and yawned. It had been a long two months since Sir Charles had offered John Smith this mission. He'd spent the time painstakingly reviewing files, interviewing intelligence officers and their FINCOs—field-intelligence noncommissioned officers. He was satisfied that all Harry's blokes in 14 Intelligence Company were clean, and MI5 had been most helpful. Unlikely that the leak was there. He had no doubt, none at all, that somewhere in RUC Special Branch a traitor was feeding info to the Provos.

It was a shame that Sir Charles had insisted on all this pussyfooting about because of the sensitivity of RUC-intelligence relations. Eric Gillespie could have found out the gen the major wanted in no time flat without them having to send Richardson in.

The major shrugged. He was thankful for small mercies. Even if Gillespie had been misled about the real reason Richardson was being trained, Eric had been useful. Very useful. That had been a hell of a performance when he'd impersonated the ex-Provo. Neither Harry Swanson nor the major himself could have been as convincing. He'd really given Richardson something to think about.

The major was quite sure that, after the way Richardson had handled himself, the young man was ready. Bursting at the seams to find the IRA bomber and his superiors.

The major picked up the dangling spool of black thread and began to wrap the thorax of the fly with patient, meticulously even turns. The time passed quickly. He paused to admire the six beautifully tied flies: two Royal Coachmen, two William's Favourites, and a pair of Renegades clipped in place in a small silver fly box. He could tie one more before Harry arrived. He selected a Mustad hook, clamped it in place, and had almost completed the fly when he heard the sound of a car pulling up outside. He went to the front door, opening it before Harry Swanson had a chance to knock.

"John."

"Come in, Harry."

The major glanced over Swanson's shoulder and saw that the car parked outside was the Ford he had ordered, repainted and with new number plates. Good. Wouldn't do to let the Provos see the same civilian vehicles in their neighbourhoods too often. Certainly wouldn't do if some sharp-eyed terrorist noticed young Richardson getting out of a car that had been identified. He followed Harry Swanson into the living room. They sat.

"So," said Swanson, "all set?"

"Yes." The major looked at his companion. Bald as a billiard ball, slim, clean-shaven, a deep dimple in his left cheek when he smiled as he was smiling now.

He said, "I didn't know you were an angler."

"Trout mostly."

"I prefer chub or dace myself. Lots of them in the canals in Yorkshire." Swanson's smile faded. "We're after bigger fish now, John."

"True. And thanks for all your help."

"I just hope it works."

"It should. It'll take Richardson a week or two to make contact. I'll have the intelligence from London by then."

"You're sure the man we're after is in the RUC?"

"Pretty much. I've asked Sir Charles to let me have the details of unexpected attacks on our forces. Missions that the Provos could only have mounted with inside gen. I particularly want to know which RUC officers would have known the movements of our people."

"You reckon there'll be a pattern?"

"Definitely. I'm betting there will be one name that stands out."

"Then what?"

"Depends on Richardson."

"How?"

"If the brave boyos do take him on, he'll have to know when raids are coming up. We'll organize a juicy bombing target that only our suspect knows about. If Richardson's told to prepare a device for an attack, he'll tell us and we'll know where the Provos got their info."

"That might just work."

The major began to attach the wings to the Black Butcher. "It had bloody well better." If it didn't he had only one other plan up his sleeve, one he had no intention of sharing with Harry Swanson. "I'll just finish this fly and then we'll be off." He cocked his head to inspect the underbelly. It wasn't quite even. Not up to his usual standards, but sometimes he had to use the best lure that came to hand. Flies really were the only sporting way to take a fish. Only a thorough rotter—he finished the knot and cut the thread—would use live bait.

TWENTY

The stink was enough to choke a cat. McCusker, in fact, had fled. Despite a streaming head cold, Davy could not ignore the acrid steam coming from four pints of his urine, boiling in a can on the stove. He sniffed, feeling the raw burning in his nostrils, the tightness at the back of his throat.

Another ten minutes should have the original eighty ounces evaporated down to eight. There would be plenty of urea in that, and one of Jimmy's mates had nicked enough nitric acid from Mackie's Foundry up on the Springfield Road. Now, if Jimmy had been successful on this afternoon's errand . . .

Davy sat at the table and waited. A few more hours wouldn't make a pick of difference. It was nearly two weeks since his meeting with Sean Conlon. A bloody long two weeks, but the job was on for this Friday. It was good to be back at work, and knowing that the target was the army helped. Not even Fiona—gone six weeks—could object to this one. Or maybe she could. She hadn't said, "Stick to being a soldier." She'd said, "The Provos or me." Davy glanced at her picture and took a deep breath, coughed as the fumes burnt his throat, and murmured, "God, I want you back, girl."

He sneezed and groped in the pocket of his brown grocers' coat for a handkerchief. He honked into the cloth and was wiping the end of his nose when someone knocked at the front door.

"Hold your horses."

Jimmy stood on the step, dressed in paint-splattered white dungarees. He looked cheerful. "Got it," he said, offering a carrier bag to Davy.

"Good man." Davy took the bag. "Come on in."

"Jesus," said Jimmy. "Smells like a French hoor house."

"How the fuck would you know? You've never been outside of Ireland in your life." Davy closed the door and followed Jimmy into the kitchen.

"I've read about French hoor houses." Jimmy peered into the can on the stove. "Looks like it's near ready."

Davy rummaged in the carrier and pulled out a tin of brown enamel paint. "For Christ's sake, I didn't send you to buy paint."

Jimmy mouthed a snatch from an old music hall song. "Do you want your oul' lobby washed down, Mrs. Brown?" He shoved his hand inside his dungaree top and produced a paper bag. "You reckon this'll do the trick?" He handed the package to Davy. "Buy paint in a paint shop, they think you're a painter. Buy aluminum powder, and you've half the RUC on your back. It's easy enough to feck a pound or two when the storeman's in the back mixing," he pointed to the can and said in a falsetto voice, "burnt ochre."

Davy looked into the bag and saw the silvery granules. "Good man." He set the bag beside the bottle of nitric acid. "Right. Give us the carboy."

Jimmy lifted a large glass bottle from the floor. A strip of gauze was tied firmly over the mouth. Davy limped to the stove, turned off the gas, put on a pair of oven mitts, and carried the can over to the table. He poured the concentrated urine through the gauze and into the bottle.

Jimmy, who had taken a seat, watched. "Jesus, Davy. You've a quare soft hand under a duck."

"Quit farting about. Hand me the nitric." He put the empty can on the floor, took off the mitts, and eyed the bottle of acid. "What do you reckon?"

"Near enough to three to one."

"Right." Davy dribbled the nitric into the urine, holding his head to one side as the mixture frothed and gave off nostril-burning yellow fumes. He put the bottle on the table and sneezed. "Bugger." He sniffed. Loudly.

"Bless you," said Jimmy, scratching his sandy hair. "Do you fancy nipping out for a jar while we wait?"

"Nah. You run on, Jim. I'm full of the cold. Anyway, I'd better not take a drink 'til I've this here finished. Away on home to your missus."

"Aye. But I'll stop in for one on the way." He chuckled, "hee-hee. The old one always looks a bit better after I've had a couple. Mind you," Jimmy was beaming, "she's been in better form this last while, ever since our wee girl wrote and said she was coming back from Canada."

"Siobhan? How long's she coming for?"

"Six weeks. She's been gone four years. She was a wee corker when she left. She'll likely be the quare lady now. I'll hardly know my own daughter. Plane comes in to Aldergrove tomorrow." Jimmy positively bubbled. "Four years is a brave long time, so it is. She's had to save up for the fare."

Davy was going to speak, but a fit of coughing cut him short. He slapped himself twice on the chest.

There was concern in Jimmy's voice. "You going to be all right?"

Davy nodded and waited for the coughing to stop. Why was Jimmy looking like a mother whose youngster had just fallen down and skinned his knees? A mother with a facial tic.

"You mean this cold?"

"Aye. And, Davy. You're getting too old to be gallivanting about with an action squad. You take care of yourself, now."

"Don't worry your head about me, Jim."

Jimmy made a sucking noise of cheek against teeth. "All right," he said, rising. "I believe you. Thousands wouldn't." He peered into the carboy. "It's coming on. I doubt there's another man in Belfast would know how to do that."

"Away on. Sure they taught us that years ago."

"Aye, and gelly and TNT and ammonium nitrate."

Davy hesitated. "Do you know anything about Semtex, Jim?"

"Semtex?"

"Aye."

"It's one of them new plastic jobs."

"I know that. Do you know how to use it?"

"Why?"

"Sean says there's a batch coming in. He wants us to do something special with it."

"Jesus. I seen a movie once. The hero had to make what they called 'shaped charges'. Made a hell of a bang in the film."

"Shaped charges?"

"Aye. But that's all I know."

"Never worry. I'll find out somehow."

Jimmy scratched his chin. "Did Sean tell you what it's for?"

"Not at all. He just said it would be an important job."

"Important?"

"Aye."

"Davy." Jimmy looked down. "Do you not think, maybe, you should tell Sean?"

"Tell him what?"

"Tell him we know nothing about Semtex."

"Look, Jim, if Sean says it's for something really big, I want in on it." He glanced back to her picture. "I want this fucking war over."

Jimmy's voice softened. "You miss her sore, don't you?" He stood and put a hand on Davy's shoulder.

Davy nodded.

Jimmy said nothing, just looked at Davy, sadness in his pale eyes.

Davy pursed his lips. "But standing here blethering about it won't get the baby a new coat. Away you on home. I've work to do."

"I'll run on." Jimmy paused. "You look after yourself, oul' hand."

Davy shrugged, touched by Jimmy's sincerity. "Aye. Right."

Davy was left to wonder if his friend had meant to look after the cold, take care on the mission—or something else. It would keep. This land mine was needed on Friday night and this time it wasn't being collected. This time Davy was going out with the Active Service Unit. Fusing mines could be tricky, and he'd have to do it on the spot. The components were a lot easier to get past the Security Forces than a completed device.

It was dark outside, but Davy worked on in the brightly lit kitchen. Urea nitrate packed a heavy punch and wasn't difficult to make; it just took time. He should have let the hot filtered urine stand for an hour before adding the nitric acid, but it didn't really matter. It cooled more quickly the way he'd done it. He'd taken his time refiltering the mixture, watching the heap of white crystals grow on the gauze. Then he'd washed the crystals and left them to dry in a dish floating in a bath of warm water.

He'd not wasted the two hours the drying had taken. The pieces for the trigger were finished. Two thin metal plates, one ten by ten, the other eight by ten, were separated by four short wooden blocks, one at each corner. He'd soldered a piece of copper wire to the top plate. It would go to the batteries. One of the wires from the detonator would run to the batteries and the other to the bottom plate. Push the pieces of metal together and the circuit would be completed. He'd leave the batteries in the torch that lay on the table and finish the assembly on Friday, at the ambush. He'd just have to nail the plates to the blocks and attach the wires to the trigger. He lifted a roll of black insulating tape and set it closer to the wood and metal. He'd need that to wrap the sides of the trigger. A bit of mud in there might stop the plates touching when compressed by the wheel of a vehicle. No contact, no explosion. And Sean was relying on him.

He went to the parlour and drew the curtains. He switched on the light, pale from a forty-watt bulb hidden in a pink lightshade. The shadows cast by the hanging silk tassels made looped patterns on the papered walls.

Davy leaned his weight against a small settee, tutting to himself when he noticed a bit of kapok sticking through the fabric where McCusker had sharpened his claws. Once the couch was against the wall he rolled back an imitation Persian rug, threadbare in the centre, colours still bright where the weave had been protected by the settee. Fiona had wanted rid of that old rug, but it had been Ma's and she had been proud of it.

The bare planks of the floor were dusty. One was loose, and he had no difficulty prying it free. The dust made his eyes water, and he sneezed, grabbed for his hanky, blew his nose, and wiped his eyes.

Only joists and boards and concrete foundations were below the floorboards. He squatted by the hole, imagining the reactions of the members of a British search team—their initial delight at finding such a poorly concealed hiding place, their frustration when they saw that it held nothing.

He slipped his hand into his coat pocket and took out a screwdriver. It took him some time to find the hole in the concrete. It was blocked with dust. The screwdriver slipped in easily, and it only took a moment to lever out a slab that had been cut with precision to fit into its niche.

He reached into the cavity. His searching fingers felt the box of blasting caps. They were safer in here than in a bag of cat food. He removed a five-pound tin of Epsom salts, a length of iron pipe, and the wooden box and set them on the floor. He opened the box and took one blasting cap from among its companions, closed the box, put it gently back into the hole, replaced the slab, and filled the nearly invisible cracks with a generous helping of concrete dust. The dust hid the crevices and—he sneezed again—would do just that to any Brit sniffer dogs.

Davy relaid the rug and heaved the settee back into place. Maybe it was the effects of his cold, but the effort had tired him. He sat on the sofa. Just for a wee breather.

And unbidden the memories came of the night of the Abercorn. Davy hunched forward, elbows on knees, big fingers massaging his forehead. Fiona's ghost sat beside him now, so real he could nearly touch her. He heard her voice, soft, contralto: "Davy, I wish you'd get out."

He stood and gathered up the components. "I can't." He sighed, a deep shuddering noise. He would put her from his mind. He had his trade, and he'd better get on with it. He switched out the light and took his equipment back to the kitchen.

He put the blasting cap and pipe on the tabletop. He used the screwdriver to lift the lid of the tin and, taking the bowl of white crystals from their water bath, tipped them into the rest of the urea nitrate in the Epsom salts tin. Now, where was the aluminum powder? The mix was four to one.

Davy sat at the table, humming to himself as he worked. The tune was one she'd loved, "Down by the Salley Gardens." Jimmy would approve. His Mr. Yeats had written the words.

Done. The pipe, screw cap fixed to one end, was crammed with the explosive; the detonator was snug at the top end, buried in the powder. The wires were coiled neatly inside. He knew he was taking a chance. Detonators and the explosives were not meant to be put together until the last moment, but he could think of no other way to hide the blasting cap. He screwed another cap onto the top of the pipe. He'd drill the holes for the wires when he reached the site of the ambush.

He looked at the assortment of objects on the tabletop. Pipe, metal plates, wooden blocks, wires, insulating tape, nails. There was nothing sinister about any of the separate pieces, unless someone unscrewed the top of the pipe. When he packed them in his toolbox, along with his drill and hammer and assortment of wrenches, he'd have little difficulty persuading any nosy security man that he was simply what he seemed to be—a plumber going about his lawful purpose. Even the batteries in the torch were perfectly legitimate—until they sent their current through the fulminate of mercury in the detonator hidden in the pipe. Assembling the device should only take about twenty minutes, and Sean had said he'd allowed plenty of time.

Davy stretched. He'd pack all this away in his toolbox. Then bed. He had nothing to do now but wait until Friday night. He sneezed, sniffed, and made one last check. Everything was in order. He'd not let Sean down. It was all going to go perfectly.

TWENTY-ONE

Cathal Fogarty finished his fifth pint, stood unsteadily, and said, "I'm away on now, lads."

Other men at the table waved or mouthed, "'Night, Cathal. See you about." One added, "And buy your fucking round next time."

He left the bar and walked through the dim night. He didn't need streetlights. He'd lived here in Andersonstown all his life and knew his way around these alleys. Not like his sister's place in Fivemiletown where he had spent the last couple of weeks. The country was spooky at night and he'd been bored silly. He was glad to be back on home territory, able to have a jar with his mates. "Buy your fucking round," indeed. That Willy Brennan was a right chancer. Cathal had used the last of the money he'd got from the peeler to buy *two* rounds.

He was in no hurry to accept any more of Sergeant Dunlop's cash. Cathal knew he'd been right to get out of the city for a while. Get away from that fucking RUC man with the red hair. Maybe the bugger would leave him alone for a bit. Cathal gave a little shudder. It was a bloody chancy business, informing. Bloody chancy.

Cathal sensed movement beside him. Someone grabbed his wrist and forced his right arm up into the small of his back. Christ, that hurt. He wriggled. A hand was clamped over his mouth, and he was shoved into the back of a waiting car.

The car drove away and turned onto a main street. He could feel something digging into his ribs. Something cold and hard. A voice said, "Keep your mouth shut," and the hand was taken from his face.

He drew in a great lungful of air. "What—"

"Keep your fucking mouth shut."

The gun muzzle ground into his side. Cathal tried but couldn't stop making soft moaning noises. He stared about him. The driver was a dark hump, silhouetted by the glare of streetlights. Two men hemmed Cathal in; the one who had snatched him and the one with the gun, a short man who carried his left shoulder higher than his right. Cathal sobbed.

"Shut the fuck up."

Cathal clapped his hand over his mouth and felt his breath hot on the palm of his hand. The car jolted as it pulled onto a rough piece of ground. He peered through the windscreen. He could make out piles of rubble and the broken walls and fallen roof timbers of a row of razed houses. They were in one of the streets that had been gutted in the riots of '69. Benweeds struggled through piles of fire-blackened bricks. Pools of muddy water sullenly reflected the headlights' glare. The car stopped.

"Holy Mary," Cathal whimpered. His whole body shook. He was fucked.

The driver switched off the headlamps. The dim glow of distant streetlights cast shadows inside the vehicle.

"Who are you? What do youse want?"

"What are you worried about, Cathal? We're your friends." The man with the gun turned. He wore spectacles and there was something odd about the left lens. His voice was low-pitched.

Cathal squirmed. "Friends? I've no friends that would take a fellow off a street like that. You're UVF."

"Not at all. Ulster Volunteer Force? We're not a bunch of fucking Prods."

Oh, Jesus. These men were Provos. Cathal felt hot tears run down his cheeks, tasted the salt.

"We just wanted a wee word."

Cathal jerked his head from side to side. He had to get out, but he couldn't. The man who had forced him into the car sat solidly, arms folded, staring ahead. The other one had the gun.

"What about?" he sobbed.

"One of the boys says he saw you in the Elbow Room a couple of weeks back."

Cathal bent forward and leaned his head on the upholstery of the seat in front.

"Well?"

He sat up. "So?"

"Says you were talking to a peeler."

"I don't know what the fuck you're talking about."

"A red-haired man. At the bar."

Cathal shook his head, sniffed, and wiped his nose on his sleeve. "Red-haired? Sure that fellow only wanted a light. I've never seen him in my life before. He's a bulky?"

"Special Branch."

"Fuck me. If I'd of known I wouldn't have given him one." He stared at his interrogator's face, trying to detect any signs that he was believed.

"So our lad was wrong?"

"Aye, certainly. Look. I'm a volunteer in First Battalion. I'd not want to be near any fucking policemen."

"It's our mistake then?"

"Aye, it is." Cathal took a deep breath. "Jesus, you'd me half scared to death there." He was going to get away with it. And as soon as he was out of here he was going to England, as far the fuck away from Belfast as he could get.

The man with the gun opened the door and slid along the seat. Cathal followed, only to be stopped when the man said, "We've to be careful, you know."

Cathal nodded. "It's all right. No sweat."

The gunman left the car. "Mind the puddle," he said, stepping aside as Cathal got out.

Cathal stood on the rough ground hauling in lungfuls of air, hardly believing his luck. He looked up and saw the stars, faint against the glow of the city.

A metal pipe with holes drilled in its sides, wrapped in cotton wool, and stuffed inside a pipe of wider bore makes a very effective silencer. The .22 pistol made only a coughing sound as Brendan McGuinness shot Cathal Fogarty behind the left knee.

Cathal screamed, clasped both hands to his leg, and toppled over to lie on the broken bricks, his head in a pool of stagnant water. He howled, high-pitched keening like a wounded hare, choking as the water blocked his throat.

McGuinness knelt beside Cathal, grabbed a handful of hair, and hauled the man's head out of the scum. "Shut up."

Cathal screamed.

McGuinness slashed the pistol butt across his mouth. Blood spurted over the youth's chin.

Cathal's screams shrank to whimpers.

"That's better." McGuinness squatted. "Now, son. How long were you working for the Brits?"

Cathal tried to shake his head, but the grip in his hair was too tight. He felt the muzzle of the pistol resting against his right kneecap. "All right. All right." His tears flowed and mingled with the blood from his smashed mouth.

"How long?"

"Six months."

"Six?"

"I swear to God. Six months."

"Who ran you?"

"Sergeant Dunlop. Springfield Road." Cathal grabbed for his inquisitor's sleeve. "Agh, Christ, please. Please!"

"Any more of our lads working with you?"

"No."

McGuinness slammed the pistol barrel against Cathal's shattered left patella. He howled, and thrashed on the ground.

"No one?"

"No! Oh, God. No. No."

"Fine." McGuinness took Cathal's hand, put a twenty-pound note in the palm, and closed the fingers around it.

Cathal Fogarty knew that it was his Judas money.

He was going to die.

TWENTY-TWO

"Is that a fact? Real cowboys?" The man standing at the bar beside Marcus seemed to be impressed. "I never knew that."

"Right enough," Marcus said, "bucking broncos and all, just like the films." Nearly two weeks gone and this was the first time anybody had even tried to talk to him. Marcus Richardson, now fully into his Mike Roberts impersonation, was determined to keep this one on the hook. "Them chuck-wagon races was terrific."

"I never heard of them."

"D'y'ever see *Ben Hur*?"

"Aye." The man, beefy face, thick lips, stubbled chin, leaned his elbow on the bar counter. "Your man Charlton Heston was great."

"Them chuck wagons is just like chariots, but they've six horses. They run like the hammers of hell." Marcus finished his pint. "You go another?"

"Is the pope Catholic?"

Marcus tried to attract the barman's attention, but that worthy was busy at the other end of the short bar, pulling a pint, working the ceramic handle of a beer pump. He looked as though his piles hurt. Marcus glanced around. The place was small, poorly lit, and half-empty. All of the patrons were men. Three stood farther down the bar, hunched over their drinks. One man, a painter by his overalls, was in front of the barman, waiting for his pint. Only two of the seven or eight tables were occupied. It was Thursday night, and Marcus had hoped the place would be packed. He should have known better. Friday was dole day.

At a table, four young lads—jeans, windcheaters—argued loudly over the prospects at Sandown Park. One with a badly repaired harelip mumbled, "Catch up in the straight? That horse couldn't catch a fucking cold."

Marcus laughed at the remark, then said, "A fellow could die of thirst in here."

The big man grinned back and yelled, "Liam."

He was obviously a regular, maybe thirty, maybe a bit older. He'd come up to the bar twenty minutes ago and called for a pint. By the time it was nearly finished he had turned and smiled at Marcus. "New here?"

"Aye. Just back from Canada." The stranger had a brother in San Francisco and was a bit hazy about geography. He'd started to ask questions and Marcus had played along.

The barman ambled up. "What do you want, Eamon?"

Eamon tossed his head at Marcus, a cowlick of dark hair swinging. "Your man here's buying."

"Pints?"

Marcus said, "Aye. Two."

"Right." Liam took their glasses and the scowl he brought with him back to the beer pumps.

"Right ray of sunshine, our Liam," said Eamon. "Probably 'cos Liam's short for William. He'd make a right good Protestant some nights. He can be sour enough." Eamon chuckled at his own humour. "What's your name, by the way?"

"Mike. Mike Roberts."

"Eamon Laverty." He held out a calloused hand. "Pleased to meet you, Mike."

The new pints arrived.

"So. What do you do with yourself, Eamon?"

"Brickie. I'm dead lucky. Most of the lads in here are on the burroo."

Marcus smiled at the Belfast mispronunciation of "bureau," the unemployment office.

"Aye," said Eamon. "Lots of work these days for bricklayers. Rebuilding, if you know what I mean."

"Right enough. I never seen anything like the Falls. Must have been bloody awful."

"It was teetotally fucking well dire, so it was. You never seen nothing like it in your life. Protestant fuckers with their petrol bombs."

"Bad like?"

"You wouldn't believe it. Fucking hoors' melts. Sooner we get rid of the Brits the better." Eamon turned and leaned his back against the bar, pint clutched in one hand. "See these lads in here? Not a one of them can get a decent job. And that Willie Whitelaw, blethering on about no more discrimination. Damn good thing he's gone." He hawked and Marcus thought that his new companion was going to spit on the plank floor. "There's still no joy for Catholics in Belfast. And this new fellow, Rees? He's only been in the job a couple of weeks." Eamon managed a credible imitation of a singsongy Welsh voice: "I'm delighted to take up the challenge as Secretary of State for Northern Ireland, working to bring harmony to the two communities." Eamon's native Belfast accent returned. "The only harmony that Welsh git understands comes from a bunch of singing miners. His da was one, you know." He took another deep swallow. "You're lucky to be out of it, over in Canada."

"I don't know about that. The winters is ferocious. Founder you, so they would." Marcus finished his second pint and waved to Liam. "Still," he laid two pound notes on the counter, "money's all right."

The drinks arrived. "Keep the change."

Liam forced a condescending smile, showing a gap where an incisor was missing.

Eamon made no attempt to protest that it was his round. "What do you do, anyway?"

Marcus lifted his third pint. He'd better slow down. His head was beginning to buzz. Jesus, but the locals drank with a grim determination to get as many pints down their throats as possible. "Oil fields." His eyes held Eamon's for a moment. "Explosives."

"Explosives? If you knew the right lads round here, you'd get a job like a flash."

"What kind of a job?"

Eamon threw his arm round Marcus's shoulder. "I'm having you on." His voice dropped. "Just you keep away from the hard men."

"What hard men?"

"Not in here, for Christ's sake. The lads wouldn't come into a place like this."

"If you say so." Marcus tried to keep the next question innocent. "Do you know any?"

Eamon pulled his arm away. "Any what?"

"You know. Provos."

"What's it to you?"

Marcus held up his hands, palms out. "The half of fuck all. Honest."

"Look, mate. A bit of advice. I know you're just back from Canada and all, but there's questions you don't ask round here." Eamon looked along the bar as if to see if anyone had overheard. "People that ask questions like that can find themselves in deep shit. D'you hear about the fellow last night up in Andersonstown?"

"No."

"One kneecap blew off and a bullet in the back of his head. They found him on a bit of waste ground. Twenty pounds in his hand. Fucking tout."

Marcus had a sudden image of the man called Fred. *If they think you're a bad fucker—head job.* Marcus took a long drink. "I don't like the sound of that." He looked round the room. Several more men were at the counter. Another three tables were occupied. The level of noise had risen and tobacco smoke fugged the air. No one was paying any attention to Eamon and him. "I'll keep my trap shut in future."

"I'd do that if I was you." Eamon finished his pint and looked at his empty glass.

Marcus waved to Liam and pulled out two more pounds.

Eamon smiled. "Aye. Well. We'll put it down to you just being back from being away and say no more."

"Right." It was time to change the subject. "I'm busting. Here. You pay." He gave the money to Eamon. "Where's the pisser?"

Eamon pointed across the room to a door with frosted glass in its top half. "Through there and across the yard."

Marcus walked past the nearest table. Harelip was stabbing a nicotine-stained finger at the youth opposite. "Away off and chase yourself . . ."

Marcus pushed his way past the other patrons. The door opened onto a small yard, lit by a single bulb behind a wire-mesh screen. At its far side a three-quarter cement wall stood beneath a corrugated-iron roof. Wiggly tin, he thought, and immediately banished the army slang for corrugated iron. Marcus Richardson might think about wiggly tin. Mike Roberts would not.

Marcus rounded the wall. A second bulb, hanging from a flex, threw a weak pool of light onto the concrete floor of the enclosure. The floor sloped down to a galvanized iron trough at the foot of the wall. A sheet of aluminum stretched from the trough to waist height. Along the top of the metal a single, verdigris-encrusted pipe sprayed a thin trickle of water down the aluminum and into the trough. A rivulet of piss and disintegrating cigarette butts flowed weakly toward a metal grille. He unzipped.

A fat man, face wrinkled like a dried-out chamois leather, came in. He ignored Marcus and looked down. "Come on, you useless bugger. I've worked for you for sixty years. You work for me."

Marcus heard the plashing and the man muttering, "Thank you." He winked. "Better an empty house than a bad tenant."

"Right enough." Marcus finished and zipped his trousers. And this undercover stuff was meant to be exciting? A whole two weeks of dingy bars, betting shops, his cruddy bed-sit. Not a decent bird in sight, unless he fancied the scrubbers that worked at the Gallagher's cigarette factory: a lovely lot with their hair under scarves to hide their plastic Spoolies hair curlers, shrill laughs that would cut tin, coarse complexions, fat calves like Mullingar heifers.

He headed back. James Bond would be in the Ritz-Carlton, vodka martini in one hand, the other up Pussy Galore's skirt. Right up. And Marcus Richardson, at least, would be in the comfort of the officers' mess.

He stopped. Dead. A rat crouched in the corner of the yard. He felt his gorge rise and hairs on his arms stiffen. He hated rats. They terrified him. The one by the wall was huge, seemed to be as big as a Jack Russell. Its fur, black in the dim light, was mottled with patches of mange and its tail looked scaly and nacreous, like the skin of a decaying snake.

Marcus hugged his arms round himself and willed the creature to go.

It sat upright and preened its whiskers with tiny skeletal hands, clearly oblivious to the man who stood so close. Marcus watched as its nose whiffled, scenting the air, scenting the man. The rat fell to all fours and hunched its narrow shoulders. He saw its teeth, yellow as the gleam in its bright eyes. It hissed.

Marcus took a step back. The rat advanced. One skittering step. Two. It sat upright, glared at him, and hissed again.

Marcus fled into the pub.

Eamon asked, "You all right?"

Marcus nodded.

"You look like you seen a ghost."

"Rat. Huge bugger."

Eamon laughed. "You're an explosives man but you're scared of rats?"

"I hate them. There aren't any in Alberta."

"You'd better get used to them here."

"Shit." Marcus closed his eyes. Rats in the yard. Pints of Guinness, a thick brickie for company, and a roomful of dull-faced men with poor haircuts. Not a woman in the place. The chances of finding out anything useful? Next to nonexistent. James Bond? Shit. He'd have one more pint—any more and he might fall on his arse, or worse, give himself away—and then home.

Eamon handed Marcus his pint. "Get that down you and never worry about the odd rat." He handed over some change. "I suppose you tip barmen in Canada. We don't. I don't want you giving Liam big ideas. He'll expect all of us to do it."

"Sorry. Cheers." Marcus was searching for something to say when someone started banging a glass on a tabletop. At one of the centre tables a small man in painters' overalls stood, waiting for something. Marcus recognized him. He'd been up at the bar a while ago. His sandy hair and narrow face, which earlier had made Marcus think of an underfed fox terrier, were hard to forget and—Christ! He'd seen that face before. In a photograph. What was the man waiting for?

"Oh God," he heard Eamon mouth. "Jimmy's going to recite."

"Jimmy?"

"Aye. Jimmy. Jimmy Ferguson. He thinks he's William Butler Yeats."

TWENTY-THREE

Two men stood side by side on the back row of the terraces, faceless at the periphery of the crowd at Dunmore Stadium. The light from the arc lamps illuminated the track but left the upper levels in darkness. As the spectators on the lower levels watched six greyhounds tear round the oval in pursuit of the electric hare, the two bent their heads close in conversation.

Brendan McGuinness wanted to leave as soon as possible. He hated public places but had bowed to his companion's assertion that the best place to hide a tree was in a forest. None of the small mob of punters stood anywhere near. There was no one within earshot. "So," Brendan said, "back of the Antrim Hills, tomorrow night. You'll arrange for our British friends to go out?"

"Aye. Two Rovers."

"Good. It's set at our end." Brendan hunched into his mackintosh. The drizzle was cold. "What about the prime minister?"

"Harold Wilson's coming."

"When?"

"Jesus Christ, he only won the election three weeks ago."

"I need to know."

"For fuck's sake, I told you it'll be April. I'll give you the word as soon as I hear. Chapter and verse."

"Do that."

Brendan's companion, a squat, broad-shouldered man, ground his teeth. "McGuinness, let's you and me get something straight. I'm the one sticking his neck out. I don't take fucking orders like some volunteer from the back of the Falls. I'll deliver, but I don't work bloody miracles. Clear?"

Brendan shrugged. It was risky working undercover. His informant had the right to be pissed off. "Clear."

"All right. Just you remember."

"I will. We need all the stuff you can give us, like the word on that wee skitter Cathal Fogarty. We seen to him."

"I heard."

"Sergeant Dunlop was running him."

"He lives in Dunmurry. Eleven Grange Park."

"Eleven?"

"Aye."

Brendan made a mental note of the address. "Dunlop's getting to be a nuisance."

"There's another nuisance. The Brits have put a fellow called Mike Roberts in New Lodge. He's to get to know the Provos. Maybe try to join."

"Roberts? He's to try to infiltrate us."

"Aye. He's been out about two weeks."

"Two weeks?"

The squat man stamped. "Jesus, my feet are foundered."

"Never mind your feet. What's this shite after?"

"The usual. Names, ammo dumps. Low-grade stuff."

"He's been out two weeks and you didn't let me know?"

"Brendan, he's not worth worrying about. He's some kind of independent. Works for a Major Smith. They're a couple of amateurs."

"You let me be the judge of that. You finger him for me, and this Roberts is going to have a motor accident."

"Not yet. Let him alone for a while."

"Why, for Christ's sake?"

"Why not wait until we could maybe use him?"

"How?"

The squat man shrugged. "Turn him. Make him a double agent. Waste him when we can set his death up to embarrass the Brits. I don't know, but we've more important things to worry about just now than some overgrown Boy Scout."

"You don't think he's a threat?"

"Not alive. If he disappears or ends up dead in the next week or two, the fucking security people'll be all over the Falls looking for him or who killed him."

Brendan realized that his companion had a point. "Tell you what. I'll have a word with the IO of Second Battalion. Have him put out the word for volunteers to keep away from strangers in New Lodge. I'll tell the IO to report to me if this Roberts does start to get close."

"Then what?"

"Give Roberts the word we want to meet him but keep him hanging about until it suits us, then him and me'll maybe have a wee chat. With a bit of luck, he'll keep until after we've got that bastard Wilson."

Down on the track, six more dogs were manhandled into their starting cages, each impatient to pursue the quarry that would soon appear.

TWENTY-FOUR

Davy huddled inside his raincoat. The night was as bitter and dark as half a yard up a chimney. What did he expect at the back end of March, a fucking heat wave? He folded his arms and tucked his chin into his collar. If the target didn't come soon, he reckoned, he was going to freeze to death. His fingers were numb and his nose, still full of the cold, dripped. He rubbed the ache in his thigh.

Jimmy's right, Davy thought. I am getting too old for this. Three o'clock in the morning is past my bedtime. I should be in my warm bed instead of lying in a ditch behind a blackthorn hedge beside a back lane in the Antrim Hills.

He wondered how Sean had found out that an army patrol would be using this road and would be coming in two Land Rovers. Intelligence must be getting better. Not that it mattered. Knowing was Sean Conlon's job; acting was Davy's. He hunched his shoulders against the March wind. A snatch of a song came unbidden. *The tans in their great Crossley tenders were rolling along to their doom.* Tonight was like the old days. Rebels lying in wait for the British . . . *With their hand grenades primed on the spot.* His two companions had grenades—old Mills bombs, relics of the First World War—to finish the job the mine would start, and their ArmaLites at short range would be lethal weapons. He preferred his Heckler and Koch MP5K SMG. It might not have the light armour-piercing capability of the ArmaLites' ·223 bullets, but it had a better rate of fire. He would soon be firing at British soldiers with the kind of weapon that was standard issue to their military police.

Davy looked over to the men with him. He didn't know their names, nor they his. The younger of the two was a right doubting

Thomas, him and his, "How do you know that the wheel of the Rover'll go over the trigger plates?" "Because," the older one had been quick to point out, "there's nowhere else for the tyres to go but in the ruts of the lane." He'd said that with a bit of respect in his voice, and added, with a sideways look of raised eyes to Davy. "It's your man's first time out."

Everyone has to have a first time, Davy thought, but it's not going to be much of an initiation if the bloody troops fail to appear. How the hell could the CO have been so sure they would come this way, and that there would be two armoured Land Rovers?

He heard a new sound above the howling of the wind in the leafless blackthorns. One of the others had heard it, too. Davy saw the man duck as a glow appeared over the top of the hill to his right. Headlights reflecting from the low clouds. Two sets. Just like Sean had said.

He hunched into the ditch, closing his eyes to protect his night vision. He heard the whine as one driver changed down to negotiate the incline. The second vehicle followed suit. Would his companions remember what to do? He'd deal with any survivors of the first Rover. The other men were to take out the second one—and its occupants.

Any minute now. He covered his ears. The sound of engines neared, he could smell the exhaust fumes, but the noises passed and faded into the distance. For Christ's sake. He opened his eyes to see taillights vanishing to his left.

The younger of the two men swore. "Fuck. The fuckers drove over the verge. They never used the ruts. Now what the hell are we going to do?"

Shit. He'd have to dig up the mine, head for the car, and get the hell out of here. Tomorrow he'd have to face Sean. "You two wait." He hauled himself upright, limped toward a gap in the hedgerow, and stepped through onto the lane, casting back and forth to make sure the coast was clear.

"Hey," one of the men called. "Hey, do you hear another one?"

Lights flashed over the far hillcrest. Was there a third Rover, a second chance? Davy turned back into the ditch, motioning with one hand. Down. He scuttled away and saw his companions crouch as he threw himself into cover and folded his arms over his head. There was something different about the engine note.

He was blinded by the glare as the mine smashed the night. The thunder of the detonation echoed from the surrounding hills. He'd got the British bastards. Davy jumped up and waved his two companions forward. "Come on."

It would take the first two Rovers ten minutes to get back here, so there'd be time to finish the one they had hit and get out. He ran from the ditch, ahead of the others, through the gap and into the lane.

He heard the staccato ripping as one of the men behind tore off a fully automatic burst. Davy slammed to a halt. Christ! It wasn't an army vehicle. A car lay on its side, one wheel spinning. A second burst tore past him, spanging sparks from the rear axle.

"For fuck's sake, stop firing!" He saw flames licking out from under the chassis. The blast had set the grass of the lane afire, red tongues casting an eerie light. A man lay beside the vehicle, howling on and on. How the hell had he got out? Davy glanced at the car. The driver's door was gone. The blast must have hurled the man clear.

Davy ran on, careless of the pain in his leg, careless of the hand trying to restrain him. He reached the man, knelt, and dropped the SMG. He smelled scorched flesh, sweet like roast pork. By the light of the flames he saw the blisters on the man's face. His trousers were shorn at the thighs, where his legs should have been. Dark stains spread slowly through his coat, dark as the earth beneath his stumps.

The man turned wide eyes on Davy. "Help me. Oh, Jesus. Help me." Over and over.

One word was torn from the vehicle, high-pitched, terrified. "Pleee-ase." A child's voice.

Davy stared up, closed his ears to the begging that had turned to racking sobs, and ran to the car. No matter how hard he strained, the rear door handle wouldn't budge.

"Pleease . . ."

He saw a face upturned, eyes reflecting the flames, mouth wide, a girl's face. A little girl's face. He saw her scrabbling at the glass, tearing her fingernails, tearing his heart. He tried again. Someone was pulling him. "Get the fuck away." He struggled but was thrown to the ground. The blast as the petrol tank blew scorched over him. Someone had him by the arm, was hauling him to his feet. "Here's your gun." He grabbed it. His companion tugged at Davy's sleeve. "Come on to hell out of it. They're coming back."

Davy saw the twin beams in the distance, knew the Rovers had turned. He stared at the inferno, heard the roaring of the flames, and smelled his own hair charring.

He stumbled after his two companions, but the throbbing in his leg was only an ache. The pain was inside his head, where he still heard, above the flames, above the rasping of his laboured breathing, one shrill word. "Please."

TWENTY-FIVE

It bothered Marcus, the picture of the bleeding heart of Jesus—face of perpetual sorrow—hanging over the iron-framed bed. The damn icon was there when he retired, there when he rose. He grasped the cheap frame, twisted the dusty cord, and faced the picture to the wall. The lime-green paint beneath stood out against the olive drab of the rest of his room. Years of dirt and neglect.

He ambled over and sprawled in a poorly sprung armchair. The fabric was faded—green with the shadows of what must once have been scarlet tea roses. The weave was frayed at the ends of the arms.

Two weeks gone now and nothing, absolutely nothing to show. As for friendly Ulster folk? The blokes who rented the other two rooms barely bade him good morning. He'd had a brilliant debate when one seemed to think that Marcus had been in the bathroom long enough.

"Would you get the fuck out of there?"

"Fuck off."

A positively riveting conversation. What was it about the inhabitants of New Lodge? They went about their cramped little streets, living cramped little lives, talking to cramped little people like themselves, folks they had known forever. They ignored newcomers. The only contacts he had made were Eamon Laverty and Liam the liverish landlord. He knew the name and the face of Jimmy Ferguson.

It irritated Marcus that he had not recognized the man immediately from a photograph the major had produced weeks ago. Once he had made the connection, he'd hoped that he might be onto something, but then he remembered that the major had dismissed Ferguson as an old has-been. All Eamon had said was that Jimmy knew more Yeats poetry than any Irishman alive. Marcus didn't doubt it. The trouble was he'd been sent out to find Provos, not music hall acts.

He was bored silly and there was no telly in his room, just an elderly wireless. He looked at his watch. Quarter past two. Damn it. He had been looking forward to a broadcast on Radio 4 and now he'd missed the overture and part of the first act. He leaned over and fiddled with the dial, found the station, and waited for the music to paint its pictures. Spain, Seville, cigarette girls, army corporals, toreadors, and the witch herself, Carmen. He still remembered the liner notes on one of his dad's records—the one with Risë Stevens singing the title role. The notes' author had stolen a biblical phrase to describe the tzigane. "She was a woman to make men run out of their wits." From what he'd seen coming through the gates of Gallagher's cigarette factory, no Carmens worked there.

Marcus had little time for the Rolling Stones or Pink Floyd, but opera, and particularly the works of Mozart and Verdi, struck something inside between his heart and his stomach. A something that seemed to lead directly to his tear glands. He could never listen to *Il nozze de Figaro* or *Nabucco* in their entirety without having to use his hanky.

He'd grown up hearing the old vinyl records that both Mum and Dad had loved, and the taste had rubbed off. He'd long ago given up trying to understand why these works affected him. He accepted it, reveled in them as a cat rolls in catnip—and kept his preferences to himself. A lieutenant couldn't afford to have his men think of him as some sort of highbrow sissy.

The music swelled and filled his room. *"Près des remparts de Séville, chez mon ami Lillas Pastia . . ."*

The soprano was a young New Zealander, Kiri te Kanawa. She had the voice of an angel. He closed his eyes and coasted on the rise and fall of the music, lost in its swells, at peace with himself and far from the cruddy bed-sit in New Lodge.

Five o'clock. Marcus was in a foul mood. He'd not been able to finish listening to *Carmen*. Halfway into the third act one of the other residents had started pounding on the wall and yelling, "Turn off that fucking row." He'd turned it down, but the banging on the wall had become more insistent. Eventually, he had given up and shut off the wireless.

Now the smell of burnt lard coming from the kitchen made him gag. It was Saturday night. He might as well go out for a bite. There was a Chinese place a couple of streets away, run by the son of Hong Kong immigrants. Yellow skin, slanted eyes, and a Belfast accent thick as champ. The restaurant served Cantonese food—and chips. The natives thought they were being starved if they couldn't have their chips.

Marcus went to the walnut-veneered wardrobe and pulled out the Calgary Stampeders windcheater. Maybe the flash of colour would provoke some interest in the boozer when he dropped in after he had eaten. Maybe.

Marcus stood at the bar, his stomach acid and heavy. The chips had left a scum of grease on his palate.

"Pint, Mike?"

Wonderful. First-name terms with lugubrious Liam. "Aye, please. Eamon not in the night?"

"He'll be in later." Liam built the pint slowly, letting the Guinness settle between pours. "Here."

"Fair enough." Marcus paid and, as had become his habit, left a generous tip. Liam pocketed the coins, making a desultory swipe at the bar top with a tea towel illustrated with scenes of Ulster, beer stains hiding Scrabo Tower and giving Lough Erne a muddy appearance.

Marcus looked over the tables. The youth with the harelip was telling the world how his horse had won at twenty to one, only interrupting his boasting to yell for "Four more Monk by the neck!" Cackling at his own humour when Liam brought the brown bottles of Wm. Younger's Monk Export without glasses, Harelip grinned at Liam. "That's a Protestant order, so it is. Four monks by the throat."

"Fuck off, Colin Heaney," said Liam.

Someone stood farther down the bar. Marcus turned, expecting to see Eamon. Jimmy Ferguson, no dungarees this time—grey pants and an old raincoat—had one short leg up on the brass rail below the bar. Marcus watched as Ferguson sank the first few mouthfuls of his pint and then tipped a glass of whiskey into the stout. Why, Marcus wondered, did the natives call that particular combination a horse's neck?

The little man looked at Marcus's red Stampeders windcheater. He cocked his head and asked, "You a Canadian?"

"Not at all. I'm from Bangor. But I worked in Canada for a while."

Jimmy moved along the bar. "My daughter's just back from Canada. Toronto, like."

"Toronto? Never been there, but we learnt all about them Great Lakes at school."

"Where'd you go to school?"

It was like strange dogs sniffing each other's backsides.

"Bangor Grammar."

"Bangor Grammar?"

"Aye. What about it?"

Jimmy Ferguson began to sidle away.

"I was the only Taig in the place. My da thought I'd get better learned there."

"So you dig with the left?"

"Aye certainly." Marcus crossed himself.

Jimmy moved closer. "You'd me going there for a minute. We don't have Prods in here."

"They'd likely have as much joy as I had at a Protestant school."

"None?"

"Jesus. None at all. Nothing open, like, but it was there. 'How do you tell a Catholic? His eyes is too close together.'" Marcus grunted derisively. "I never fitted in. I'd of been far better at Saint Columba's." He nodded at Ferguson's glass. "Another?"

"Better not. The missus is expecting me." Jimmy hesitated. "Still— just the one won't hurt. Just a wee Jameson. A wee half-un. It's not often a man comes in here that's been to Canada. Jimmy Ferguson, by the way."

"Mike Roberts." Marcus signalled to Liam. Jimmy reached for his fresh drink. "Thanks very much—Mike."

Marcus saw Eamon come through the door. He raised his hand in salute. Eamon stood at Ferguson's other shoulder. "How's about you, Jimmy?"

"Rightly. Just having a *craic* with your man here. Mate of yours?"

"Aye. Mike Roberts. Did he buy you a jar?"

Jimmy nodded.

"Don't think you've to buy back, like. He's loaded. Makes a million in the Alberta oil fields. Mine's a pint, Mike."

Jimmy asked. "What do you do, Mike?"

Eamon let out a guffaw. "He'd've been a brave useful lad to your lot twenty years ago, Jimmy Ferguson." He dropped his voice to a stage whisper. "He's an explosives expert."

It wasn't the way Jimmy's jaw shot forward, but more how his pupils constricted—only for a split second. He was quick to recover. "Away off and chase yourself, Laverty. I've been out of that for years." Jimmy must have noticed Marcus's look. "I was one of the bad boys. Years ago." He turned to Eamon and snapped, "And you just keep your big trap shut about that."

"I was only joking."

The major had written Jimmy Ferguson off. By whose word? A double agent. Was it possible—just possible—that Ferguson was a Provo?

"There's some things you don't fucking well joke about." Ferguson's voice had risen.

"Look. I'm sorry, Jim. All right?" Eamon looked like a whipped Labrador.

"It's just not funny, so it's not."

"How many times've I to say I'm sorry? Do you want me to cut my fucking throat?"

Marcus interrupted. "Mr. Ferguson. Look. It's none of my business, but if Eamon means what I think he does"—he looked directly into Jimmy's eyes—"it's fine by me. I'd've been on your side."

Jimmy's voice lost its hectoring tone. "Aye. Right. But we don't talk about the likes of that. Them days is over for me."

"I understand. It's none of my business anyhow. Would you go another, Mr. Ferguson?"

"I'd better be getting on, like. Herself'll be on the warpath if I'm late the night." He turned to go, then swung back. "It's Mike, isn't it?"

"Aye."

"I'd love another jar. Tell you what. Come on round to my place. We'll have a wee one there. I want to hear more about how much Yeats you know. Siobhan'll be pleased to meet someone else from Canada."

"Siobhan?"

"My wee girl. I told you. She's here on her holidays." He looked at Eamon. "She should get a chance to see there's one educated man round here."

"I'd like that, right enough," Marcus said, hoping his voice held sufficient respect. This Ferguson could just, just, be someone worth getting to know better. "Hang on a wee minute. I'll settle up." He paid. "'Night, Eamon."

"Aye," said Eamon, hunching over his pint. "Any rats at your place, Jimmy?"

"What?"

"Your man's heart scared of rats." Eamon chuckled.

"Fuck off, Eamon," said Marcus.

Marcus followed Jimmy onto the road. New Lodge at night. Neon street-lights, cluttered gutters, terraces, the incessant sounds of cars, lorries. He watched a bus pass and read the exhortation on its side to phone Belfast 652155 to report any suspicious activity. Confidentiality assured.

"Where do you live, Jimmy?"

"Ten Hogarth Street."

Marcus knew the place. Terrace houses set back a few yards behind tiny box hedges stunted by the fumes of the traffic. Shrubs in New Lodge clung to a precarious existence like the tobacconists' and corner grocery stores, hanging on to their roots with grim determination.

They turned past a two-foot brick wall onto a narrow path. The garden, dimly seen in the streetlamp's glow, was a slab of concrete with a rosebush skulking through a diamond-shaped hole in the middle. Jimmy pushed a key into the lock. "Come on in."

Marcus followed into the narrow hall. He could smell cabbage water. "I'm home."

A female voice answered, "About bloody well time."

Jimmy rolled his eyes. "I've a friend with me."

A large woman, pink fluffy slippers, bare shins mottled with too much sitting in front of a fire, calico pinafore, appeared from the other end of the passage. She ignored Marcus. "Where the hell've you been?"

Jimmy tried to plant a kiss on her cheek. "Come on now, don't be at it, dear. This here's Mike. From Canada."

"That's nice." She swung on Marcus. "I suppose it's your fault he's half cut."

"Ah. Come on now, Mrs. Ferguson. He's only had a couple. It was me that was on for getting stocious. Jimmy said I should pack it up and come round here for a cup of tea."

"That's right. Mike and me was just after a wee cup in our hand."

Her fleshy face softened. "I believe you. Thousands wouldn't. Go on into the parlour. I'll bring you a cup, seeing you're from Canada and all."

Jimmy scuttled past her, and Marcus followed.

"Good thinking about the cup of tea," Jimmy said in an undertone as he switched on the light. "Mind you, I'd rather have a wee half."

The room was tiny but tidy. Antimacassars were draped over the backs of two red-velvet armchairs and a matching sofa, and the walls were papered with a climbing flower pattern. Over a polished iron grate, where paper and sticks and black coal were laid ready to light, a flight of three china mallard climbed through the blossoms.

"Sit down. Sit down." Jimmy pointed to one of the armchairs. "Jesus. You saved my bacon there. Hold on a wee minute, Mike. I'll light the fire."

"Never worry, Jimmy. I'm warm enough."

"Right enough. I suppose you get used to the cold in Canada. Siobhan says it's ferocious." He took the other armchair. "She lives in Toronto, but she come home here on Thursday. Her ma and me's quare pleased to see her."

Siobhan? If she was a cross between Jimmy and Mrs. F., she'd look like a heifer with the face of a stoat. Stifling the thought, Marcus picked up on something Jimmy had said earlier. "Canada? It can get parky enough. Particularly if you're out on the permafrost."

"Must be dangerous, your work?" Jimmy sat forward.

"Not at all. Just took a while to learn. Folks reckon explosives is risky. They just take a bit of getting used to. That's all."

"Can't say I fancy messing about with nitroglycerine. I seen a film about that once. One shake and kaboom!"

Marcus laughed, looking the little man straight in the eye. "Jimmy, we don't use nitro any more. Do most of the work with dynamite. Once in a while we get to use plastic explosives."

Jimmy's pupils contracted, a tiny twitch. That chap Warnock from the SAS had been right. Watch the eyes to gauge interest. "Rather you nor me, Mike." Jimmy nodded his head at the corners of the room. "Not a bad wee place, is it? Missus keeps it lovely."

Marcus was disappointed. The earlier questions could have been simple curiosity. "Right enough. I like the ducks. I like the shape of the fat one at the back."

"Got them for the wife for her birthday a brave few years back. It is a grand shape, right enough." Jimmy cocked his head and said, "I seen another movie. One of them war ones. Your man—the hero—he had to make what they called 'shaped charges' out of plastic. What you said about the wee duck brought that to mind."

"We do the lot, shaped ones, hollow ones, ribbon charges. All depends on the job. Bloody powerful, so they are."

"Shaped, hollow, and ribbon." Jimmy hee-heed. "Sounds like a set of Irish dances." Twitch went Jimmy's jaw.

Marcus heard the front door open, someone walking back to the kitchen, and Mrs. Ferguson making welcoming noises before saying, "Take that along to your da. He's a friend with him."

Jimmy was on his feet. "That'll be Siobhan. She must have been out. I thought she would have stayed home with her ma."

The door was opened by a young woman carrying a tray. Marcus stumbled in his hurry to stand. Jimmy said, "Siobhan, this is Mike Roberts."

Marcus barely heard Jimmy. He wasn't sure if it was Siobhan's waist-length blond hair catching the light or the light catching her dark blue eyes that took his breath away. His words caught in his throat. "Pleased to meet you." He knew his accent had softened. He did not want her to think him a boor.

She smiled. "Hi, Mike." Just a tiny transatlantic twang. Where in the name of the wee man did she get those eyes? Somewhere between moonrise and star rise? "Do you want me to pour, Dad?"

Please pour, Siobhan Ferguson. Please stay. All Marcus Richardson's thoughts of bombers and the Provos fled, burned away by the radiance of her.

TWENTY-SIX

Davy McCutcheon and two badly scared men tried to keep warm, huddled under a pile of cut turf. They had been there since they bolted from the botched ambush, Davy following blindly as they charged through the fields back to the farmyard, where the third member of the action squad was waiting with the car.

The younger men had wanted to drive off at once, and they'd wasted valuable minutes arguing. Davy took an automatic from the bewildered driver—its possession would guarantee his conviction when the car was inevitably stopped and searched—and told him to drive away slowly. His job was to act as a decoy while the other three found somewhere to hide.

As soon as the car had turned onto the road the headlights of the army patrol swung after it. The bleak hillside would soon be crawling with soldiers. It was a bloody good thing that this was where he had trained, back in the late forties. He still knew the country. He'd led his companions inland through the gorse and peat bog, running like bejesus through the dark night, away from the dying flames of the farmer's car. Away from the little girl.

They found what Davy was searching for, a pile of cut turf bulking darker against the ebony sky. His companions needed little urging to help him burrow into the damp peat, hollowing out a chamber in the heart of the mound, stacking the soft blocks behind them to hide the entrance. Davy had just begun to catch his breath as the first helicopter roared overhead.

The warmth of his exertion soon wore off. His leg pounded, his sweat congealed, and soon he was shuddering. By morning the stink of fear and piss mingled with the all-pervading smell of turf. By ten o'clock on Saturday night the young man on his first mission had suggested that it was time to go.

Davy turned on him. "You're out of your fucking mind. The Brits don't give up that quick."

"But I'm foundered."

"You'll be colder by tomorrow."

"Ah, Jesus."

Davy couldn't see the youth's face. He reached out, found an arm, and held it in a crushing grip. "We're staying here 'til tomorrow." His voice was low and venomous. He had enough to think about without having to deal with this wet-behind-the-ears kid and his sniveling about being cold. "Now shut the fuck up and try to get some sleep." Davy released the arm. He heard the youngster sniff and sensed him move away. "And keep quiet. There could be half the fucking British army outside."

Maybe the lad would be able to doze. The other fellow seemed to have nodded off. But Davy knew there would be no sleep for him—not as long as he kept seeing flames, smelling scorched flesh, and hearing a high-pitched, supplicant, "Pleeease."

Far removed from the squalor of the turf pile, Brendan McGuinness sat comfortably at a table in the drawing room of 15B Myrtlefield Park. Sean Conlon paced up and down. He stopped, turned to face McGuinness, and said, "So you reckon they're still out there?"

McGuinness nodded. "We'd a report from the driver. He's not sure what went wrong. All he knows is they missed the troops and had to run. Your man, McCutcheon, sent him off. He got stopped but the soldiers believed his story."

"Do you think someone tipped the army the nod?"

"I doubt it. I'll tell you one thing, though"—and there was pleasure in his voice—"it wasn't that cunt Fogarty."

"I heard." Conlon's words were flat. He understood the need to deal harshly with touts but could not approve of McGuinness's obvious enjoyment. "There's no word of any arrests?"

"That's right."

Sean leaned over the table. "Davy knows that part of the world. He'll have gone to ground somewhere."

"Aye, and he's got two of my men with him—and a couple of ArmaLites, a Heckler and Koch, and a Colt."

"Shit, Brendan. Davy and your men are more important than a couple of guns. Is there anything we can do to get them out?"

"Don't worry about them, Sean."

"Why the hell not?"

"They may not have got the soldiers, but remember why we sent them out in the first place?"

"To test your gear."

McGuinness smiled. "Aye. And it's working. The soldiers'll pack up the search tomorrow."

"How do you know?"

"Because," said McGuinness, "I heard them give the orders half an hour ago."

"So you reckon Davy'll be all right?"

"Bugger McCutcheon. The stuff works."

TWENTY-SEVEN

McCusker looked up and opened one eye as if to say, "So. You're back."

"Aye," Davy croaked. His tongue stuck to the roof of his mouth. He was cold, exhausted, filthy, unshaven, hungry, and desperately thirsty. His leg throbbed. He would kill for a cigarette.

Kill? He had done.

Here it was, late Sunday afternoon, and both the poor bloody animal and he had been without food since Friday night. "I'll get your grub in a minute."

The cat rose, arched his back, and gave a little shudder and a great yawn.

"Hang on, McCusker. Wait 'til I get myself a drink." God, but he was thirsty. He wanted a bath and a shave, and sleep. But first, water. Davy filled a tumbler from the tap and drank, great gulping swallows. He went over to the dresser, opened the drawer, and rummaged about until he found a bottle of aspirin and the Woodbines. He swallowed two of the white tablets, then lit up, hacking as the smoke burnt his dry throat.

He returned to the sink and set his empty glass on the counter. He saw his face in the window. Gaunt, grey-stubbled cheeks, red-rimmed eyes, dark circles under. His eyes looked into their own reflection. The wee girl wasn't your fault, he told himself. And he saw the lie for what it was.

He inhaled again. He'd better see to the cat. "All right, McCusker." Davy filled the bowl and stood watching as the animal wolfed the pellets.

He shrugged out of his coat and hung it on the peg. No wonder he smelled like a barnyard. He'd not had the coat off since Friday. It was covered in mud stains and smeared with patches of dried cow clap. He lifted the left sleeve. Torn all to hell. That coat was going into the rubbish.

Davy refilled his glass and gulped. God, but that was good, and the aspirin must be working. The pain in his thigh had lessened. It was a pity that aspirin didn't work for heartache. He felt his fingers, cold where water had slopped over the rim of the glass. Some of the mud on his hand had been washed away, and he saw white streaks through the dirty brown. He put the glass down, held the cigarette between his lips, and rinsed his hands under the cold stream. He lifted a cake of Sunlight and scrubbed with the coarse soap until his skin was red and the dirt gone. In his mind he heard Father Dominic's soft southern brogue as he'd stood at the front of Davy's class, thirty years ago, reading the Easter story. Pontius Pilate washed his hands.

His own hands trembled as he shook the drops off with heavy flaps of his wrists and groped for a tea towel. He'd not wash away that wee girl's blood so easily. He stood, head bowed, eyes closed, fists clenched about the rag. Davy spat the fag into the sink. What a fuckup.

It was all the "ifs." If the Rover had behaved as he had anticipated. If the soldiers hadn't known to avoid the ruts in the track. If there had been mud between the trigger plates. If the shattered man and his family had not been on the lane. If he could have run faster. If she hadn't screamed. If she hadn't screamed, "Pleeease . . ."—fingers bloody, clawing at the glass.

He heard McCusker eating, making crunches like the snapping of small, brittle bones.

Davy dragged at the piece of cloth in his big hands and heard the fabric rip. The tap still ran. Water be damned. He threw the torn rag onto the counter, turned off the tap, opened a cupboard, and took out a half bottle of Jameson. The neck of the bottle chittered against the glass as he poured.

He pulled out a chair and sat, drink held in both hands, angry and bone-weary. He sipped at the neat spirit, feeling its heat. Something landed in his lap. He gasped and started, nearly spilling the whiskey. He recognized McCusker's soft warmth as the cat settled and began to purr.

"You stupid bugger. You near scared me to death."

McCusker looked up languorously, thrusting his head against Davy's hand.

"It's all right for you. You think when I stay out all night I'm on the tiles. How would you like to spend two nights huddled under a turf pile?"

McCusker butted insistently. Davy fondled the cat's ears.

"We'd to wait until it was safe to send one of the lads to phone for a car, and we'd to leave the guns and grenades under the turf."

McCusker buried his pink nose in his paws.

Davy finished his whiskey. His eyes felt as if someone had poured sand from Ballyholme Beach under their lids. He yawned. He must have a bath before bed. Food could wait. He stood slowly, decanting the cat onto the linoleum floor.

The room was darker now as the shadows lengthened outside. Davy put the bottle back in the cupboard. He heard a single mew and turned to see McCusker looking, hope in his eyes, at the bag of cat food in the cupboard. Davy shook his head. "No more in there for you tonight."

Aye, and maybe no more missions for Davy. Certainly not the big one.

What the hell was Sean going to say? He'd been relying on Davy. Relying, for Christ's sake, and he'd been let down. Davy McCutcheon had never let Sean down. Never. The CO'd give the plastique to someone else. And he'd be right to. But it would rankle. A man still had his pride.

Davy hesitated as he closed the cupboard door. He wasn't sure if he really cared about the Semtex. He could still hear the "pleeease . . . ," smell the roasting flesh, see the little hand. He closed his eyes, trying to banish the scene that had played in his head, over and over, while he'd huddled under the turf.

He told himself, rubbing his leg, that he knew better than most what explosives did to flesh. He wasn't a child. But the "pleeease . . ." echoed. She was a child. And children didn't need to die for Ireland. Not like that.

He turned and saw Fiona's picture. He shook his head. "I should have heeded you, girl." Davy made a strangled noise, deep in his throat. "The Cause?" For the first time in nearly thirty years, Davy McCutcheon began to doubt the rightness of it. He felt like a priest in a leper colony, seeing the evil of the disease and questioning the goodness of God Almighty.

"Jesus, Fiona," he muttered. "Maybe Jimmy's right. I should get out."

TWENTY-EIGHT

The major massaged his temples and tried to concentrate on the chart on his desk. The conundrum was worse than the *Times*'s cryptic crossword puzzle. He tapped the end of a pencil against his teeth and looked again at the lists he had drawn up. Looked at them for what seemed like the millionth time.

Sir Charles had phoned yesterday morning to say that his people had finally found all the information the major had wanted. He felt the beginning of a headache, dull behind his eyes as he recalled Sir Charles's parting remarks. "Nothing new at your end, Major? No? Oh, well. Soldier on. Don't want to put you under any pressure." That man could exert more pressure with his understated civility than a hydraulic ram at Belfast Shipyards.

The paperwork had been choppered into Thiepval at seven, and the major had been trying to make sense of it all morning. Trying to link the names of Special Branch officers with knowledge of troop movements prior to raids on army personnel.

He had drawn a chart of potential RUC suspects. There were four columns of Special Branch men who worked in the most troublesome parts of the city. Each column represented the police station to which the men were attached. Of the fifty-eight potential suspects, fifty-five were scratched off for one reason or another.

The major ran a hand across the back of his neck, feeling the tension in the muscles. The other three men? Damn it, that was where the whole thing started to unravel. Each of the RUC men was Catholic. It was more likely that the sympathies of a Catholic officer would be Republican. All of them worked undercover and had ample opportunity to have contacts in the Provos. They were all attached to the Springfield Road station, deep in the heart of PIRA territory. Two of the three had known about one or two of the impending security operations. One, Sergeant Samuel Dunlop, had known about five. Sergeant Samuel Dunlop. So far, so good. But—and it was a big but—none had known about all twenty. The pattern of one man's knowing and being in a position to tip off the terrorists, the pattern he was counting on discovering, simply wasn't there.

He mumbled the names of the three detectives. "Dunlop, Logan, or O'Byrne? Dunlop, Logan, or O'Byrne? Eeny, meeny, miney, mo." He was missing something, but what? He threw down his pencil. What was he missing? His stomach growled. Lunch, and the morning paper. That was what he was missing.

He thought about crossword puzzles. How many times had he been absolutely stuck. Four across: "Ophidian summer (5)." Ophidian summer? Ophidian? Eventually, he would put the paper down in desperation, walk away, mind on other things, and somehow, in the mysterious way of synapses and little brain circuits he did not understand, the answer would appear unbidden: "Adder."

He stood. He'd take a couple of aspirin before the ache turned into a real throbber, wash, and head over to the officers' mess for lunch.

Marcus had pissed away twenty pounds at an off-track bookmaker's. Two bookie's clerks stood behind a grille, happily taking the punters' money, stacking the notes in drawers beneath the counter, then waiting as the race came up on a television screen mounted high on another wall.

Men in cloth caps and mufflers, worn suits, or threadbare jackets and moleskin trousers sat on wooden benches watching the tiny horses fly round a track at Aintree in England. Men with dull eyes and lifeless faces. When a race was over, one or two bettors would rise, go to the wickets, and collect their winnings. The rest seemed untroubled by their losses. They had been losers all their lives.

These men had no jobs, no prospects of jobs, and they lived in even worse accommodations than Marcus's shitty place, lived on fried bread and potatoes, stayed cold and damp all winter. Their only respite was a cigarette, a pint, and a bet on the races. And they'd never known anything else.

He'd been unemployed for only a couple of weeks and was just about ready to climb the walls. Marcus Richardson was used to action, and he surmised that Mike Roberts, explosives man, would have been equally browned off.

Men went to and came from the pub next door, their breath heavy with the smell of stale beer. This was how they spent their afternoons, had done since they were old enough to drink and would do until they were too feeble to walk to the betting shop. These men weren't Provos; they didn't give a shit for the Cause. They just wanted to draw their dole, smoke their fags, sink their pints, and put a few quid on the next race.

Marcus wondered why the major had told him to frequent these places. He was as likely to meet a Provo here as he was to find a Greek shipping magnate. He supposed it was all part of trying to become accepted in the neighbourhood. But despite his best endeavours to seek advice or congratulate some of the winners, he had been rebuffed. He was a stranger, as out of place as a Shinto priest in a Benedictine monastery.

To hell with wasting any more money here. His supply was running low and he'd need a few quid tonight. He glanced at the TV screen. The three o'clock was under starter's orders, so he'd three more hours to kill until he picked up Siobhan at six.

He'd hardly dared hope, when he asked her out on Saturday, that she'd accept. But she did, and tonight—although Mike Roberts might feel at home in the crud of New Lodge—Marcus Richardson was going to treat himself to the kind of comfort he was accustomed to. Good food, dim lights, a bottle of wine, and the company of the most stunning creature he had ever met. He pictured her velvet-blue eyes, her cascade of long blond hair, her trim figure. Beautiful.

He heard a man beside him say, "Ah, fuck!" The race had finished, and obviously his horse had not come in.

"Tough titty, mate," Marcus said and was rewarded with a scowl. "Never mind. Maybe one of us'll get lucky in love."

TWENTY-NINE

Mrs. Gordon peeped out between the curtains of 12 Grange Park in Dunmurry. A man carrying a rolled rug was coming up her drive. She went to answer the door.

He stood there, looking at a piece of paper. "Sorry to bother you, missus."

She caught a glimpse of Mrs. Dunlop from across the street. Nice woman, for a Catholic. Her husband was a policeman, and her two little girls were very polite. Mrs. Gordon waved. The wave was returned. She turned to the man on her doorstep. "Can I help you?"

"Aye. I've the car parked one street over and I've walked miles. I'm looking for Fifteen Grange Crescent."

"I don't think I know that street."

"Here." He offered her the piece of paper. "Have a wee look."

"Oh dear. This is Grange Park. You want Grange Crescent. That's in Dundonald."

"Dundonald's miles away. Ah, Jesus. Sorry, missus, I'll never get this there tonight." He peeped over her shoulder. "Could I use your phone? Call the shop?"

She hesitated. The television was always telling people not to let anyone they didn't know into their houses.

"Please, missus? I could lose my job over this."

She thought he looked a decent young man, and it would only be for a second or two. "Come in."

. . .

The major decided to have a brandy after lunch. He went through to the anteroom, sat in a leather-upholstered armchair, gave his order to a white-coated mess steward and picked up the folded paper to scan the lead story. He shook his head. Another one early Saturday morning. Four dead. Mother, father, ten-year-old girl, and a babe in arms. The PIRA had already issued an apology. An apology, for God's sake. It seemed they'd been after an army patrol. He turned the paper over. The attack had been made on a deserted road in the Antrim Hills.

Someone coughed discreetly. The major looked up.

"Your brandy, sir."

"Table."

The steward placed the snifter on a low rosewood coffee table, slipped a mess chit beside the glass, and quietly withdrew.

The major signed the chit, lifted the glass, and sipped. The newspaper report was pretty sketchy, but he sensed that this was another of those PIRA jobs planned and executed on information received. He rose and carried his glass and the newspaper to where the two fellow officers, a staff colonel and a military police captain, stood.

"Afternoon, gentlemen."

"Afternoon, Smith." The staff officer, who had a chubby face and a florid moustache and looked like a pallid Sir John French, moved aside. "Join us?"

The major held up the paper. "Just wondered if either of you knew anything about this."

"I didn't do it, guv. Honest." The military police captain's pseudo-cockney accent was slurred. "It was me, bruvver."

The major smiled at the weak humour. "Just curious."

"Bloody good thing our lads weren't hurt." The staff officer was taking the question more seriously. "Pity about the locals."

"Indeed." Smith hesitated. "What was the patrol after?"

"An ammo dump."

"Ammo dump?"

"Mmm. Seems for once the RUC decided to let us in on something."

The major halted his glass, halfway to his lips. "RUC?"

"Someone in their upper echelon got the word from one of his informers. Last night. Notified our HQ. Gave us the location of an arms dump. Asked for a fastball with a couple of Land Rovers."

"Fastball?"

"You know. Immediate response to an emergency situation. No time to assemble the whole might of our troops. Just shove in what's handy."

The MP officer chuckled. "Sounds as if it was a flexiplan to me. AKA no bloody plan at all."

His companion coughed. "All a bit embarrassing. After the explosion, the Rovers were able to get turned around and race back. Of course, we send out Royal Engineers to look for explosives. Not really combat troops."

The MP gave him a dirty look, clearly disliking any disparagement of soldiers who were not members of line regiments. The staff officer ignored the look. "They couldn't find anything but the civilians. Some signs there'd been an ambush, not just a random bomb. The grass was flattened behind a hedge. Spent ·223 cases all over the place. No sign of the brave Irish." His moustache bristled. "Just the poor devils in the burnt-out car."

The MP added, "And when the RE squad went in to dig up the cache from under a potato clamp, they found potatoes. Nothing but spuds."

"That is disappointing." The major wanted to know more. "Were our blokes playing nursemaid to the coppers?"

The staff officer snorted. "No. On their own. Actually, I think the lieutenant in charge was rather pleased. Our lads get a bit pissed off looking after the RUC. They get paid twice as much as our troops."

"That's why I joined the MPs. For the money." The captain sank his drink and rolled his eyes.

The major ignored his colleague. He'd more important things to think about. He'd have to get the details of this attack. The RUC had set it up, and yet there was no munitions dump. Now, had a member of the constabulary deliberately planted the gen, or had he been fed duff info by a tout? It certainly had the smell of a decoy operation. The major badly needed to know which RUC officer had called for the strike. Dunlop, Logan, or O'Byrne? He turned to the staff officer. "I don't suppose you know who our RUC liaison was?"

"Matter of fact, I do. I was duty officer last night. Just a sec. I'm rotten at remembering names."

If the major had to bet he'd put his money on Dunlop.

The staff officer frowned. "Bugger it. Gone completely. Tell you what. Finish your tot and we'll head over to my office. I'll look up the log."

.   .   .

Sergeant Sam Dunlop waited for the light to change. He'd be heartily glad to be back in Dunmurry, a quiet lower-middle-class suburb on the way to Lisburn. Too quiet. Sam was a Catholic and most of his neighbours were Protestants. They were polite enough when they met him in the street or nodded over the fences while mowing their lawns, but there wasn't much chat. He missed the easygoing friendships of his younger days, growing up near Leeson Street in a small Catholic enclave known as the Pound Loney. If this fucking traffic would just get a move on, he'd be home in half an hour.

The major waited while the staff officer rummaged through a pile of papers. Dunlop, Logan, or O'Byrne?

"Here we are. Friday. 2355. Call logged in from an E Branch fellow. He'd just had a tip about an arms cache. See?" The staff officer shoved the papers under the major's nose.

Damnation. The name he was looking for wasn't there. The call had come from Detective Superintendent Eric Gillespie. The major shook his head, trying to cover his disappointment. "Thanks very much. Sorry to have bothered you."

"No bother, old boy. None at all."

Only five more minutes and Sam would be home. He hoped Mary would have a decent stew on, with dumplings. Sam Dunlop loved dumplings. And he loved Mary. Married ten years and he still got a tingling in his pants just thinking about her. Where a girl reared in a convent school had learned to be such a sexy woman he didn't know. Didn't want to know. Some of the things she did he'd only read about in a dog-eared copy of a Victorian sex manual called *The Red Light* that had done the rounds when he was a recruit.

He hoped she'd be in the mood tonight. He'd know as soon as he got home. She'd be wearing a skirt, high heels, and black stockings—not those awful tights. Sam fiddled with the front of his pants at the thought of running his hand up Mary's thigh, over the silky fabric to the warm woman flesh above, and above further still.

He accelerated. It was her joke, her code to let him know how she felt before the kids went to bed. She'd let him get himself worked up into a right old lather before she would let him near her, once the girls were asleep.

The major walked slowly back to his quarters, head bowed, hands clasped behind his back. Damnation. He'd been so sure the RUC man would have been one of his three suspects. But Gillespie? According to Sir Charles, Eric Gillespie was one of the RUC's best men, even if he couldn't be told everything because of RUC-army mistrust. So it probably was planted info from a tout. Eric had got it wrong for once, except . . . something was niggling. Something didn't fit. Something to do with timing.

Sam Dunlop swung into Grange Park, reflexively noting that no strange cars were parked there. Policemen could never be too careful. He parked in his drive. Mary was waiting on the doorstep, one of their daughters holding onto her left hand. Sam switched off the ignition, threw the door open, slammed it, and stood looking at his wife and daughter, happy to be home and randy as a buck hare. He glanced down and grinned from ear to ear to see how her long, black, gift-wrapped legs glistened in the evening sunlight.

Mrs. Gordon's eyes bulged. She tried to move, but the ropes tethering her in the chair were too tight. She could hardly breathe past the dish-cloth stuffed into her mouth and bound in place with a tea towel. All she could see was the unrolled carpet on her front-room floor and the man's back as he knelt motionless by the open window.

There was a loud noise like a car backfiring. Her nostrils were filled with the bitter smell of burnt powder. The man rose, turned, rolled his rifle in the rug, and said, "Don't bother to see me out, missus. I'll go out the back."

The major strolled along a tarmac path. Something to do with the tim-ing? Tout to Eric. Eric to Lisburn HQ. Headquarters agrees to mount a fastball. He stopped and moved a few chips of gravel with the toe of his shoe. They made the path's black surface untidy.

It was something the staff officer had said. "Brave Irish." He walked on. "Brave Irish?" The major stopped dead. That was it. The staff officer might speak disparagingly about the Provos' courage, but they were not stupid. The bullet casings were clear evidence that someone had fired on the bombed car. A ·223-calibre round was fired by an ArmaLite, the Provos' favoured weapon. They wouldn't go to the trouble of mounting an ambush unless they were sure that the patrol would appear on time. And who would know the timing? An informer could not have. All he would know was that he had passed information. He'd have no idea how the Security Forces would react. So it had to be someone who had known the timing. The duty officer who authorized the patrol's dispatch would, and the members, obviously. They would hardly ask the Provos to attack. The only other person in the know was the RUC man who had asked for the mission in the first place. Eric Gillespie.

The major frowned. It couldn't be true. Sir Charles had sworn by the man. He was one of the RUC's best and had a track record as long as your arm. A brilliant track record. And yet. Why had that stupid crossword puzzle clue intruded? Ophidian summer? A summer was someone who added things up—an adder. Ophidian? Pertaining to snakes—an adder was also a kind of snake.

Christ Almighty. Was Eric the snake? Eric Gillespie—Detective Superintendent Eric Gillespie—as a senior RUC officer would have had access to the information about all the attacks that interested the major. Superintendents attended briefing meetings for their divisions every morning. And Gillespie knew all about Mike Roberts.

THIRTY

Marcus and Siobhan left the bus near the city centre. A heavily armed RUC constable, bulky in his flak jacket, patted Marcus down at a gate in the security fence, then opened Siobhan's handbag and shuffled through its contents. "Right." He motioned them on.

Siobhan shuddered. "I'm glad we don't have to go through that sort of thing in Toronto."

"Or Calgary. Come on." He hurried her along a poorly lit street. "It's not far."

Another search outside the restaurant, this time by a tall skinny private security woman, perfunctory, disinterested. Marcus watched as the guard ran her hands over Siobhan's body. With a bit of luck he'd be doing the same later tonight.

"Upstairs," he said, pointing up a narrow flight of wooden treads.

She went first. He followed, admiring the bright cascade of hair, the curve of her calves between red high heels and coat hem, the fluid sway of her slim hips.

She let him take her coat and sat waiting for him to join her at the table. He sat opposite and watched her look around the small room. A narrow bar stood at one side. Rows of bottles on shelves were reflected in a mirror mounted on the wall behind them. There were six tables, each with four chairs, white linen, silver place settings, a small candle, and, alone in a narrow Waterford cut-glass vase, a single red rose. The lighting was pleasantly dim. Three other tables were occupied. Men in suits, women in cocktail dresses. Marcus, who normally would not consider going to a place like this without a jacket and tie, felt underdressed in his Stampeders windcheater.

The waitress handed them menus. "Something from the bar, sir?"

He looked at Siobhan.

"Please. A small gin and tonic."

"Sir?"

"Have you Guinness?"

"Yes, sir."

"Pint, please."

Marcus could not stop looking at Siobhan. Her eyes, indigo tonight, were oval, slanting slightly. Her cheekbones had the planes and contours of a Slav. Above her right eyebrow, a tiny dark mole sat alone on pale, flawless skin. Her nose was delicate, tip-tilted, her lips generous and smiling. Except for pink lip gloss, she wore no makeup. She didn't need to. She radiated a deep stillness, calm and profound as a trout pool.

"You have interesting taste, Mike Roberts. Not what I'd expected of a lad from New Lodge."

Nor was she what he had expected to find in that working-class district. "I'm from Bangor."

"And Canada changes you, too."

"It does. We head down to Calgary when we get leaves from the rigs. Me and some of the other lads go to a place called the Owl's Nest. I thought you'd like something better than a pub."

The drinks arrived. "I'll give you a minute to look at the menu." The waitress lit the candle and withdrew.

"Cheers."

"Cheers." She sipped. A trace of lip gloss remained on her glass. She pushed her hair back with her left hand and picked up the menu.

"Looks lovely."

"So do you."

She did not blush, as he had hoped, but simply said, "Thank you, kind sir."

A very self-possessed twenty-three, he thought. She might not be the pushover he'd been counting on. He scanned the list of starters and main courses. Nothing had changed since the last time he had visited the Causerie, here on Church Lane, the last Saturday night out of barracks before the bomb in the blue van had gone off. He knew he was taking some risk that the waitress, Peggy, might recognize him, but that risk added to the pleasure of being here with Siobhan. Certainly

Peggy had not seemed to know who he really was. The long hair and the moustache hid a lot of his face.

"Well," he said, "what do you fancy?"

"I'd like a shrimp cocktail and a steak."

He waved to the waitress.

"Ready to order, sir?"

"Please. The lady would like a shrimp cocktail and I'll have half a dozen oysters. Fillet steaks for two." He looked at Siobhan. "Medium rare?"

"Please."

"Would you like a glass of wine?"

Siobhan nodded.

He said, "I'm not very good at wines." He looked up at the waitress. "What do you suggest?"

"The Pommard's good with the steak, sir."

"Fine." He looked back at Siobhan. She was watching him, a suggestion of an upward tilt to the corner of her lips, little laugh lines at the corners of her eyes, the flame of the candle reflecting from deep within the blue. "What's so funny?"

"Nothing. I thought you were going to try to impress me. But you didn't mind telling the waitress that you don't know about wines." She touched his hand. "I like that." She tossed her hair. "Canadian men can be a bit—you know."

He tingled to her touch and wanted her to put her hand back on his. He felt himself start to blush. Siobhan Ferguson. He may not have impressed her, but she sure as hell had turned the tables. He'd only known her for a few hours and already was basking in her presence.

She'd refused an after-dinner liqueur and had finished her coffee. Marcus had lost track of time. Perhaps his oysters had been tasty; he'd hardly noticed. Half of his steak had grown cold as he sat listening to the music in her voice, watching the play of candlelight on her face, her hair. He had paid no attention to the room filling up, the other diners.

He'd learned that she had emigrated to Canada, with her older brother Fergus, in 1970. Her mum and dad had wanted the children out of the line of fire. At first they had lived with her dad's sister in Toronto.

Siobhan had trained in Belfast as a secretary, but her auntie persuaded her to spend a year at Ryerson taking an executive secretarial course. She now worked for a firm of Bay Street financiers. She lived alone in a small apartment on Eglinton Avenue. Fergus had gone into car sales and was doing well somewhere in the Niagara Peninsula—Welland, she thought—but they had never been close and had not kept in touch.

He told her about growing up in Bangor. He was more circumspect when it came to providing details about his own doings in Canada. It would be too easy to slip up with someone who actually knew the country.

"So," she said, "what brought you back?"

"I dunno, really. The winters were pretty tough . . ." He put both hands on the table and leaned forward, lowering his voice, "You may not like this, but I've always been a bit of a Republican. I wanted to see for myself what was going on in Belfast."

"Mike, my dad was in the IRA."

He said, "You know, I'd love to meet someone who is involved. Find out what's really happening here before I go back to Alberta."

"You surprise me."

"Why?"

"How long have you been in Canada?"

"Years."

"And you still think that the rubbish going on over here matters?" There was a tiny wrinkling of her brow.

"Well. I—"

Her frown deepened. "Ulstermen! Heads stuffed with romantic visions. If you've any sense, you'll go back to Alberta and leave the Ulster Troubles to the men who haven't enough sense to stop fighting a dead war."

"Do you not think the Brits should get out?"

"I don't know. All I do know is innocent people are being killed and mutilated every day. And for what?"

"Ireland," he said, knowing that would be the response of Mike Roberts. It sounded odd, he thought, coming from a British officer.

"Ireland?" She shook her head. "Ireland?"

"Yes."

"I'd rather be in Canada. No one's getting shot there."

"Maybe you're right."

She put her hand on his, looked into his eyes, and said, "It's only a three-hour flight from Calgary to Toronto."

He saw her face, the smile lines back round her eyes, and heard the promise. He wanted to get to know this Siobhan Ferguson—and get to know her very well.

Something distracted him. At a table in the corner, a man in a blue blazer was staring at them. Marcus recognized him. Knox. Robby Knox. Captain, 2nd Para. Marcus hadn't seen him come in. He looked away, avoiding the man's gaze. Christ, if Robby came over, Mike's cover would be blown. Good-bye mission, good-bye SAS, and probably good-bye Siobhan. She was not the sort of woman who would tolerate being deceived.

Marcus stole another quick glance. Robby was rising. Marcus stood. "Excuse me. Got to shed a tear." He headed for the toilet. From the corner of his eye, he saw Robby following.

Marcus pulled his fringe down further, hunched his shoulders into his windcheater, took a deep breath, and unzipped. Christ, and the major had said to keep away from places like this. He felt a presence at his shoulder, heard the plashing and a puzzled voice say, "Marcus?"

He ignored the man.

"Marcus Richardson?"

He turned and thickened his Belfast accent to a slur. "You talking to me?" He looked Robby Knox directly in the eye. "My name's Mike, so it is."

"Dreadfully sorry." Knox smiled weakly. "Mistook you for somebody I used to know. Chap was killed, actually. Thought I'd seen a ghost."

"No problem. Guinness'll do that to you." Marcus hawked, spat into the porcelain, and zipped his fly. "Fellow the other night thought I was Elvis Presley. Take it easy, oul' hand." He turned and left without washing. His palms were sweating.

Siobhan smiled as he took his seat. "Better?"

"Oh aye." Marcus looked up as the Para captain passed and nodded. He gave Knox a broad grin.

"Friend of yours?" she asked.

"Not at all. Some English chap. He thought I was someone else."

"Oh." She smiled. "It happens to me, too. A youngster in Toronto Airport wanted my autograph. He thought I was that girl in ABBA."

"Silly boy." Marcus took the rose from the vase and handed it to her. "You're much more beautiful."

This time she did blush.

She sat close to him on the bus ride home, hand in his, head resting on his shoulder, her warmth and musk exciting him. He held on to her hand as they walked from the bus stop.

It was dim in the little concrete garden. She fumbled for her key, turned, and kissed him, softly, chaste eiderdown on his lips. He held her, feeling her breasts against his chest, her breath warm on the side of his neck.

"Thank you, Mike Roberts, for a lovely evening."

He pulled her to him, lips on lips, soft, enticing. The tip of her tongue met his, and he trembled.

"Siobhan, I have to see you again."

Her reply was a kiss, longer, deeper. She pulled away. "I really have to go."

"How about the pictures tomorrow night?"

"I'd love to." She pushed the door open, light from the hall spilling in a pool round her, dancing in her hair and on the crimson rose in her hand.

"Six?"

She blew him a kiss. "Six."

He stood looking at the closed door, the light gone, and Siobhan gone.

Marcus Richardson walked slowly through the dimly lit streets back to his grubby bed-sit. He could still feel the softness of her, her warmth, could still taste her. Careful, boy, he thought, there could be more to this than you can handle. A lot more. Christ. That had been close with the Para captain. The major would not have been happy if Marcus's cover had been blown because he had decided to take a girl into downtown Belfast.

He turned a corner, lost in his thoughts of her. In the distance, far away on the other side of Belfast Lough, he saw the undersides of the clouds lit by a garish glow, and moments later the slopes of the Cave Hill close behind him echoed a rumble like the clap of doom.

THIRTY-ONE

Davy stared through the window of the Malone Road bus. Strange skeletal bronzes hung on the wall of the Shaftesbury Square side of the Northern Bank. No human ever looked like those things. He'd never understood modern art, and at the moment there was a hell of a lot more he didn't understand—like whether he wanted to go on fighting. He wished he could have a cigarette. It seemed to be taking forever to get to Myrtlefield Park.

The Club Bar came into view. Ten thirty and already a couple of Queen's University students—he recognized their green, blue, and black scarves—were pushing their way through the swing doors.

The bus stopped outside the main university gates. Davy could see the cenotaph in the forecourt. A memorial to the Ulstermen who had died fighting for the enemy in both World Wars. There'd be no memorials to the girl he'd murdered in the wee hours of Saturday morning or to the Brit bastards that fell in Ulster. This conflict was no heroic struggle, honourable and glorious. It was like all civil wars: long, brutish, vicious, and dirty. It had just got a lot dirtier.

He'd been deluding himself, pretending that he was fighting the troops of the occupying power. The bombs he and Jimmy made must have killed and maimed scores of civilians. Civilians like the Mary Hanrahan girl. He'd read her name in the *Telegraph*.

The bus jerked to a stop at the front of the David Keir Building. The words FACULTY OF SCIENCE. DEPARTMENT OF CHEMISTRY were chiseled into a marble slab over the doors. Maybe, he thought, he should be teaching in there. He was a damn good practical chemist. Not smart enough to make Semtex, mind you, but there was someone in that building who would know how to use the stuff. He could just see himself talking to one of them professors. "'Scuse me. Could you tell me how to make Semtex work?" The idiocy of the thought brought a smile to his lips. It faded fast.

Well, maybe he wouldn't have to find out. Sean had said Davy's chance to use the plastique depended on how well the last attack had gone. He sighed. Did he give a fuck about the Semtex?

Yes and no. Yes. It was a matter of pride. Yes. He owed Sean Conlon. Sean had had faith in Davy, a faith that should be repaid. Yes. Semtex was always kept for special attacks, attacks on soldiers or peelers.

No. He never, ever wanted to hear, as he still heard Mary Hanrahan now, another little girl screaming, "Pleeease."

He looked out the window. Fuck it—he'd missed his stop. He yanked the string that looped along the sides of the bus.

He dismounted, lit a smoke as he waited for the 71 bus to move off, crossed the Malone Road, turned right, and limped toward Myrtlefield Park.

"Come in, Davy." Sean Conlon remained seated at the big table.

Davy crossed the carpet, pulled out a chair, and sat, back to the window, hands on the tabletop, the oil of his fingers making little blurred ovals on the polished wood.

"How are you?" The CO's voice was level.

"I've been worser."

"You're back in one piece, anyhow."

"Aye." Davy picked at a fingernail. "I'm sorry I fucked up."

"You didn't, Davy. It wasn't your fault."

"It was. I let you down, Sean."

"The fuck you did." Davy saw no condemnation in Sean's eyes. "You did the best you could. No one's blaming you here." Sean's gaze held Davy's. "All right. Now, just so you know, we've already had the other lads in."

"What lads?"

"The ones you were out with. They all said you done good, that they'd be in jail up the Crumlin or in Long Kesh if you hadn't kept your head."

Davy shrugged.

Sean rose. "There's someone here just wants to ask you a few questions."

"Who? What questions?"

"Come on, Davy. You know the form. The information officer needs to debrief volunteers after a raid."

"Oh. That." Only a postmortem. He'd been to enough of those. "Fair enough. Go and get him. And, Sean. I'm sorry about the fuckup."

"Give over, Davy. It's done."

Davy watched as Sean walked to the door and left the room. He looked up at the great chandelier hanging over the table. Decent of Sean not to lay blame, but Davy knew very well where the fault lay. Both failing his CO and—ah, shit, he didn't want to think of her now. Anyway, someone was coming.

The man who accompanied Sean was not 2nd Battalion IO. The newcomer was thin, dark-haired, and wore spectacles with an eye patch. Davy saw in the eye behind the wire-rimmed glasses the colours of a dead fire. And about as much warmth. Davy began to rise in the presence of a strange senior officer.

"Stay where you are, McCutcheon," the man rasped.

Davy lowered himself into his chair and let his hands fall limply into his lap.

Sean and the other man sat opposite.

Sean spoke. "Davy, this is Brigade IO."

"Brigade?" Davy looked questioningly at Sean.

Sean gave a reassuring twitch of his head. "He just wanted to meet you. Clear up a few things. Tell us exactly what happened. Take your time."

Davy ran quickly through the events of the weekend, truthfully, accurately, answering the occasional question, letting no hint of his feelings show.

The IO pulled his glasses from his nose; held them by one leg, his own elbow resting on the table; and said, "How do you think the Brits avoided the booby trap?"

Davy looked away from the man's puckered eye socket. "Buggered if I know. One of the other lads said they drove on the verges."

"Could anyone have tipped them off?" The light from the window made little flashes sparkle from the lens as the IO swung his spectacles.

Davy thought for a while before saying, "I doubt it. If they'd known what we were up to, the Rovers would never have come down the track. The Brits would have been looking for us with helicopters, night-scopes, the whole fucking army."

"Aye." The IO sucked on the end of his spectacles. "That's what we thought, Sean."

Sean nodded.

Davy looked from one man to the other. Where the hell had he seen the IO before?

The IO asked, "Do you think we can recover the weapons?"

"Aye. They'd be a bit rusty, but one of the Active Service lads could show you where we left them. They're well hid in the turf." He could smell it, as if there was a pile of damp peat in this room.

"Not like to go for them yourself, Davy? Maybe the old leg . . . ?" The IO pulled his lips back in a tiny smile, and Davy saw the man's irregular teeth.

"There's fuck-all wrong with my leg." Davy noticed green discolouration of the IO's incisors. McGuinness. Brendan McGuinness. It was the teeth Davy remembered. He'd met the man years ago, sometime after 1962 in Bodenstown, County Kildare, at an annual Wolfe Tone commemoration service. McGuinness had only been a youngster then. Not even in the IRA. A hanger-on. He had both eyes back then. Now he was Brigade IO. Jesus.

McGuinness rehooked the wire earpieces of his spectacles around his ears and settled the frames on the bridge of his nose. "All right, McCutcheon."

Davy glanced at Sean, who shook his head.

Davy stayed put as McGuinness turned to Sean and spoke to him as though Davy had ceased to exist.

"Pity your people didn't get the Brits. A younger man might have hung around. The group should have had the firepower to knock out two armoured Land Rovers."

Davy flinched. He hadn't even considered that option.

Sean kept his gaze on Davy's face and said, levelly, "They did not. We lost our RPG-7s in the ammo-dump raid. A couple of hand grenades won't stop a moving Land Rover. The lads did their best. The commander on the ground has to make decisions fast."

"Aye. But age slows the reflexes. McCutcheon's getting on. You've to be choosy who you send out."

Davy sat bolt upright. McGuinness was having a go at Sean, and using Davy as a weapon. He saw Sean's eyes narrow. "I am choosy. Very. You're one of my best men, so you are, Davy," Sean's voice was measured.

A vessel throbbed at Davy's temple. Sean Conlon understood the meaning of loyalty. So did Davy. And whatever was going on between these two, it was his fault that McGuinness was scoring points.

Davy leaned across the table. "Stop you picking on my CO."

"Pardon?" McGuinness's upper lip lifted. His words were sibilant. "McCutcheon, I'll ask your advice when I want it. Sit you there and keep your mouth shut."

Davy felt the flush start from beneath his collar. Fucking whippersnapper. Wet behind the ears. Talking to a Fifties Man like that.

"It's all right, Davy." Sean spoke rapidly.

"Anyway, Sean, even if McCutcheon didn't hit the primary target, the end result was very satisfactory."

"Jesus Christ." Davy thrust his chair back. "Satisfactory. Satisfactory? Have you ever seen what a bomb does? That wee girl was ten years old. Ten, for fuck's sake. Her da had both legs blew off. They're all dead." He wiped the spittle from his chin with the back of one hand.

McGuinness smiled his rat smile. "Pity your Second Battalion men are a bit undisciplined, Sean. McCutcheon should understand about casualties. And that there are other matters that don't concern him."

"Understand?" Davy felt his nails digging into his palms. "Understand casualties? I *was* one, when you were in nappies. We didn't murder children back then. We didn't have to apologize like Army Council. How the fuck do you say 'I'm sorry' for killing a wee girl?"

"Davy!" Sean's voice cut across the table.

Davy lowered his head and took several deep breaths. "Right." He looked up. "Sean, you know very well I don't think we should hit soft targets. Look. Jim and me makes explosives. We don't ask what for, but I'm telling you now," his gaze darted from the CO to the IO, "I'm going out on no more missions unless it's against the peelers or the army. I've half a mind not to go on at all."

"McCutcheon," said McGuinness, "you'll do exactly as you're ordered. Volunteers don't pick and choose their operations." He glanced at Sean. "At least not in First Battalion."

Davy stiffened. "I do exactly what my CO tells me."

"Not quite." McGuinness's dark brows lifted. "He told you to take out an army patrol."

Sean swung on McGuinness. "That's enough."

McGuinness held up a hand.

Davy waited, willing his rapid breathing to slow, feeling the sweat beneath the collarless neckband of his shirt, inwardly thanking Sean for coming to his defence.

"All right." Sean turned back to Davy. "I told you about the big job coming up, Davy. We still need you for it."

"Is he up to it?" Davy saw McGuinness leaning back in his chair.

"I'm able for anything my CO needs."

"I hope so." McGuinness rose and left.

Davy watched the man go. Little shit. He waited for Sean to speak.

"Sorry about that, Davy. Brigade IO and me . . ." He let the words hang. "You got stuck in the middle."

"Never worry. Brendan McGuinness doesn't bother me."

"How the hell do you know who he is?"

"I met him years ago. I don't think he remembers me. What's going on with the pair of you, anyway?"

"Either him or me's next in line for OC Belfast Brigade. He wants it."

"Do you not?"

"I'm not fussed. I'm like you, Davy. I just want to get the job done and over."

"Aye. Right." Davy hesitated. "You know, Sean, after that wee lassie— I came here and I was nearly going to ask about getting out. The screams of her were fucking dire."

"Giving you nightmares?"

"Aye."

"You'd not be the first." Sean looked directly at Davy. "It wasn't your fault."

Davy snorted.

"Do you want out?"

"If I did?"

"It would be a bugger for us. We've lads out in Libya training, but you're still our best man in Belfast."

"Aye, well." Davy inwardly thanked his commanding officer for the words of praise.

"Davy, the big one's still on. The one with the Semtex."

The Semtex. Jimmy had said to tell Sean they didn't know how to use the new plastique. Davy started to speak, but Conlon carried on, "I can't tell you the target. Yet. But it'll be fair game, I swear to God. It could even be the one to finish the whole damn war."

"Finish the war?" Jesus. Fiona. And after the way Sean had stood up to McGuinness, how could he not do as Conlon asked? "All right."

"Good man."

"Sean?"

"What?"

"It'll go right."

"I know that, Davy." Sean had a tired smile.

Davy said nothing. He waited until Sean said, "You'll be going out in a week or two. 'Til then keep your head down."

"Right."

"And, Davy?"

"What?"

"You'd be happy enough about using Semtex?"

"Sure. I told you, it's no sweat."

THIRTY-TWO

Siobhan watched Steve McQueen and Gregory Sierra race through the jungles of some South American country. She smiled at Sierra's ungainly lope. *Papillon* had been Mike's choice of film, but she was enjoying it thoroughly. She hadn't told him she'd seen it in Toronto last year. She knew that first run in Belfast usually meant at least a year old. She'd wait until the spears of the mantrap skewered Sierra before she snuggled up against Mike. That would give him a chance to put his arm round her. It was like being sixteen again, lurking in the dark back row of the Capitol.

She'd been surprised that he hadn't made a move already, or even last night. In Canada men had embraced the sexual revolution and believed that an expensive dinner was a ticket straight to bed. Mike hadn't. He'd been a gentleman. She smiled to herself at the old-fashioned word. She'd read Germaine Greer's *Female Eunuch* and fully subscribed to the ideas of the women's movement—even to the extent of not wearing a bra tonight. She might let Mike know that later.

On the screen Sierra's face contorted as pointed branches slammed into his chest. She squealed and leaned her head against Mike's shoulder. His arm slipped round her. She could feel the muscles through his windcheater. He was a gentleman and a sexy man. His hazel eyes had tiny gold flecks in the irises, and she thought he'd look even better if he shaved off that silly moustache. It had tickled when he kissed her last night and—she sensed him moving toward her—it was tickling now, but his lips were gentle on hers. She moved toward him and felt her nipples harden against the silky material of her blouse.

The house lights went up.

She pulled away, seeing a shocked look on Mike's face. A man in a dinner suit appeared on the stage in front of the screen. The cinema's manager. He spoke into a microphone. "Ladies and gentlemen, please do not panic. We have received a bomb threat."

People scrambled to their feet. A woman screamed.

"Please, ladies and gentlemen, please make an orderly exit."

"Come on." Mike was on his feet tugging at her hand.

"Right." She stood and followed as he crabbed along the row. A fat woman in front pummeled the man beside her. "For fuck's sake, hurry up."

More screams, drowning the manager's pleas for calm.

Mike reached the aisle. He held on to Siobhan's hand and stood like a rock in a torrent, back thrust against the press of bodies, clearing a passage for her. She left the seats and at once they were swept toward the foyer by a human flood. Siobhan lost a shoe and yelped as a foot squashed her toes. Her hands were sweating, and it was difficult to breathe. She stumbled, but Mike hauled her upright.

Bodies jammed the doors onto the Antrim Road. Mike pulled Siobhan to him. "Hang on," he said, lowering one shoulder and driving it hard into the back of a smaller man wedged in the doorway. The man popped through like a cork from a bottle, and they were in the open air.

People ran, women screamed, men swore. A door went down with a crash of splintering glass. From behind Siobhan came a dull rumble. She turned to see part of the cinema's flat asphalt roof rise lazily, tear apart, and collapse into itself. A dense column of smoke spiraled upward.

And still people spilled through the doors. Some were coughing, others' faces were soot-stained. Women cried. One man yelled "fuck it, fuck it" over and over. A short youth beat at his woman companion's smouldering hair with his cloth cap. Siobhan felt Mike pulling at her hand. "Come on, Siobhan."

"Mike, we've got to do something."

"What?"

"Help."

She saw him stare above the smashed doors where the marquee sagged drunkenly, the neon PAPILLON flashing on and off, sparks jetting from loose wiring. The short lad and his sobbing girlfriend stood beneath the marquee. It groaned and sagged. They seemed unaware.

"Wait here," Mike said, dropping her hand and pushing his way through the press of bodies.

She watched him force his way forward toward the broken building. There was a screech of tearing metal as the signboard started to tear free from its moorings. Mike darted beneath, grabbed the woman by one arm, yelling something at her dazed companion. Siobhan couldn't hear him over the crackling of the flames, the sobbing and cursing of the throng, and the howl of the sirens of ambulances and police cars.

Mike dragged the woman onto the street. The short youth stumbled after. The marquee parted from the wall and smashed to the pavement.

Siobhan ignored the cold in her shoeless foot. She noticed, quite dispassionately, that she was trembling and yet she was not scared for herself. She realized she had been terrified for Mike's sake.

He stood by her side, panting. "I don't think we can do much more here."

The crowd had thinned. Funny, she thought. In Toronto spectators always gathered to rubberneck at accidents or fires. Here in Belfast almost everyone had disappeared except a few small knots of people who clung to each other and stared with glassy eyes at the ruined building. She guessed they were waiting for those who had not made it outside.

"Come on," he said. "Time to get you home." He pointed to her shoeless foot. "You'll not be able to walk very far like that."

"Rubbish." She bent and slipped off her other shoe. "I'm not helpless." She had stopped trembling. She had been proud of what he had just done, but was damned if she was going to play the damsel in distress.

"All right. Just don't step on any broken glass."

"Right." She was grateful that he had not tried to be Sir Galahad.

"I'll go first," he said, turning and starting to walk toward New Lodge. "I'll warn you of any bad bits."

She followed, feeling the roughness of the pavement through her tights. She stared back over her shoulder. Two red fire engines had arrived. Firemen, helmeted, bright in their yellow oilskins, uncoiled hoses. Two were shrugging into self-contained breathing gear. Policemen herded the remaining victims away from the scene as two ambulance attendants knelt over a woman who lay very still. Siobhan stumbled on a broken piece of concrete, stubbing her toe. "Ouch."

He was at her side. "You okay?"

She bit her lip and mumbled, "Fine."

He took her hand, and together they walked along the Antrim Road, away from the wreckage. Mike blasted a piercing whistle and waved at a taxi heading north along the Limestone Road where it crossed the Antrim Road. The cab slowed, turned, and headed toward them.

"Get in," he said.

She climbed aboard and he followed, giving Jimmy Ferguson's address to the driver. Siobhan heard the driver ask, "What's going on up there?" and Mike's reply, "Bomb in a cinema." The driver muttered, "Ah, shit."

She turned and saw Mike looking at her, concern in his eyes. "Thanks, Mike," she said.

"For what?"

"For getting me out of there."

"They teach you to move fast in explosives school."

"I suppose so, but you didn't have to go back for that couple."

"If you hadn't told me we'd better do something, I'd have got us away as fast as I could." It was a matter-of-fact statement.

She liked his modesty. She said, "Thanks for not playing the knight in shining armour."

"Good God." She heard the surprise in his voice. "Why would I?"

She took his face in both her hands and kissed him long and deeply.

"We're here, mate," the driver said. "Two pound forty."

Mike paid the man. He walked beside her up the path. "Are you sure you're all right?" he asked.

Her toe throbbed, but she said, "Fine."

"Sorry about the way things turned out tonight."

"It wasn't your fault."

"I know, but . . ."

"Mike, it was bloody awful. I wonder how many people were hurt."

"Dunno. It wasn't that big a bomb."

"It was terrible. There'll be folks dead, or all broken up, and just because they wanted a night out at the pictures." She began to tremble. "How's that going to win their stupid war?"

She moved against him, feeling some of the tension in her dissipating, her body comforted by the nearness of him. "And you wanted to find out what was going on over here? Now you know. That bomb was in a cinema. It wasn't a Catholic cinema or a Protestant cinema."

He held her to him. She looked into his eyes. "Now do you still want to get to know the Provos?"

"I'd need to think about it."

"Why? What the hell must it be like living with that sort of thing every day, year in, year out? Provos on one side, Loyalists on the other, everyone else stuck in the middle?"

"Pretty rough."

"And you need to 'think about it'?"

He screwed up his face.

"All right," she said. "You give it a bit of thought. My mind's made up."

"Siobhan?"

"What?"

"It's just . . . Would you not want to get a dig at the bastards who put the bomb in there?"

"I would not! And I hope you wouldn't."

He looked at her like a chastened child.

"Think about that, Mike."

"I will. I promise." He held her more closely, saying, "I don't want to spoil it."

"Spoil what?"

"You and me."

"Nor do I."

He bent and kissed her, and she responded to his lips, wanting him, and yet . . .

He said, "I want to see you again. Very soon."

"I can't." She felt him flinch. "At least not until Sunday. I have to go to Ballymena to visit one of Dad's sisters." She felt him relax and kissed him.

"Sunday?" He cupped her chin in his hand. "You make a picnic. I'll bring a car."

"All right."

"Aye," he said, "I'd like to get out of Belfast for a day."

She kissed him hard, then said, "Not just for a day, Mike. If you've any wit, you'll get out of it for good."

THIRTY-THREE

The major let Harry Swanson drive. It was a different car this time, an old Ford Consul, built like a half brick sitting on a brick. Harry turned onto the Grosvenor Road. "I thought you might like to get a look at the Falls."

"Fine." The major peered through the window at the mean streets of cramped terrace houses. Ahead in the distance at the corner of the Grosvenor Road and the Falls he could see the red-brick bulk of the Royal Victoria Hospital, its slate roofs glistening in the drizzle. "I appreciate you taking the time to see me."

"No problem." Harry braked as a red bus slowed at the curb. "I wondered how your lad was getting on."

"That's the problem. I haven't heard."

"How long's he been out?"

"Nearly three weeks."

Harry shrugged. "I wouldn't worry. One of my best blokes spent six weeks before he made contact with anyone useful."

The car passed Devonshire Street, Cullingtree Road, Servia Street, and the little playground at Dunville Park where drunks often slept away the small hours in the bus shelter opposite the Royal Victoria.

"It's a bit more than that, Harry." The major tried to keep the concern from his voice. "I've been chewing this one over since Monday. I'd appreciate your thoughts."

"Fire away."

"I think I've identified the bloke I'm after."

Harry whistled as he signaled for a right turn onto the Falls Road. "So you want to move on part B of your plan and set the bugger up, but you can't until you hear from Richardson?"

"That's part of the problem."

Harry smiled, the dimple deep in his left cheek. "Reckon one of my chaps could find him. New Lodge's not that big."

"I'd appreciate it if you would."

"Done. Stupid bugger." Harry braked as a lorry cut in front.

The major had no way of reaching Richardson unless he made contact, and he knew, if Gillespie was a traitor, the boy should be told to get out. Immediately. But then there'd be no chance to nail Gillespie the way the major had planned. His suspicions were simply not enough to build a watertight case.

Harry pointed to a multistorey building where communications aerials stuck up like ungainly Christmas trees from the flat roof. "Divis Flats," Harry said. "One of our most important surveillance posts. Keeps an eye on the buggers in there." He pointed to the left to the narrow streets that ran from the Lower Falls to the concrete peace line.

The major nodded and then said, "Harry. I think the mole may know about Richardson."

"Christ. Then you've got to extract your man."

"You think so?"

"Too bloody right."

"I thought you'd say that, but I'm not so sure."

"Why the hell not?"

"If I'm right, the bloke I suspect has known about Richardson from the day he went out."

"Three weeks?"

"Give or take."

Harry stopped at the lights, waiting for the traffic to move on Royal Avenue. "Three weeks. And as far as you know, Richardson's all right?"

"I think so. No one's turned up dead."

The car moved across the main Belfast thoroughfare and onto High Street. Harry said, "If your suspect has known this long and done nothing, Richardson is probably fairly safe." Harry signaled for a right turn at the Albert Clock.

The major had hoped that would be Harry's opinion. Without Richardson, he knew he hadn't a snowball's chance of nailing Gillespie. Harry drove along Donegal Quay, past the Queen's and Albert Bridges.

Harry said, "Who is your suspect?"

"I'd rather keep that to myself a bit longer."

"Close bugger, aren't you?"

The major said nothing.

"Fair enough." Harry ran a hand over his pate. "If Richardson has been sussed out, I don't see how he's going to get anywhere near the senior Provos."

"I know," the major said, "but I'm going to leave him in play. I'll think of something. I'll bloody well have to."

On the way back to Thiepval they drove along Oxford Street, past the ruins of the bus station where, on July 21, 1972, a bomb hidden in a Volkswagen had killed two soldiers and four civilians. On that day, in incidents all over Belfast, twenty bombs were detonated by the PIRA in sixty-five minutes. Nine people were killed and 130 maimed. July 21 had been a Friday—"Bloody Friday."

THIRTY-FOUR

Davy closed his front door. He'd time yet before Jimmy came and he'd nothing in the house to offer him. It would be good to see Jim. He hadn't been over since the pair of them had built that fucking mine. He usually popped in on Saturday, but Davy had been otherwise engaged last Saturday—in a turf pile.

And apart from his trip to Myrtlefield Park on Tuesday, he had barely spoken to another soul since. This Che Guevara "cell" business was good for security, but sometimes Davy missed being able to have a bit of a yarn with other men in the battalion. Like the old days.

Four doors down from his house he limped past Mrs. Cahill as she knelt scrubbing her sandstone step, grey sudsy water dripping across the pavement and into the gutter.

"'Morning, Mr. McCutcheon."

"'Morning."

Farther along Conway Street an Inglis bread van surrounded by a knot of housewives was parked beside a lamppost. Huey the driver—known here in the Falls as Shooey—on his weekly round. He'd stopped his vehicle away from the curb to avoid the shards of broken glass from the shattered light above. He'd be selling pan loaves, soda farls, potato cakes, Veda bread, barmbrack. Jim always liked a bit of barmbrack.

Davy walked along the pavement, nodding to a group of five men, one standing with a leg crooked against a red-brick wall, the rest gathered round, smoking, talking, wasting time and their unemployed lives. Young Donal Donnelly, whose dad was in Long Kesh on a possession-of-firearms conviction, hung about at the fringe of the group. Davy heard him trying to cadge a fag. Crooked Leg told Donal to bugger off.

Two boys of five or six ran one after the other, the pursuer screaming in his bird's voice, "Come back here, you wee shite. I'll fucking kill you." He collided with a girl jumping over a skipping rope chanting, "One potato, two potato, three potato, four . . ." They went down in a tangle of skinned knees, tearing her tartan skirt. She started to howl.

Davy tried to block out the image of another little girl howling. He'd promised Sean four days ago, so he'd better forget about the Hanrahans and concentrate on the next job. Davy hoped Jim might have some ideas about Semtex. Shaped charges? They might as well ask him to build a fucking spaceship.

The steeple of the chapel at the far end of the terrace cast its shadow over the narrow street, and Davy felt a chill as he moved from the sunlight into the shade. He glimpsed a Saracen rumbling along the Falls Road, past the mouth of Conway Street. Two Paras in their red berets stood in the open tailgate, quartering with SLRs. The back of the bread van was open. He joined two women and waited his turn, eavesdropping.

"He never did! The dirty skitter."

"My husband? He did so. A white pan loaf please, Shooey."

"My God. He should be put away. That's diabolic, so it is."

"Thanks, Shooey. I'll say so."

They walked away, shopping bags on arms, the younger—the one with the husband—full of righteous indignation, her older, plump friend solicitous, nodding her head in sympathy.

Davy smiled. Belfast. Belfast people. They never changed. Talkative, contentious, getting on with life, trying to ignore the war. His war.

"'Morning, Davy." The bread man, white coat, peaked bus-conductor's cap, pencil stuck behind one jug ear, leaned against the side of his vehicle. He held a long-handled stick for pulling loaves from the depths. "Grand day."

"Right enough. Have you a barmbrack?"

Huey pulled a sliding shelf from the van and picked up a dark, flat, round loaf studded with nuggets of raisins. "Here y'are."

Davy gave the bread man a pound and waited as he rummaged in his leather satchel for the change. "Is that it? I'll not be back 'til next Saturday."

"It'll do rightly. Just me and McCusker now, and he doesn't eat raisins."

"Aye. I was sorry to hear about Fiona."

"Aye. Well." Davy collected his change and limped home. He saw Jimmy approaching and hurried to meet him.

"How's about ye, Davy?"

"Rightly. Good to see you, Jim. You're early."

"Aye. Them black taxis is great. Better than the bus. Just as cheap, run on time, and half the money goes to battalion."

"Come on in." Davy opened the door. "D'you fancy a cup of tea and a piece?"

"Great."

Jimmy sat at the table, smoking, while Davy put on the kettle, sliced the barmbrack in half, and slipped it under the grill.

"Here," said Jimmy, offering a packet of cigarettes. "Have a Green. They're better than your oul' Woodbines."

"Thanks, Jim."

"I missed you last Saturday, Davy."

"I was out." Davy kept his back to Jimmy as he pulled the loaf from under the element and dropped the warm 'brack onto the counter. "Hot."

"C'mon, Davy. We've been mates a brave while. Are you all right?"

"What do you mean?" Davy spread butter.

"I read about the Hanrahans."

The knife slipped from Davy's grasp. He lunged for it, but it clattered to the floor. He bent and straightened, holding the knife.

Jimmy coughed. "Bothered you, didn't it?"

"How do you know that?"

Jimmy's jaw twitched. "Ah, Jesus, Davy. Neither one of us likes hitting civilians."

"Right."

"I thought so." Jimmy stubbed out his cigarette. "You mind I was talking about getting out? Why don't you pack it in?"

Davy drew on his smoke. "No."

"Davy?" Jimmy took a deep breath. "I've just about had enough." He pointed at the photographs. "Your da would understand."

"Maybe." Davy looked at the picture as he said, "Jimmy, I killed a wee girl. I had to leave her to burn."

"Jesus."

"I'll tell you this, and I'd tell no one else. I'd to go and see Sean. I'd half a mind then to tell him I was quitting."

"Why the fuck didn't you?"

"I don't know. First of all, he was with that shite McGuinness."

Jimmy sucked in his breath.

"Aye. McGuinness was having a go at Sean, blaming him for my fuckup with the land mine."

"Why?"

"Doesn't matter. Sean needs to put that skitter McGuinness in his box. He wants our help for a big job, and he's always stuck up for us."

"And that's important?"

"For God's sake, Jim, if it's not, what the hell is?"

"Davy." Jimmy nodded at the other picture. "No harm to ye, but I mind Fiona said she'd have you back if you quit. That would be more important. To me anyway." His jaw shot sideways. "I ran into her the other day in Smithfield Market."

Davy's hands shook. "Is she well?"

"She was asking after you."

Davy closed his eyes. He could see her. Dark hair. Laughing eyes. He swallowed. Hard.

"She said to say hello."

"Here." Davy handed a plate of barmbrack across. "Eat that up." Jesus. She'd asked after him. He tossed his butt into the sink. He felt like a schoolboy whose friend had just told him that the girl in the front row thought he was smashing. She'd said to say hello. Maybe there was still a chance. Aye. And there was still a promise to Sean.

Davy carried two cups to the table and sat opposite Jim. He saw Jimmy's look, like a hopeful child. "Here's your tea."

"Why don't you phone her?"

"I can't, Jim."

"Why the fuck not?"

Davy clenched his teeth.

"Davy, why not?"

"Look. You just said it. She'd have me back if I quit."

"So?"

"Sean says the next one's so big it could win the war."

"Ah, Jesus, Davy. I suppose you believe in leprechauns, too."

"I believe Sean Conlon," Davy snapped.

"Well, I've had enough."

Davy held Jimmy's eyes with a cold stare. "You have not, Jim. Maybe after this one."

"What's so fucking great about it that's more important than having a word with Fiona?"

"A whole lot of things."

"Like what?"

"I told you, I promised Sean."

"He'd understand if you backed out."

"I doubt it. Anyway, it's not just that. I've believed—fuck it—*we've* believed in the Cause for twenty-five years." He struggled to find the words. "I've done bugger-all but think about that wee girl since I killed her. I've started to feel like a priest who's stopped believing in God. I can't let that happen." His right hand clenched over his left. "Jimmy, the bloody war's near won."

Jimmy put one hand on Davy's. He was grateful for his friend's touch.

"It still means that much to you, Davy?"

"Jesus, I hope so. And Jim? I need to say 'sorry' to the wee Hanrahan girl."

"What the hell are you on about?"

"Look. If I quit now, then all I am is a murderer."

Jimmy sat quietly.

"I want to win this war. I want Ireland to be free." Davy shook his head. "Fuck it, I'm starting to sound like one of them stupid movies—but if I can do a big one, one that really matters, then—I don't know. Somehow, somehow her dying would have been more like an accident."

Jimmy squeezed Davy's knuckles. "I don't understand, but I'll see you right on this one. Just this one, mind."

"Thanks, Jim." Davy forced a laugh. "I never thought you'd have to nurse me again. Not since the Sperrins."

"Water under the bridge."

"Not for me, Jim."

"Look, Davy. Do this one, but then"—he hesitated—"ah, for God's sake, call her. She's living with her sister."

Davy took a deep breath. "I might."

"No 'might' about it. Do it."

"We'll see, but Jim, there's a wee problem with the next one."

"What?"

"I've to use the Semtex."

"So?"

"You know bloody well I can't make shaped charges."

"Hee-hee. No sweat."

"What do you mean?"

"What kind of shaped charges? Hollow. Ribbon? One, or a bunch in sequence? Or maybe you'd just like to stick a fucking great lump of the stuff on and hope for the best?"

"How do you know about all that?"

"I don't, but there's this young lad, Mike Roberts."

"Never heard of him."

"He's just back from Canada. Davy, he's a fucking explosives expert."

"So are half the British army."

"You'd need to get a look at him. I never seen a fellow looks less like a soldier. Hair like Mick Jagger and a moustache like Pancho-fucking-Villa. Him and me had a brave wee chat the other night. He told me that he'd be in the Provos if he lived here. Davy, he told me the names of them charges."

"Could you get him to tell you how to make them?"

"Indeed I could or, if I can't, my Siobhan can. You should've seen his face the first time he seen her. He looked like he near took the rickets. He's been out with her a couple of times." Jimmy picked his nose. "Do you want to meet him?"

"I'm not sure. How much do you know about him?"

"Not a whole hell of a lot. But he's in the pub every Saturday. I'll get a word with him the night."

THIRTY-FIVE

"How're you, Mike?" Jimmy motioned to an empty seat.

Marcus took the chair. "Grand, Jimmy. How's Siobhan?" He'd rather be with Jimmy's daughter right now. Still, he'd be seeing her tomorrow.

"She doesn't think a whole hell of a lot of Belfast. Not after Tuesday night. I seen in the paper there was three people killed in that cinema."

"Pints, Mike?" Liam stood by the table.

Marcus glanced at Jimmy's glass. "Jimmy?"

Jimmy nodded. "You done good getting her out and bringing her home." He hee-hee'd. "She was fit to be tied. She thinks we're all fucking mad."

"She's a great girl."

"I know."

Marcus saw the pride in the little man's eyes.

"Where's Eamon, Jimmy?"

"He'll be in. He can smell a free pint six streets away. You should let him buy his shout once in a while, so you should."

Marcus grinned. "I wouldn't want him to take a heart attack."

"Right enough. Eamon could peel an orange in his pocket so he wouldn't have to share." Jimmy lit a cigarette. "Busy the night. Usual mob."

Marcus looked around. Harelip and his friends. The older man who'd been in the pisser telling his willie to get a move on. Familiar faces. "Who's that up at the bar?" Marcus inclined his head to a young man standing by himself.

"Who?"

"The young lad. The one with the green and white scarf footering about in a wee knapsack."

"Celtic colours? No idea. Never seen him before. Probably drowning his sorrows. Ards beat Celtic 3–0."

Liam arrived. "Here y'are." He waved away Marcus's fiver. "Settle up before you go."

"Right." No doubt about it, Marcus thought, I'm one of the lads now. Wonderful. "Cheers, Jim."

He watched Eamon push his way through the small crowd. Heard him say, "How's about you?" Bovine. Smiling.

"Sit down, Eamon. Pint?"

"Aye," said Eamon. "So, what's new and exciting?"

"Celtic got beat again." Jimmy stubbed out his smoke.

"Jesus," said Eamon, "and the Germans lost the war. Tell me something I don't know."

"Your fly's undone," said Jimmy. And hee-hee'd mightily as Eamon looked down and his hands flew to his crotch.

"Stop codding about, Jim. It never is."

Marcus drank, ignored Jimmy and Eamon's banter, and let his gaze wander round the bar and his mind dwell on Siobhan. Her dad was right. She was a gazelle. High-spirited, likely to dart away if approached too suddenly. She was the most lovely creature he had ever met. And she had pretty strong views about the civil war. She'd forced him to take stock. That was the first time he'd actually been there when a bomb had wreaked havoc on a civilian target. Usually his squad arrived in time to defuse it or wasn't called if it had already blown. He did not like what had happened on Tuesday night. Not one bit.

He'd found himself agreeing with her. The years in England had distanced him from his birthplace. Since he'd seen more and more of the effects of the Troubles firsthand, he had become disgusted with the hard men. They were making a charnel house of Ulster, and Ulster was his home. He'd been foolish to pretend it wasn't. He'd grown up here, felt comfortable with Eamon and Jimmy, even if they did come from different backgrounds.

"Do explosives make you deaf?" Jimmy said.

"What?"

"I just said, 'I'm for another.' " Jimmy held up his empty glass.

Something Marcus couldn't put his finger on bothered him like a vague toothache.

"Mike, for fuck's sake. Do you want another?"

"Right."

"It's my shout."

"Sure." Marcus could hear Eamon blethering on but paid no attention. He glanced over to the bar. Something was missing. There was no flash of green and white. The Celtic supporter was gone but beneath the bar counter, where the young man had stood, lay his knapsack. Marcus could see the straps and brown canvas webbing between two pairs of trousered legs. No sign of the bag's owner. Still, he'd probably just nipped out for a pee. Marcus shook his head. Nothing to get excited about. Marcus glanced at his Timex. Eight thirty-two. Give him a wee while.

"You're quiet the night, Mike." Eamon leaned back in his chair.

"Not like some," Jimmy said.

Marcus saw Eamon smile as he said, "Away off and chase yourself, Jim."

There was still no sign of the green and white scarf. Marcus remembered his "Special to Theatre" course. A captain asking, "What's the fastest game in the world?" and Al Cowan answering, "Pass the parcel in an Irish pub." It hadn't been funny for armless, eyeless Cowan two months later.

The knapsack shouldn't be there, yet Marcus didn't want to make a fuss, didn't want to draw undue attention to himself. He rose. "I'm going to shake the dew off the lily."

Eamon cackled and Jimmy hee-hee'd at the old chestnut.

Marcus pushed his way past the men at the bar and into the cramped backyard. He glanced in the corner where he had seen the rat. Nothing. He hurried to the urinal and looked behind the wall. No green scarf. He hurried back into the bar, head darting as he scanned the room. No green scarf. He took a deep breath and headed for the counter, elbowing aside one of the men who stood close to the brown bag. He ignored the, "Watch it, for fuck's sake," and knelt beside the knapsack.

The bag was held shut by a single leather strap. Marcus lifted the strap gingerly, scanning its underside for hidden wires. Nothing. Not surprising. These types of bombs, if that was what it was, were usually booby-trapped on the inside. He unbuckled the strap and slowly lifted the top flap. Enough. Just enough to see the ends of six red cylinders and the top of a saltcellar.

Thundering shite. Dynamite and a saltcellar trip switch. Jiggle that, close the circuit, and good night.

Now what? His immediate thought was to get everyone out. He wanted nothing to do with trying to defuse the bloody thing. And yet . . . He would put his stock up with the locals if he did. That might even lead someone to approach him. The sooner that happened, the sooner he could get on with his mission and the sooner he could leave bombs behind for good. Was it worth the risk? Inside his head, he heard a voice whisper, "Don't be a sissy."

He exhaled, replaced the flap, and stood slowly, careful to place his legs astraddle the bag. He did not want the men beside him to disturb it. Not at all.

"What are you up to?"

Marcus saw a questioning look on an acne-pitted face. He forced a smile. "Just a wee minute." He beckoned to Liam. The bloody man dismissed the summons with a flap of his hand.

"Liam. Come here, fuck it."

He felt Acne Face start. "It's all right," Marcus said, as the level of noise fell and questioning faces turned his way.

Liam strode along behind the bar. "Who're you yelling at?"

"Liam. Get everyone out."

"What the fuck are you talking about?"

Marcus felt the man on his left shift. He ignored Liam and reached out his hands to hold on to the coat sleeves of the men hemming him in. He kept his voice low and steady, but loud enough that Liam and the two could hear him. "You two. Move away very slowly. There's a bomb on the floor. Between my feet."

He felt both men pull back and saw them stare downward. Saw the scarred one's eyes widen. Heard him whisper, "Fucking Jesus."

"Keep your mouth shut and move slowly," said Marcus. "Very slowly." The men backed off.

Liam craned over the counter, eyes wide, mouth open. "You sure that's a bomb?"

"Dynamite. Can you get them out without starting a stampede? If they shake it too much it'll go off."

Liam's whistle, shrill, piercing, echoed from the low ceiling. Marcus looked over his shoulder. All faces were turned to the barman. Liam spoke. "Right." He pointed at Marcus. "Your man here's found a bomb."

A low muttering filled the little room. Several men started to rise. Marcus saw big Eamon's mouth open in a perfect O.

"Shut the fuck up." Liam sounded like a sergeant major and was obeyed with the same kind of unquestioning servility. "He says if we jiggle, it it'll blow. I want everyone out, quietly, and, for fuck's sake, walk lightly."

Men made for the door. Marcus watched them go. If he'd any sense he'd go with them.

Liam picked up a telephone.

"Who are you calling?"

"The army. I don't want my bar blew up."

"They'll take too long to get here. Have you pliers?"

"Pliers?"

"Jesus, Liam, I work with explosives."

"Can you fix it?"

"I can try."

"Right," said Liam, "they're in the back."

"Quick as you can." Marcus stood for a moment. He glanced round. Everyone was out—yes, Eamon and Jimmy were gone—except him and Liam. What the hell was he doing? To hell with it. He'd made his decision. He'd have to live with it—he hoped. He knelt beside the bag, regretting that he was not wearing his Kevlar armour.

A voice said, "Here. Pliers."

Marcus took the tool. Good, there was a built-in wire cutter. He laid the pliers close to hand. "Get out, Liam."

"Right."

Marcus took a deep breath and exhaled slowly. He reached for the flap, noticing the slightest tremor in his fingers. He lifted the flap. Let's see. Charge? Six red sticks. Detonator? Nothing protruded from any of the dynamite. The blasting cap must be down there somewhere.

The damn saltcellar was buried in a rat's nest of red and blue wires. Far too many for a simple circuit. Lots of extra wires to confuse any bomb-disposal expert. Detonator below somewhere. No chance of simply cutting a wire. He'd have to untangle the whole bloody lot to find the right ones.

He straightened his back. That saltcellar contained a ball bearing. If the thing was dislodged, it would fall and land on two metal terminals and the circuit would be completed. He gave a small, involuntary shudder. He couldn't simply pick up the bag and carry it into the backyard. The metal ball might fall. For a second he gave a thought for the Protestant paramilitary man who had brought the bomb in here. It would have been easy enough to transport the thing with the saltcellar upside down. The ball bearing would be snug against the narrow end of the glass. That's what he'd been doing fumbling in the bag. Putting the bloody booby trap the right way up.

And Marcus had never heard of a device like this rigged only with a saltcellar fuse. There had to be a timer in there somewhere, too.

So. Dynamite. Two detonating circuits and a mess of wires. The saltcellar would fire nothing, as long as it wasn't moved. It would be nice to get it out of the way, though, then go after the timer.

He reached gingerly forward, surprised to see that now he was immersed in his work the tremor had vanished. He grasped the top of the cellar. Holding it firmly, he moved the wires aside. He worked his fingers lower, feeling the wires against the back of his hand. Under the cellar, he turned his hand.

Crafty buggers. He couldn't tell how many wires were soldered to the metal base. It wouldn't be a simple snip-snip to disable it. It could take quite some time to sort out which wire was a dummy and which was live. He didn't have that kind of time.

His hand burrowed more deeply, searching, until his fingers hit something round and smooth. There was a tiny knurled button at one side of the circumference. Wristwatch timer. Set to go off when? The last time he had looked at his own watch, it had been just after eight thirty. He could see its face now, on his left wrist, six inches from where his fingers were clamped round the saltcellar. Eight fifty-five. He'd bet his life the timer below was set for nine. A tiny smile touched his lips. Bet his life. Five minutes.

He willed his breathing to slow. Christ, his fingertips had started to sweat. He shifted his grip on the cellar and heard a tiny, tinny noise. The ball bearing had shifted. He froze.

Eight fifty-six. Gently, gently, he started to withdraw his right hand, moving the wires as little as possible. The timer in his fingers followed. Gently. It snagged. He pushed his hand more deeply into the satchel, paused, withdrew at a different angle, and gained another two or three inches before the damn thing snagged again.

Eight fifty-seven. Back in. Different angle. Withdraw. It was coming. His fingertips appeared above the surface of the tangle of wires. He could see the face of a cheap wristwatch. The minute hand had been removed and a brass screw driven into the face at exactly nine o'clock. Hour hand touches screw: kablooie. It was 8:58.

He pulled. The watch came closer. He could see the wires attached to the back of the case. Two of them. Marcus laid the watch on top of the tangle and reached for the pliers. Damn it, he was hamstrung. He daren't let go of the saltcellar and yet he'd need one hand to steady the wires from the timer and one to work the wire cutter.

Less than two minutes. If he ran he might have a chance of getting clear. He mouthed, "Fuck it," let go of the saltcellar, and heard the tinny sound again. He ignored it.

Eight fifty-nine. Marcus lifted the watch, slipped the pliers beneath, and severed one of the leads. He bent it away from any possible contact with the watch case. He snipped the other and dealt with it. He held the watch in his hand, exhaling deeply as silently, jerkily, the hand advanced and stuck on the top of the brass screw. Beat you, you bastard.

Now. That booby trap. It worked if the ball bearing inside fell down. That should be fairly simple to deal with by making down up. Marcus grasped the satchel in both hands and inclined it sideways. Gradually, he increased the angle until the bag lay on its side. He paused and wiped his hands on his trouser legs. He took hold of the bottom corners and turned the thing until it was almost inverted. Not completely. At this angle the ball bearing could not roll to the business end of the salt-cellar.

Marcus took a grip on the dynamite sticks. They moved fairly easily. The dynamite came loose. He inhaled. He could see the blasting cap sticking out from one of the sticks. He laid the bundle on the floor and eased the detonator free. He exhaled.

He wasn't out of the woods yet, though. If the switch made its connection, there was enough force in the fulminate of mercury to blow off his hand. He laid the detonator on the floor, hunted for the pliers, found them, and severed the leads to the blasting cap.

Marcus Richardson stood slowly, feeling the kinks in his knees and the stiffness in his back. His hands, which for the duration of the work had been rock-steady, were shaking again. He was proud of having forced himself to confront and master his fear, but he knew that nothing on God's green earth could persuade him to carry on as an ATO. He hoped his heroics had been worth it. Ignoring the materials lying beside him, he walked through the deserted room. He saw unfinished drinks at every table, a pool of Guinness, black and scummy, on the floor where a glass had been overturned.

The street outside was deserted. In the neon glow, he could make out a familiar face peering round the gable end of a house. He heard Jimmy's voice. "Mike. Get over here."

Marcus crossed the road to where a clearly agitated Jimmy waited.

"You all right?"

"Aye."

"You fix it?"

"I did."

Jimmy beamed. "So you weren't just blowing about being an explosives man?"

"No."

Jimmy had a strange look on his face. A cross between respect and concern. "Right," he said, grabbing Marcus's arm. "You and me had better get the fuck out of here."

"Why? It's safe now." He followed as Jimmy hustled them along.

"The fuck it is. Liam phoned the peelers."

Marcus could hear the "nee-naw, nee-naw" of sirens. "We've done nothing wrong."

"Jesus," said Jimmy, halting for a moment. "Nothing wrong? What're they going to think when they find out a local lad defused the bomb?"

Marcus hadn't considered that. It could get messy if he was held for questioning. And he would be. Here in New Lodge, anyone with explosives expertise would be suspect. Suspect PIRA. He didn't have time to bugger about with the Security Forces. "Come on then, Jimmy." He started walking rapidly, his longer strides forcing the smaller man to trot to keep up as they crossed several streets before turning onto Robina Street. Marcus could hear his companion's laboured breathing. "Do you reckon we're far enough away, Jimmy? I live up here."

"Aye." Jimmy gasped. "I need a wee breather."

Marcus halted. Jimmy stood beside him, bent over, hands on his knees, sucking in air like a marathon runner at the finish line. Finally, he stood erect. "Fucking cigarettes." He shot his jaw. "Jesus, Mike, you done good there the night. Bloody quick off the mark to spot what was going on."

"I got lucky, Jim."

"Bloody good thing you did. If it hadn't been for you, we could be all over the place like raspberry jam. But you done enough just finding the fucking thing. Why did you bother staying to fix it?"

"Seemed like the right thing to do."

"Rather you nor me. You could have been killed."

Marcus knew that too well but said, "Jim, my job's to use explosives to blow up rocks and tree stumps. If that bloody thing had gone off, it would have killed people, a bunch of folks I've got to know, like you and Eamon."

Jimmy lit a cigarette, coughed, spat, and said, "And you, too."

"Aye. It would." Marcus controlled his desire to shudder. He had to be Mike the cocky Ulster-Canadian explosives expert.

"Liam'll be quare grateful."

"I suppose so. Anyway, I'd not want to see them Prod shites get lucky."

Jimmy stopped the cigarette halfway to his mouth. "I hope the peelers don't come looking for you."

"They can't. Nobody knows I live here." Marcus grunted. "Hardly anyone knows I even bloody well exist."

Jimmy threw his fag into the gutter and stood, head to one side, looking at Marcus.

"What did I say?"

"Nobody knows you."

"It's true. If it hadn't been for you and Eamon, I'd still be sitting talking to myself."

"So, I tell you what. You come round to my place on Monday morning."

"What for?"

"I want you to meet somebody."

THIRTY-SIX

He was going to be late. Marcus jammed the Morris Mini in gear and drove to the exit of McCausland's car-hire parking lot. He forced his way into the traffic, but something was stopping the line of cars. He banged his fist on the steering wheel, "Come on. Come on." He wound down the window and craned out. Bugger, bugger, bugger. Ten cars ahead he could see a couple of Saracens parked across the road. A police Land Rover stood at the curb. Uniformed police in bottle-green flak jackets, Ruger revolvers in waist holsters. A sergeant carrying a Sten gun walked along the row of cars, stopping at each, bending, looking in the windows. Mike watched the man approach.

The sergeant peered through Mike's open window. Sweat streaked a haggard face under a peaked cap. Even in late March, the sun was warm.

"Yes, officer?"

"May I see your licence, sir?"

"Sure."

"Canadian, sir?" he asked as he scrutinized the plasticized card.

"Not at all. I'm from Bangor. I just live in Canada."

The licence was returned. "Sorry about the delay. There was a near thing in New Lodge last night."

"Right enough?"

"Aye. Bomb in a pub. Someone defused it."

"Oh," Marcus's hands tightened on the wheel but he forced a yawn. "That's nice."

"Shouldn't hold you up much longer." The policeman adjusted the sling of his weapon. "Do you think there'd be any jobs in the Mounties?"

"Dunno."

"Just asking. I'm fucking sick of this." The sergeant waved Marcus on.

"Have a nice day," he called out of the window, and drove on, wondering if the officers had been looking for the bomber or the man who had defused the bomb. Good thing he'd not worn his Stampeders jacket last night. Someone might have given that bit of information to the police.

He parked outside Jimmy's house and ran up the path.

Siobhan answered his knock.

"Sorry I'm late. I got held up by a police roadblock." He scanned her face for any signs of irritation.

Siobhan smiled, sunshine in her violet eyes. "That's all right. Happens all the time round here, Dad says. But he'll be sorry to have missed you. He'd to go to see my uncle Davy."

"I'll see your dad again. I'd rather be seeing you," he said. "How was Ballymena, anyway?"

"Boring," she said, "but nice and peaceful."

"Come on," he said, taking a small rucksack from her, thinking for a second of last night's rucksack and the bomb in the cinema on Tuesday. Ballymena might have its charms after all. "Picnic in here?"

She nodded and asked, "Where are we going?"

"Have you ever been to Gransha Point?"

The Mini bounced over the rough grass of a lane between whin bushes, bright yellow flowers clean against dark green spikes. The stunted evergreens bloomed year-round. He remembered something his mother had once said. When the whins are out of bloom, kissing is out of fashion.

He stole a quick glance to where she sat beside him, hair in a long ponytail, hands clasped in the lap of her black stirrup pants. Apart from remarking how sad it was that three people had been killed in the cinema bombing, she'd hardly spoken during the drive here. Marcus hadn't minded, as long as she was there. Her blond hair was yellow in the sunlight. Whin-flower yellow.

A rusting five-bar gate blocked the path. He parked the car before the gate. "We're here." He leaned over into the back, opened the rucksack, pushed in a bottle of wine and two plastic glasses, and took the satchel and a blanket from the seat.

"Here," she said, "let me take something."

He gave her the blanket and slung the rucksack on one shoulder.

The gate's hinges squealed. He took her hand, warm in his, and walked with her through the March noontime. Ahead, the mile of Gransha Point bent crookedly into the ruffled waters of Strangford Lough. The south wind made his hair dance on the collar of his denim jacket. The breeze pushed small whitecaps against the shore, and waves rocked the tide-mark of bladder wrack and kelp. A rusted oil drum riding high on the rising tide scraped and clanged on the stones. Overhead, a flight of ducks beat into the wind, sunlight shining from the green of the drakes' heads.

"Mallard," he said. She seemed uninterested. He pointed at another flock of small, busy birds strutting like avian marionettes along the shoreline, dun-coloured, long sharp bills probing in the weed. "Those are dunlin. Watch." He clapped his hands. The flock rose, wheeling and darting in unison like a wisp of blown smoke. "Pretty, aren't they?"

He turned to her. "My da used to bring me here when I was wee." He could picture his father standing, shotgun crooked over one arm, shaking his head, saying, "How many times have I to tell you, pick a bird; don't blaze away at the whole flock?" Marcus bent and plucked at the top of a grass tuft. "I'd come down on my own when I was older, whenever I wanted to get away from Bangor." He decided not to tell her he had been a keen wildfowler. He knew Siobhan would not approve. "I've always loved the quiet of the lough and the birds."

Siobhan said, "I didn't know you were a bird fancier."

"Indeed, I am. And not just the ones with feathers."

She tried to pull her hand from his. "I am not a 'bird,' nor a 'chick.'"

He wouldn't release her hand. "No, you're not. I'm sorry."

He led her over the sea grass, past a peat-brown pool. He could see the Mourne Mountains, cloud capped, sombre where the clouds' shadows fell. Between the mountains and Gransha, islands lay green and lapped by waters as blue as the painted Plasticine he had once seen beneath a ship in a bottle. Blue as her eyes.

Ahead, a rough heap of stones made a lee. He remembered sitting beside it with his father, drinking lemonade and watching shelducks flying. He set the rucksack down, took the blanket from her, and spread it on the turf beside the rock pile, "So? Do you like it?"

"Yes," she said. The sunlight was caught by her eyes, her hair— sapphires and burnished gold.

"I thought you would." The words caught in his throat as he looked at her. "Come on. Sit down." He sat on the rug and held his hand up to her, taking hers and pulling her beside him, seeing the smallness of her feet in flat-heeled shoes, the tautness of her legs under the black stretch fabric as she sat, legs tucked, and he thought of the tail of a mermaid.

"This is what Ulster should be like," she said, "beautiful and peaceful. Why do people want to spoil it? Thank you for bringing me." She kissed him, but her kiss was perfunctory.

Perhaps she was still upset that he had called her a bird. He leaned toward her, but she moved away, reaching for the rucksack. He sat back and waited until she opened the satchel and pulled out greaseproof-paper-wrapped bundles. "Ham with lots of mustard. Cheese and tomato. Hard-boiled eggs. Apples. And"—her eyes widened as she produced the bottle of wine—"Pommard?"

"Same one we had at the Causerie." As he leaned across her to find the plastic glasses, he smelled her perfume, sweet against the salt of the day. "Presto." He produced the glasses and a Swiss Army knife, took the bottle from her, drew the cork, and poured. "You're quiet today," he said.

She took the glass and sipped. "Here." She handed him a ham sandwich and took the other herself, biting into it, chewing. He watched the lines of her throat moving as she chewed and swallowed. "Come on. Eat up."

He ate, all the while watching her, puzzling over her silence, as curlews cried overhead and the breeze blew to him the nectar scent of the whin flowers.

She wrapped the empty wine bottle in the sandwich papers and pushed it back into the bag. "I feel much better now." She smiled and stood, brushing white bread crumbs from her black pants. Marcus rose, relieved to see her smile. She was half a head shorter, and he had to bend to find her lips.

He held her, kissing her mouth, her eyes, her hair. He stroked her hair, soft beneath his fingers. He unzipped the front of her anorak as she stood, head bowed, and he felt her breast beneath his palm.

She turned her head from him, leaning it against his chest. "Mike."

He held her at arms' length and looked into her blue eyes. He saw them mist, the early tears turning the sapphires to opals.

"What's the matter?"

She shook her head, ponytail swinging. "You," she said, "and the stupid things you do."

"What? What stupid things?"

"God, Mike, you were great on Tuesday, getting those people into the clear, but then you said you'd have to think over whether or not you still wanted to find out about the Provos."

"Maybe," he said, knowing he was lying. "Maybe that wouldn't be such a good idea."

"It's not just that. Did you have to be a hero last night?"

"In the pub?"

"Yes. In the stupid pub. Dad told me what you did."

"But . . ."

"No 'buts.' You could have been killed."

"Come on. That was just like what I do for a living in Alberta."

"I know that." He saw her tears fall through her smile and wiped them away as she said, "Mike, I'm sorry. It's just—"

"Just what?"

She closed her eyes. "Mike, I could fall in love with a man like you, but I couldn't bear wondering every time he went out the door if I'd ever see him again."

"But it's not like that."

Her tears flowed. "But it will be."

"What are you talking about?"

He heard a shrillness in her voice. "You want to meet someone in the Provos?"

Marcus's breath caught. He nodded, as a cloud veiled the sun's face and cast its shadow over Gransha Point.

"Dad's arranging for you to see somebody tomorrow." She pulled away.

"Come on. I'm just going to meet someone. Talk to them."

"About the Troubles. Did you not see enough on Tuesday?"

"That was different."

"No, it wasn't. I hate the violence. I don't care about a united Ireland. I don't give a damn about Catholics and Protestants. I wouldn't care if you were a Protestant. I wouldn't care if you were a general in the British army . . ."

God, if she was serious it might not be as difficult as he had anticipated, once his mission was over, to explain to her why he had been pretending to be another man. "Do you mean that?"

She shook her head. "It doesn't matter. You want to meet the Provos."

"But—" His mind was as troubled as the waters frothing against the shore.

"You'll meet them, you'll join them, and you'll be as evil as the rest of them. I want to love a man who does his job—not who fights a holy war. You saw what happened on Tuesday. Is that what you want?" She moved away from him and stood staring out over the lough. "I want to love you, Mike Roberts. I want to, but I can't."

THIRTY-SEVEN

Belfast Waterworks lies off the Antrim Road, near New Lodge. There are two reservoirs, disused since the water from the Silent Valley in the Mournes started to provide for Belfast's needs. Few people went there, except for some hardy water-polo players who thrashed in the frigid ponds on summer evenings. At break and lunchtime and after school, small knots of boys from Belfast Royal Academy, recognizable by their maroon and navy caps, would huddle against a hedge, furtively smoking. It was a good and private place.

Davy waited on a bench, watching the rain circles and rings meeting and overlapping on the oily surface of the pond. He remembered a day Da had taken him here. It had been raining and Da said the sky was crying for Ireland.

Jimmy should be here soon. He'd been bubbling with excitement yesterday morning, telling Davy how Roberts, the man he'd mentioned the night before, had defused a bomb in the pub. Jimmy was certain that if Davy wanted to know about Semtex, Roberts could tell him. He was bringing him here.

Davy hunched his shoulders. It was a grand day for ducks, but the rain was seeping through the fabric of his new raincoat—the old one had gone into the rubbish—and his leg throbbed. He looked out over the water and saw two men walking quickly around the granite-block banks of the reservoir. That looked like Jim, raincoat collar turned up, duncher pulled down. The other man was taller than Jimmy. Long dark hair, funny-looking moustache, the kind favoured by some of the younger Active Service lads. His jeans were dark from the rain and he wore a bright red windcheater.

Jimmy stopped in front of the bench. "How's about ye?"

"Rightly."

"This here's Mike Roberts. Lad I was telling you about."

The younger man smiled and offered his hand. "Pleased to meet you,"

Davy took the hand, noting its softness. "Oil man, are you?"

"That's right."

"Where?"

"Alberta."

"Hands is very soft." Davy kept his gaze fixed on Roberts's eyes.

The lad laughed. "I'm a specialist. Explosives."

"That's right," Jimmy added. "Your man here knows all about Semtex, so he does. You should have seen him on Saturday night."

Davy looked up at Jimmy. "Sit down and shut up like a good lad." Davy turned back to the man who called himself Roberts. "Defused something, did you?"

"Aye."

"You'd've been better off to run."

"You're right."

Davy detected a note of sincerity but said, "Aye. Well." He saw how Roberts stood, shoulders hunched to the rain, but otherwise relaxed. Roberts seemed innocent, but Davy was not taking any chances. "I'm going to ask you a few questions."

"Fair enough."

"Where do you live?"

"Robina Street."

"You're from Northern Ireland?"

"Bangor."

"Where'd you live there?"

"Victoria Road. Number 4."

"Semi?"

"Not at all, them's all big tall terrace houses."

"Are you a Catholic?"

"No. I'm a fucking Hottentot." Roberts grinned and crossed himself. "Hail Mary, full of grace, the Lord be with Thee; Blessed art Thou amongst women, and blessed is the fruit of Thy womb, Jesus. Holy Mary, mother of God, pray for us sinners—"

"—now and at the hour of our death." Davy finished the line. "Son, I never seen you in my life. Jimmy here thinks I can trust you. He says you want to meet the Provos."

"I do."

Davy stood. He was only an inch taller than Roberts. "Well, if you do, sit you there beside Jimmy and answer the questions."

The young man sat, one shoulder facing his interrogator, legs crossed, arms folded, looking up warily from under his wet donkey fringe.

Davy began. "What's the difference between guhr dynamite and straight dynamite?"

"Guhr dynamite has an inactive base. Straight dynamite has an active base. Forty percent straight dynamite's forty-percent nitro, forty-four-percent sodium nitrate, fifteen-percent wood pulp, and one-percent calcium carbonate."

"That's right."

"Jesus, mister. It's the first thing they taught me."

Jimmy held up a finger. "I told you he knows explosives."

"Whist, Jim." Davy ignored Jimmy's spluttering. "What's the minimum initiating charge for TNT?"

"Fulminate or hexamethylene triperoxide diamine?"

"Fulminate."

"Zero-point-two-six grams. If it has a reinforcing cap."

Davy recognized the man's knowledge of these conventional explosives was as good as his own, but the Security Forces might have trained an infiltrator in the making of unconventional charges, too. "Suppose you had some nitric acid, sulphfuric acid, and some methyl alcohol, could you get an explosive out of that?"

"Dead easy."

Davy stiffened. "How?"

Roberts flipped his hair aside and grinned. "I'd give it to a bloke like you and ask him to make me a bomb. For God's sake, mister, how the hell would I know? We buy our stuff. We don't fucking well make it."

Davy saw Jimmy laughing and could not help laughing himself. Maybe the lad was on the level.

"Say your name was Mike?"

"Aye."

"All right, Mike. Why do you want to meet someone in the Provos?"

"It's kinda hard to explain. I grew up in Northern Ireland. I never thought much about politics, but I never got used to getting the shitty end of the stick because we were 'Fenians.' It wasn't much fucking joy being a Catholic at a Protestant school."

Davy saw how the youngster's lip curled. "Go on."

"My da took us to Canada. Do you know, it didn't matter if you were Catholic or Protestant there. No one gave a shit. It was great."

"That would be nice."

"Aye. But, you know, you miss your own. Them Canadians have no sense of humour. I sorta stuck with the rest of the Irish lads. I met a fellow from Monaghan. He said he was in the IRA before he emigrated."

"Go on."

"He told me all about why he'd fought to free Ulster. I thought he talked a lot of sense. Sounded exciting, what he did. He'd to run because someone thought that the Brits had sussed him out. I thought I'd come and see for myself. Get it from the horse's mouth, like."

"Would you help out?"

"I might. It's still my country."

"And you know about Semtex?"

"Mostly C4."

"Not Semtex?" Davy scowled at Jimmy. Had he come here on a wild-goose chase?

"I've used C4. I know about Semtex. It's popular stuff with terrorists, if you know what I mean." He grinned a big open smile. "It's very hard to get your hands on in civilian work."

Davy grunted.

"There's not a lot of difference. Plastique's plastique."

"Tell me about it."

"I will. If you'll tell me about what's really going on. I might even join up. I just wish to hell you'd tell me in out of the rain. I'm fucking drenched."

"You'll not melt. Tell you what. You tell me about Semtex. If you are serious about joining, I'll ask about." The hell he would, but he was going to learn what he wanted to know.

"Semtex-H? The Czechs make that in a place called Pardubice-SemtÍn. It's a plastic explosive. Eighty-two percent cyclonite, and eighteen-percent paraffin wax. C4's ninety-one percent cyclonite, that's the only difference. They dye Semtex orange so if it doesn't go off it's easy to find. You can set fire to it, and nothing happens. Set it off with a detonator, and the gases expand at 26,400 feet per second."

"Could you make a shaped charge?"

"Sure. But that's not how you use it. Not all the time. It depends on what you want to blow."

"Go on."

"Look, say you wanted to knock down a concrete pillar. If you use C4, the best bet's an offset charge. You need one pound of C4 for every foot the thing's thick. You divide the C4 in half and fix half to one side and half to the other. Detonate them at the same second, and that'll take out anything to four feet thick."

"Sounds simple."

"It is. Now suppose you want to break a steel beam, up to two inches thick. You'd use a ribbon. You make it twice as thick as what you want to cut and run it from one side to the other. Stick the primer in one end. That'll go through an I bar like a hot knife through butter."

"So you'd not need too much plastique?"

"The whole idea's to use as little as possible. Like I said, it depends what you've to do. There's all kinds of formulas to figure it out."

"Formulas?"

"Aye. Like P equals R cubed KC."

"P equals what?"

"P's the pounds of TNT. R's how big you want the hole. You've to cube that. Then you multiply by K. That's the material factor. It's different for all kinds of things. There's a table. K for rubble's 0.32, so you'd be cutting the amount by a third. It's 1.76 for ferro-concrete, so you'd need about twice as much. Then C's the tamping factor. You need twice as much if you don't bury the charge."

"Jesus." Jimmy was right. This young fellow could be a gold mine of information.

"Aye, and once you've calculated P, that's the pounds of TNT a job would take, then you divide by RE."

"What the fuck's RE?"

"Relative effectiveness factor. TNT's given a factor of one. If you're using Semtex, the RE's 1.6. So if you figure out you'd need sixteen pounds of TNT, divide by 1.6. You'd only want ten pounds of Semtex. See?"

Davy shook his head.

"It's not as bad as that. I could write it out for you."

"Who said I wanted you to?"

"Suit yourself."

"Tell me more."

"All right. Sometimes you don't have to do the sums. If you wanted to hole a fuel container and set fire to the fuel, a platter charge can do it from up to fifty yards away, but you'd need up to six pounds. You can get the same effect with a soap-dish charge stuck on the side of the fuel tank. Mind you, you'd have to add thermite to the plastique."

"Is that what they call a shaped charge?"

"Not at all. Shaped charges is linear, cylindrical cavity, or conical." He rubbed his arms with the palms of his hands. "Look. I'm fucking foundered."

"Just a wee minute."

"Jesus. All right. You have to get the size of the cavity just right. They work because making a hole in the plastique focuses the force. In a conical charge, the angle of the sides of the cavity has to be thirty to sixty degrees and the explosive twice as deep as the depth of the cone. Then you have to figure out the standoff."

"Standoff?"

"Aye. You don't put the explosive right against the target. You set it back. The formula's once or twice the diameter of the cone."

Davy was used to learning by doing. He frowned. "Tell me that bit about shaped charges again."

"Look, if you really need to know, it'd be far easier for me to show you with a lump of putty."

Davy smiled. "Aye. Right enough. I'll maybe get ahold of you. You said you lived on Robina Street?"

"I did."

Davy was getting cold. He'd learn no more today. Time for home. "You and Jim run on."

"But what about my questions?"

Davy shook his head. "I'm not a Provo."

"But you said . . ."

"You never met me. Go on now."

Jimmy stood. "Come on, Mike. It's cold as a witch's tit."

Davy watched them walk away. At least now he had some notion about what was involved in working with plastique. And it was fucking complicated. Maybe he would have a word with Sean about Mike Roberts. Sean and McGuinness could worry about why a fellow who claimed he worked in the oil fields would know not one but two ways to blow up petrol tanks. Davy didn't think there'd be much use for that skill in the oil business.

Maybe he'd take a chance. Why should he let McGuinness know that he'd been bluffing when he'd sworn he knew all about Semtex? He could get young Roberts round to the house and have him demonstrate. The putty was a good idea. Jimmy would have plenty. Davy shrugged. He'd have time to think that over, but damn it, he didn't want to let McGuinness in on this. The thought of that shit's contemptuous smile, and the way he'd have another excuse to have a go at Sean. Davy could hear the bastard now. "So your old man didn't know how to work with plastique."

He walked slowly toward the exit, right leg dragging, wondering if he could learn enough before the shipment Sean had spoken about arrived from Dublin. Schoolboys watched him pass, hiding their smokes, conducting their clandestine business in the rain at the Belfast Waterworks.

THIRTY-EIGHT

Brendan McGuinness's communications room in 15B Myrtlefield Park was getting crowded. Four wooden crates were stacked against a wall. Each contained thirty one-kilo blocks of an orange-coloured material wrapped in a pink plastic sheet. There were six crates containing ArmaLite rifles, and twenty squat ammunition boxes of ·223 ball cartridge. The long tubes of eight RPG-7s lay in a corner. The Belfast Brigade was resupplied, thanks to the efforts of Turlough Galvin, who was down in Dublin for meetings with Army Council, the governing body of the PIRA.

Turlough was being briefed about the decision to begin a campaign on the British mainland. He wondered about the wisdom of such a move. Two foreign corporals had tried to have a go at the Brits in their own backyard. One hadn't been able to cross the English Channel. Nelson's navy had seen to that. The other had thought he could bomb England to her knees. He hadn't come close. Hitler had tried sending his Luftwaffe to blitz Belfast in the Easter of 1941. The Catholics and Protestants had come together as one community in the face of a common enemy.

The British government was trying to get them to come together again. Provisional Army Council had no time for that. They wanted the Brits out of the sovereign state of Ireland, a state that should have thirty-two, not twenty-six, counties.

If the senior Provos wanted to mount raids in England, that was their decision, but Turlough had more faith in the effects of the war in the north. Brendan McGuinness had been silent recently about the big raid he had mooted several weeks ago, and he'd refused to identify the target until he had all the details. Turlough decided not to discuss it with Army Council until he had something more concrete to propose. For the time being, he would listen and carry out his orders. At least he had been able to expedite the shipment that his men in Belfast so desperately needed.

In the drawing room, rays from the cut-glass chandelier were reflected in irregular patterns onto the high ceiling. They reminded Sean Conlon of Mister Eyes, a game he'd played as a child. Circles of light thrown from a shiny surface could be made to run and dance over the walls.

He sat in a comfortable armchair, close to the ornate fireplace, waiting for Brendan to finish in the other room. He had to admit, taking this furnished flat on Myrtlefield Park had been a stroke of genius. No one in this line of work was ever completely secure, but he was closer to feeling safe than he had since he joined the Provos back in 1970. The ordnance would be safe here, too. And they were going to need some of it very soon.

Sean yawned. It had been a long day, and he wished that Brendan would get a move on. No doubt the new source of intelligence was proving very useful, but the information obtained took time to analyze. *Match of the Day* would be on the telly shortly. He thought that Manchester City were playing 'Spurs. He would enjoy watching the game, but there would not be time if Brendan didn't shift himself.

Sean hoped to God that Brendan was finally going to sort out the mysterious "big one," something that would grate on the Protestants and the English like nails on a blackboard. The Republicans had to keep the pot boiling. Sean wanted union with the Republic, and as far as he was concerned, the best way to achieve that was to hit here in Northern Ireland. Hit hard, again and again, until the Protestants—the Reverend Ian Paisley and his like—reared up and refused any further cooperation with the British, the province became ungovernable, and the Brits finally gave up.

He let his gaze wander round the spacious room, marveling once more at how the upper crust lived. Clean white walls, adorned with paintings—originals, at that. Four Milliken watercolours of game birds. He admired the one of the autumn trees stark against the bracken below, with a cock pheasant rocketing through the bare branches. He'd enjoyed a shot, before the Troubles. Rabbits mostly. Pheasants were for the gentry. That would change when Ulster was free. He'd maybe get a go at what now were Lord Dufferin's birds but then would belong to everybody. Until that day, Sean would have to content himself shooting at bigger game.

It was a superb picture. Sean envied the artist his skill. He'd wanted to be a painter himself, had been a student at Belfast College of Art when the Troubles started, but the IRA was a family business and he'd had no choice. Sean's own da had been in the Officials in the fifties. He'd been younger than Davy McCutcheon's father, but the two men had been comrades. Davy had kept an eye out for Sean in his early days with the Provos, before his rapid promotion.

He was a sound man, Davy, but the stupid bugger insisted on blaming himself because the raid on the Rovers had gone sour. Sean had sensed that Davy would need to have his confidence restored. Sean knew he'd been hasty, telling Davy that he'd be using the Semtex on an important job, when in truth, until McGuinness identified the target, Sean had no idea what the job might be. Still, the offer had produced the right response. The last time Davy was here, he'd left showing the right degree of determination.

Davy had given everything for the Cause. He deserved the rewards. Just as Sean had been forced to give up his art, Davy had lost his woman. Sean had met her once. Fiona Kavanagh. Black hair and a smile like a sunrise. Maybe he could go back to his painting, once the Troubles were over. Maybe Davy could go back to his Fiona. Sean heard the door open and turned to see Brendan, coatless, sleeves rolled up, eye bright behind his spectacles.

"Sean, it's on. I've just got the word. This is fucking ginormous."

"Get a grip, Brendan." For a moment Sean wondered why he put up with McGuinness. He could be as vicious as a bull terrier, but there was no doubting the man's commitment. "What is it?"

"Harold Wilson."

"Harold Wilson?" Sean whistled. "Wilson? The PM?"

"Aye. Himself."

"Jesus Christ."

"Not Jesus. *Wilson*. The bastard's coming here."

"Hang about. I'd need to think about that for a minute."

"Take your time, Sean. But I'm telling you, we can get him."

Sean wondered if Brendan was having a fit of the head-staggers. The security surrounding the visit of a British prime minister would be tighter than a duck's arsehole. The idea was daft. There'd be no way to get at Wilson. None at all. Unless? Ah, no. The Provos weren't like the PLO with their suicide squads—and yet if there was a way . . .

Sean asked, "Do you know when he's coming?"

"Aye. April eighteenth."

"That's just a couple of weeks." Sean had no reason to doubt Brendan. Intelligence was getting better. Much better. Even if Davy and his squad had failed to get the Land Rovers, they had been exactly where Brendan had said they would be.

"Wilson's coming, Sean."

"Jesus. We'd better have a word with Turlough about this. He'll have to get Army Council approval."

Brendan smirked. "He'll not be back for a few days. We'll have to start planning now."

"How the hell could we get to Wilson? The Security Forces will be all over the place."

Brendan took off his glasses. His single eye sparkled. "We have the Semtex. We have an expert—if McCutcheon's telling the truth."

"He is, for Christ's sake."

"I believe you, Sean. Thousands wouldn't. In a few more days I'll know Wilson's exact movements. If he has to take a drive anywhere, we can put the Active Service Unit in a safe house near the route. Even a week or so before."

"Could we use something with a timer?"

"I doubt it. The Brit bomb-disposal boys will be everywhere. It's going to take someone on the spot."

Sean bit his lip. He didn't like it. Not one bit, and yet the target was too good to miss. "We might not be able to get the attack squad out."

"So? McCutcheon's expendable."

"He is not," Sean's voice was icy.

"It's not for you or me to decide. That'll be Turlough's call." He draped one arm round Sean's shoulder. He flinched from the man's touch. "Come on, Sean. Sooner or later, Davy's really going to fuck up. I told you he's past it. We might as well get some use out of him now." He took his arm away and moved toward the big Philips television set. "Anyway, the lads'll be back from Libya after the middle of this month. We'll have more explosives experts than we'll know how to use."

Sean said levelly, "You are talking about a no-hope mission."

Brendan smiled. "Not at all. We'll get started on the logistics tomorrow." He turned the on switch. "*Match of the Day*'ll be on in a minute," he said, "'Spurs and Manchester."

THIRTY-NINE

Marcus sat in the frayed armchair, feet propped up on the candlewick bedspread, and wondered what the hell he had let himself in for. For two months he had become another man. Mike Roberts might have developed more sophisticated tastes in Canada but would be no stranger to squalor, scruffy boozers, and the premises of "turf accountants," as bookies styled themselves.

Living as a slum Catholic for the last month had been an eye-opener. Marcus could understand now why Captain Warnock had said it was more attractive for men to be PIRA volunteers than unemployed greyhound walkers.

And Mike had new friends, big Eamon and wee Jimmy, and an avowed interest in joining the Provos. He had fallen hopelessly for Siobhan Ferguson, but was the kind of man who would be too proud to go begging her to reconsider what she had repeated three days ago when he had brought her back from Gransha, that she thought it better if he didn't come round anymore.

Never mind Mike Roberts. Marcus Richardson loved Siobhan, and she was wrong about him. He knew he was a different Marcus from the apolitical ATO who had come back to Ulster. He hadn't been able to ignore the daily carnage in the streets of the city. *His* city.

He'd felt completely at home on Gransha, with its peace and its memories—or had until she'd knocked his world askew. His Ulster roots went deeper than he had recognized. And he'd come to understand from what he saw daily, and from his conversations with Eamon and Jimmy, that the situation in Ulster was more complex than a simple Catholic-versus-Protestant-faction fight with the army in the middle.

Great wrongs had been done to the Catholic minority. The scars and the wounds went back so far, and recent history was nothing to boast about. Since partition in 1922, the Orange Order had ruthlessly kept the Fenians in their place. There had been anti-Catholic discrimination in jobs and in housing, Gerrymandering—the redrawing of electoral boundaries to ensure that the Catholics could never form majorities—was rampant.

At first sight, it seemed simple to characterize the Protestant Loyalists as evil men. They weren't. They were scared men, terrified of the prospects of a united Ireland in which they would become a minority in a Catholic country. Scared men do evil things. They were wrong to try to cling to power like the white South Africans, but, like the Boers, the Protestants had been in the country for hundreds of years, and it was as much their home as it was the Catholics'. Loyalist paramilitary organizations, the Ulster Volunteer Force, the Red Hand Commandos, and the Ulster Freedom Fighters had been formed to oppose the PIRA and to keep Ulster part of Britain.

The violence was the work of a small number of hard-liners on both sides of the sectarian divide. The great majority of the population abhorred the killings and wanton destruction, wanted to live in peace and find a politically workable solution. But no one could see what that solution might be. Marcus certainly could not. He still wanted to nail the bomber and his superiors, and not just so he could hold the major to his promise about the SAS. It wouldn't halt the war, but he was convinced that, however the conflict was to be resolved, bombings were not the way to achieve political ends.

Marcus had known fear when the van bomb blew in the Falls. He'd had to force himself to go under the cinema marquee. It had been hairy enough defusing the pub bomb, but at least he was trained for that kind of work. Civilians weren't, and they must live with fear every day of their lives.

He ran a hand through his hair. What a cock-up. Ulster and its complexities, Siobhan gone, and as far as his mission was concerned, he was getting nowhere. Meeting McCutcheon had been promising, but that fizzled out when McCutcheon had had his questions answered. He'd said he might ask about, but how close was Marcus to meeting senior Provos? He hadn't a clue. Certainly he hadn't learned enough to bother making an appointment with the Dr. Kennedy who was to be Marcus's contact with the major.

Marcus stood up and toyed with a photograph that lay on his table among the books about Alberta and the green folder. The Mike Roberts folder. That face in the snap, he looked at it closely, belonged to the man the major thought was one of the M62 bombers. There'd been no sign of him in the pubs or bookies'. No Provos, no idea when or if he'd hear from McCutcheon again, and no Siobhan. Bugger it.

He looked over into the corner where he had piled his dirty clothes. He really should take them to the launderette. He'd get them washed on his way to the pub. He'd have to go down there again tonight and pretend to be enthralled by Eamon's repartee. Maybe Jimmy would be in. He'd not been for the last couple of nights. Marcus could at least ask him how Siobhan was. Maybe enquire obliquely about McCutcheon. And then what?

He moved to the window, pushed aside the grey net curtains, and peered down the length of narrow Robina Street. A young woman was walking toward number 10. She had long blond hair, and—he sighed— for a moment she reminded him of Siobhan. He watched her approach, seeing her hair—wishing. Christ. It *was* Siobhan.

Marcus dropped the curtain. He grabbed his notes and the photographs from the table. He shoved the papers under his bed, reached into the corner of the room, and stuffed his dirty clothes in after the green ring binder.

Someone knocked on the door. "Coming."

The bloke who had been pissed off because Mike had been too long in the bathroom stood there. "Roberts?"

"Aye."

"There's a bird to see you."

"Thanks." He pushed past and saw her standing on the pavement. "Siobhan?"

"Can I come in?"

Two miles from Robina Street, the air in another room was warm and muggy. A chlorine stink filled Brendan McGuinness's nostrils. He sat on a slatted, backless wooden bench dressed in nothing but a damp towel that bore the slogan, "Ormeau Baths. Property of Belfast City Corporation." He had difficulty seeing because the humidity fogged the lens of his spectacles. His feet rested on duckboards, and he had an uncomfortable feeling that he might catch athlete's foot.

He squinted through the fog. None of the changing cubicles was occupied. A fat man with sagging breasts, his torso as hairy as a gorilla's, rotated under a freshwater shower. The sound of the spray echoed from the tiled walls. Brendan had not expected the place to be busy on a Wednesday. He'd been right.

The door of the changing room opened and a towel-clad newcomer crossed the duckboards and sat on the bench beside Brendan. He carried a second towel and began to dry his short-cropped hair, the towel over the sides of his head effectively shielding his face from the man in the shower.

Brendan had to strain over the splashing of the water to hear the newcomer's words.

"Wilson hits Thiepval at ten on the eighteenth. They'll take him by a roundabout route to Hillsborough, but he'll have to cross the Ravernet River. The convoy'll be two army Saracens and an armoured Mercedes. He'll be in the Merc. He'll be on the Ravernet Bridge between eleven thirty and twelve." The short-haired man stared at the floor as the fat man left the shower and went into one of the cubicles, closing the door behind him. Then he asked, "Any sign of Roberts?"

"Roberts? The Brit? Aye. The information officer of Second Battalion and me had a word."

"What about?"

"One of our New Lodge fellows, Colin Heaney"—

"Lad with a cleft lip?"

"Aye. He'd reported to his battalion IO that some fellow in New Lodge, back from Canada, was an explosives expert. He defused a bomb in their pub. Heaney wanted to know if he should try to recruit him."

The short-haired man grunted. "And?"

"The IO said to hang on 'til he'd spoken to me. I told him to tell Heaney to keep an eye on Roberts but to keep away from him for a wee while."

"Fair enough. Now you know where he is, you can sort him out whenever it suits us."

"He'll keep 'til I'm ready."

"Right. Now, Ravernet Bridge, eleven thirty to noon on the eighteenth."

Brendan nodded once to indicate that he had heard clearly, then rose and walked to a cubicle. As he dried his left foot, he peered balefully at a bunion and hoped to God he had not picked up any fungus in these grotty public baths.

Marcus tried to apologize because his room was so dingy, but she brushed aside his protestations. He took her coat and hung it behind the door. She'd taken the armchair, leaving him nowhere to sit but on the bed.

"Would you like a cup of tea?" he asked, hoping she'd say yes.

"No thanks."

"Oh."

"I didn't come for tea."

"I'm glad you came."

She shook her head and he wondered how many times he'd seen her toss her bright mane.

"I had to talk to you," she said. "It's stupid."

"No, it's not."

She crossed her legs, folded her arms, put a hand on each shoulder, and leaned her face against a forearm. "I shouldn't have come."

"Siobhan."

She looked into his eyes. "Damn you, Mike Roberts. I've cried myself to sleep every night."

"I'm sorry."

"Don't be. I'm the one that should be sorry."

"Why?"

"Because I thought I meant what I said, except I didn't get it quite right." She unfolded her arms and rubbed the back of her neck. "I said I could fall in love with you."

He slipped off the bed and stood close before her. "I love you, Siobhan."

"I know. I know." He saw her tears start.

He bent and kissed her and the kiss was returned.

"I love you, Mike." She stood and he held her to him, lips on hers. His hand found her breast, soft through the stuff of her blouse, the nipple hard beneath his palm. He felt her teeth on his lower lip and her breath sweet on his.

She stepped back and he watched her undress, without coyness, without false modesty, baring her body for him: alabaster skin, coral nipples—pink reefs in the shining sea of her long, gold hair. He brought her to him, soft against his shirt, and brushed her lips with his, tasting her, the sweet and the salt of her, breathing the perfume of her, feeling her yield to his touch. He put his mouth to her nipple, taking in the firmness of the rosebud and soft strands of her hair. She shuddered and pulled his head against her breast.

"Siobhan," he murmured, "Siobhan," as he stripped and, naked himself, enfolded her, holding his hardness against the softness of her belly.

She surprised him with the ferocity of their first lovemaking, pulling him to her, onto her, into her, ravenously wanting, taking until both were spent, humid and drowsy, lying on the small bed. She surprised him with the tenderness of their second lovemaking, seeking, exploring, learning, finding out. Languorous, rhythmic, timeless.

He lay, head on her breast, fondling the curve of her hip, looking at the beauty of her, taking her in with all his senses. He knew, beyond doubt, with a certainty that scared him, that life without Siobhan Ferguson would be no life at all. "I love you," he said.

When she said, later, that she really must go home, they dressed, and he walked her to her house, held her, and kissed her, feeling their parting like a physical pain, knowing then that he would never find, nor want to find, another Siobhan.

He wandered back to Robina Street, thoughts flogging like a headsail with a broken sheet. He knew he must stop lying to her, prayed that she would understand when he eventually explained who he was. Had she really meant what she had said on Gransha, that she wouldn't care if he was a British soldier?

FORTY

Davy leaned against the wall beside the makeshift bar, sipping his stout. He looked at the other men in the room, seated at tables or standing in knots around the walls. It was the same old crowd and some younger ones he hadn't seen before. There was no sign of the singer.

One of the newcomers, a lad of nineteen or twenty, with a pasted-on sneer and a ferocious squint, harangued the rest of his party, declaiming his loyalty to Ireland and his hatred of all things British. The little shite would ignore his disapproval when it came to accepting his dole money.

Jesus. Words. The country was drowning in words. Davy ignored the tirade.

Through the smoke haze he could see tears in the wallpaper where strips hung down, limp and ragged. Someone had tried to brighten the place up by tacking posters to the walls. A man with muscles like an ox held a surprised-looking carthorse above his head with one hand on a poster proclaiming: "Guinness is good for you." It is, Davy thought, in good company.

He was here because his house had become cramped and empty all at the same time. Cramped because for the last week, since he had met young Roberts, he had seen, more clearly than ever before, the narrowness of his own horizons. It was something the youngster had said about Canada. "No one there gives a shit if you're Catholic or Protestant."

The Cause and all that went with it; hard men in luxury flats, ammonium nitrate, urea nitrate, dynamite, nitro, blasting caps, ArmaLites, constant guard, skulking and subterfuge, death and maiming . . . dead ten-year-old girls. Even now, the Land Rover raid more than a fortnight gone, he could hear her "pleeease . . ." in the small lonely hours of his nights.

The hollow times between the action. Nowhere to go but the back-streets of the Falls or an unlicenced drinking den full of broken-down relics refighting battles of a forgotten, failed war, men with whom he had nothing but a past to share. No friends except Jimmy and a scruffy ginger cat. No contact with the rest of his battalion save Sean and Brendan McGuinness.

Days spent in a cramped, two-down-two-up, empty house—empty because Fiona wasn't there. He had lost count of the number of times he had set out, determined to phone her. And he had reason now. He'd do the big one. His mind was set on that. It might win the war, but even if it didn't, it would be his last.

He would call her when it was over and done with for good. Next time he saw Jimmy, he'd find out more about Canada. That Roberts lad knew an IRA man who'd moved there.

Davy was impatient. Impatient for the summons from Myrtlefield Park. Until then, he had no way of contacting the CO. No way of getting it over with. And now, now that his mind was made up, he wanted it finished.

He was impatient to talk to her again, face-to-face, not on the impersonal telephone. Maybe they could start a new life in Canada. He wasn't too old. She would have to enquire at the Canadian consulate if her teaching certificate from Stranmillis College would be good enough for a Canadian school.

He shifted the weight from his bad leg. Dream on, Davy McCutcheon. What if she says, "No, I don't want to go to Canada"? He'd not think about that now. He'd dream. You're good at dreams, Davy, he thought—dreams of Celtic Twilight, dreams of a new life in a new country, dreams of Fiona. He hawked, the spit bitter in his throat. Dreams, Davy. They're all you've got.

He swallowed Guinness, the bottled beer more bitter than the draught he preferred. He wondered if he would be able to get a decent pint in Canada. He should have asked Mike Roberts. He'd been living there for years. Or so he said. The youngster certainly knew his explosives. As soon as Davy got the word and the plastique from Sean, he'd have Roberts round. Forget buggering about with learning on putty;

Roberts could make the real thing. There was no need to mention anything to Sean Conlon. Roberts could fix the Semtex charges, and Davy would deliver them. The Active Service Unit would go out well equipped, and Davy would have kept his promise to Sean, with that shit McGuinness none the wiser. The plan seemed watertight and pleased Davy.

And then—Fiona. He hugged the thought, a smile playing on his lips.

Sean Conlon had no smile on his face as he paced up and down the big drawing room. "Fuck it, Brendan. We can't go ahead without permission from Army Council."

Brendan sat in an armchair beside the carved fireplace. "As far as I know, we've got it."

"How the hell can you tell? Turlough was meant to bring back the word from Dublin."

"He can't, can he, Sean?"

"How the hell did the Brits know he'd be crossing the border at Dundalk yesterday?"

"You tell me."

"Jesus, Brendan, Turlough's the third OC Belfast Brigade they've lifted." He counted on his fingers, "Adams, Bell, and now Turlough."

"Yes," said Brendan, "and you'd better have a look at this." He handed Sean a piece of paper. "It's from Army Council. They've confirmed me as OC, Belfast Brigade."

Sean stopped pacing and scanned the note. "Congratulations," he said coldly as he handed the paper back.

"I'm sure we'll work together very well. I'll carry on as IO until we find a new one. It won't interfere with my duties as OC, and I say we're going ahead."

"On the British prime minister?"

"Jesus, Sean, at the first meeting of Provisional Army Council they said that action could be left to the discretion of local leadership." His voice hardened. "And that's me."

And likely to stay that way, Sean thought, if you pull this one off. Pity the PIRA doesn't hand out medals. You'd like that, Brendan, wouldn't you? Sean let his head bow. "All right."

"Great." McGuinness stood. Just for a moment Sean wondered if McGuinness had had prior knowledge of Turlough's impending arrest and kept quiet about it, either to improve his own chances of promotion or to ensure that there would be no interference with his plans to go after Harold Wilson. He could be devious, but surely not *that* devious.

"We need another big victory. Remember what Chairman Mao said about power coming from the barrel of a gun? We've got our tails up now. Look. Peter McMullen, the ex-para, got four bombs into Claro Barracks in Ripon in Yorkshire on March 26; we set off fourteen bombs in London stores on April 6, aye, and two in Manchester and three in Birmingham. Incendiaries took out half the city centre in Armagh yesterday. Ten shops gone in Market, Scotch, and Thomas Streets."

"And you think wasting Wilson would help?"

"Yes, for fuck's sake. You know what our New Year's message said?"

Sean quoted, "We look forward with confidence to 1974 as a year in which the British rule in Ireland shall be destroyed and the curse of alien power banished from our land for all time."

"'Banished for all time'! We can do it, Sean. Kill Wilson, and the Prods'll start tearing the province apart. Paisley would go fucking Harpic."

Sean smiled at Brendan's allusion to the Harpic lavatory cleaner's slogan: "Clean round the bend." And he might just be right. It could be the final nail in England's coffin. Perhaps when Sean had told Davy that this one could win the war, he hadn't been too far from the truth. "So, where do we go from here?"

"I've just heard. Wilson's going to helicopter into Thiepval and be driven to Government House at Hillsborough on the eighteenth. Lisburn's in First Battalion's area of operations, so we don't have to clear it with the County Down boys. We just need to finish the final arrangements, then get your man McCutcheon up here."

Davy drained the glass and moved to the front of the bar.

Paddy Flynn said, "You're looking cheerful the night, Davy. Another?"

"Aye."

"Here y'are." Flynn uncapped the dark bottle and took Davy's money. "Haven't seen you in for a brave while."

"I've been busy."

"Right enough?"

"Aye."

"Full of chat, as usual. Jesus, Davy, you'd talk the hind leg off a donkey."

Davy craned over the bar. "Doesn't seem to have fell off yet, Flynn."

The barman guffawed. "You're so fucking sharp you'll cut yourself."

"Aye."

Davy moved back to his place against the wall. He tilted his glass, tide-marked with grey-white rings of foam, and poured from the bottle, slowly, watching the black beer rise, thinking of Fiona's black eyes.

The patriot with the squint pushed past on his way to the bar. He jostled Davy's elbow, spilling some of his beer. "Easy, son," Davy said.

"Who the fuck're you calling 'son'?" The youth turned on Davy, forcing him to push back against the wall.

Davy could smell the whiskey on the boy's breath, see the red vessels in the whites of his eyes. The wee shite needed a shave. He needed to learn some manners, too, but Davy was in no mood to teach him. "Forget it."

"I said"—the youth swayed. His eyelids drooped. "I said, who the fuck are you calling 'son'?"

"No one."

A hand thumped into Davy's shoulder, slamming it against the wall. He heard the crash as his glass hit the floor. He turned his face away to avoid the spittle as the drunk yelled, "Don't you fucking well call me 'son,' you old cunt."

Davy saw Flynn moving round from behind the bar, yelling, "Get you to hell out of that, Seamus Rourke." Flynn could put an end to this.

"Look at me when I'm fucking well talking to you." Rourke grabbed Davy's hair. "Fuck, you. Look . . . at . . . me!"

Davy looked. Hard. His stare bored into the bloodshot eyes, six inches from his own. His voice was level. "Take your hands off me."

"Fuck you." Rourke darted his head forward. Davy pulled aside, but the hand in his hair held him. He managed to move so Rourke's skull missed the bridge of his nose. He felt the smash on his right cheekbone.

He lashed his knee into Rourke's crotch, feeling the crunch against the man's pelvis and the pain flashing along his own badly set thigh bone. Hot breath whistled past his ear, the breath of a shriek cut short as Rourke tried to inhale and failed as he doubled forward, clutching his groin.

Davy lifted his right hand like an axe, fingers extended, the edge its blade, and aimed a vicious chop at the side of the man's neck. Before making contact, he checked the swing, jerking his hand back up and away.

Rourke collapsed and lay on the floor in the spilled Guinness and broken glass, curled up like a baby, gasping like a stunned mullet. Davy lifted his knee to smash his boot into Rourke's face and hesitated as the fighting madness flowed from him. He stood breathing deeply.

"You all right, Davy?" Paddy Flynn kicked the fallen youth in the ribs. "See you, Seamus Rourke? Youse is barred."

He drew back his leg to kick again but Davy grabbed his arm. "Let him be, Paddy."

Flynn spat on Rourke. "You, Arthur, get him the fuck out of here."

The man called Arthur bent over Rourke, ignored his whimpering, hauled him to his feet, and yelled, "Give us a hand with this stupid—oh, Jesus."

Rourke puked.

"Get him out." Flynn snarled.

Davy clenched his teeth, trying to ignore the ache in his thigh, the throbbing in his cheek. The silence was broken only by weak retching sounds from Rourke. Davy heard Flynn say to the crowd, "That's it. It's all over. Pay no heed."

Faces turned away. The hum of conversation started slowly and gradually rose. Arthur and another man dragged the semi-conscious Rourke toward the door.

"Sorry about that, Davy." Flynn looked worried. "Did he get you?"

"I'll live." Davy rubbed his cheek, feeling the heat in the bruised skin, satisfied that the cheekbone was intact.

"Here." Flynn slopped a generous measure of Bushmills into a glass. "Here, get this down you."

"Thanks." Davy took the glass, noticing how his hand shook. He drank the neat spirits.

"Shook you up a bit, Davy?"

"Aye."

Flynn poured one for himself. "I thought you were going to murder him." He sipped the whiskey. "When I seen the rabbit punch coming, I thought your man was a goner. You'd've broke his neck. Fucking good thing you pulled back."

"Aye," said Davy. "Aye. It was."

FORTY-ONE

"You look like shit, McCutcheon." McGuinness's eyebrow rose.

"Some puppy took a poke at me in Flynn's last night."

"He must have fetched you a right one." McGuinness's lips smiled. His eye was flat.

"Aye. Head butt."

McGuinness tutted. "I hear there was a time you'd not have let him do a thing like that."

"I hear there was a time that young lad sang bass." Davy's gaze held McGuinness's. The threat was in Davy's voice: step outside anytime, boy. Anytime at all.

Sean sat with his back to the window, the afternoon light casting his long shadow across the tabletop.

Davy limped over. "Good to see you, Sean."

"Are you all right, Davy?"

"Oh, aye."

"Good. Sit down."

Davy sat and waited for McGuinness to be seated opposite, beside Sean. McGuinness leaned forward, elbows resting on the table, one hand enfolding the other, cracking his knuckles.

"We need you now," Sean said. "The big one's set for the eighteenth."

Davy glanced at McGuinness and back to Sean Conlon. "Military target?"

Sean nodded.

"What?"

"A convoy."

Why the hell was that old song buzzing in Davy's head again? *The*

tans in their great Crossley tenders were rolling along to their doom . . .
Soldiers. "Sounds like an important one."

McGuinness spoke softly. "It is, Davy. It is."

"Good," said Davy. "I'll make the bombs for you. Have you the Semtex?"

"We have." Sean Conlon coughed. "But we'll need you to do more than make the bombs, Davy."

The red velvet curtains were closed against the dark outside. A map of Ulster lay unrolled on the table. McGuinness had gone next door. Sean stood at the far side of the table. Davy thought the CO looked tired, worried. "Cheer up, Sean. It'll work."

"What?"

"It'll work."

"Davy, I'm sorry to ask you to go out alone on this one. Honest to God I am."

Davy shrugged. "Jimmy's as well out of it and you've no other choice. You need an explosives man to set the charges. It's not just a big bang you want. That bridge'll have to come down at the right time. I'll have to get the measurements of the span to figure out P." Davy tried to recall the formula for calculating the amount of explosive.

"P?"

"Aye, the number of pounds of TNT."

"But we're giving you Semtex."

"I know, Sean, but you calculate the amount of TNT, then divide it by 1.6." He congratulated himself for remembering that much. "Semtex is about one and a half times more powerful than TNT."

"Oh," said Sean, obviously impressed. "So do you reckon about sixty pounds would be enough?"

"Why sixty?"

"Because the stuff comes in thirty-kilo boxes and that's just a bit more than sixty pounds."

"Dead-on," said Davy, hoping he was right.

"Sixty pounds is a fair load. Are you sure you won't need backup?"

"Jesus, Sean have we not just spent the last three hours thrashing this out? Look." Davy pointed at the map. "The convoy leaves Thiepval Barracks on the eighteenth, right?"

Sean nodded.

"You want the target hit as it crosses this bridge between eleven thirty and twelve, so that means we can't use a timer. Someone's going to have to push the button at just the right minute. How many men does it take to push a fucking button?"

"One."

"Right. Now, there'll be heavy security and no decent cover near the bridge, so nobody can get near with an RPG or a mortar. Mortars is too inaccurate anyway."

Sean nodded again.

"Someone'll have to measure up and make the charges. I can do that a few days before." Davy let the lie roll off his tongue. He knew damn well he had not fully understood what Roberts had tried to explain. Trouble was, he wouldn't be able to get Roberts to prepare the charges in advance. He'd figure that out later. "All I have to do then is set the charges. If I can't carry sixty pounds by myself, I should have packed this up years ago. I reckon I'll get the Semtex in the night before. What are you looking so worried about?"

"What if the Brits sweep the bridge just before the convoy comes?"

"Christ, if the target's as important as you say, the security people will go over the bridge with a fine-tooth comb days before, and it'll be clean then. They'll come back nearer the time, but they won't be expecting to find anything. Not after their thorough search. Their dogs can't sniff out Semtex, and I'm losing my touch if I can't camouflage the plastique well enough for the kind of quick once-over the place will get the second time." He smiled. "You don't find things you know aren't there."

"I suppose you're right."

"I am. Now, if it takes one man to set the explosives, the same man can watch for the convoy from that empty farmhouse."

"Right."

"So if I move in a few days in advance, I'll be inconspicuous."

"True."

"By the same token, when the charges blow, the Brits'll be all over the place like wasps from a broken nest. Do you reckon one man or a squad would have a better chance of getting away?"

"That's another thing," Sean said. "The getaway. You should be able to get out the way you went in, but just in case"—he pointed to the map where a cluster of symbols indicated a wood—"can you ride a motor-bike?"

"Aye, certainly."

"We'll leave one inside that wood. If you can't get out by car, head for the wood and take the bike."

"You'd only get a whole action squad on a motorbike if they were in Duffy's Circus."

"All right, Davy." Sean laughed at the allusion to the little one-tent show that still toured the country districts in the summer months. "You've made your point, but this is strictly a volunteer mission. You can back out now."

"I want this one." Davy hesitated. "You said this one's so big it could win the war for us."

"It might."

"I've not asked you why, and I won't, but after this one I want out."

"You what? Jesus, Davy, don't say that in front of Brendan."

"Sean, how you sort him out is up to you, but I mean it. I've had enough. I'm out after this one."

"Davy, you've been in all your life. We're going to win. Why the hell do you want out now?"

Davy ran a hand through his hair. "Sean, I want a free Ireland as much as you. I don't want it at the price men like McGuinness want to pay. Ten-year-olds and babies. And, Sean? You met Fiona once." Davy knew that a pleading tone he had not intended had crept into his voice. He ploughed on. "She'll have me back if I quit."

Why was Sean staring at the painting of the pheasant and nodding his head? "All right, Davy." Sean leaned across the table, hand out-stretched. "I understand."

Sean's palm felt dry. "I'll not let you down on this last one, Sean."

"I know."

"Right," said Davy. "I'll away on and get my bus."

Brendan came into the room. "All set?"

Sean said, "He'll do it all right. He's a proud man, Davy. He insists on going in alone."

"Good."

"Could we not give him any backup?"

"We can do two things."

"What?"

"We'll set up diversionary raids all over the province the week before. Keep the Brits unsettled."

"Have we time to arrange that?"

Brendan laughed. "It's arranged already. For Christ's sake, Sean, I want this to work. Now look," he pointed at the map, "see that other farm there?"

"The one half a mile down the road from the bridge?"

"Aye. There's a back road that swings by Davy's farm just beyond it. Now. The first Saracen might get over the bridge. It could head for this road and cut him off from behind."

"Shit."

"Not if we put a squad in there."

"What with? RPGs?"

"Sheep."

"What?"

"Sheep. If the lads fire a rocket grenade, they'll give themselves away. But if they let a flock of sheep onto the road, the Brits would be tangled up long enough, and there's no law against sheep."

"That's bloody brilliant." Sean smiled. "And I thought you were going to leave Davy on his own."

The bus stopped at the end of the Lisburn Road before joining the traffic moving slowly round Shaftesbury Square. Davy sat on the upper deck thinking about his orders. The map with the directions to the farm was folded in his inside pocket. He put a hand to his left breast and felt the crackling of the paper. An old van, the kind farmers used, would be delivered to his house. The Semtex, remote-control detonator, and a weapon for Davy would be hidden in the van. Sean had smiled when Davy asked for a Heckler and Koch and told him he'd have to be satisfied with an ArmaLite.

Davy looked along the bus, distracted by the efforts of a mother to make her youngster sit down and stop making faces at the man in the seat behind. For a moment he wondered, but he knew the answer—Fiona would be too old for kids. He regretted the time they had wasted, but he'd waste no more. Now that he knew when it would be over, there was no reason not to phone her. He'd call tonight.

He told himself to forget about her and think about the job. He'd need his tools and some paint. Jimmy could get the paint. A wee lick of the right colour and the Semtex would look just like bits of the bridge supports. That would be the easy bit. The difficulty was figuring out how to destroy the bridge.

Davy understood that the size of the thing to be demolished influenced the size and weight of the charges. Without knowing the bridge's dimensions, Roberts couldn't prefabricate anything. There was a solution. Roberts would have to come on the raid. He'd said he wanted to help. Let him. Davy knew bloody well that McGuinness would have a fit if he found out. Sean wouldn't be too happy, either. No one was meant to be involved in the PIRA until they had been thoroughly screened. The most destructive spies were ones on the inside. The fucking British were forever trying to infiltrate the Provos.

But if Davy told Roberts he was being taken to meet the CO, he'd get into the van like a lamb. Once in a farmhouse in the middle of nowhere, who was he going to tell? And come hell or high water, Roberts would make the charges.

The bus passed the end of the Grosvenor Road. Davy noticed that *The Sting,* one of last year's big films was showing at the Grand Opera House. Paul Newman, Robert Redford, Robert Shaw, Charles Durning. Cast of bloody thousands. Not like next week, when there'd just be him and Roberts. And the convoy.

The phone box stank of piss. Davy thumbed through a damp telephone directory and found Fiona's sister's number. He dialed and closed his eyes, shutting out the square window frames—frames from which the glass had been smashed for as long as he could remember—"Brits Out" and "Fuck Paisley" daubed in black on the peeling red paint.

The line crackled.

"Hello?" He knew her voice at once. "Hello? Belfast 642376."

"Hello. Fiona?"

"Can you speak up please? It's a terrible line."

"Fiona, it's me. Davy."

"Davy? Are you all right?" He heard her concern but refused to play on it.

"I'm fine. I just need to talk to you. Just for a wee while." He waited, his fingers grasping the receiver.

"I see." Her voice was noncommittal. "Well. I'll listen."

"Not on the phone. I—I need to see you."

"Something's wrong."

"Not at all."

He heard a chuckle. "God, but you're still a stubborn, proud man, Davy McCutcheon."

"Aye. Well."

"But not too proud to ask for help?"

"No."

"All right. What do you need to see me about?"

It wasn't likely that public phones were bugged, but . . . "Look, I've one more wee errand to run." She'd understand. He waited. Nothing but the crackling in his ear. "Once it's done, I'm handing in my cards. For good. Jimmy said he seen you in Smithfield and you said—" He couldn't finish the sentence.

"I meant it." He heard a catch in her voice. "I'm still in love with you."

"Oh, Jesus, Fiona." Davy's knees felt weak. "You mean it?" And he cursed himself. Fiona Kavanagh had never said anything she didn't mean.

"It's not what I mean, Davy. It's what you do."

"I am finished, after this one."

"What are you up to tomorrow? At four?"

"Nothing."

"Do you remember where you took me for tea the day we met?"

"God, aye."

"I'll see you there tomorrow. At four."

FORTY-TWO

Davy had hardly slept, and all morning he prowled round his home, changing the sheets, dusting, vacuuming, tidying. If McCusker hadn't fled, Davy would have dusted the cat. He polished the glass of Fiona's picture twice. He kept thinking the twinkle in it, from the sunshine fighting in through the window, was the sparkle in her eyes.

He walked down to the shops and bought two lamb chops, enough fresh broccoli for two, and a ten-pound sack of potatoes. He picked up a bottle of Harveys Shooting Sherry at the off-licence. Fiona rarely took a drink, but sometimes, on special occasions, she'd have a glass of sherry. On his way home he got a haircut in the barber's shop with the chipped red and white pole outside and two creaky old chairs inside, along with three pairs of scissors and two combs in a glass cylinder full of disinfectant, posters for Brylcreem tacked to the walls.

At one o'clock he took a bath and changed into the shirt with an attached collar, the one that went with his only suit. He stood in his shirt-tails ironing the pants of the suit, smoothing until he was satisfied with the sharpness of the creases. He slipped his trousers on, laced up his polished boots, and tugged a V-necked sweater over his head.

He combed his new haircut and looked at his face in the mirror, seeing the grey of his freshly trimmed moustache and the black, now turning to yellow, in the bruise under his left eye.

The suit jacket was shiny at the elbows. He tutted, put it on, took one last look at himself in the mirror, collected his raincoat—his duncher was in the pocket—and left the house. He knew that he would be too early, but he couldn't bear to wait any longer. Maybe if he arrived before four o'clock, so would Fiona.

. . .

He sat at a table in the corner of the little tearoom. He was on his third cup of tea and fourth cigarette when she came through the door. He slammed the cup into the saucer, slopping tea over the rim; crushed out his cigarette in a tin ashtray, burning a fingertip in his hurry; and stood.

She smiled at him, and he saw her damson eyes, crow's-feet at the corners, and her jet-black hair, streaked with silver like a stoat's tail tip in winter, cut to frame her face. His heart swelled at the loveliness of her.

"Well, Davy," she said, her words melodious.

"Aye." He stumbled in his haste to pull out her chair. "Thank you for coming."

She sat and set her handbag on the tabletop.

"Would you like a cup of tea?" he asked, and she laughed, warm and throaty, melting him with memories of her.

"That's what you said all those years ago."

He blushed. "I know."

"I'll help myself."

Davy watched her pour and admired her short fingers, nails cut blunt. No nail polish. No rings. He handed her the milk.

"Thank you." She took the jug, brushing her chilled fingers against his.

"Your hand's frozen."

"Rubbish," she said, and chuckled.

Davy sat drinking her in as she drank her tea, waiting for her to speak, feeling as tongue-tied as a fourteen-year-old on his first date.

"What happened to your face?"

"Some eejit took a poke at me the other night. It's nothing. I stopped him." He wanted to tell her that he had been proud of himself for pulling his punches, that he was a changed man.

"So," she said, "you're getting out?"

He nodded. It was just like her, a few pleasantries and then straight to the point.

"Why?"

He told her, haltingly, in veiled terms—it was a public place—about the botched attack. Davy spoke of the Hanrahan girl, and waited for her to say it was about time he recognized what his work did. He should have known better; Fiona had never played the "I told you so" game. He looked up into her eyes and saw sadness.

"Ach, Davy. It's been hard for you."

"Aye, well. It'll be over soon."

"Why not right now?"

"I promised a man."

Her lips curved in a little smile. "And you've always kept your word?"

"Something like that." He footered with his empty teacup. "It's more than that."

"Go on."

"Fiona, it's the real thing this time." He couldn't give any details in public about the upcoming attack. "I need to do one right. Just one."

She put her hand over his. "And you think you'll find absolution for the little girl and the ticket man and his little girls?"

How had she seen that so quickly? He knew. She had always been able to look deep into him. "Aye."

"I don't think you will, Davy," and he flinched at her words, "but I understand. I'll not hold it against you."

He rolled his hand over and twined his fingers with hers, holding her hand as a child holds its mother's for comfort. "I'll make it up to you. God, but I've missed you, girl."

"I've missed you, Davy. I told you, I still love you."

Her words engulfed him like warm surf on a soft beach. He pulled her hand to his lips.

"I know," she said.

He lowered their hands to the tabletop and sat in the silence between them. "More tea?" he said.

She shook her head. "When?" she asked. "When will you be finished?"

"Next week."

"Good." Her eyebrow lifted in question. "Then what?"

"Jimmy's been talking about going to Canada."

"Canada?"

"Aye. I thought maybe—" He waited.

She smiled, and its radiance lit up the tearoom. "You thought maybe we could go, too?"

"I did."

"I'll need to find out how we'd go about it."

Davy leaned across the table and kissed her. "Bless you, girl."

Her smile faded. "But only if you get out, Davy."

"I swear to God."

She laughed. "And you always keep your word."

He realized she was teasing him. "Aye. I do."

"Good. I'll wait for you."

He looked down at the table. "Fiona, I've a couple of lamb chops at home." He looked up. "McCusker misses you. I don't suppose—?"

"Not tonight. I keep my promises, too. I meant it. Only when you're out."

He stifled his disappointment. The one kiss had brought the memories of the sweetness of her, the joy of their loving, and he wanted her now, tonight, and forever. "All right," he said, "but let me take you to your sister's place."

"I'd like that, Davy. I'd like that a lot."

He paid the bill, held the door for her, then took her hand. Together they walked to the bus stop, Davy lost in the nearness of her and his dreams of their future, with barely a thought for the last job still to come.

FORTY-THREE

Marcus shrugged into his Stampeders windcheater. "'Vesti la giubba'—on with the motley, the paint, and the powder." He mouthed the clown's aria from *Pagliacci*. Marcus felt like a clown.

He'd not heard anything more from Davy McCutcheon, and he'd been as successful at meeting other Provos as an angler fishing in a winter-killed lake. How was he ever to make contact?

He zipped the jacket front. Sitting in this cruddy bed-sit would solve none of his problems. He might as well go for a walk.

He let himself out, still trying to decide what to do next. For two pins he'd pack up the whole bloody spying thing now. Except he had come to like John Smith, did not want to let him down. How the hell could he keep the man's respect if he quit? And how could he keep Siobhan if he didn't?

He felt something squish underfoot and glanced down. He'd stepped in a pile of dog turd.

Davy stood washing the dishes. He'd eaten both chops wishing Fiona'd been with him but content that in a week she would be. He regretted that he'd agreed to go on this mission, wondered if he could tell Sean he didn't want to. Davy shook his head. It had to be done, and that was an end to it. He put his knife and fork on the draining board. He'd worry about it no more.

He stiffened and cocked his head. From Conway Street, faint at first, then rising, a clamour swelled until his ears were assailed by the din of women's screams, hoarse men's commands, the crash of hobnail boots on the street. And over all rang the clatter of stick on dustbin lid as the women of the street beat out a wild tattoo, announcing that the Security Forces were up to something more than a routine patrol.

Were they chasing suspects? When that happened, the people of the Falls were quick to respond, hindering the efforts of the troops by chucking broken concrete and homemade Molotov cocktails, finding back doors and alleys for the fugitives.

He knew he should keep his head down, but curiosity drove him into the front room. The racket was louder, and through the drawn curtains the flames outside threw flickering shadows on the walls. He parted the curtains to peer outside. A mob, fifty or sixty strong, stood on the street, hurling abuse and jagged missiles at an army platoon. Overhead, the comet tails of petrol bombs arced through the darkness, crashed to the tarmac, and spread pools of fire. A soldier, hampered by his flak jacket, helmet, and body-length Perspex shield, stooped, grabbed an unbroken bottle with its wick still alight, and hurled it at his tormentors. Davy watched as the flames from its burst engulfed a young man, listened to the shrieks.

Soldiers deployed on both sides of a Saracen and, led by the "Pig," charged, holding their shields before them, lashing out with heavy truncheons. He saw two, three men go down, the blood from their split heads black in the garish light. The mob retreated, and over it all—the yells of the troops, the roar of the Pig's engine, the curses of the mob, the howls of the wounded—the clatter of stick on bin lid filled Davy's ears, as the smell of melting tar and burning petrol filled his nostrils and anger filled his heart. This was slaughter. And for what?

Then he saw. Opposite, a door lay wide open. Soldiers crouched on either side, backs to the wall, 7.62-mm SLRs at high port, moving back and forth, quartering the street, oblivious to the battle. One of the shits had a CS gas projector, another the wide-bore Webley-Schermuly gun that fired the hated rubber bullets. The troops were protecting something—or somebody.

Christ Almighty, the Brits were on a house-to-house search. The fuckers were rounding up suspected PIRA sympathizers. He watched as three soldiers hustled a man into the back of a Saracen. Davy let the curtain swing shut when he saw a sergeant and his squad run across the street.

Davy glanced down. He hoped to God the cache of blasting caps was safe. He limped back to the kitchen, then heard his front door crash against the wall, boots thumping along his hall, feet clattering up his stairs. Two paras, a private with an SLR and a corporal carrying an L3/4A1 SMG, burst into his kitchen. Just like John-fucking-Wayne.

The corporal yelled, "Hands on your head!" slammed his back to the wall, and menaced Davy with the automatic. Davy obeyed—slowly, deliberately, looking into the corporal's face. The NCO's teeth were bared, his nostrils flared. He was right to hate and to be scared in bandit country deep in the Falls.

"Right, then." The corporal jerked his head to the other soldier. "Get on with it."

"Right, Corp." He slung his rifle, wrenched out Davy's kitchen drawers, and dumped their contents onto the linoleum floor. He attacked the cupboards, scattering china, the bag of cat food, pots and pans onto the growing heap of Davy's possessions. The racket, for a moment, stifled the din of wrecking coming from overhead.

"Nothing here, Corp."

"Dresser."

The private bent, opened the doors, and peered inside. He dumped the two small drawers on the shambles below, swept the china away, grunted, and overturned the dresser. As it toppled sideways, the bottle of sherry tumbled off and the dresser's corner ripped Fiona's picture from the wall.

Footsteps pounded down the stairs.

Davy stood immobile, hands on his head, watching. These khaki-clad English bastards, Cockneys by the sound of them, playing hell with Davy's home as their lords and masters had run roughshod over Ireland for eight hundred years. This was the enemy. He was careful to let no hint of the anger show; he'd not give the fuckers the satisfaction of thinking they were getting to him—nor any reason to search more thoroughly. He heard a yell from the parlour.

"In here quick, Corp. Bring the paddy bastard with you."

Davy kept his eyes downcast, his face impassive, but his interlocked fingers tightened on top of his head.

The private grabbed Davy's arm. "Move yer arse."

Davy shrugged the hand free as a horse would flick away a botfly. He stood, big, solid, quietly menacing. "Get your hands off me."

The private grabbed for his slung rifle.

Davy's slow smile held the contempt of all oppressed for their oppressors. "You'll not need your gun, sonny."

He stopped in the parlour doorway. The corporal stood inside the room. Two other soldiers searched. The pink lightbulb was drowned by the glare of flames in the street, flooding through the windows. The curtains, ripped from their rails, lay crumpled over the settee, upended against one wall, plaster dust flowing over the ragged fabric where McCusker had clawed. The armchair was cast aside and the rug crammed in a corner.

The dark blotches of the soldiers' camouflaged smocks looked like the blood he had seen spilled by the truncheons of the riot squad. Davy wanted blood. Soldiers' blood. This was his house, fuck it. His ma and da's house. They'd no right. No fucking right . . .

"Loose board here, Corp."

"Where?"

Davy didn't look. He heard the corporal say, "Everyone out," and watched as the two squaddies sidled past to join their mate in the hall. The corporal moved to the doorway, turned, covered Davy with his weapon, and shouted staccato commands. "You, Thompson. Backyard. White. Lyons. Street. Nail this bastard if he tries to come out." He bared his teeth and lowered his voice. "All right, Paddy. I'm off. When I'm gone, you lift that board." He took two paces back. "I hope there's no little surprise under it—for your sake, mate."

Davy waited, breathing deeply, telling himself to let his rage abate, not to do something stupid because he felt violated. They were getting cleverer, these Brit bastards. There could be a booby trap under a loose board. Could be, but there wasn't. Only the blasting caps under the concrete.

He bent and lifted the loose plank, leaving sweat stains where his hands held the wood. He stood, cursing under his breath, waiting for his enemies—his real enemies—to return.

Outside, he heard the steady growling of Pigs' engines, more muted now, distant yelling from the Falls Road at the end of Conway Street. The soldiers must have forced the mob there. The dustbin lids had fallen silent. The dying flares of burning petrol hissed in the rain. He looked through the window, seeing rubble, broken glass, tendrils of CS gas leaking from a spent canister.

"Good lad." The corporal had returned. "That wasn't too hard, now was it?"

"Fuck you."

The corporal made a sucking noise, pressing his upper buckteeth against his lower lip. "You a bit pissed off then, Paddy?"

"Fuck, you."

The corporal shook his head, helmet exaggerating the movement. "Not very polite. I'd not want to black your other eye, mate, so watch your fucking mouth." He turned to the hall. "In here, White. Keep an eye on Sunshine."

The private stood in the doorway, insolent and in charge.

"Right then," said the corporal, "let's be having a butcher's." He lay on the floor and peered into the hole. "Hang about." He produced a torch, shone the beam into the cavity.

Davy waited, teeth clenched. He wished he had the faith to pray, but his faith had gone with his da on a rainy night in the Sperrin Mountains.

"Fuck it. Nothing in here." The corporal stood, switched off the torch, stowed it back in his pack, and dusted off his hands. "Looks like you're clean after all, mate. Sorry about the inconvenience. Aren't we, Private White?"

The private laughed, a harsh, grating guffaw. "Dead sorry, corp."

"Come on, then. Next door. You and Thompson, up the apples and pears. Me and Lyons'll do down."

Davy followed them into the hall and slammed the door behind them. He was shaking. Relief, delight at having fooled the bastards mingled with hot rage inside him. *Get out of my house. Get out of my country. Get out. Get out.*

He went back to the kitchen and surveyed the wreckage. All his china was smashed, the pots dented. A shattered sherry bottle had turned the spilled cat food into a soggy mess. Oh, bugger it. Bugger it.

He pulled Fiona's picture from the heap, shaking the broken shards of glass from the frame. He spoke to her softly. "Do you not see, lass? These are the hoors I'm fighting. Not wee girls. These arrogant, booted, armed men. Britannia's Huns." And he saw her face in the frame, white gashes in her black hair where broken glass had torn the glossy paper. He saw her smile.

He righted a chair, put it by the table, and sat for a long moment, bent forward, her picture held in his big hands. "Fiona, I did it once. I turned the other cheek to that wee skitter who wanted to fight. I'll do it again. Girl, I want to fight the fuckers that did this to my house, to all the houses in the street, but they're not worth it. Not if it means you'll not come back."

He set the picture on the table where her eyes could not see his. "Och, but—it's a close thing. I'd like to kill the bastards. All of them." He felt his nails digging into his palms. "One more night like tonight. One more invasion by the fucking Brits, and I'd change my mind about quitting." He knew it was the truth.

Someone was knocking at the door. He skirted the debris, limped along the hall, and opened the door.

"Mr. McCutcheon?" It was Mrs. Cahill from four doors down, a tartan shawl hooded over her head, her arms crossed over her chest, holding the plaid to herself.

Davy forced himself to speak calmly. "Yes, dear?"

"Like, could you come down the street for a wee minute?"

"What for?"

"Mr. McCutcheon, I think it's your McCusker."

"McCusker?"

She reached out and took his hand. "Come on."

"McCusker?" He followed her through the rain and the rubble.

"There." She pointed along the gutter.

In the dim light he saw a dark lump huddled against the curb. "McCusker?" He knelt.

McCusker lay on his side, his back twisted at a grotesque angle. Cat shit fouled the fur of his hind legs. His eyes were open, and he made a low mewling. He scrambled with his front paws against the hard pavement. His back legs moved not at all.

"Ah, Jesus, McCusker." Davy fondled the animal's head but he spat and tried to bite.

Mrs. Cahill said, "I seen one of the soldiers fetch him a powerful boot." She bent closer. "Do you think he'll be all right?"

"His back's broke."

"Jesus, Mary, and Joseph."

Davy grasped the cat's back paws in his left hand and stood, holding McCusker at waist height, head dangling, howling. Davy lifted his right hand. One short chop to the back of the neck, and the howling stopped.

Davy, standing in the rain, cheeks wet, holding the corpse of his friend, knew the kick that had snapped the cat's spine had nearly broken more: it had nearly broken his own resolve to get out. He'd taken the wrecking, the jibes, the mocking. He'd taken them all. But he had taken enough. He would still quit after Sean's raid, but he'd go gladly on that one, hoping the squad who'd desecrated his home would be on the bridge when the Semtex blew.

"Thank you, Mrs. Cahill," he said. "Away you on home, dear." He wondered why she was looking at him, as if he had threatened to kill her, too.

FORTY-FOUR

"I don't give a bugger how tired you are, Conlon. Get a van organized." McGuinness slammed the door behind him as he returned to the communications room.

Sean Conlon massaged his shoulder with one hand and wished that McGuinness was not such an abrasive bugger. Despite his dislike of McGuinness, Sean had to admire the man's tirelessness; he could even understand Brendan's bitterness.

He hadn't been bitter until he lost his eye. Late in 1971, Brendan had been set on by members of a "tartan gang"—Protestant youths who wore tartan scarves in memory of three Scottish soldiers who had been killed by the Provos. The Prod bastards dressed up in their scarves and balaclavas and beat the shit out of any Catholic they encountered on a deserted street. Brendan, in the wrong place at the wrong time, had been lucky that an eye was all he lost.

Sean knew it was Brendan's hatred of the Prods that made him so committed to the Cause, to the goals they both pursued, but since his promotion to CO, Brendan had become arrogant.

Sean had swallowed his irritation and worked with McGuinness to organize the details of the assassination of the British prime minister. They'd worked out the diversionary raids and the attack.

The diversions were aimed at keeping the Security Forces off-balance. Some would be targets of opportunity, others mounted on information from Brendan's inside man or from the electronic equipment manned round the clock by 1st Battalion. The province would be a hot spot next week. White-hot.

The attack on Harold Wilson needed a great deal of organization.

The action squad that would move into the farm to herd the sheep had been selected and would be briefed next week. Tomorrow night, two of Sean's 2nd Battalion men would drive to the deserted farm beside the Ravernet Bridge and provision the place. Sean and Brendan had decided to put Davy in on Sunday night, and he'd need enough grub to see him through until Thursday. The provisioning team could nip back later next week to hide Davy's backup getaway motorbike in the little wood. If they put it in place too early, someone might find it or, in the damp of the Ulster spring, something important might rust.

A van must be stolen to transport Davy and his tools. Arranging, that was Sean's next task. He picked up a telephone and began to dial.

Davy had been getting his place redd up when a dicker arrived and handed over an envelope. So, he was to go in on Sunday, two days away. A camouflaged van would be brought round on Sunday morning, loaded with the Semtex and other tools of his trade. He told the dicker to nip round to Jimmy's and ask him to come over.

While Davy waited, he dragged more wreckage into the backyard. The dustbin was full. There had only been room in it for some broken china and poor old McCusker.

Davy barely listened to Jimmy's sympathetic noises about the damage the buggers had done, his rabbitting on about how he and the missus were going to go to Canada, his patent delight with the news that Davy had seen Fiona, was going to quit, and hoped to follow Jimmy to the land of the maple leaf and beaver. That wasn't important now.

What was important was that Davy needed to paint the Semtex to make it blend in with the bridge. Jimmy had answered that at once; he'd get Davy some white enamel and tubes of tinting to mix with the paint and produce any required colour. He was grateful that finding the gear was to be his only contribution. Jimmy had had enough and didn't mind saying so, nor did he mind telling Davy that he had taken leave of his senses to risk his chance of a new life with Fiona.

Davy ignored Jimmy's concern and asked him to contact Mike Roberts and tell him to be at the corner of Albert Street and Cullingtree Road at five o'clock on Sunday evening. He was to be told that the CO of 2nd Battalion wanted to meet him. Davy brushed aside Jimmy's questions about why Roberts was to be told to bring changes of clothes and his toilet gear.

The major fretted and twisted his ring. Richardson had been out of touch for five weeks. He might as well be dead. He wasn't, and that was a relief—one of Harry Swanson's blokes had identified Mike Roberts in a pub in New Lodge. The sergeant had seen Roberts keeping company with Siobhan, the daughter of that old Official, Jimmy Ferguson.

It was all very well for Richardson to be having fun, but he'd been sent out there to do a job, not get his hand up some girl's leg. Sir Charles had been busy. Eric Gillespie had been privy to information about all the incidents where the Provos had hit selected targets. The major was certain Gillespie was the mole. He just needed one more tangible piece of evidence, evidence that Richardson was meant to provide, albeit unknowingly, to hang the bastard.

And time was of the essence. Sir Charles had phoned last night to say that his patience was running out. He had given Major Smith ten more days to solve the problem or forget all about it, and a commission, permanently.

The spectre of being rusticated to Bourn hung like the sword of Damocles, and there wasn't a damn thing the major could do until Richardson made contact with the Provos' upper echelons—if ever he was going to.

FORTY-FIVE

Marcus arranged to take Siobhan to lunch tomorrow, kissed her good night, and walked down the path. He heard a voice calling his name.

"Mike. Could I have a wee word?" Jimmy hurried along the path.

"Sure, Jimmy." What could he want?

"Brave nice night," Jimmy said.

Marcus did not think Jimmy wanted to discuss the weather.

"You and Siobhan have a nice time?"

"Oh, aye."

Jimmy shot his jaw. "Listen. You mind the man we seen at the water-works?"

"Aye."

"He wants to see you tomorrow."

"Oh?" Finally.

"Do you know the corner of Albert Street and Cullingtree Road?"

"I'll find it."

"Fair enough. Be there at five. And he says to bring a wee bag and clothes for a few days."

"Am I going on my holidays?" Marcus tried to make light of the situation.

"It'll be no holiday. Your man's CO wants to meet you."

"Great."

"I hope so, for your sake. I'd not—" Jimmy shook his head.

"Not what?"

"Never mind. You look after yourself. Siobhan wouldn't want anything—"

"I'll be grand, Jimmy."

"So you will. Mind now, five o'clock. Cullingtree Road and Albert Street."

"I'll be there. Thanks, Jimmy."

"Don't thank me. Take my advice. Do what your man wants and then get the fuck away from them fellows."

"Jimmy. Do me a favour? Don't say nothing to Siobhan. She doesn't like all this stuff. I'll tell her tomorrow."

"Fair enough." Jimmy held on to Marcus's sleeve. "You take care, now."

"I'll be fine. I'd better be running on."

Marcus set off to walk home. At last. He was going to get on with things. The sooner he got this charade over with, the better. At least if he met some senior Provos he'd be able to finish his mission properly and, as Dad always used to say, "If a job's worth doing, it's worth doing right."

He wondered what his next moves should be. He'd have to explain to Siobhan. For a moment he considered making up some plausible excuse, but he soon dismissed the thought. That he was not Mike Roberts was going to be tough enough to explain when the time came; he must be completely truthful with her in all else. That he wasn't exactly sure what was happening would be the truth, although Captain Warnock had explained that potential Provo recruits were usually screened for several days by the intelligence officers.

Should he contact the major now that he had something to report? Of course he should, but before or after tomorrow night's meeting? He weighed the options. He'd have a lot more information after. He should probably hang on until then. Certainly this was not the time to rush up to the nearest bobby yelling the password, "whigmaleerie," nor to use the last-resort telephone number, Lisburn 574669. The GP, Dr. Kennedy, whose surgery on the Antrim Road was to have been used as a rendezvous, would be unlikely to be open on the weekend.

He turned into Robina Street and suddenly felt chilled. Tomorrow he was going to meet a man who did not trust Mike Roberts, who would take him to meet one or more equally suspicious hard men for an unspecified time in an unspecified place. The major wanted the bomber and his superiors. If Marcus did get into bother with the Provos, he might not come back. He inhaled deeply. That was not a thought to relish. It would be prudent to contact the major and at least let him know that Mike was making progress.

Marcus let himself into the hall of his digs. There was a communal telephone. He looked up the GP, Dr. Kennedy, in the telephone book. Beside his surgery number was a listing, "After hours and weekends." He inserted the coins and dialed.

"Contactors' Bureau," said a female voice.

"Hello," he said. "I'm a patient of Dr. Kennedy's."

"What seems to be the trouble?"

"I'd like to leave a message."

"I'm sorry, sir, but we're very busy. What seems to be the trouble?"

"Listen. I need to leave a message for Dr. Kennedy."

"Contactors' Bureau only provides locum cover for outside-hours emergencies. Call his surgery on Monday."

"I won't be able to. Can you give me his home number?"

Marcus heard a giggle and realized he might as well have asked the operator for the Queen Mother's private line. "Sorry, sir."

"So I can't leave a message and I can't reach him tonight?"

"That's right. If you'll excuse me, sir—" The line went dead.

He replaced the receiver. Typical bloody army SNAFU—Situation Normal. All Fucked Up. Set up a system that doesn't work.

FORTY-SIX

The Presbyterian church at Killinchy had been there for two hundred years, its granite blocks softened by the gentle country rains, its slate roof moss-covered and bowed at the peak, its stained-glass windows faded. It was a place of contemplation, a peaceful place for the Sunday-morning service that was now ending.

Justice William Boyes, sixty-nine years old, helped his wife, Alice, out of the front pew, glad of the weekend's respite from his duties on the bench, grateful that today he did not have to listen to another prosecution of a gunman. He'd lost count of the number he'd sentenced, Republican and Loyalist paramilitary alike, to years of incarceration in Crumlin Road Jail or Long Kesh.

Alice's arthritis was getting worse, and Judge Boyes waited as she picked up her walking stick and hobbled along the nave, pausing on the steps to exchange a few pleasantries with the minister. As they spoke, Judge Boyes nodded at Detective Constable Hogan, the plainclothes man assigned today for the judge's protection.

"Next Sunday then, Judge?" Reverend Borland asked.

"Yes indeed, Mr. Borland." He took Alice's arm to help her along the gravel path toward the lych-gate, where they would wait for Constable Hogan to bring the Bentley as close as possible.

Standing under the crossbeam of the gate, the judge hoped the warm sun would be good for his wife's aching joints. The damp weather played hell with the old girl's hips.

Before he could wonder what was keeping Hogan, a black Austin with mud-caked plates slowed down as it passed the gate. A hail of ·45 bullets, fired from a Thompson gun by a young woman in the passenger seat, knocked the judge sprawling. Alice's cane was shattered, and two slugs tore holes in her chest.

Constable Hogan, hearing the shots, threw open the door of the Bentley and hurled himself behind the wheel. He slammed the driver's door, forgetting in his haste that standard police procedure was to start a car's engine with the door open, a precaution that would dissipate the force of any booby trap. He shoved the key in the ignition and turned it.

The blast of gelignite wired to the starter scattered pieces of the Bentley, and Constable Hogan, over the hedge and into the nearby field, scaring the living bejesus out of a herd of Hereford bullocks.

Brendan McGuinness's diversionary campaign had started.

FORTY-SEVEN

Marcus stood in the pouring rain and watched a grey van pull up to the curb. He opened the passenger door and nearly choked. Dear God, the stink would gag a maggot.

"What the hell's that?"

"Get in." Davy McCutcheon stared ahead.

Marcus held his breath as he slid into the passenger seat, slammed the door, and immediately wound down his window. "Jesus. That's ferocious."

"Aye. Pig manure." Davy drove off.

Marcus looked at Davy. There was a fading bruise on his left cheek. Marcus remembered his own bruises, the ones he'd got two months ago when the bomb in a van much like this one blew. He grinned. At least pig shit wasn't going to explode.

"Do up your belt. No need to give the peelers an excuse to stop us."

Marcus fumbled with the webbing, trying to ignore the all-pervasive stench. He distracted himself by watching the rhythmic to-and-fro sweep of the windshield wipers, the terrace houses, tobacconists', dreary pubs—the monotonous sameness of the slums of Belfast—while he waited for the driver to say something.

The van headed south, too far south for the Falls or Ballymurphy. Much too far south for Andersonstown. Davy turned onto the M1, toward Lisburn. "See that there?" he pointed out over the Bog Meadows to rows of gravestones on a hillside. "That's Milltown Cemetery."

"So?"

"They bury Republican heroes up there. Green, white, and gold flag on the coffin. Honour guard. Volley of rifle fire."

"That's nice." Marcus would rather not think about burials. He slid down into the seat. They were heading into the country, where he'd be cut off from army patrols and the police. At least the smell didn't seem to be quite so overpowering, though—he was becoming inured to manure.

Up ahead, Marcus saw the row of stopped cars and heard McCutcheon's muttered "fuck" as he geared down.

"Roadblock?" Marcus sat erect.

"Aye. Now listen. Say nothing unless you're asked. You're my cousin and we're on our way back to my farm near Hillsborough. We've been picking up this pig manure from my brother's place outside Dunmurry. You got that?" He brought the van to a halt at the end of the line of vehicles.

"Just one wee snag," Marcus said.

"What?"

"If you were my cousin I'd know your name."

"Davy McCutcheon." He lifted his hands off the steering wheel but did not offer to shake hands.

Marcus could see damp sweat patches on the wheel. "Pleased to meet you, Cousin Davy."

Marcus wiped condensation from the glass with the back of his hand. There was no sign of troops or police moving toward them. They must be up ahead at the front of the queue, examining each vehicle as it passed. The van advanced. He saw a lorry pulled off at the side of the motorway. A soldier wearing a Denison smock and red beret stood beside the open rear doors. The man was a para, and they were tough bastards.

Davy banged his fist on the steering wheel in time with the wipers, then rolled down his window. An officer, bulky under his rain-slicked waterproof cape, stuck his head inside. It was Robby Knox, the captain who'd approached Marcus in the Causerie. The one who had mistaken Mike Roberts for Marcus Richardson. He shrank back in his seat, holding his breath, and stared straight ahead.

An English voice said, "Oh, shit."

"Aye," said Davy, "pig shite."

"Out of the van. Both of you."

Marcus heard Davy's door open, and the van lurched on poorly maintained springs. Marcus climbed out and hunched his shoulders against the rain, trying to hide his features. He sensed movement. The captain stood one foot away.

"Have you some identification, sir?"

Marcus reached for his wallet.

"I say. Haven't we met?"

Marcus looked the young officer full in the face and let a smile of recognition play on his lips. Please God, don't let the captain go into his "thought you were someone I knew in the army" routine. "Aye. A while back. In the Causerie."

"Right. You were with a smashing blond."

"Aye." Marcus lowered his voice. "Don't mention her. She's a Protestant. We're Catholics. My cousin Davy would go bananas if he knew about her."

The Para captain grinned. "See what you mean." A heavier-than-usual rain squall slashed along the road. "Go on." He gestured to the van. "Sorry about this. Routine, you know."

"Thanks." Marcus nipped back inside and slammed the door. "Get us out of here, Davy."

"What did that fucker want?" Davy drove past a parked Saracen.

Marcus watched the man's face, the way he sat. He was tense, angry. Marcus said, "The usual, but he thinks we're a couple of farmers. Didn't go much for the stink."

"Good." Davy's smile was obviously forced. "Grand stuff, pig shite. Attracts flies but keeps the soldiers off."

"Off what?"

"Off our case. Jesus. You think this is some kind of game. You don't understand, do you?"

"Understand what?"

"Oh, for fuck's sake, you know I'm a Provo."

Finally. The man had admitted it.

"If the soldiers had found that out, were after me—where do you think that would have left you?"

"In the back of the van."

"What are you talking about?"

"In the shite, Davy. In the shite." Marcus's voice held a trace more sincerity than he had intended.

"It's no time to be buggering about," Davy laughed. What Marcus had just said must have struck home. Perhaps it was a release of tension—the wisecrack hadn't been that funny—but Davy threw back his head and guffawed. "Right enough. That's just where we'd have been." His big shoulders shook under his waterproof jacket. "In the shite." He chuckled for a moment longer, then said, "You're a cool bastard, aren't you, Mike Roberts?"

Marcus's own relieved laughter died away. "Probably don't know enough to be worried."

"Unless them lads in camouflage suits is your mates."

"Aye. Right enough. I was in the Chinese forces before I went to Canada."

Davy looked puzzled. "Chinese—?"

"The Foo-king arm-ee."

"The—?" McCutcheon laughed again. "All right. We'll say no more."

Marcus listened to the engine, the sounds of the tyres on the wet road, the ticking of the wiper blades. At least he'd made McCutcheon laugh. They sat in silence, and Marcus was able to contain his curiosity now that he knew where they were heading. Hillsborough. Government House was there. He did not think they were going to pay a social call. More important, something had happened at the checkpoint. Was it because Davy had opened up enough there to give his name, because they had shared a laugh, because Davy had admitted he was PIRA and said he believed Mike's story—or because, for a moment, each for his own reason had been scared silly?

Marcus looked over at the big man beside him. Something about the way he was sitting, one arm resting on the window edge, wheel held loosely, told Marcus that Davy had sensed it, too. Good. If he was satisfied, that would make it easier with the Provos. Whenever they finally met them.

He watched the trees flash by, lime and apple green in their early spring foliage, sheep huddled against a hedge, the little fields. The van turned onto a country road, narrow and tree-lined; jolted over the potholes; slowed; and entered a lane leading to a grey farmhouse.

"We're here," Davy said as he parked in the farmyard.

"Right." Marcus was alert, anticipating the meeting. He remembered the SAS man's instructions. Take a good look around and study your surroundings. You never know what might be important if you have to get out in a hurry.

McCutcheon had left the van and hurried through the rain to the door of the farmhouse. Grey stone. Two stories. Sash windows with green frames, the paint blistered and peeling. Two slates were missing from the roof. Telephone wires ran from white ceramic insulators under the eaves to a bare pole standing starkly among a windbreak of tall poplars. The trees marched from the corner of the house along the lane to the country road a hundred yards away. The phone lines were strung on telegraph poles among the trees.

Marcus retrieved his knapsack, opened the door, and stepped out into the mud of the farmyard. There was no dog, and that was strange. All farms had dogs. Border collies, usually.

He turned to get his bearings. The house fronted onto a yard of mud and straw. A blackthorn hedge bordered its near side. Across the yard an open barn, rusting corrugated iron sheets held up on wooden posts, sheltered a Massey-Harris tractor. He could see empty stalls at the back of the building. No animals, and by this time of the evening the cows should be in for milking. No dog. No cattle.

"Will you come in the fuck out of the rain?" Davy stood inside the doorway, beckoning.

Marcus squelched across the yard. Something nagged at him. It wasn't that the place seemed to be deserted . . . He stopped. There were no other vehicles. How had the men he was to meet got here? He pushed past Davy.

In the dim light coming from the two windows behind him, Marcus could see that there was no hall. He had entered the main room. A sink set into a countertop, cupboards above, took up space on the wall to his right. Past it he could see a staircase. To his left a range bulked black. Beside it was a pile of turf, which filled the space between the range and a huge open fireplace, visible directly ahead, behind the plain wooden table and chairs in the middle of the room. Where did that door beside the fireplace lead to? Black cast-iron gallows stood out from the sides of the hearth. There was no fire. And there was no one else there. Marcus spun round and saw Davy standing by a cardboard suitcase on the slate floor. Davy said, "Cold in here."

"Cold? Never mind that. Where the hell is everybody?"

"Nobody lives here. The owner, Sammy McCandless, died a month ago."

"I don't mean that. You said I'd meet the senior men. Where the hell are they?"

"They'll be along."

Marcus sensed that Davy was lying but said, "Jesus Christ, I came here to meet people. I should have listened to Siobhan."

"What?"

"I was out with her for lunch today. I told her I was seeing you again this evening."

"You told her?"

"Come on, Davy. Jimmy's daughter's not going to blow the whistle."

"Mebbe."

"She says I'm daft. I should forget about you lot and go back to Canada with her."

"Mebbe you should."

"Look. I want to find out what's going on."

"You will. We've to get this place ready for them."

"All right."

"Put down your bag and give us a hand."

Marcus set his knapsack on the planks of the tabletop, seeing the dust of disuse on the wood. "What do you want me to do?"

"Get a fire lit. I'm foundered." Davy produced a box of Swift matches.

Marcus took the matchbox, moved round the table, and knelt at the hearth. Someone had laid a fire. Bunched-up balls of newspaper supported a pile of fresh kindling. Two bricks of peat perched on top. Dust on the tabletop but a freshly laid fire? It was like *Alice in Wonderland*—curiouser and curiouser. He struck a match and held the flame to the paper. The kindling began crackling. Marcus heard Davy say, "Give us the matches," and stood to hand over the box.

Davy held a brass kerosene lamp in one hand; the funnel and globe lay on the tabletop. He lit the wick, slipped the funnel over, and covered it with the glass globe. The light was bright and threw shadows on the white plaster walls. "That's better." He opened his waterproof coat, took it off, and said, "Here. Gimme yours."

Davy shook the rain off both and hung them on a coatrack tucked in between the front door and a large chest of drawers. Marcus asked, "What now?"

"We'll have to wait." Davy lit a cigarette. He seemed to have found something of interest on the floor, and he was scratching his nose.

Pinocchio. The SAS chap had said that when men lied they often touched their noses. Marcus felt an alarm bell ringing in his head. The same one that went off when he sensed all was not well with a fuse, and when that happened, you got the hell out—fast.

"How long?" Marcus looked directly at Davy.

His stare was returned. "Until we do a wee job together."

"A what?"

"A wee job." Davy smiled and there was a challenge in his smile. "With Semtex."

Davy stood by the door watching Roberts's response.

"A job? With Semtex?" was all the younger man said. Either Roberts was a bloody good bluffer, or he had meant what he'd said about joining up.

"Aye. Semtex. That's what's under all the pig shite."

"Wait a minute. You told me you were going to introduce me to higher-ups in the Provos. You never said nothing about a fucking job."

"Would you have come if I had?"

"No bloody way."

"But you're here now, and you are going to give me a hand."

"Do I have a choice?"

"What do you think?"

The lad fidgeted, rubbing one foot back and forth over the slates. "I don't suppose I do, do I?"

"That's about the length and the breadth of it."

Roberts surprised Davy by saying, "I'm your man, then."

"You *will* get to meet my CO—once it's over." Davy looked into the younger man's eyes. "I suppose you'd want to know about the job?"

"Not at all. I'll just stand here, both legs the same length, picking my fucking nose."

"You do that. I'm for making a cup of tea. There should be a food safe out the back. See you if there's milk in it."

"What about the Semtex?"

"Take your hurry in your hand. We'll have a wet first."

"All right."

Davy watched Roberts go through the back door and stood, waiting to see if he would try to bolt.

He returned and closed the door. "Got it."

"Set it over there by the sink."

Roberts put the milk bottle down on a shelf beside a tapless chipped sink and asked, "Is there a pump out there?"

"Should be." Davy picked up a heavy, soot-blackened kettle. "Away off and fill that up."

"Right."

Davy was stooped, stirring the turf with a poker, when Roberts returned. Davy took the kettle, hung its handle on one of the gallows, and swung the arm over the heat. "Not be long." He held his hands to the warmth. "Jesus, that's better." Christ, Davy thought, the last time I was near peat I was hiding under it. After the fuckup. After that wee Hanrahan girl. He turned and said, "Picked your nose enough, have you?"

"Och, come on, Davy. You know bloody well I want to know what's going on."

"And I'll tell you. When we get the tea made." Davy busied himself. He wanted to see how well the lad could contain his curiosity, and make sure there was nothing fishy about Mike Roberts's story. He asked, "Did you say you went to Bangor Grammar School?"

"Aye. And I told you I'm not a Prod."

"Is Bangor Grammar the one with the red and green school caps?"

"Away off and chase yourself. Bangor Grammar's blue and yellow."

"My mistake."

"D'you ever go to Bangor, Davy?"

"Aye. When I was a wee lad. The BCDR—"

"Belfast and County Down Railway."

"That's it. They had a slogan, 'Bangor and back for a bob.'"

"Queens Quay Station, the one they bombed a while back, to the top of Main Street, Bangor."

Davy thought, Queen's Quay. The one he'd bombed a while back that nearly cost him Fiona. "Aye. I suppose so. Here." He handed Roberts a cup of tea. "Come on and sit down, Mike. That's what they call you, isn't it?"

"It's better than shitface, Davy. It's my name."

Davy laughed, choked on his tea, and coughed. "You're no dozer, are you?"

"No."

"All right. You want to know?"

"Aye."

"This farm's not far from Lisburn. Do you know what's there?"

"No."

"Thiepval Barracks. You'll see the yellow arc lights when it gets dark. It's British army headquarters. The General Officer Commanding Northern Ireland and the headquarters of Thirty-nine Infantry Brigade's there."

Roberts said nothing.

"Down to the southeast of that's Government House, in Hillsborough. There's a lot of traffic back and forth."

"So?"

"Between Lisburn and Hillsborough the road crosses a bridge over the Ravernet River."

"And you want to take out the bridge?"

"I do."

"And you need Semtex charges to do it?"

"Aye."

"And you want me to make the charges?"

Davy swallowed his pride. "That's right."

"No sweat."

"Dead-on," said Davy. "We're going to pull one off in the Brits' own backyard, right between Government House and their fucking army headquarters. Four days from now."

"Why four days?"

"There's going to be a convoy on the bridge."

It took them two hours to unload the van. They stowed the Semtex under sacks of manure, in one of the stalls of the barn. The detonating apparatus and Davy's tool kit were taken into the farmhouse. The last thing Davy unloaded was an ArmaLite—one from Howa Machinery in Japan, not the American modification of the M16—·223-calibre, folding-stock, with single-shot, semi- , and fully automatic capability. The Provos called the weapon the widow maker.

During those two hours, Marcus worked out a plan. Having come this far, it seemed a pity to ruin his chances of meeting the senior Provos by making a run for it when Davy was asleep, or by trying to overpower the man. Davy wanted Marcus to make a bomb. He'd do it, but he'd build in a defect so that it wouldn't explode. No one in the convoy would get hurt, the man Davy thought of as Mike Roberts would have shown loyalty and willingness, and Davy would have to keep his word about making the introductions in the not-too-distant future.

Marcus knew that he would have to keep his guard up. That business about the colour of the caps worn by pupils of Bangor Grammar School hadn't been a slip of Davy's memory. He'd been testing, and he'd probably test again. And Marcus, unless he wanted to be the proud possessor of a ·223-calibre bullet in his brain, had better pass every test that Davy set.

FORTY-EIGHT

Davy rose on Monday morning and washed in a basin on his dressing table. He dried his face, noticing a framed print of the Madonna hanging above. "Hail Mary, full of grace—" He crossed himself, turned away, and pulled on his trousers, hoisting the braces over his shoulders, tucking in the tails of his shirt, buttoning the fly. He'd never liked zippers.

Davy moved to the window and drew the curtains. Through the pouring rain he could see a ploughed field that marched along the back of the farmyard. Three hundred yards away the field met the main road to the village of Ravernet—the road that linked Thiepval with Hillsborough.

To his left a wood bordered the road at the side of the field. The wood where Sean's people would leave the motorcycle. To his right the river flowed past the field. A low hedgerow marked its near bank and two large elms grew in the hedge, not far from the bridge. There was a gate between the trees.

The main Ravernet Road crossed the river at the far corner of the field. The bridge, the all-important bridge, and the approaches from Lisburn were clearly visible from Davy's room. The convoy would come along the road and onto the span, moving across from right to left. There was a clear line of sight from the bedroom window. The remote transmitter worked on line of sight.

A secondary road ran from the main Ravernet Road to the lane to the farmhouse. It started half a mile from the bridge, passed the farmhouse where McGuinness was going to put his sheepherding men, and skirted the wood. Past Davy's hideout the back road followed a curve in the river and crossed it five miles upstream. That would be important when it was time to run. It would be a ten-mile round-trip for anyone leaving the site of the ambush to get onto the back road at its far end and drive to the farmhouse.

When the Semtex blew under the vehicle in the middle of the convoy, the lead Saracen would either be disabled by the blast or stuck on this side of the demolished bridge. There was a deep, wide ditch between the ploughed field and the Ravernet Road. It would take more than a Saracen to cross that.

If the armoured personnel carrier followed the main route to the back road, it would be held up long enough by the flock of sheep to give Davy time to slip down the farm lane, screened from the main road by the poplars, then along the back road and onto a connecting road that headed away from Lisburn.

The rear escort would be stranded on the other riverbank. Its troops might be able to ford the river, but in the inevitable confusion that would follow the explosion, Davy would be long gone by the time they crossed the ploughed field on foot. It was a good escape plan. Davy would make it all right. If nothing unexpected happened.

The Massey-Harris tractor jolted over the furrows. Davy sat on the perforated metal seat, steering as best he could with the weight of Mike's hands on his shoulders. The rain sleeted past. Davy set a course to skirt the field. His knowledge of farming was sketchy, but he couldn't believe any farmer who'd ploughed such straight rows would churn them up by running the tractor's huge rear wheels across the results of his labour.

He headed along beside the hedge that bordered the field and separated it from the river. He could see the bridge up ahead, its outline blurred by the driving rain. He pulled the tractor into the shelter of one of the elms and switched off the engine, glad to be rid of its noisy clattering. He sat motionless. Something was not right. He listened and realized he was missing the sound of city traffic, but there was another sound that he could not place. It wasn't the wind in the trees. It was a rushing, roaring noise. He turned to Mike. "D'you hear that?"

"The river. It's coming down like a steam engine."

"Will we take a gander?"

"Aye." Mike jumped down and Davy followed, clambering from the tractor to the grass verge at the edge of the field. The gate between the elms was made of five horizontal bars of galvanized metal braced with a diagonal cross-strut. Mike climbed over the top of the gate. Davy untwisted the wire fastening, hauled the gate open, and joined Mike on a broad, tyre-rutted riverbank. A hundred yards to his right, he could see a concrete blockhouse. The letters UDA and UVF were daubed in black paint on one wall. He scowled. Protestant bastards. Tyre tracks led to the blockhouse. It was probably an implement store.

"Davy, for God's sake, are you going to stand there all day? We came to look at the bridge."

"We did." Davy peered downstream.

The spandrel bridge stood solidly, twenty yards away, one single granite-block arch marching from bank to bank. The roadway was hidden behind a sandstone-capped parapet. How the hell were they going to knock that down? "What do you reckon?" Davy asked.

"Don't know."

"What do you mean, you don't know?"

"I mean I don't know—yet."

"Oh."

Mike stood staring upstream. "Fuck." He shook his head.

"What's wrong?"

"Look at the bloody water."

The river was in spate, brown water roiling, white wave caps churning as the stream fought against the wind. A dead tree swirled past, gnarled roots grasping at the air like a drowning man's fingers.

Mike muttered, "There's no fucking way we can get under the arch."

Davy looked downstream. The tree was jammed against the masonry. The trunk thrashed and bobbed until it was swept under the span and on downstream.

"Right enough."

Mike said nothing. He stepped back under the lee of the hedge and squatted on his haunches, ignoring Davy, staring at the bridge.

Davy stood fidgeting. "Can we do her or not?" He tried to keep the worry out of his voice.

"Aye."

"Good."

"If the river goes down."

"It'll slack off when the rain stops."

"I hope you're right." Mike pointed at the masonry. "We'll need to get under to put charges below the keystone. Knock that out, and the whole fucking thing'll come down."

"I know."

Mike's grin was wolfish. "Won't do anything on top of the road a whole hell of a lot of good either."

"That's why we're here."

"There's not much call to take out bridges in the oil business," Mike said.

"You've never done a bridge?"

"No, but we had to knock out a fucking great lump of the Swan Hills to get a road into a drilling site. Should be dead easy if we can get in under, but we're stuffed 'til then." He stood. "Wait you here. I'll go and measure up."

Davy waited as Mike clambered up the embankment and walked to the centre of the span. He watched as Mike used a carpenters' metal tape to measure the height from the top of the parapet to the undersurface of the arch and from the roadbed to the top of the parapet. He disappeared as he crossed to the other side. Davy guessed that Mike was determining the width of the structure.

Mike reappeared and slid back down the embankment. "Time to go back to the house. Come on."

And Davy, after one last look at the bridge, followed in the younger man's footsteps.

FORTY-NINE

The kitchen smelled of cooking fat, damp raincoats, and burning peat. Homey smells. Supper was finished. Marcus opened the front door and looked out. The rain had stopped but the dark clouds were heavy, and threatening. He closed the door. "I think it's clearing."

"I hope so." Davy put the last plate on the draining board and dried his hands.

Marcus wandered over and sat at the table. Davy joined him. "So," he said, "tell me about Canada."

"Why?"

"Just curious." Davy sounded wistful. "Jimmy's going to emigrate."

"He'll like it there—lots of our lot in Ontario. There's a few in Alberta, too."

"Aye?"

"Aye. I used to go out at night with a lad from Monaghan Town from one of the derricks. Him and me used to go for a jar when we were down in Calgary. He told me what was going on over here. He got me thinking of coming back."

"Oh," Davy said without much enthusiasm. "What's the weather like out there?"

"In Alberta?"

"Where you live."

"Takes a bit of getting used to. Winters go on for fucking ever. The summers is great in Alberta, but I hear it gets very muggy in Toronto, where Jimmy's going."

"Can you get a decent pint?"

"Not at all. Canadian beer's awful. Labatt Blue's like butterfly pee."

Davy chuckled. "What's the people like?"

"Decent enough. You'll not get much of a laugh out of them, but they're good to work for. Wages is great."

"Were you happy there?"

"Happy enough. It's a great place for giving a fellow a chance. I'd not have done near as well for myself back here. Another thing—they don't give a shit what foot you dig with. I still remember what it was like being a Catholic at a Protestant school. There's none of that kind of buggering about in Canada, so there's not."

Davy grunted. "I'd believe that when I saw it. Us Catholics have always been shit on."

After what Marcus had learned in the last month he could sympathize. He said, "It's a good country. Jimmy and his missus'll do rightly there, so they will."

"Like Siobhan?"

"She loves it. Thinks Toronto's great."

"Are you in love with her?"

Marcus swallowed as he sought for an answer.

"Well?" Davy's eyes held the same intensity Marcus had seen on the day when the man opposite had been testing him about his knowledge of explosives.

"I'm daft about her." And as he spoke he could see her. "She's a great girl."

"She is that. I've known her and her brother Fergus since they were wee." Great open smile. "They called me Uncle Davy."

"You've no kids?"

"How the fuck do you think a fellow like me could get married, never mind have a family? Fergus and Siobhan were as close as I got." Davy sniffed. "Is she in love with you?"

"God, yes. It's great."

"And she doesn't think much about you getting mixed up with the likes of me?"

Marcus hesitated before answering. "I told you her and me's talked about it. She thinks the whole thing's crazy. She wants to go back to Canada."

"Would you go with her?"

"I want to, but—"

"Take my advice, son. Once this lot's done, get Siobhan as far away from Northern Ireland as you can."

"But you said you'd take me to meet the big fellows."

"Aye. Well." Davy lowered his eyes. "Jimmy says you've cowboys in Alberta."

"What's that got to do with me and the Provos?"

Davy looked Marcus right in the eye. "The fight between the Provos and the Brits isn't cowboys and Indians. People get killed."

"I'm not scared."

"I wasn't thinking about our side."

"You don't give a shit about the Brits, do you?"

"The Brits? Not at all."

"Who then?"

"Civilians."

"Do you not think that's worth it?"

Davy muttered, "Sometimes I wonder. I suppose it's all right to die for your country. It's a different matter to make somebody else do the dying."

Marcus put his hand over Davy's. It was cold.

Davy started, as if unused to human touch. "Aye. Well. I'll say no more."

For a second Marcus had been permitted to glimpse another side of the usually closemouthed Davy McCutcheon—the Provo who was also Siobhan's "Uncle Davy." He found himself warming to the man and decided not to ask for an explanation. "If you say so, Davy. You're the boss."

Marcus was surprised by Davy's look of gratitude. He heard Davy say, "Thanks, son."

Engine noises, very close engine noises, intruded. Marcus said, "What the fuck's that?"

Davy eye's narrowed. "Someone's coming down the lane."

"Coming here?"

"Aye. Fuck it."

"Were you expecting somebody?"

"Not at all."

The engine noises grew louder, then stopped. "Jesus," Davy whispered. "They're in the yard."

He jumped from the chair. "I'm off upstairs. You get rid of whoever it is." He raced to the staircase. "Remember what I told you about the fellow who owned this place."

"But—" Someone pounded on the kitchen door.

"Who is it?" Marcus felt sweat on his palms.

"Police."

"Hang on." Marcus took a deep breath, exhaled, crossed the kitchen, and opened the door.

"Evening, sir." A heavily built RUC constable stood on the threshold.

"Evening, Officer." A Hotspur Land Rover was parked in the farm-yard. A private of the Ulster Defence Regiment sat behind the wheel. Marcus knew that these part-time soldiers served as armed escorts for the police. "What can I do for you?"

"Mind if I come in, sir?"

"Not at all. Just kick the mud off your boots." Marcus nodded to a cast-iron boot scraper at the side of the doorway. He stood aside to let the man see into the empty kitchen.

The policeman smiled. Big, circular, jowly face; eyes flickering around the room in front of him; fair hair sticking out like a badly stooked hay-stack from under his green peaked cap. "Right enough. It's quare and mucky out in the yard, sir. You'd not want all that clabber inside." He looked embarrassed. "Tell you what. I'll just ask you a few questions."

"All right."

"Who are you?"

"Mike Roberts."

"Haven't seen you about the place."

Local officer. He'd know everyone. "I don't live here."

"Oh?"

"Just come down from Belfast."

"What for?" The man's right hand now rested on the butt of his re-volver.

Think, Marcus told himself, think. "To give this place the once-over. The fellow that owned it died." Jesus. What had Davy said the previous owner was called? The policeman looked tense as a wound-up spring. "My cousin," Marcus added, then the name finally came back to him. "Sammy McCandless."

"Sammy was your cousin?"

"Aye. I'd a letter." Marcus rummaged in his pocket and produced his Canadian passport.

"Can I have a look at that, sir?"

Marcus handed it over, inwardly blessing the major's thoroughness, and Davy's hint about the dead farmer.

"You live in Alberta?"

"Aye."

"Don't suppose you know my brother? He's in Halifax."

Marcus laughed. "You live closer to him than me."

It took a moment for that to sink in, then the constable's booming laugh drowned Marcus's forced chuckle. "Right enough. It's a brave big country."

"It is that."

"You'll be here long?" He returned the passport.

"Maybe a couple of days. The rent's good."

"What?"

"It's free."

"Right enough." The policeman laughed again, an open, trusting laugh.

"I was surprised there's no beasts here. By the look of the byre, Sammy kept cows," Marcus said, hoping he was not overembellishing his spur-of-the-moment story.

"He did. Aberdeen Angus. They're over at the Johnston's place. Norman's a decent man. He's minding them until after the estate's sorted out."

"I'll maybe take a run-race over to see them. Johnston's?"

"Aye. About half a mile up the road, sir. You can't miss it. There's a big red barn. Norman keeps a lot of sheep."

"Thanks."

The constable started to move away. "I'll maybe look in again, sir. The name's Young, Constable Young. Sorry to have bothered you, Mr. Roberts, but we have to be careful over here."

"Aye. I've heard."

The policeman shrugged, the movement exaggerated by his flak jacket. "There's some highheejin coming in a day or two." He pointed to the Rover. "That's why me and him's out here bothering you."

"No bother. You lads have your job to do."

"I'll be away on, sir." The constable squelched back to the Land

Rover. Marcus looked down and saw two other distinct sets of foot-prints in the mud. His own and Davy's irregular strides. Don't look down, he thought, willing the constable to keep moving.

He gave them a cheery wave as the vehicle pulled away. Jesus, for a minute or two that had been close. For his mission and for Davy.

Why, he wondered, was he worried about McCutcheon? He'd better be careful. He was starting to like the man.

Marcus went back into the kitchen. He heard Davy moving about upstairs. The phone on the dresser caught Marcus's eye. He glanced upward. More noises from overhead. Davy was in his bedroom.

Marcus lifted the receiver and put it to his ear. The dial tone was music. The phone had not been disconnected. It was unlikely he would need to use it, but it was good to know it was there if needed. "It's OK," he yelled, gently replacing the receiver, "they've gone." He hoped his shouts would cover the faint "ting" as the phone settled in its cradle.

FIFTY

A tractor rumbled down the Newtownards Comber Road. Its front-mounted hydraulic arms carried a deep metal bucket, tangy with a load of seaweed harvested from the mudflats of Strangford Lough. The driver and his mate sat in the cab.

Behind the slow-moving vehicle a row of cars followed, some drivers exasperated by the hold-up, most well acquainted with the realities of rural Ulster life. If it wasn't a tractor it would be a horse box or a herd of cows slowing things down. And Tuesday was market day in Comber.

The major had not heard from Richardson, and Harry Swanson had reported that his man in New Lodge had not seen Marcus since Sunday. It was a mark of the major's concern that he had phoned Harry this morning. The deadline set by Sir Charles five days earlier was approaching. To make matters worse, the senior civil servant had arrived in Ulster last night and summoned the major to a meeting this morning at Stormont Castle—or, to be more precise, his secretary had. It was the first time that Sir Charles had not spoken personally to Major Smith.

Woman Police Constable Mary Young retreated upstairs, heading, she said, to the bathroom. She had just started her shift and already she was feeling peevish. It was bad enough being stuck behind the desk of the Comber police station without the attentions of that bloody man, Sergeant Crawford. He didn't seem to be able to take no for an answer and the last thing she wanted was to accept his invitation for a drink after work. She knew damn well what he was after. And he was married.

She could hear him below, telling one of his crude jokes to the other two constables on duty. Mary Young was no prude; she could have a laugh with the lads, but not today. Today she felt claustrophobic. The two-storey, grey building hemmed her in. It squatted behind a twenty-foot high-wire-mesh fence. The doors were of reinforced steel and every downstairs window had steel loopholed shutters.

The armoury held racks of Sten guns, CS gas projectors, and Webley-Schermuly riot guns that fired plastic bullets. She thought it was silly. This wasn't Crossmaglen or Springfield Road. Comber was a small country town, eight miles from Belfast on the Belfast–Downpatrick Road.

Sir Charles came straight to the point. "The PM's coming over here on Thursday."

Harold Wilson's impending arrival was news to the major. "Can't dissuade the silly bugger," Sir Charles continued. "He's determined to have it out with the Unionists. Harold knows Paisley's lot are trying to arrange a general strike. Apparently the PM thinks he can lend the moderate Unionist faction a bit of moral support by his presence here." Sir Charles looked as aquiline as ever. An eagle with badly ruffled feathers.

"Yes, Sir Charles."

Sir Charles glared over his desk. "All hell's broken loose since my boss, Merlyn Rees, announced in the Commons that the British government legalized Sinn Fein and the Ulster Volunteer Force." He snorted. "Two bunches of thugs, Catholic and Protestant. And the government's going to begin a phased release of IRA internees. Paisley's fit to be tied."

Sir Charles shook his head and pinched the bridge of his nose between a bony thumb and forefinger. "As if that wasn't bad enough, our dear Secretary of State for Defence, Roy Mason, has just dropped another brick." Sir Charles took his hand from his nose. The exasperation in his voice was palpable. "He said in the House that there's widespread feeling among the British public that the troops should be withdrawn from Ulster. Paisley, Craig, and West and the rest of the Loyalists are having a field day. Yelling that they're going to be sold out. Harold's tried to calm things down. He's announced that the troops will have to stay for as long as the security situation demands."

"I'm not quite sure what this has to do with me, Sir Charles."

Sir Charles's face darkened, a dusky hue tinging the wattles at his throat. "I'll tell you precisely what it has to do with you, Smith."

Mary Young sighed and tried to ignore the guffaws from below. She couldn't stay up here all day. Women's Lib might have arrived in America, but the Neanderthals downstairs hadn't heard of it. If she kept turning Sergeant Crawford down, he'd probably try to club her and drag her off to his cave by her hair—which reminded her, she'd better wash it tonight.

She looked out through the window. At least the sun was shining. A line of cars had stopped at a traffic light. The second vehicle was a tractor with its bucket full of seaweed. Something caught her eye. There was more in the bucket than wrack. She could see quite clearly from her vantage point that at one side of the bucket the kelp had shifted, and beneath was a brown gunnysack. No farmer would stink up whatever was in the sack by dumping a load of wrack on top.

Sir Charles had spoken for several minutes without interruption. "Harold's promised that the terrorists will be crushed." He glowered at the major. "That's going to be damn difficult, as long as the Provos have a direct line into the Security Forces. That's been your job—finding the bugger—for quite a while now, and frankly I'm disappointed."

"Sorry, sir."

"Sorry's not good enough. I'm taking enormous stick. I expect results. I don't care how, as long as it's soon." Sir Charles waved a dismissive hand. "I'd suggest you ask Gillespie for a hand."

"But I thought—"

"Don't think, Smith. Get on with it."

"I'll meet with him today, sir."

"Right." Sir Charles began to read. He glanced up. "I'll be going back to London on Thursday with the PM. So will you, although you'll be travelling economy, if you haven't got some answers by then."

. . .

The driver waited for the light to change, then moved the tractor slowly forward. He glanced at his companion. "Are you right?"

The man nodded and slipped a hand down to the floor of the cab to lift an ArmaLite. The driver looked to his right where a red Ford was parked. The driver of the Ford held one thumb up.

"Now." The passenger cradled the rifle as the driver slammed his foot onto the accelerator and aimed the vehicle straight at the wire fence surrounding the barracks.

Woman Police Constable Young stared in through the window of the tractor's cab. God Almighty, that was a rifle the passenger was holding. "Sergeant," she yelled, hauling out her ·38 revolver. "Sergeant! We're under attack."

She steadied her right wrist with her left hand and triggered one shot. The bullet missed the driver, but it shattered the glass, and a flying shard sliced into the man's left eye. He screamed, clapped both hands to his face, and lost control. The tractor skidded broadside into the mesh fence and stalled.

"I'm fucking blinded."

"Get out," the passenger yelled, tugging at his driver's sleeve. "Get out." He ducked as rounds spat from the police station and whined off the tractor's body. If one of them went into the bucket . . . He slipped from the cab and took cover behind the tractor, laying the ArmaLite on the mudguard and loosing off an automatic burst.

Chips of brick flew from the station's wall. Bright stars of steel shone through the grey-painted shutters where the rounds had hit. The racket of firing drowned the driver's howls. The muzzle of a Sten gun slipped through an aperture in one of the shutters and winked yellow flame. The driver convulsed like an electrocuted rag doll, his howling cut short.

The man with the ArmaLite crabbed sideways, keeping the body of the tractor between him and the front of the police station. He stared off to his right. The red Ford pulled away from the curb, heading his way. One door was open. Bullets cracked overhead. As the car came abreast, he hurled himself through the open door. "Get the fuck away to hell—"

A row of slugs stitched him from hip to shoulder and punched neat holes in the red metal of the car. One round in the burst struck a nun in full habit as she cowered on the pavement opposite, killing her instantly. The red Ford sped away, heading for Belfast, as its driver sobbed, "Oh, shite. Oh, shite."

Woman Police Constable Young could not stop trembling. Her nostrils were assailed by the acrid smell of gun smoke, her ears still rang from the clamour of the now-silent automatic weapons. From below, she heard Sergeant Crawford's voice. "Jesus Christ, there must be half a ton of ammonium nitrate in this bucket. For God's sake, get the bomb squad." She heard footsteps on the stairs. Sergeant Crawford stood in the doorway. "God, Mary, you done good." His arms were wide open. She fled to the comfort of him.

FIFTY-ONE

The major waited in his office. He'd had hell's delight getting a message through that he needed to see Eric Gillespie. Sir Charles had insisted that the major use the RUC man, and that was precisely what he intended to do—although not in the way Sir Charles intended. Richardson would be the key. It would be an outside chance, but, given the major's mandate, he would have to take chances. Or, to be more precise, Richardson would.

Since this morning's meeting, when his deadline had been reduced to three days, the major had rapidly reviewed his options and decided on a course of action. Harry Swanson's sergeant had not seen Richardson for a couple of days. Did it mean that he had been picked up by the PIRA? If he had and was still alive, there was an outside chance that the major could still use Richardson the way he had originally planned. Eric, and only Eric, would be notified about an imaginary British operation. One that would be easy to attack. Gillespie would be unable to resist notifying his controllers. If they went ahead planning an attack and used Richardson as their bomb maker, he would pass the word back to the major. And as there was no real target and only Gillespie would be privy to the information, only Gillespie could tip off the Provos. Two plus two equals four.

Most probably the Provos would eventually kill Richardson. But he'd only been missing for forty-eight hours, and they usually interrogated suspected British intelligence operatives for days. Of course, Richardson was a soldier, and as far as the major was concerned, death was an occupational hazard. He could regard the possibility of Richardson's demise with detached equanimity, provided it led to the attainment of the objective.

It might be even more helpful if he *were* killed. Apart from Harry, Harry's operative, and the major, no one knew that Richardson was undercover—except Gillespie. If Richardson's corpse showed up in the next day or two, it could be used to the major's advantage. He would simply have Gillespie arrested on the suspicion that he had used his knowledge to tip off the Provos about Richardson.

At the moment, any link between Gillespie's knowledge and the possible demise of Richardson was tenuous, and, even with the circumstantial evidence that Gillespie had known about all of the twenty planned Provo attacks, it would not be enough to convince a jury. But Gillespie would not face a jury. Under the Northern Ireland Act, which had come into force on August 8, 1973, suspected terrorists could be tried in secret by a judge alone—a judge who was sympathetic to the Security Forces. The Diplock courts.

There would be a witness to Gillespie's arrival for the meeting tonight. The major could swear he had briefed Gillespie about Richardson's true mission. No mole could ignore that. That line of reasoning should be enough to convince a judge. The major would satisfy Sir Charles, gain his permanent commission, and be able to visit the rustic peace of Bourn only when on leave.

The major answered a knock. An MP corporal stood outside the door. "Someone to see you, sir."

The major ignored the NCO. "Come in, Eric. Sorry to drag you here." He closed the door.

"What do you want?" Gillespie looked tired. Those dark bags under his hard eyes had not been there the last time they had met. Was he tired from his routine work, or from the stress of leading a double life?

"Would you care to sit."

"No. What do you want?"

"You remember Richardson?"

"Your man I roughed up?"

"Yes. He seems to have disappeared."

Eric narrowed his eyes. "When?"

"A few days ago."

"It's none of my business."

"I know, but I wondered if your people could sniff about. See if they can find him. I'm a bit worried."

"Do you think the Provos have lifted him?"

"What do you think?"

"They might."

"You're the expert, Eric. If they have, what will happen?"

Gillespie said in a matter-of-fact voice, "Either they'll let him go or they won't."

The major produced a convincing shudder. "Is there any way you could find out what's happened to him?"

"I can have my people keep an eye out for him. If we're wrong about his being lifted, or if he reappears, I'll let you know."

"I'd be most grateful."

"Aye. And if he contacts you, let me know. My men have better things to do than waste time looking for some bloody amateur."

The major ignored the jibe. "Fine. Eric?"

"What?"

"Do you think, if the Provos do have him, they'd kill him if his story doesn't hold up?"

Gillespie snorted. "No, they'd give him a thousand pounds and send him off on his holidays. Of course they'd fucking well kill him."

"I know." The major sounded contrite. "You'll tell me at once if you find a corpse?"

"Of course."

"Thanks." The major forced a weak smile. "Silly of me to worry, but one does get attached to these young chaps."

"Jesus Christ. You should have thought of that before you sent him in."

"I know. Still, he's probably all right."

Gillespie shrugged. "Is that all?"

"Yes."

"I'm off then. I'm up to my neck arranging security."

"Oh?"

"Aye. Harold Wilson's coming here on Thursday."

"Really?"

"Aye." He turned to the door.

The major opened it. "Corporal Arbuthnot." The MP trotted down the hall. "See Superintendent Gillespie to his car."

"Sir."

The major shut the door. He congratulated himself. The pieces were in place. Arbuthnot could confirm that Gillespie had met with the major tonight. The major would swear that he had asked the RUC man here for his help in locating Richardson, which was perfectly true. The major would also testify that he had explained Richardson's mission—to find the Provo bomber and his superiors—in detail to Gillespie. If Richardson's body was found, the finger would point at one man. Gillespie would naturally deny that he had been briefed, that he was PIRA, but it would be his word against the major's. And who would the judge believe—an Ulsterman, or an officer and a gentleman?

FIFTY-TWO

The good black earth in the ploughed field glistened through the steam of its drying. The level of the Ravernet River was falling. As soon as it was dark, Marcus and Davy would get in under the bridge to complete the measuring that Marcus had begun yesterday. The charges would be set tomorrow night, but it was time to start their construction. The two men stood together at the table surveying the components that would form the firing circuit: blasting caps, spare batteries, and a small transmitter and receiver. A galvanometer lay close by.

Marcus said, "Fulminate of mercury caps. Sixes. Have you any delayed-action caps?"

Davy shook his head.

"Pity. If you had, we could have the charges go off in sequence, put a couple of laterals to fire first. That would increase the force of the central charge."

"Will it matter if we can't?"

"Not at all. We'll make the middle charge hollow."

"All right."

Marcus picked up the receiver. "What's this?"

"Model-aeroplane control." Davy pointed at the little box. "The transmitter moves levers inside. If we make them part of the circuit, we can close it from up to six hundred yards way."

"Have you given it a try?"

"Not yet."

"Here, hold this." Marcus handed Davy the receiver. "Take it over to the far side of the room."

Davy carried the flat metal box. It had a tiny aerial at one end, two wires dangling from the other, one coated in blue plastic, the other in red. Beyond the coloured insulation, copper filaments, bright and braided, shone in the evening sunlight that streamed through the window.

"Far enough." Marcus held the transmitter in one hand. "Put the ends of the wires together."

"Right."

Marcus flipped a switch. A bulb on the box in his hand glowed red. "Spark?"

Davy shook his head.

"Put the ends closer."

Davy did so.

"Spark?"

"Nothing."

"Where's the galvanometer?"

"On the table."

"Give us the receiver."

Davy limped back to the table. "Here." .

Marcus connected the wires to screw terminals on the galvanometer. The needle did not move.

"Well?" Davy asked, and Marcus could hear the anxiety.

"Let's see." Marcus took a screwdriver and pried the back from the box. He pulled a battery free, loosened the receiver from the galvanometer, and put one of the meter's wires on the anode, the other on the cathode of the battery. The needle whisked across the dial. "Not the battery."

"Jesus, without that receiver the Semtex is about as much fucking use as putty."

"Cheer up, Davy."

"What?"

"You've a face on you like a Lurgan spade." Marcus fiddled inside the receiver. "Aha."

"What?"

"See that there?" Marcus indicated a wire lying beside one of the clips that would hold the battery in place. "Wire's loose."

Davy produced a piece of solder and a soldering iron from his kit. "Here."

"Nice piece of equipment, Davy. There's one wee snag."

"What?"

"It's an electric iron."

"Fuck it. There's no electricity here."

"Never worry. I'll bet you were using solder before all these high-powered whigmaleeries was invented."

"Right enough." Davy went to the fireplace, picked up a poker, and brought it back to the range. He thrust the poker inside. "Just a minute."

"No rush."

Davy waited for the poker's end to glow cherry-red, then carried it to the table.

Marcus grasped the wire with a pair of needle-nose pliers. He touched the end of the solder to the poker and, as the amalgam melted, guided a molten drop over the terminal and the wire. He held the wire in place with the pliers until the silver metal hardened. "That's her now."

Davy moved the poker aside.

Marcus slipped the battery back into its nest and reconnected the galvanometer. Davy made a phewing noise as the needle flicked across the dial. "Good man. You'd me going for a minute there."

Marcus slipped the cover back in place. "Let's give it another go."

"Right." Davy carried the receiver back to the shelf, pausing on his way to replace the poker in the fireplace. Marcus threw the switch, and a spark crackled between the wires.

Davy grinned. "Dead-on. Good lad."

Marcus smiled back. "Right enough." He smiled because he had found what he had been searching for. The way to disable the system. "It'll soon be dark enough to go and take a look at the bridge."

Davy crouched under the lee of the ivy-covered abutment. The stones of the pier were damp, and moss grew between the granite blocks. The mortar in the cracks was old and pried loose easily with a screwdriver. The bridge had probably been there for two hundred years. It was seventy feet from bank to bank, the roadway fourteen feet wide. Six feet or so from the water to the highest part of the undersurface. Eight feet from the riverbed.

They'd timed it well, moving round the edge of the field in the gloaming, the trees at the gate on the far side easy to identify, dark against the indigo sky. There'd been a nasty moment when a Lynx helicopter had whisked low overhead, and they'd cowered in the hedgerow, hidden from prying eyes even if the aircraft's observers were equipped with infrared sniper scopes. Marcus knew it would have been a different matter if the helicopter had had thermal imagers aboard. Those bloody things could pick up the heat from a man's body through foliage.

Davy looked up. There was no moon, but the stars were beginning to appear, cold white points against the darkening sky. There was the Plough, Cassiopeia, Venus. Do they have the same stars in Canada? he wondered. He remembered the night he took Fiona to the beach at Tyrella and made love under the stars on a soft summer evening—the sand dunes, breeze in the coarse grass, and the bowl of the sky star-bright and distant.

Davy stiffened. In the distance a light brightened the edge of the sky. Was it a car, or a Land Rover or a Saracen? The light was coming this way. He scrambled to the bank, pulled his waders up his thighs and slipped into the water, feeling the current pushing him toward the bridge. He worked his way along the edge of the abutment, cursing as he stumbled and an icy wavelet slopped over the top of a boot.

He crept beneath the arch, moving deeper under the overhang. There was Mike, silhouetted against the dim light at the far end of the tunnel. He must be standing on a rock. He'd seemed at first to be enormously tall as he held his hands over his head to feel the masonry above.

"Mike." Davy kept his voice low-pitched. "Mike."

Mike stepped into the water and started to wade upstream, forcing his way into the current.

Davy moved downstream. The river was frigid. A stone rolled under his foot and he flailed his arms, trying in vain to keep his balance. His head went under. He gasped, pulling water into his lungs. He tried to cough and thrashed, feeling the stones of the riverbed hammering him as he was tumbled along. Finally, his head broke the surface. He tried to get a lungful of air, but there was nothing but strangling water as he was pulled under again. Although the river was only two feet deep, the current was too strong. His chest was bursting. A red haze blurred his vision, and Davy McCutcheon knew that he was drowning, held under by the weight of water in his boots.

Something grabbed him by the left arm and lifted his mouth above the surface. He felt a wrenching on his hair and thought of old myths of water kelpies—evil river spirits—but he didn't care. He could breathe. Greedily. Noisily. Wheezing and retching. The red blur faded. He realized that Mike was holding them both against the masonry of the bridge. The thing pulling his hair was Mike's hand.

Davy tried to find a footing but skidded off a slippery rock, and would have fallen but for Mike's grip. Managing to get his feet under him, Davy stood, crouched, gasping. Jesus, he was freezing. The pain in his left leg gnawed like the teeth of a rat.

"Oh, shit. Oh, shit." He retched, spewing up river water into the blackness under the bridge. "Oh, shit." His teeth chattered, and Davy did not know whether it was from cold or from fear.

"You all right?" Mike had his head bent close to Davy's ear.

"No, I'm fucking well freezing. Have you done?"

"Aye."

"Come on to hell out of here." Davy worked his way along the arch, pressing his palms to the rough stones, moving his feet cautiously. God, but his waterlogged boots must weigh a ton apiece. Davy's breath rasped in his throat. He didn't think he would have made it up the bank if it hadn't been for a heave in the small of his back. He rolled onto dry land and heard Mike scramble out of the river.

"All right, Davy?"

"Hang on. I need to get my boots off."

"I'll give you a hand."

Mike's tugging overcame the suction created by the water in the boots. One and then the other came off. Mike, bless him, lifted each by the toe and upended them, waiting for the water to cascade out.

"Here. Get those back on you."

Davy struggled to force his damp socks into the wet waders, stood, and turned down the tops of the boots, the thigh parts hanging as flaps below his knees. "Come on." He set off toward the gate, limping, trying not to let his teeth start chattering again.

He thanked God for the fire and for Mike Roberts. Davy sat on a stool in front of a blazing heap of turf, letting the warmth soak into him. His bare feet tingled painfully as the circulation returned. The ache in his left thigh ground on and on. Mike had half carried him, half dragged him for the last hundred yards. The tea in the mug he held in both hands was life-saving, hot and sweet. His sodden clothes hung steaming over chairbacks. He remembered being stripped by Mike, toweled dry, bundled into this coarse blanket, and set in front of the fire. The tea had appeared moments later. Mike was upstairs now, changing his own soaked clothes. He must have been frozen, too, but had paid no attention to his own needs, not until he had seen to Davy.

He watched Mike come downstairs carrying his shirt, sweater, trousers, and underwear. He wore a pair of jeans and a dry pullover. His long hair was sleek, ragged at the ends and still not dry.

"All right, Davy?"

"I'll live." Davy massaged his thigh with his left hand.

Mike hung his wet things on a chairback. "Enjoy your swim?"

"Piss off. I fell in."

Mike pulled a chair over beside Davy and sat, leaning forward, holding his hands out to the warmth. "I noticed. For a minute I thought you were the biggest salmon in Ulster." Mike laughed. "You went down with a powerful spraughle."

"Mike, I damn near drowned. If you hadn't . . ."

"Och, the hold I had on your hair, you came nearer to being scalped."

"Are you trying to spare my feelings?"

"Not at all. You fell in. It could have happened to a bishop." Mike rubbed his hands. "Boys-a-dear, that's great. I was cold there myself."

"Thanks, Mike." Davy touched Mike's arm, feeling the tight muscles, envying the man his youth. "Thanks for the haul home, too."

"Aye. Well. I couldn't help but notice the scars on your leg. It's a bloody miracle you can walk at all. What happened?"

"Tell you what. Find me a fag."

Mike rose. He lifted a packet of Woodbines from the table. "Here."

Davy lit up and coughed. "Thanks."

Mike took his seat.

Davy stared into the fire. "Nineteen fifty-seven. One of mine went off too soon."

Mike's breath made a little whistling noise as he inhaled sharply.

"Aye. Killed four men—and my da."

"Your da?"

"Aye." Davy lowered his head. He felt a hand on his shoulder. "Aye."

The moisture in his eyes had not come from the river. Davy sniffed and wiped his nose with the back of his hand.

"I'm sorry, Davy."

Davy inhaled smoke. "Water under the bridge," and before he could help it, found himself smiling at what he had said. "Water under the bridge." He knew his laugh must sound hysterical, but he couldn't stop, peals echoing from the rafters as tears ran down his cheeks.

FIFTY-THREE

WEDNESDAY, APRIL 17

"Trace this call," Ulster television reporter Jack Henderson scribbled on his pad, handing the note to his producer. His fingers tightened around the telephone. "I'm sorry, sir. Would you mind repeating that?"

He heard a mocking chuckle at the other end. "Aye. I would." The line went dead.

It was a hell of a way to start a Wednesday. "Get a camera crew ready," Henderson said as he dialed the number pinned to a corkboard above his desk. The number was in bold black numerals on a yellow card bearing the title: "In case of bomb threat."

Even though they had both retired early last night, Marcus knew that Davy had slept badly. He'd been up to take a leak and had spent a fair bit of time downstairs. Probably making himself a cup of tea. The sound of the lid of the range being lifted had rung metallically from below. He'd said very little since the pair of them rose this morning.

Marcus finished his breakfast and looked across the table at Davy. The bruise on his cheek was still there, and now the left side of his forehead was raw and abraded. His eyes were bloodshot, and the three days of grey stubble made him look like an old man.

Marcus felt the cold through his shirt and nipped upstairs to get a sweater. He glanced out the window to the bridge. Something was going on. "Davy. Get up here. Quick." He heard the scrape of a chair on the slates, Davy's uneven footsteps as he crossed the floor.

Davy appeared. "What is it?"

"Dunno. C'm'ere 'til you see." Marcus stood by the window. "Look. Down at the river."

British soldiers were posted at both sides of the bridge, crouched in the hedgerows, rifles covering the road. There were more men on both riverbanks. In the distance he could see two Saracens and a half-tonner parked. "What do you reckon?"

The desk sergeant took the call from the reporter. The message had been accompanied by the correct password. This was no hoax. Only the Provos knew what the identifying word would be, and they thoughtfully supplied it to the Security Forces so that when a message was received, the police or the army could be in no doubt about its origin.

"Thanks, Mr. Henderson. We'll get onto it."

The sergeant issued his orders. Get the nearest car round to the Shankill Road and have the officers clear McGuiggan's greengrocer's shop and the premises on both sides. Get more officers into the area for crowd control. The shops would be busy. Notify the army to send in an EOD squad to deal with the device, although it was unlikely they would arrive in time. The message had said the bomb would blow at 9:45. He looked up at the clock—twenty-eight minutes. It would be up to the soldiers to decide whether to have a protective infantry detachment go with the bomb-disposal boys. Call ambulance control, just in case. Notify the fire brigade. And one more thing—tell the senior officer on the spot to keep Henderson and his camera crew well away.

Marcus watched as a corporal walked an Alsatian sniffer dog in a harness. The dog trotted, nose down, tail waving, along one side of the bridge. For a moment Marcus thought he might be watching some of his own mob, 321 EOD Company. They were headquartered at Thiepval, but the RAOC didn't use sniffer dogs. This was a detachment of the Royal Engineers.

He glanced back to where vehicles were parked. No Goblin or Gobbler load carriers. The RAOC weren't here—not yet—but the Royal Engineers blokes would send for them if something was found. He should know. He'd been out enough times at the Royal Engineers' behest. Whenever they found a bomb, it would be some poor ATO's job to defuse it. Someone Marcus would know. When the time came, he'd better make bloody sure the Semtex was harmless. He comforted himself with the thought that he had determined exactly how the receiver's wiring could be short-circuited. Now, making sure the thing did not go off was one less cause for concern. He turned as Davy muttered, "Looking for bombs."

The Wolseley Saloon pulled up against the curb. Two constables dismounted. One, carrying a megaphone, said, "You, Peter, inside Mc-Guiggan's. Get them out."

The second constable elbowed his way through the shoppers who thronged the pavements—women in head scarves and curlers, shopping bags on arms. At least the Shankill was Loyalist, and he didn't have to put up with jibes and catcalls the way he would have on the Falls.

From far away the sirens of the ambulances, police cars, and fire engines wailed like demented donkeys. A Mercedes-Benz, Felix the Cat sticker on one door, swung round a corner. The EOD squad had arrived. They parked beside a van with a dish aerial on its roof. The UTV camera crew had arrived, too.

The constable went into the greengrocer's and began shepherding customers, shop assistants, and the protesting owner out onto the Shankill Road. His companion yelled at them through his megaphone, telling them to clear the area as quickly as possible or to take shelter behind a large metal rubbish container. The skip sat in front of a slum-clearance site on the other side of the road. Its cast-iron sides were rusted and covered in brick dust from the broken walls that had been dumped into its capacious hold.

An officer of the Royal Engineers, dressed in anglers' chest waders, slipped into the Ravernet River and made his way under the span. From where he stood, Marcus could make out the flash of a torch beam in the darkness under the bridge.

Davy said, "I hope they're happy at their work. They'll find bugger all."

Marcus watched the patrol. "What'll we do if they come here, Davy?"

"Give them a cup of tea. Like a couple of good farmers." He did not seem to be perturbed. "And wait for them to piss off."

"Does it not bother you?"

Davy shook his head. "I'd have been worried if they'd come after we'd set the bomb. If they come back again now, they won't be so thorough, and that suits us fine."

"Can't be much joy, looking for bombs," Marcus said.

It wasn't. Back on the Shankill, an ATO struggled into his EOD suit. He wished that when the bloody Provos gave a warning they'd be more specific about the positioning of the device. It was all very well to say it was in a greengrocer's shop. Where exactly in the shop was going to be his problem. He checked his watch. 9:41. He had four minutes.

He paused, helmet in his hands, and looked about. McGuiggan's was empty. He could see in through the window, past the wire-mesh grille that was meant to protect the glass from drive-by firebombings. Lettuces and cauliflowers, brussels sprouts, turnips, and mounds of spuds sat on racks. People ran from the adjacent shops, a cobbler's and a chemist's.

The yellow Northern Ireland Hospitals Authority ambulance was parked behind his Mercedes. Blue-uniformed attendants lounged against the ambulance's mudguards, one smoking, the other holding his peaked cap in his hands. Firemen waited, two in the cab, the rest perched on the big red fire engine pulled up alongside the skip.

Two police Hotspur Land Rovers had arrived, and policemen were erecting barricades at each end of the street, keeping newcomers from entering the cordoned-off area, hustling those who had been in the nearby shops to safety on the far sides of the barriers.

The television crew had set up their equipment behind the skip. A cameraman peered round its metal side, lens focused on McGuiggan's. An infantry platoon moved in. Their officer decided that the lee of the heavy metal container would provide sufficient shelter for his men if the bomb in the grocer's did go off.

At 9:45, two hundred pounds of ammonium nitrate, mixed with sump oil, blew the skip and the morning apart.

Brendan McGuinness had planned the ambush precisely so that those seeking refuge would move directly into the eye of the blast.

FIFTY-FOUR

"So," said Marcus, "we've to take out a car when it crosses the span?"

"Aye." Davy looked at the thirty blocks of Semtex stacked on the kitchen table. "Do you think we've enough to do her?"

"Aye, certainly. If we use crown charges under the centre of the span. Look. The roadbed's three-feet thick, and we'll call it good masonry, so the material factor is"—Marcus scratched his head—"0·48. We'll not be able to do much tamping, so that gives us a tamping factor of 1·8. So"—he scribbled on a scrap of paper—"we'd need just under twenty pounds of TNT."

"Aye. But you've to divide by 1·6 because we're using Semtex."

"Right. That works out at just under thirteen pounds per charge."

"Per charge?"

"We'll need three charges so that their cavities overlap and the whole fucking issue collapses."

"I see."

"So. Two side charges and one in the middle, and we'll shape that one."

"Good."

Marcus smiled. He knew he was taking some risks, building demolition devices exactly to the correct specifications, but he was determined that, once he'd secretly sabotaged the thing by disconnecting the soldered wire in the receiver, Davy would have no grounds for complaint about Mike Roberts's workmanship and would still have to keep his side of the bargain. Marcus stood and separated the Semtex into three heaps of ten orange blocks. "Come on," he said, "let's see what we can find in the barn."

. . .

It took a while, rooting about in the open structure, to find exactly what Marcus needed to make shaped charges: a length of copper piping, some wooden dowels, plywood. He was not surprised that the bits and pieces were readily available. Farmers kept all kinds of junk lying around.

Marcus knew he was being melodramatic, impressing Davy by making a shaped charge. A solid one would have been nearly as effective if the explosion was truly going to go ahead as planned, but he wanted Davy to be convinced that Mike Roberts had really done his best.

He worked steadily until the job was done. Marcus looked at his handiwork again. It had been a slow business.

But there the charges sat. Waiting. All that was required was to pop in the detonators and wire them to the receiver. Well, not quite all. Their bright orange hue would stick out like a sore thumb. Davy cocked his head to one side. "Just have to give them a lick of paint." He went to fetch the white enamel and the coloured dyes that Jimmy had provided.

"It's not as easy as that, Davy."

"What?"

"You can't paint Semtex."

"So what do we do?"

Marcus opened a drawer, pulled out the contents, and removed the liner paper. "Wrap them in that and paint the paper."

"All right." Davy began to work.

Marcus sat and watched Davy calmly painting the undersides of the now-wrapped charges. Davy was not a man to be fooled by a shoddy job. Not yet, anyway.

When Davy finished, he looked at Marcus. "I never really thanked you for fishing me out of the river." His voice was soft.

"Never worry. You'd have done the same for me."

"Aye, Mike. I would."

Marcus heard the catch in Davy's voice. "I could take a shine to you, you old bugger."

"You're not such a bad lad yourself."

"Fuck off." Marcus laughed and said, "Try not to fall in again tonight."

"I will." Davy paused. "Does all this not bother you?"

"Why should it?"

"Because when we blow the bridge, the soldiers will be rushing round like chickens with their heads cut off."

"What soldiers? You've not seen what this stuff can do. Anyway, I'm with you."

"So?"

"Jesus, Davy. How long have you been keeping away from the Brits? Twenty years?"

"Aye. Give or take." Suddenly, Davy looked even older and more tired. "A brave wheen of years."

Marcus chuckled. "You must be good at it, then." He watched a look of pride cross Davy's face. "One of the best."

"Away on."

It was funny how the big man could be embarrassed. "Should be exciting."

"You like a bit of excitement, don't you?"

Marcus nodded. It seemed simpler to agree. His taste for peril had diminished since that van bomb.

"That's why you defused the bomb in that pub, isn't it?"

"Aye." It wasn't, but Marcus was not going to tell Davy that either.

"Son, you could've been me twenty-five years ago. I thought it was a game."

Marcus was surprised to feel Davy's hand on his arm. He looked up and saw sadness in the man's eyes.

"It's not a game, Mike. We've a job to do." He hesitated. "It'll be my last one."

"What?"

"You heard."

"But—"

"No buts. I've had enough." Davy's fingers tightened. "Take my advice. Make it your last one, too."

"I suppose that's up to you. I still want to get involved."

"Jesus, I knew you'd say that. I suppose I'd have been disappointed if you hadn't."

"Why?"

"I've been watching you. You've guts. I don't want to see them spilled."

"Come on now, Davy." This was crazy. Marcus was setting Davy up to be arrested, yet he felt pleased that he had not "disappointed" the big man, had enjoyed his praise and his concern.

"I mean it, son. I mean it, but it's your choice. I'll put in the word if you want me to." Davy nodded toward the plastique. "Maybe we should get started."

"Great." Marcus hummed the first bars of the triumphal march from *Aida*, then realized that it was not the kind of thing Mike Roberts would know and changed to a pop song.

"What's that tune?"

Marcus's smile was very wide. "It's called 'Spinning Wheel.'" He began to sing the words. "What goes up, must come down—"

FIFTY-FIVE

"So far, so good," Brendan McGuinness said.

Sean said nothing.

Brendan grinned. "We got the judge and we scared the bejesus out of the peelers in Comber."

"We lost three men yesterday—two dead, the other one picked up at the Holywood Arches."

"You get casualties in a war."

"Give over, for God's sake."

Brendan sat. "This morning went off like a breeze. The paper said we killed four soldiers, a fireman, and that bloody reporter." He jabbed his finger on the tabletop. "Do you know how many of the Security Forces were up the Shankill this morning?"

"No."

"Thirty. Peelers, soldiers, bomb-disposal men. And that's only a start. We'll be able to get nearly a thousand tied up tomorrow."

"Good. Davy's going to need all the help he can get."

"He'll have it. Have you organized the sheepmen?"

"Aye. The action squad goes into Norman Johnston's farm at four tomorrow morning. They'll have plenty of time to get the flock ready. What about the motorbike?"

"It'll be delivered tonight. I doubt if he'll need it, but it'll be there. Just in case. I just hope your man McCutcheon will be up to his job tomorrow."

"Don't worry about Davy."

"I won't. I've more to worry about than him. My man called."

"Oh?"

"He's been busting his arse. The bloody MPs wanted to take the direct Lisburn–Hillsborough road. He had to work like hell to persuade them that if there was going to be an attack on Wilson, the best way to avoid it was to use an unexpected route."

"Good for him."

"He told me something else." Brendan had decided that now that the Wilson attack was almost over, it was time to tell Sean about the new British agent. There was no reason for him to know that Brendan had known about the bastard for weeks.

"The Brits have a new undercover man in New Lodge."

"Fuck."

"Some lad who calls himself Mike Roberts. I'm going after him once the big one's over."

Marcus sat in the kitchen as he and Davy waited for dark. "So," said Marcus, "what'll we do to while away the shining hour?"

Davy shook his head. "You're still not one bit bothered, are you?"

"Not much. I was pissed off at first when you told me I wasn't going to get to meet the big lads for a while, but this here's great, so it is."

Great? Jesus, Davy thought, as he packed the charges and the wires into his canvas carryall. "The detonators and the receiver'll fit in my tool kit." He hesitated as if coming to a decision. "I'll do the rest myself."

"Worried I might blow myself up?" Marcus did not want to seem too eager, but he knew he had to get to the receiver to disable it.

"I shouldn't have brought you. It's not your fight. I want you out of here."

"Fuck off."

"Don't worry. I'll find you when it's over. I'll put in the word with the CO."

"Shit, Davy, I'll not be used. You couldn't make the charges, so you kidnapped me to do it for you."

"Aye."

Marcus stabbed a finger at Davy. "You owe me the chance to finish the job. And what the hell are you going to do if you fall in the fucking river again?"

Davy said nothing.

"Davy, two of us can do the job in half the time."

"Aye. Well."

"You know it. Don't you?" Davy was backing down. "Davy, I want to help."

Davy pushed the carryall aside and sat silently before saying, "On your own head be it."

Marcus grinned. "Thanks."

"But I'll carry the detonators."

"Fair enough—Mammy."

"Mammy?"

"Aye. You're trying to look after me like an old broody hen. I know about the risks of fulminate as well as you do."

Davy offered his hand. "Thanks, son."

They shook, and Marcus, not knowing what to say, let the silence hang between them.

Davy coughed and held his fist before his mouth, using his curled index finger to smooth his moustache. He turned and faced Marcus. "I don't know about all the stuff going on now."

"What about it?"

"Army Council. They reckon we can make the Brits go home if we cost them too much. Wreck businesses and fuck up civilian life. The more we bomb, the more it costs, the more fed up the Brits get."

"Do you not think it'll work?"

Davy snorted. "I doubt Army Council ever heard about Dunkirk. The harder you push the English, the tighter they hold on. They don't have a fucking bulldog for a mascot for nothing." He put his hands in the small of his back. "Jesus, I gave that a right wrench last night. Anyway. I don't think hitting soft targets is right."

"But you're not worried about tomorrow?"

"The army's fair game. It's probably some general'll be in the car." He hesitated. "As long as it goes all right."

"Why shouldn't it?"

"The last one was a right fuckup. Right bollocks."

Silence.

Davy moved back to the table. He stood, resting his hands on the edge. He pushed out his lower lip. "I'm going to tell you about a wee girl—a wee girl in a motorcar."

"Davy, you don't have to." Marcus shifted uncomfortably. He was unused to older men unburdening themselves.

"I want to. By God, Mike, I want you to understand."

Marcus listened, heard the story, heard Davy's remorse. When the big man finished, Marcus groped for the right words, knowing that any suggestions that the Hanrahan girl *had* been a casualty of war would be dismissed. Yet he knew he had to try.

"Come on, Davy. You know it was an accident."

"There's been too many accidents. I want no more. I'm finished after tomorrow. Fiona and me's going to Canada."

Fiona? Who the hell was Fiona? Leave it, Marcus told himself.

Davy said, "I've had enough. I'm telling you this because you're a decent lad. I wanted you out because there's no need for you or Siobhan to get tied up the way I was. No need for you to be a fucking murderer."

"Davy. You're not a murderer. You're a soldier." Marcus searched for the right words, "One of the Fianna."

"Aye. Finn MacCool's bodyguard. Right enough."

Despite the bitterness in Davy's voice, Marcus could see that the thought had comforted him.

"I think you're a good man, Davy McCutcheon." And Marcus knew that he meant what he had just said.

Davy laboured along and envied the easy lope of the younger man as he made his way through the furrow closest to the hedge. The night was clear, and a clear night meant dew. Unless they kept out of the grass they would leave a shining trail—like the path laid by a snail, and just as obvious in the sun's morning rays.

It was heavy going in thigh boots, the mud of the field clinging to their soles. Davy found relief in remembering Mike's words. "I think you're a good man, Davy McCutcheon. You know it was an accident." Decent of the lad to say that. It helped. Just a bit. But it hadn't been an accident. Davy knew he was guilty as sin. Tried and convicted in his own soul. And if there was the hell that the bloody priests ranted on about, that's where he was going.

The toe of his boot snagged in a root. Davy stumbled and clutched the toolbox tightly to his chest; then his shoulder hit the soft earth as he measured his length. He lay still for a moment, letting out his breath in a long gasp. Jesus. Going to hell? If the jolt of the fall had fired the blasting caps, he'd be there now.

"You all right?"

"I'll live." Davy stood.

"At least you don't have to swim in a field. Here, give me the tool-box."

"Be careful with that." Davy immediately regretted his words. How careful had he been? "Come on." He rubbed his palms together to wipe away the mud and set off for the gateway.

It was dark as the pit of hell beneath the bridge. Mike was saying something. Davy bent his head to hear.

"Can you hold on to the toolbox and give me a hammer and a big screwdriver?"

Davy took the box and opened the lid. The receiver, wires, and caps were snug where he'd put them, in a nest he'd made of strips torn from an old towel. "Here."

"Thanks."

Davy heard a scraping noise overhead. Mike must be loosening the mortar round one of the granite blocks. The scraping went on and on, the only sound louder than the gurgling of the stream against his legs.

Clangggg. Jesus. Mike had hit the screwdriver a clout with the hammer. The noise was magnified under the bridge, and in the stillness of the night Davy was sure the racket must have been heard in Thiepval Barracks, only a few miles away. *Clangggg.* Davy crouched and turned to look out into the night. No signs of life. No headlights. *Clangggg.*

"Out of the way, Davy."

The granite block splashed into the water.

"One," said Mike. He was panting. "Here, gimme the box."

Davy handed it over.

"Where'd you put the staples?"

"Top end."

Davy waited, flinching with every hammer stroke as Mike pounded in two rows of staples, one on either side of the cavity. Nylon rope from the barn would be strung between the staples to support the charges.

"Done," said Mike. "Your turn."

Davy followed Mike to the far side of the centre of the arch. He had a hand over his head, the pale skin just visible in the darkness. "This one."

Davy felt the rough, clammy stone and the raised and cracked cement that bound it to its fellows. "Right." He began to work and was amazed at how easily the mortar fell away, but the work took longer than he had thought. The stone was well anchored. Davy was sweating by the time he was able to rock the block in its bed. "Give us a bit of that cloth packing." Davy bound the rough material round the head of the hammer. "Out of the way." He held the screwdriver firmly and hit it an almighty belt. The noise was less, muffled by the toweling.

"I should have thought of that," Mike said.

Davy smiled. The old dog could still teach the pup a trick or two. He grunted and swung the hammer.

The final block to be removed was a hoor, smack in the centre of the span. Mike swayed as he scraped. After twenty minutes he climbed down. "I'm buggered. You have a go."

Davy took the screwdriver, felt for the groove above his head, and began to work. The perspiration from his previous efforts had not dried, and when he started to chip away at the mortar, he was cold. Half an hour later, the sweat blinded him, his shoulder was on fire—but the stone was loose.

"Hammer." He took the heavy tool, steadied himself, and belted the head of the screwdriver. Cement rained onto Davy's head and the block tore free, plummeting down and hitting him a glancing blow on his thigh. The twisted bone protested, and he fought not to cry out. Biting down hard on his lower lip, he screwed his eyes tight shut and waited for the pain to pass. There'd be a bloody great bruise there tomorrow.

"You all right, Davy?"

He felt a steadying hand on his arm. "Aye. Just a minute." The pain was less now. Bearable. Davy leaned on Mike's shoulder and stepped down into the water. "Jesus, that rock hit me a queer dunt."

"Here. Take the toolbox. I'll knock the staples in and make the grooves for the wires."

Davy moved to the side of the stream and leaned against the abutment, taking the weight off his bad leg. He could hear the scraping as Mike dug channels between the blocks. The wires from the receiver to the detonators would be hidden in there.

Davy froze as the barking of dogs tore the night, becoming louder, more insistent by the moment. A man yelled, "Shut the fuck up, Landy." A door slammed, and the dog obeyed its master.

Davy held his breath for a long time. Mike must have crouched. Davy sensed the movement as his companion straightened up and said, "Fucking dog. I near filled my pants."

"Me, too." Davy allowed himself a dry laugh. "Sounds carry at night. It must be away to hell and gone."

"Come on, let's get finished and out of here."

"Right," said Davy.

"I'll only be a minute."

Davy waited as Mike moved upstream to collect the carryall. "Come on," he said as he stepped back under the haunch. Davy followed. "Here," said Mike, "hold you the bag."

Davy took it and tightened his muscles. Sixty pounds of Semtex was heavy enough.

Mike reached into the bag and produced the first charge. He lifted it over his head and said, "Fits like a glove. Give us the rope."

Davy pulled a length from the bag and handed it over. He waited, knowing that Mike would be anchoring the plastique into the cavity left by the granite block.

"Done. Next." Mike moved downstream. Davy followed.

Setting the charges didn't take long. And it was a good thing, too. That fucking Landy might start howling again. "Detonators?"

"Aye."

Davy waded back to the bank. The ache in his leg was there, but, thank God, not as insistent. He'd known worse. He lifted the lid of the toolbox and took the blasting caps and their attached wires from their toweling nest. Three number 6 detonators connected in sequence, and the command wires to go to the receiver. One last check. Davy touched the wires to the posts of the galvanometer. He couldn't see the needle in the dark. It had been all right when they'd tested the circuit back at the farmhouse, but you were always meant to run a final check before the detonating circuit was fitted to the charges.

"Mike."

"What?"

"I can't see the galvanometer."

"Hang on."

Davy heard the gentle splashing.

Mike said, "Have you a match?"

Davy rummaged in his pocket.

"You watch the dial, Davy."

"Right."

Davy heard the scrape, saw the flare and the flicker of the needle across the dial. "It's OK."

Fitting the detonators to the charges and burying the wires in their precut grooves took little time. The two men brought handfuls of mud from the riverbank to plaster the dark earth around the edges of the three charges and along the grooves where the wires ran. Davy hoped that it would dry slowly and still hide the wires—at least until midday tomorrow.

Together, they ran the command wires into the ivy that covered the abutment. The receiver would be well hidden among the leaves, just the tip of the tiny aerial sticking out.

Mike grunted. "Where's the whigmaleerie?"

Och, Mike, Davy thought. He was never able to be serious for too long. It was a bit like having Jimmy along, him and his always acting the buck eejit. Mind you, now that they were nearly finished, Davy could feel his own tension ebbing. "It's in the tool kit. I'll get it."

Davy handed the receiver to Mike, who made the final splice to the command wire. "That's her," he said. "Have you the screwdriver?"

"What for?"

"Just want to check that joint we soldered."

Davy laughed. "I checked it last night. And I soldered the back of the receiver shut."

FIFTY-SIX

It had been so simple the way he'd planned to slip off the back of the receiver and snap a wire. Marcus sat by the embers in the fireplace, berating himself. He'd painted himself into a hell of a corner.

Last night when he'd heard Davy working at the range, he'd assumed the man was making tea. He'd been soldering the back onto the receiver. To waterproof it, he said.

Jesus Christ on a crutch. Now the pair of them were stuck in the farmhouse, and under the bridge was a perfectly constructed line of demolition charges—set, wired, live, and ready to blow the span, the army convoy, and the VIP all over the fields of County Down. Marcus felt like the crazy colonel in *Bridge on the River Kwai*, working like a beaver for the enemy. He should be whistling "Colonel Bogey."

He watched Davy pour boiling water into two glasses. The older man had his back turned, and Marcus wondered if he could take Davy by surprise. Probably, but that would put paid to any hopes of introductions to the senior Provos. Now that he was so close to completing his mission, Marcus was determined to see it through. There had to be a way to stop the explosion yet still retain Davy's trust. There might be a way— if Marcus could get to the phone.

Davy came over with a couple of glasses. "Here, get that into you."

"What is it?"

"A wee hot half."

The whiskey, sugar, and hot water smelled good. "*Sláinte.*"

"*Sláinte mHaith.*" Maybe, Marcus thought, if Davy gets a few into him he'll get drowsy.

"I was wrong," Davy said. "I couldn't have fixed it by myself. I owe you."

"Away on."

Davy drank. "Exciting enough, was it?"

Marcus laughed. "When that bloody dog started—" And when he'd found the receiver soldered shut.

"You done good. I've known men run when they got a shock." Davy leaned forward. "You'd be a useful man to the Provos, but I still think you should forget it. For Siobhan's sake. You love her, don't you?"

"Very much."

"I know how you feel."

"Have you a girl, Davy?"

"I bloody well hope so."

"You mentioned Fiona last night."

"Fiona. There's music to that name, son." Davy looked into the embers and said softly, "You should hear her laugh."

"Tell me about her."

"We lived together before one of my specials killed the da of a couple of kids in her class."

"She's a teacher?"

"She is."

"What happened?"

"She gave me the choice: her or the Provos. I chose. She left." Davy smiled, "But I saw her last week, and she'll come back if I quit."

So there was more to Davy's wanting to get out than guilt. "What'll you do?" Marcus asked.

"It's likely just a dream, but we want to go to Canada." Davy looked up. "Do you think a fellow like me could make a go of it there?"

"I don't see why not. In the oil fields, maybe. Tell them you learned about explosives on the North Sea rigs."

"I could, couldn't I?"

"And you learn fast. I watched you with the Semtex. I could teach you more."

"Would you?"

"Aye, certainly." There was hope in Davy's eyes. The man was hearing what he wanted to hear. It seemed a shame to lead him on.

Davy looked wistful. "I think Fiona and me could be happy in Canada."

"Davy?" Marcus hesitated. "I don't suppose you'd think about not going ahead tomorrow?"

"What?"

"I just thought, after what you said, like, maybe it wasn't so important anymore."

Davy shook his head. "I've always delivered. Have you heard of Danny Blanchflower? Best soccer player Northern Ireland ever had. He scored two goals in his last game."

"And you want to go out with a bang?" Marcus chuckled at his unconscious pun.

Davy had had a smile on his lips, but it faded. "Desperate thing, pride, and it's not just that. I promised a man."

"I could stay here and fire the Semtex, let you get away tonight. To Fiona."

Davy rose. The big man's eyes were misted. "Son, you don't know what you've just said. Thank you. But I want this one. I owe the Brits; I owe it to myself to get this one right." He spoke as if to himself. "And Brendan McGuinness can go and fuck himself."

Brendan McGuinness. Marcus stored the name. The major would want to know. "All right, Davy. We'll do it together, but when we're done, maybe I could help you find a job in Alberta. Put the word in with the company I work for. Like you're going to do with—what's his name—McGuinness?"

"The IO? Shite."

IO. Information Officer. Marcus knew he was getting closer and did not want to seem too forward. "Tell you what. When we get out of here, I'll make a few phone calls to the oil people."

He was pleased by Davy's grateful smile and wondered how the big man would have looked had he known that Marcus had decided to make a phone call all right. To the major's emergency number.

Davy stretched. "I'm knackered. I'm going for a pee, then I'm off to my bed."

"I'll be along in a wee minute." Marcus sat rigidly, listening to the uneven footsteps, the door opening and shutting. He leapt up and strode toward the phone. Something moved at the foot of the dresser where the phone sat. Oh Christ. A rat. A fucking great rat. Marcus inhaled, clamped his jaws so tightly that he heard the joint at his temple creak, and took a step forward. The rat scuttled in under the dresser.

Marcus's hand shook when he grabbed the phone. Fucking rats. He dialed the number he'd mentioned. Three double rings and a metallic, recorded female voice saying, "You are in the Lisburn area. Do not dial 084-62."

He redialled, the phone's action slow as molasses on a cold day. A male voice said, "Thiepval HQ."

"Mike—Sorry, Lieutenant Richardson. Connect me with Major John Smith. In a hurry."

A clipped voice said, "Smith."

"Major, I've only a few seconds. I'm in a farmhouse between Hillsborough and Lisburn. Near the Ravernet bridge. I'm with a Provo and we've mined the bridge. Target: some VIP tomorrow."

He heard an indrawing of breath.

"I can't disarm the charges, but I'm close to the top men. Their IO's called Brendan McGuinness."

"McGuinness?"

"Right. Now, John, stop the convoy, but do not, repeat, do not raid the farm. I'm going to need my contact to get the rest of the names."

"Well done."

Marcus put the phone down and flinched as it tinged, sure that Davy would have heard the noise as loudly as the tolling of a funeral bell.

FIFTY-SEVEN

The major replaced the receiver and swung his legs out of bed. Richardson had resurfaced as unexpectedly as a German U-boat in the middle of Belfast Lough. He was not dead, and for that the major was grateful because, by circumstances the major could only guess at, Richardson's situation was perfectly tailored to the major's needs. The lad was smack at the heart of the Provos' most spectacular attempt to date, had compromised it, and no one knew but Major Smith.

The snare that had been set for Eric on Tuesday was no longer operative. It hinged on the supposition that Richardson was dead. Palpably he was not, and his present circumstances had given the major the key to the conundrum, a key of such amazing simplicity that he felt as though he had just won the triple chance on the football pools.

The target, which Richardson had called "some VIP tomorrow," was the British prime minister, Harold Wilson. Saving him would be a huge feather in the major's cap, and might by itself make Sir Charles sufficiently grateful to forget his threat of dismissal.

Killing Wilson would be an enormous propaganda coup for the Provos. The political fallout hardly bore thinking about. But failing to kill him, and being incontrovertibly identified as the perpetrators of such an assassination plot, could do the Provos huge damage in the arena of public opinion.

It would be simple now to reroute the PM and to have the bomb under the bridge discovered, but if that was all that happened, the PIRA would deny all knowledge of the device and try to divert blame to any one of the other paramilitary organizations operating in the province. If, on the other hand, the bomb—and the Provo who was to have fired it—could be taken, his presence would stamp the PIRA's signature on the attempt as clearly as if they had taken an advertisement in the *Belfast Telegraph*. And they would not want that to happen. Not at all.

If they found out that the whistle had been blown and that the Security Forces were going to raid the farm, they would cut their losses—they'd have to—by pulling their bomber out. And how would they find out? Any raid on the farmhouse would be mounted by the army, but there would have to be representatives of the civil authority. Detective Superintendent Eric Gillespie had said he wanted to hear when Richardson reappeared. He would hear. But not yet, not until time was so short that when he acted on the information and warned his controller, there would be no chance to muddy the trail.

The major yawned, set his alarm for 3 A.M., and headed for the bathroom to take a pee. He hummed a little tune. "A-hunting we will go."

The major sat on the side of his bed, cigarette in one hand, the telephone receiver pressed against his ear with the other.

"What's up?" Gillespie sounded drowsy.

God, but his Ulster accent was even more grating, distorted as it was by the telephone wires. "Spot of bother. My man's just reported in." The major blew a smoke ring directly into the face of the bedside alarm.

"And?"

"Seems the bold boyos are going to have a go at the PM tomorrow. From a farmhouse."

"What? Shit. Where?"

"Near a place called Ravernet."

"Ravernet?"

"They've mined a bridge."

"Ravernet. There's only one bridge there."

"Could you pop over to Thiepval this morning? Have a word with one of the infantry chaps? Thought we might pay a visit to the farmhouse. You'd make the arrests."

"Right. Your troops are here to support the civil authority."

"Of course." An edge crept into Major Smith's voice. "Be here at 0400."

"You're not giving me much time."

"Sorry about that." The major grinned. "One more thing, old boy. Do keep it to yourself." The major hung up, slid off the bed, stubbed the smoke in an ashtray on the bedside table, and went into the bathroom to shave. It wouldn't do to be scruffy-looking at the upcoming briefing.

The major thought about Richardson. He was a smart lad. As far as he knew, his mission was to identify senior Provos. Of course, he'd not want the farmhouse to be raided. If the PM simply didn't show, the Provo Richardson was with would have to put it down to bad luck. He and Richardson would vanish, and sometime later he'd make the introductions Richardson had been instructed to seek.

But Richardson did not know that the real reason for his mission was mole catching, and for that to succeed Major Smith knew that a raid would have to be mounted. They probably wouldn't catch the Provo. As soon as he was warned, he'd scarper. But it was the warning, and the trail leading directly back to Eric, that interested the major.

He'd have to try to ignore the obvious snag in the arrangements. Major Smith had known for several weeks that Richardson's cover had been blown, that the Provos knew who he was. How he had managed to find himself in such a strategically important position was unclear, but how did not matter now. That he was in that position did matter, and that posed something of a problem. When the Provo in the farm got the word to run, he would be ordered either to waste Richardson or to bring him out for in-depth interrogation. Either way, the young man's future looked cloudy in the extreme. Pity, Major Smith thought, as he finished lathering his face, but there really wasn't much he could do about it. The razor made a grating noise as it sliced through his unwanted stubble.

FIFTY-EIGHT

"Come quick, Brendan." One of the communications centre's night-duty men wakened McGuinness.

He groped for his spectacles. "What time is it?"

"Three thirty."

"Shit. It'd better be important."

The man flinched. "The Brits know about the attack on the prime minister."

"What?"

The smaller man crouched into himself. "The Brits know. There's an informer called Roberts with Davy."

"There's a what? An informer? Roberts?"

"Aye—and the soldiers're going to raid the farmhouse."

"Fuck." McGuinness sat bolt upright. "Fuck." He swung his legs to the floor. "Get to hell out while I get dressed."

"Will I wake up Sean?"

"No. I'll be there in a minute."

"Right." He left.

Brendan struggled into his pants. He managed to get both feet into one of the trouser legs and almost fell. Shit! Now. The first thing to do was get the action squad out. The lads who were to herd the sheep at Norman Johnston's farm. They were to move in half an hour. There was bugger-all they could do now. What about the diversions? Later. He'd think about that later.

McCutcheon? With an informer? What the bloody hell was going on? How in the name of thundering Jesus had McCutcheon got tied up with the Brit Roberts? Roberts wasn't supposed to be approached until

Brendan had given the OK. No one would have told McCutcheon that, because Sean kept his old bomber isolated. But why would the stupid shit have taken Roberts to the farm?

Brendan decided that the answers to those questions would have to wait. Right now he had to work on damage control. If the Brits attacked and found no one in the farm, they'd know that Davy had been tipped off. And that could compromise Brendan's source. The source of information was more important—vastly more important than a broken-down old Fifties Man.

McCutcheon would have to stew in his own juice. McGuinness finished dressing and went to his control centre. He was very wide awake.

No one slept in the farmhouse. Davy tossed and turned, impatient as a girl before her first Communion, willing the time to pass. Only a few more hours and he'd be finished, on his way to a new life with Fiona.

Marcus lay and stared at the ceiling. Tomorrow was going to be an anticlimax now that the major was tipped off. And Marcus didn't mind. During the weeks of being Mike Roberts, Marcus had noticed that his own attitudes were altering, as if the man in the green binder was trying to take over. He'd been doing it again this morning. Marcus the officer knew very well where his duty lay. Once this morning's non-event was over, he must continue as ordered, meet the senior Provos, and turn them, and the bomber, in.

And after that? He'd missed Siobhan dreadfully since he'd been here. Once he'd satisfied the major, he would go to her, tell her the truth, and hope to God she would forgive him. Just like Davy's Fiona would forgive him.

But Mike Roberts, the wee lad from Bangor, had grown to like the old terrorist during their forced comradeship. Davy did have a sense of chivalry, even if it was misguided, and whatever he had done in the past, Davy was unlikely to be a threat in the future. Mike and Marcus agreed on what to do about Davy McCutcheon. Marcus had decided to go ahead with getting Davy to make the introductions, but afterward he'd let him have his chance to break with the Provos and go to his Fiona.

Which was all very well. None of that would solve Marcus's worries about how to explain to Siobhan who and what he really was and how she would react to the news. He was no closer to puzzling that out as he looked at his luminous watch, saw it was 3:45, and drifted off into a troubled doze.

At 0355, the major entered a briefing room. He carried a rolled-up map under his arm. He finished pinning it to an easel as the door opened and Captain Robby Knox came through the door. The major nodded toward a seat.

The captain sat. "Morning, sir."

"Morning, Knox. Sorry to haul you out of bed."

Knox yawned.

Eric Gillespie walked in, said nothing, and took a seat beside the Para captain.

"Morning, Eric," the major said. "Detective Superintendent Gillespie, Captain Knox."

The two men shook hands.

"Right," said the major. "I need a rapid-reaction force on the ground here," he pointed at the map to the Ravernet Road. "There's a mine under the bridge, so keep your men away from it. We'll send in the RAOC to deal with it later.

"The RAF will have to lay on a Wessex to transport a second team here, because in this farmhouse is one of the Provos' top bomb men. See to it, Knox."

"It'll take an hour or two."

"Be ready by 0900."

"Yes, sir."

The major turned to Eric. "That's your backup organized. Are you bringing anyone else?"

"You told me to keep it to myself. I'll go on my own with the soldiers in the chopper."

The major asked Knox, "Leave Thiepval 0900, on the ground by?"

"Before 0930, sir."

"Good. Now. There will be two men in the farm. The younger one's a British officer. I'd like you to get both out in one piece, but particularly my agent. His password's 'whigmaleerie.'"

"'Whigmaleerie'? Right, sir." The captain rose. "I'd better get moving."

"Hang on a moment, Knox." The major spoke directly to Eric. "Do you have other arrangements to make?"

"Aye."

"Use my office. Three doors along the hall."

"Right." Gillespie left.

The major said to Captain Knox, "For reasons which don't concern you, I want this operation kept absolutely hush-hush until you and your men have left Thiepval. Clear?"

"Sir."

"I'll tell you, Knox, and no one else, the buggers were going to have a go at the PM."

Captain Knox whistled.

"Quite. I don't want any possibility that our hand will be tipped to the Provos, so we'll keep that to ourselves until after you've hit the place. Have your wireless operator call in when you get started. Soon as I hear, I'll arrange to have the PM rerouted."

"Right, sir."

"Good man. Off you go. And, Knox? Good luck."

By 8:45 Brendan had finished. He'd sent a lad to Johnston's farm. The three men of the action squad had been intercepted at the end of the lane and told to head back to Belfast. It had taken longer to reach the others. Brendan had made no idle boast when he told Sean that he expected to have a thousand Brits tied up. His plan would have caused chaos and diverted troops and police away from the bridge and the land mine.

Thirty men and women had been briefed earlier in the week to telephone from public facilities, starting at nine o'clock. Each message was supposed to have been to the RUC, the *Belfast Newsletter,* and the *Telegraph*, smaller regional papers like the *County Down Spectator,* and the television and radio stations. Each call was to be prefaced by a code word so that the recipients would know it to be genuine. Each was to warn of a bomb. After the explosion on the Shankill Road yesterday, the Security Forces would have had to respond. But now that the attack on the British prime minister was off, there was no point wasting a previously unused diversionary tactic. Brendan left the control room and went through to the lounge.

Sean stood by the window, back to Brendan. He turned. His face was clouded. "What the hell's happened?"

"Things go wrong."

"Why didn't you call me?"

"What for? It's all taken care of."

"Christ, Brendan. Our most important attack's blown and all you can say is 'it's taken care of'?"

"What do you want me to say, that I've been telling you all along that McCutcheon was past it, that your favourite Fifties Man has fucked us up royally?"

"What the hell are you talking about?"

"According to my source, your old comrade took a friend along. A British army bomb-disposal expert. Maybe McCutcheon needed a hand with the Semtex."

"Jesus. Davy'll have a bit of explaining to do."

Brendan polished his spectacles. "Not to us. Their man's tipped the Brits off. They have a squad heading for the farm."

"What? I thought you said it was all fixed."

Brendan shrugged, hooked one leg of his glasses over an ear, adjusted the frames on the bridge of his nose, then fitted the other leg in place.

"Brendan!"

"I didn't bother to get McCutcheon out."

"Why the hell not?"

"That would tip our hand. Let the Brits know we had a source."

"Maybe."

"Look. I told you McCutcheon was past it. It's not our fault he screwed up again. He's not worth risking anything more for. We need the information we're getting a damn sight more than we need McCutcheon. The new explosives lads're coming back from Libya on Monday."

"We can't ditch Davy."

"The fuck we can't. We'd be better off without him."

"Look, get Davy out. Have him bring the Brit bastard with him."

"What for?"

"Do you not think you could get some information out of him?"

"Oh, aye," said Brendan. "I'd enjoy doing that."

Sean shuddered. "Even if aborting the mission lets the Brits suspect we've an inside track, they've no way of finding out exactly what it is. Have they?"

Brendan pursed his lips.

"Well. Have they?"

"They might."

"I don't give a shit. Look, if Davy's not there, they'll find the bomb, but they can only try to pin it on us."

"What do you mean?"

"Christ, Brendan. If Davy's taken, they'll have proof that it was a Provo mission. If he's not, we can have Army Council deny it."

"Maybe."

"No maybe about it."

"No. Leave the old bugger there."

"I will not."

"You forgotten who's acting CO? You'll leave him there."

Sean moved very close to the shorter man, looked down on him, and said, quietly and with utter disdain, "I've not forgotten. I've not forgotten Davy, either."

"You've your orders, Conlon."

"Go fuck yourself."

FIFTY-NINE

The phone in the farmhouse rang. Davy's head jerked toward the sound. Another double ring. Who the hell could that be? The bell jangled. Davy saw Mike's questioning look as he said, "Expecting a call?"

Davy shook his head.

"Are you going to answer it?"

Davy limped to the dresser, back turned to Mike, and lifted the receiver. "Hello."

"Davy?"

"Sean?"

"Aye. Davy, get out. Now."

"What?"

"Listen. The lad with you's a Brit. He's shopped you."

"Jesus." Davy stared at the wall. He did not trust himself to look at Mike. A Brit? Oh, fuck. "You sure?"

"Definitely. Don't let on you know. Bring him with you. McGuinness wants a word with him. You've not long. Get out and bring him to Myrtlefield."

"Right."

"Good luck, Davy." The phone went dead.

Davy's hand shook as he replaced the receiver. He knew he was in deep shit, and if that wasn't enough, Mike was a fucking British agent. McGuinness wanted a "word" with him? Oh, Jesus. McGuinness would grill Mike over a slow fire. There wasn't time to worry about that now. They had to get out. Davy took a very deep breath. "That was Brigade HQ. We've to run. We've been rumbled."

"What?" Roberts leapt to his feet. Davy saw the look on the lad's face as he obviously tried to control himself. "What?"

"You heard. Come on." Davy strode to the back door and wrenched it open. "Come on, for Christ's sake."

A raucous clattering battered Davy's ears. Low over the farmyard a Wessex helicopter swooped, making for the field behind the poplars. He slammed the door and limped rapidly across the kitchen to the front door. He hurled it open. In the distance across the bridge he saw two Saracens. Men in combat gear spilled onto the road and into the field on the far side of the river. Avoiding the bridge.

Davy slammed the door. He was trapped. "The fuckers are all round us." He had to yell to make himself heard above the noise of rotors. If he ever wanted to see Fiona, Davy knew he had to find an escape route. And fuck McGuinness. Davy had no time to bother with getting Mike Roberts out to satisfy that one-eyed shite in Myrtlefield Park.

"What are we going to do, Davy?"

Davy felt a hand on his sleeve. He turned on Roberts. The bastard was still playing his stupid game, trying to keep Davy occupied while the Brits attacked.

"Let go."

Roberts tightened his grip.

Davy fetched the younger man a fierce open-hander. "Let go."

Roberts's head rocked. He hunched into a boxer's crouch. The helicopter's engine roared. It must be taking off. Davy knew it would have deplaned a squad. "You shite. You British shite."

"What are you on about?"

"You're a Brit, you fucker."

Roberts dropped his guard. He looked as if he was going to deny the accusation, but Davy didn't care. The roar of the rotors forced him to shout. "I trusted you, you fucker, and you've dumped me in it." Davy pulled back his fist.

Roberts stood his ground, yelling back, "Give up, Davy. You haven't a hope in hell."

A megaphone bellowed: "Come out or we're coming in."

Davy lowered his fist. Roberts wasn't worth it. Anyway, there was no time for a fight. He had to run. Had to. He shook his head and said softly, "Get out. Go to your British friends." He didn't care if Roberts heard over the racket.

"You, in there. Come out. You've three minutes." The voice came from overhead. From the helicopter.

Roberts shouted. "Make it easier on yourself, McCutcheon. Give up. Fiona'll wait for you."

"For twenty years?" Davy shook his head. "I've to run."

"They'll kill you if you try."

"Two minutes."

Davy turned on his heel. "Get out of my sight, you bastard." He felt a hand on his shoulder.

"Davy. I'll not let you do this."

Davy spun, saw the punch coming, blocked it with his forearm, and rammed a stiff jab into Roberts's stomach. Davy heard the younger man's gasp and watched him double over, knees sagging as he struggled to breathe. "Fuck you, Roberts."

Davy turned and climbed the stairs. He locked the bedroom door, grabbed the ArmaLite in one hand and the remote in the other, moved to the window, and knelt. And all the while the helicopter roared. The man with the megaphone yelled, "One minute."

Fuck them all.

Davy stared through the grimy window. Two Saracens were parked well back from the bridge. The troops had formed a skirmish line along the hedgerow on the far side of the river. They'd not risk being shot at, just lie there and wait for the buggers behind to flush him out. The ones from the Saracens were backstops.

He sat with his back to the wall. Damn you, Mike Roberts. Damn you to hell. Now there was no chance to avenge Da, no chance to make it right for the mistake with the wee girl, no chance to keep his promise to Sean.

The voice in the sky roared, "We're coming in."

Davy turned back to the window. The Brit shites were still behind the hedge. He scanned the ditches. There were no troops on the Ravernet side of the river. He closed his ears to the din and concentrated. There might be a way to get to the wood and the motorbike.

Marcus retched and tried to haul in a lungful of air. All his years boxing and he hadn't seen that one coming. He was still struggling to draw breath when the door slammed back. A paratrooper and a man in a dark green RUC uniform stood in the open doorway. He could not make out their features in the kitchen's dim light but could see the Ruger revolver in the policeman's right hand. Marcus's password came out in a strangled whisper. "Whigmaleerie." He saw a rifle muzzle swinging in his direction. "Whigmaleerie, for Christ's sake." He swallowed as the soldier lowered the SLR.

"You the British agent?"

Marcus nodded.

"Where's the other bloke?"

Marcus hesitated. Was there a chance Davy could make a run? He saw the paratrooper glance up the stairs. Marcus shrugged and said, "In the bedroom."

He watched the soldier race up the stairs two at a time. The impatient bastard should have waited for backup. Another trigger-happy hero. Marcus tried to follow but he was still winded. He struggled to yell at the RUC officer, "Davy's no chance of getting out. Tell that soldier not to—" He heard the calico-ripping noise of automatic fire, harsh against the basso thrumming of the helicopter's blades.

Another sharper-sounding burst, a muffled yelp, and the para's body smashed against the bannister, spread-eagled like a sagging crucified Christ. His SLR crashed to the kitchen floor.

Marcus spun on the RUC officer. He'd moved closer. Jesus, he thought it was the man who had called himself Fred, the one who had interrogated Marcus and split his lip. "What the hell are you people doing?"

The RUC man holstered his gun and stood, legs braced, hands behind his back. "Our job, son."

"Christ, man, I told the major not to mount a raid. Now I've no bloody chance of contacting the senior Provos."

"Is that what you were meant to be doing?" The officer strolled to where the dead Para had dropped his rifle.

"No. I was looking for fucking leprechauns." Marcus lowered himself onto a chair, nursing his bruised gut. Why should he even give a damn about contacting more Provos? Now that he was safe, he'd get out of this stupid cloak-and-dagger business. Perhaps the major would be satisfied that Harold Wilson was safe. Marcus sincerely hoped so. He looked up and shuddered as he saw the dead para, and he wondered what was happening to Davy McCutcheon.

Marcus watched the RUC man stoop and carelessly pick up the SLR. "Are you going after McCutcheon?" Marcus asked.

"No."

Davy crouched in the corner of the bedroom and stared at the splintered wood round the door lock where the Brit had tried to shoot the door open. Stupid git. Davy's return burst, fired blind from his ArmaLite, had punched neat holes in the paneling and been rewarded by a satisfying yell. One of the bastards down, but there'd be more coming. And soon.

Davy shook his head. His ears rang from the row of the recent gunfire and the incessant thunder of the helicopter overhead. It was time to get away the fuck as fast as possible. He crawled to the window and raised his head. Good. The troops were all still on the far riverbank. And that was where the shites were going to stay.

Davy dropped the automatic rifle, grabbed the model aeroplane control, looked out through the window, pointed the transmitter, and pressed the button.

He watched sixty pounds of Semtex erupt in a red, black, and orange fireball. The blast drowned the sounds of the chopper. As the span rose lazily, then blew apart, blocks of masonry crashed into the river and onto the road. Shrapnel peppered the hedgerow where the soldiers lay. That would give the buggers something to occupy them while he made his dash for the wood.

Davy glanced back at the framed Madonna, her eyes full of all the sadness of the world, then crossed himself. The old, oft-spoken words of the Hail Mary gave him no comfort.

He left the ArmaLite on the floor. He couldn't hope to shoot it out in the open with half the British army. The weapon would be nothing but an encumbrance. He hurled up the window sash, crawled through the window, hung by his outstretched arms, let go, and dropped heavily to the ground. He felt the shock jar through his leg and screamed as the bone snapped.

"No!" Davy lay on the ground. He tried to stand, but his leg would not take his weight. "No!"

In the distance he could see a line of soldiers moving toward him across the ploughed field. The blast might have taken out one or two, but not enough. They'd forded the stream and were coming for him.

He started to drag himself toward the wood, inching along a furrow, useless leg jarring, sending bone-grating shocks through him. It was hopeless and he knew it.

He lay on his back, hands clasped round his thigh. Closing his eyes, he remembered what Fiona had said, how she knew he was trying to atone for the death of the Hanrahan girl. One good raid would wipe the slate clean.

He opened his eyes and saw moss on the eaves and above the blue of the heavens. He was on his way to his personal purgatory with no hope of absolution. He'd see that little girl for the rest of his life. He'd have plenty of time to think of her. He'd been betrayed by a man he'd come to trust, and because of Mike Roberts—or whatever the bastard's real name was—Davy would have all the time in the world to mourn for the Hanrahan girl, and to grieve for the life he might have had with Fiona. There was nothing but time in the British jail at Long Kesh. Maybe McCusker had got off easy.

Marcus's ears rang as the sounds of the chopper were drowned by an almighty thunderclap. He flinched. The windows rattled and two cups tumbled off the dresser.

"That was the bridge." Marcus knew precisely what the charges he had built would have done and he'd have to answer for that at the inevitable debriefing. "Stupid. There was no need for that to happen." He looked up at the RUC man who stood at the far side of the table, SLR held loosely across his body. Marcus glanced at the open door. "Where the hell's the rest of your squad?"

The RUC man put one foot up on a kitchen chair. "I ordered them to wait outside."

"Christ. You reckoned the pair of you could take out a committed Provo? You've got one soldier killed. McCutcheon was waiting for you. Someone tipped him off about your raid."

The RUC man lifted his foot from the chair and stood erect. "How do you know that?" Marcus heard the same tone in the man's voice that he'd used during the mock interrogation.

"Because somebody phoned McCutcheon and told him."

"You sure?"

Marcus looked up into a pair of hard, lifeless eyes. "Of course I'm bloody well sure."

"That would interest your major." The eyes narrowed.

"Maybe, but he was after senior Provos."

"Is that what he told you?"

"Yes."

Fred shook his head. "You were had, son. I think he was after informers." Eric Gillespie snapped the SLR against his shoulder and put one 7·62-mm full-metal-jacket round between Marcus Richardson's staring hazel eyes.

SIXTY

Major Smith walked up the steps of the Clinical Sciences Institute and stopped at the hall porter's office.

"Orthopaedics?"

"Ward eighteen." The porter pointed to a staircase and said, "Up two flights and follow the corridor."

The major walked on. It was a shame about Richardson. According to Gillespie, the paratrooper had been shot by the PIRA bomber and spun and fired as he fell. Richardson was killed instantly. And no way to prove it hadn't happened exactly as Gillespie had reported. The Provo—Gillespie said his name was Davy McCutcheon—had broken his leg trying to escape, was captured and taken to the Royal.

Things had not worked out the way the major had planned. Not at all. He had expected the farmhouse to be deserted yesterday morning, clear evidence that someone—to be precise, Eric Gillespie—had warned the Provos off. The bomber and Richardson were there when the attack went in. Either they had not been warned or the warning had come too late. Richardson could have told the major what had transpired, but Richardson was dead. Conveniently dead, as far as Gillespie was concerned. But McCutcheon might have the information, and if he did the major would get it out of him. He permitted himself a tight smile as he strode along a rubber-tiled corridor. He'd wring McCutcheon dry.

Siobhan had slept late. She hadn't slept well since Mike had gone off on that stupid business with Uncle Davy. And Dad had been no help. He hadn't a clue where they were. Didn't seem to care. All he could think about was how soon he and Mum could leave for Toronto. They were out at Canada House this morning finishing up their paperwork. Dad was right about emigrating. The sooner the whole family and—she smiled in spite of her concerns—that pigheaded Mike Roberts were in Canada, the better.

She took a cup of tea and the newspaper through to the parlour, sat, balanced the cup and saucer on the arm of the chair, and glanced at the front page. More bloody violence. She glanced at a clean-cut British officer staring at her from a head-and-shoulders photograph.

She tutted as she read the story. There'd been an attempt on the life of the British prime minister. A British agent, Lieutenant Marcus Richardson, had infiltrated the PIRA and uncovered the plot, but was killed in the attack that captured the man who was to have assassinated Harold Wilson. She felt a pang of sorrow for the young man, glanced at his photograph again, lifted her teacup, and read on.

The story said that a terrorist, David McCutcheon, had been arrested. Uncle Davy? Good God. Uncle Davy? And Mike was with him. It couldn't be. She stared at the picture. The long hair and ridiculous moustache weren't there, but she recognized the eyes, Mike's eyes. Mike Roberts had been a man called Marcus Richardson?

The teacup slipped from her fingers. This couldn't be true. She looked hard at the face before her. Sweet Jesus, no matter what his real name was, she was looking into her Mike's eyes. Mike was dead? He couldn't be.

She stood, laid the paper on the seat, knelt, and busied herself picking up the broken china, piece by piece. She'd have to get a cloth and clean up the spilled tea. The milk in it would stain the carpet if she didn't hurry up. She put the shards on the newspaper and saw his picture again. It was Mike. She knew it was Mike. She hugged herself, keening as she rocked and whispered his name. "Mike." And her tears flowed like Mourne freshets after the cold Ulster rains.

A pair of blue plastic swinging doors opened onto the main corridor of the Royal Victoria Hospital. Light filtered in through skylights and dappled the hospital-yellow-painted walls. Nurses in blue uniforms, orderlies, white-coated doctors, members of the public jostled each other as they passed to and fro. There was an antiseptic smell. The major made his way through the throng. He could see the ward numbers on small plaques above the doorways. Ward 9. Not far to go.

What a waste. Weeks of planning, waiting, and now, unless Mc-Cutcheon cooperated, nothing to show for it that would satisfy Sir Charles beyond reasonable doubt. Admittedly, Richardson's intelligence had aborted an attempt on the life of Harold Wilson, and the major had been able to give Harry Swanson the name of Brendan Mc-Guinness. If Harry's boys grabbed McGuinness, it might be enough to keep the major in the army, but he still wanted that bastard Gillespie. McCutcheon had better give.

The major turned onto ward 18. He could see the rows of beds in the public area. Two armed constables stood outside the door to a private room. A handsome dark-haired woman argued with one of the policemen. "I've every right to see him. I'm his wife."

"Sorry, madam. No visitors."

The major approved. It wouldn't be the first time the Provos had sprung a wounded member from hospital, or killed one in his bed if they thought he might give away vital information. And they were not above using women as assassins. He produced his pass and handed it to one of the policemen.

"Thank you, Major Smith."

The woman stepped in front of him. "You're an officer. Tell this man to let me by."

He was struck by the deepness of her black eyes. If she was the Provo's wife, the major could almost feel sorry for her. More to the point, he might be able to use her. "What's your name?"

"Fiona."

He did not know if McCutcheon was married, but this woman obviously cared for him. He said, "Wait here," as he pushed the door open.

McCutcheon's bed was surrounded by curtains hanging from a rail suspended from the ceiling. The major stretched out his hand.

The lace bedroom curtains of 18 Myrtlefield Park hid two men from enquiring eyes. Stark on its tripod, a Nikon with a telephoto lens was aimed at the front door of 15B across the street.

"That's him," the shorter of the two watchers said as a dark-haired man wearing spectacles, their left lens replaced by some opaque material, came out through the door opposite. The shutter clicked and the automatic mechanism whirred as the film advanced.

They'd been in the bedroom since last night, when they had been told by their CO, Harry Swanson, that a suspect he was after had been spotted in Andersonstown and trailed back to Myrtlefield Park. It had taken some very persuasive talking to coerce the owner, a retired banker, to let the surveillance team move into his house. He'd not be sorry to see one of them go to deliver the film to HQ. The other would keep a watching brief behind the lace.

The major pulled the bedside curtains back and looked down on McCutcheon. His left leg, swathed in a plaster cast and hanging from a gantry, was suspended by wires attached to a steel pin that seemed to go right through the lower end of his thigh bone. An intravenous solution dripped from a bottle. McCutcheon's eyes were open but looked unfocused. The major guessed it was an effect of morphine. That might be helpful. The man's guard would be down under the influence of the narcotic.

Major Smith sat on a chair beside the bed. "McCutcheon?"

McCutcheon's head turned. He blinked. The man's pupils were tiny, but his stare said, "Fuck you."

The major had not expected this interrogation to be easy. "You're David McCutcheon?"

No reply.

"Of Conway Street."

Silence.

"McCutcheon, you shot one soldier. There were two killed in the explosion. You'll get life. I can make it easier for you. Answer one question."

McCutcheon closed his eyes.

The major stood, leaned over, grabbed the stainless-steel pin, and shook it. The jagged bone ends inside the cast would grate.

McCutcheon opened his eyes and moaned.

"Were you warned about our attack?"

A bead of sweat appeared on the Provo's forehead.

The major felt the steel pin, cold in his hand, and yanked. Hard.

"Were you?" He listened to the throaty whimper and the harsh sound as McCutcheon ground his teeth. There were no more beads on McCutcheon's face. The drops had coalesced to form a sweaty sheen. He said nothing.

Tug. "Were you?"

McCutcheon's words were slurred. "Fuck . . . you."

The major took a deep breath. He knew that men who would break because of physical pain did so early. Others could hold out for days. McCutcheon was clearly one of the latter, and the major was running out of time. He bent over and whispered into McCutcheon's ear, "Fiona."

"What?"

"Fiona's outside."

McCutcheon's eyes widened. He muttered, "Fiona."

"Would you like to see her?" The major waited. He'd be surprised if a fully alert McCutcheon would say yes, but he was muddled by the morphine. "Would you like to see Fiona?"

McCutcheon's nod was nearly imperceptible.

"Were you warned?" The major saw the big man's eyes mist as he clamped his mouth shut.

"Davy," the major said gently, "unless you tell me, you'll never see her. I'll get her as an accomplice. She'll do twenty years." It wasn't true, but McCutcheon might believe him. "Twenty years, Davy."

"You cunt."

"Twenty years."

"Fuck you to hell, you British bastard. I was phoned."

The major smiled. He'd got him. He'd got Gillespie. Someone had warned McCutcheon. "That wasn't too hard, Davy, was it?" The major turned to leave. He had never enjoyed seeing a man cry.

As he passed the sentries, the woman named Fiona blocked his path. "I want to see him."

The major shook his head. "Sorry, dear. The constable was right. No visitors."

SIXTY-ONE

Brendan McGuinness bent over the mahogany table staring at a newspaper lying on the polished wood. He knew that he stood accused by the headline—"Provos Try to Kill Wilson"—and the subhead, "Attack Foiled by Senior RUC Officer with Help of Army. Terrorist Taken." The news had been all over the television this morning. The Brits' propaganda machine was rubbing the Provos' noses in their own dirt.

Brendan screwed his good eye shut and rubbed at the itch in the empty socket under the leather patch. What a fuckup—and all because Sean Conlon had been softhearted about that broken-down old bastard McCutcheon. What did it matter if McCutcheon had been taken? The explosives team that had been training in Libya would be back in Northern Ireland next week. McCutcheon was expendable. They were well shot of him. At least the old bugger would know enough to keep his mouth shut—not tell the Security fuckers about Sean's stupid warning phone call.

Damn Conlon. He'd disobeyed a direct order, challenged Brendan's authority. He'd have to be brought to heel. Brendan began to pace—short, angry steps. He'd been right to send Sean to Dublin to brief Army Council. That got the insubordinate shite out of the way, gave Brendan time to decide how to deal with the man. Forget about Conlon, he told himself. Think about what can be salvaged.

It was unlikely that their ability to monitor British signals traffic would be compromised. There could be no suspicion cast on Gillespie—indeed, the media were making him out to be a hero, the man who'd saved their prime minister. So what if the carefully planned attack hadn't got Wilson? There would be plenty of other targets and the

Brits' little propaganda victory would soon be old news. Brendan allowed himself a suggestion of a smile. The war wasn't lost. Not by a long shot.

The major spoke softly into his office phone. "Thank you, Sir Charles, although saving the PM was an extraordinary bit of luck . . . Yes, it is a great pity about young Richardson. Brave chap."

The major half listened as Sir Charles explained the difficulty his office was going to have in breaking the news to the young man's parents. That was Sir Charles's problem. As far as the major was concerned, it was like the parachute jumps in Borneo. "You can't make an omelette," and all that. He waited until Sir Charles had finished.

"Actually, sir, I phoned to tell you I've got our man . . . the mole . . . Yes, I'm sure . . . senior RUC officer . . . I know, sir. It'll cause a bit of a stink when you have to tell the chief constable. I fully understand. Perhaps it would be better to say nothing until it's all sewn up—but it will be. I just need a day or two . . . I will, sir. You'll hear the minute I've got the final bits of evidence . . . Thank you, Sir Charles. Thank you very much."

The major hung up and said softly, "Lieutenant Colonel Smith." He smiled. *Lieutenant Colonel.* And the man who was going to make it happen, that abrasive bastard Gillespie—the media's current darling—was waiting in a detention cell. Gillespie had come to the major's office in response to an earlier phone call. His "you're out of your mind" had cut no ice with the two MPs who hauled him away. Major Smith hoisted his feet onto his desk and lit a cigarette. Gillespie could wait—just a little longer.

The one-tonner swung into Myrtlefield Park, stopping in the middle of the street. Six armed soldiers dismounted, led by Harry Swanson, and doubled into the garden of number 15. Swanson pounded on the front door. A man appeared and immediately tried to slam the door, but Swanson smashed it back and disappeared inside, followed by three men. Three more soldiers crouched in the garden covering the housefront. Another squad had been posted at the rear of the building.

Someone was clambering through a downstairs window.

"Oi, you." A soldier swung his SLR. "Freeze."

The shot from the Provo's automatic missed the soldier and shattered a window in the house opposite. The sound of breaking glass was drowned by the crack of an SLR and the howling of the would-be escapee.

Harry Swanson ignored the racket outside. A short man, bespectacled, one lens of leather, sat at a long table. "What the fuck?"

"Stay there," Swanson yelled. "Hands on your head. You." He pointed to the second man in the room. "Against the wall."

The man obeyed.

"Sergeant. Watch them. Corporal. With me." Harry Swanson strode into the room next door and halted. He stopped, eyes wide. He recognized the Howa Machinery ArmaLite crates stacked along one wall. Two boxes in the far corner were labeled in Czech. He had stumbled onto a cache of Semtex. And rocket-propelled grenades. Their tubes were in a corner.

The rest of the equipment in the room puzzled him. An electrical panel sat on a desk. From a communications board on the desktop, red and blue wires equipped with male connectors ran to sockets in the panel. He was in a telephone exchange.

"Jesus," he said quietly, "Jesus Christ. A PIRA communications centre."

Harry smiled. Not a bad catch. The bloke next door was Brendan McGuinness. The bold boyos would sorely miss their arms and explosives cache, and this telephone setup must be important.

He might pick up some useful information if the board was active. He slipped on a set of earphones. His ears filled with a static hum, then an English voice said, "Right, Sergeant. Send Two Platoon to Crossmaglen. Get one of your Saladins back here to Thiepval HQ." There was the sound of a telephone connection being broken, more static, then the whirrs of a number being dialed.

"Hello? Palace Barracks?"

"Yes, sir."

"Brigadier Hutchinson here, Thirty-nine Brigade. Put me through to your officer of the day."

Swanson clamped his hands over the earphones, listening, concentrating, wondering. It couldn't be. It couldn't. The bloody Provos had a tap into the Thiepval Barracks switchboard. The enormity of his discovery hardly bore thinking about. No wonder the Provos could strike at will. He removed the headset.

Swanson smiled. John Smith would be delighted. Of course, because the PIRA had been using such sophisticated surveillance methods, they wouldn't have needed an inside man. Poor old John. He'd been so utterly convinced he'd been on the track of a mole, was going to pull off the intelligence coup of the war. Swanson's smile faded. He had to feel sorry for his colleague. All that effort, all the man's hopes pinned on catching a nonexistent informer. And the answer had been here in Myrtlefield Park, right under their noses.

No wonder the Provos had known when a patrol would go out looking for a decoy arms dump, were able to set a mine under Ravernet bridge. Crafty buggers. John Smith would be very interested in this setup—and, Harry thought, without John having named McGuinness, they would never have stumbled onto it. Perhaps the old SAS man could still get some of the recognition he so much wanted.

The major shifted on the wooden chair. It was cold in the cell and they'd been in there for four hours. The glare of the overhead light cast his shadow on the metal table on the far side where Eric Gillespie sat, dressed only in his shirt and beltless pants.

He was coldly defiant now, but the major was determined to make the bastard crack open like a rotten walnut. Although the circumstantial evidence was strong, very strong, the major wanted a confession. He wanted to see Gillespie abased. He rested his elbows on the tabletop, folded his hands, and leaned his chin on his fingers.

"Eric, you could save us all a lot of bother if you'd tell me the truth."

Gillespie sat, arms folded, and met the major's stare.

"You were the only one outside the army who knew we were going to raid the farm."

Gillespie said nothing.

"McCutcheon told me they were warned. Who else could have tipped them off?"

"I've no fucking idea. It wasn't me."

"It was, Eric."

Gillespie examined the quick of a fingernail and ignored the major.

The major rose. "I'm off." He shivered. "Cold in here. I think I'll have a bite and a bath." He moved to the door and knocked. "Corporal." The major turned to Eric, glanced down at his bare feet, and said, "Do try to keep warm."

It was cosy in the major's office. He'd popped in to collect some notes, then he'd be off to have that meal and a bath. He'd turn in early tonight and continue Gillespie's interrogation tomorrow. The MP had orders to ensure that the prisoner did not sleep. Tomorrow morning, Gillespie would be cold, hungry, tired, and, in consequence, more vulnerable.

The major wanted that.

He stretched, picked up the file, and started for the door. Someone knocked.

He opened the door. "Harry?"

"Sorry to disturb you, John."

"Come in, man."

"I wanted you to hear this as soon as possible." Harry smiled and his dimples deepened. "We got McGuinness. Nasty piece of work. Shame he tripped getting into our one-tonner. Doc says he'll be laid up for weeks with a fractured skull. His trial'll have to wait 'til he's better."

The major spared little thought for one PIRA man. If Harry's squaddies had beaten the hell out of McGuinness, it was none of the major's business. "Blokes like him should watch their steps."

Harry laughed. "We found something else."

"Oh?"

"McGuinness's mob had a direct phone tap into Thiepval."

"Really?" The major tried to sound interested.

"Don't you see? All this mole business was a red herring."

"Would you mind repeating that?"

"The Provos had a telephone tap into the Thiepval switchboard. We found the equipment in their flat. They've been listening to our conversations for months."

"I don't see what that has to do with my mole." The major wondered if he was being deliberately obtuse, but he could not—or would not—see what Harry was driving at.

"Look, John. Your job was to find a leak. You've found it. Not what you expected, but it's how the PIRA were able to keep one jump ahead."

"Rubbish. Gillespie's the mole."

"I'm sorry, John. There never was a mole. It was a bugging operation."

"Gillespie's as guilty as sin."

"You really think so?"

The major sat heavily in his chair. "Of course I do. Gillespie knew about every one of the raids I examined. He was the only one who knew we were going to attack McCutcheon in the farmhouse."

"He wasn't. Anyone listening to the telephone traffic from HQ would have had exactly the same gen, including Richardson's warning call from the farmhouse. It came through Thiepval switchboard."

The major's head drooped, and for several moments he said nothing. "Harry, I know, I bloody well *know* Gillespie's as guilty as bedamned." He could feel his prize slipping away like a trout that has snapped the leader.

"He may be, but how can you make it stick? The tap gives a perfectly reasonable explanation for the leaks. Have you any other hard evidence?"

The major set the file he had been carrying on the desktop. He ignored the question. "Go on." He forced his words to be calm.

"Not even a Diplock court would convict him now. I'd leave him alone if I were you."

"Would you?"

"Bloody right. Have you any idea how arresting him would bugger up army-RUC—"

"He's in my custody."

The major saw Harry take a step back, as a healthy man will avoid a leper. "Oh, Christ."

John Smith's head drooped. He could see little sympathy on Harry's face but still had to ask.

"You're absolutely sure?"

"Absolutely."

Smith hesitated, then said stiffly, "Thank you, Harry. You've been a great help." He reached for the phone. "If you don't mind, I'd like you to leave. I've some phone calls to make."

SIXTY-TWO

"I didn't bring you here to London, Swanson, to have you make excuses for Smith. Your loyalty to him is commendable, but I have to clean up the god-awful mess he's created. My minister is livid."

"Yes, sir." Harry Swanson could not meet Sir Charles's glare.

"It's a bloody shambles. The RUC are barely on speaking terms with the army. One of their best men arrested by some unheard-of, self-appointed James Bond. Christ Almighty." At least, Sir Charles thought, news of Gillespie's arrest had not been made public—yet. "We have to restore some semblance of working relations."

"It'll be tricky, sir."

"I'm well aware of that. Come on, man. You're supposed to be an expert on Ulster. Think."

Harry Swanson took a deep breath. "Have you seen today's papers, sir?"

"No."

"According to the *Sunday Telegraph,* Eric Gillespie should get a pension and a gold clock. The 'ero who save our 'arold."

The Yorkshire man's accent was grating, and that was no way to refer to the PM.

"Mr. Harold Wilson, I think you mean."

"Sorry, sir. But *The Mail on Sunday* wants Gillespie knighted."

"You mean we should fete the man?"

"Yes, sir. Maybe the RUC would see that as a kind of atonement for our sins."

"Smith's sins."

"Sir."

Sir Charles nodded once, sharply. But I think a CBE should be enough. I'll see to it. I'll let Sir Graham Shillington know—if he'll talk to me—have him pass the word to their chief constable." Sir Charles liked the idea. "You know, Swanson, we might just go one better. If we really get the PR people working—gallant RUC officer, brilliant detective work, typical of the calibre of the Ulster police—it could smooth quite a few ruffled feathers. They might even consider promoting Gillespie."

"I think I'd leave promotion up to them, sir. The coppers don't take kindly to being told what to do."

Sir Charles raised one eyebrow. "Nobody's going to tell them—but a hint or two in the right places . . ."

"Yes, sir."

"Excellent." Sir Charles fiddled with the knot in his tie. "Now that only leaves one more problem. I asked Sir Graham for quite a bit of help—names of RUC personnel who knew about army operations. It wouldn't be too difficult for him to wonder why and to whom I was passing the information."

"Do you think he could connect you to—"

"Don't be ridiculous. Of course he could."

Swanson took a very deep breath, lowered his head, then looked directly at his superior and said, "You could try coming clean, sir."

Sir Charles glared at Harry Swanson as a bull might a matador. "Tell Sir Graham that Smith was my man? Rubbish."

"Smith was once very sick with malaria."

Sir Charles's eyes widened. There might be something here. "Malaria, eh? Can it spoil a man's ability to think straight?"

"Apparently the high fever affects the brain, sir."

"I could use that. Suggest that he'd broken down on the job. Temporary loss of his faculties. In Ulster on a simple fact-gathering task. Exceeded his remit. I like that Swanson. I like that." Sir Charles clapped Harry on the shoulder.

"Thank you, sir."

"Pity about Smith. It'll be the end of him—but you know the old saw about omelettes and eggs." He removed his hand. "Right. Off you go, back to Belfast. I'll sort things out at this end."

As Sir Charles watched Swanson leave, his thoughts turned to his next interview. And he was not looking forward to it.

. . .

In keeping with civil service regulations, the heat had been turned off in Sir Charles's office since the first of April, and the chill in the room reflected the iciness of the worlds spoken by a tall, hazel-eyed man sitting, arms folded, at the opposite side of the desk.

"The whole thing's appalling. Simply appalling. First, we're told our son has been killed in a bomb blast—months ago. Then, out of the blue, you phone to say he was shot dead last Thursday and my wife and I should come to London for a full explanation—and his funeral."

Sir Charles cleared his throat. "It's not the sort of thing one can explain over the telephone."

"I don't see that it can be explained at all. How do you think his mother's taking this?"

"I understand."

"I don't think you do. She wasn't coming here today. I had to leave her in our hotel. I could hardly bring myself to see you." Professor Richardson's voice cracked. "He was our only child. We were proud of him."

"So are we, Professor Richardson. Very proud. His sacrifice saved the life of the prime minister."

"Yes. Well—"

Sir Charles sensed a softening in Marcus's father. "The army is putting him in for the George Cross."

"It won't bring him back."

Sir Charles let the silence hang, then said, "I really think it might help if I told you what happened."

Professor Richardson unfolded his arms and laid his hands palm down on the desktop. "Go on." His gaze held Sir Charles's.

Sir Charles lowered his eyes and said softly, "When Lieutenant Richardson survived the explosion, it was decided that your son might be able to serve his country better as an intelligence operative. It was for his protection that the story about his death was fabricated."

"Surely you could have told his mother and me the truth?"

"Not my call, I'm afraid. The intelligence chaps are a very secretive bunch," said Sir Charles. At the same time, he thought, *I will not accept blame for Mr. John Smith's incompetence.* "Marcus made his own decision," he said, "although I can tell you he was very worried about your being kept in the dark."

Sir Charles wondered why the suggestion of a smile touched Professor Richardson's lips. "It wouldn't have been the first time."

"I beg your pardon?"

"Nothing. Please go on."

"Yes. Well. Marcus volunteered to try to penetrate the Provos—you've no idea how vital such intelligence can be to our forces in Ulster—and he succeeded. I can't tell you how, but it took enormous resourcefulness and courage of a very special kind."

"I know about his courage," Professor Richardson said softly. He looked down at his hands as he rubbed one palm across the other. "You wondered what I meant when I said it wasn't the first time he'd kept me in the dark."

Sir Charles waited.

"When he was very little—five or six—I asked him to walk on a wall. He wouldn't. He was frightened." The professor looked straight at Sir Charles. "Marcus went back by himself, walked on the damn thing, and never said a word to anyone."

"How—"

"How did I find out? Bangor was a small town then. Someone who saw him told me." The professor's voice cracked. "I never told him I knew. Now I never will."

"A truly remarkable young man."

"I know."

"I did not have the privilege of knowing your boy, sir, but without him, there's absolutely no doubt—none whatsoever—that Mr. Wilson would have been killed. Your son has earned the gratitude of the entire country." Sir Charles leaned forward, his right hand almost touching the professor's. "And you and Mrs. Richardson have my deepest condolences." He steeled himself to deliver his next words. "And my most sincere apologies for the way you have been misled."

The professor said nothing.

Sir Charles withdrew his outstretched hand, dropped it into his thigh, and rubbed aimlessly as he searched for his next words.

"Sir Charles, I'm not entirely satisfied—I never will be, but I think I can help my wife see that our boy's death did have a purpose."

"Thank you."

"I accept your apology—with reservations." Professor Richardson rose.

Sir Charles stood. "Under the circumstances, sir, you have been more than gracious." He moved round the desk and offered his hand. Professor Richardson's grip was firm. As the professor turned to leave, Sir Charles said, "There is just one more thing."

"Yes?"

"The funeral. It's tomorrow. In Bangor. The army will fly you and your wife over, of course."

The professor's lips tightened before he said in a low voice, "I hate funerals."

"We'll send a car to take you to the heliport. Ten thirty."

"My wife can't possibly go on her own."

Sir Charles could see the effort the man was making before Professor Richardson said, "We'll be ready."

SIXTY-THREE

The coffin was draped in a Union Jack. The rain lashed down in stair rods blackening the reds and blues of the flag and drenching the guard of honour and the huddled mourners. The army chaplain's words were barely audible over the soughing of the wind in a nearby stand of elms.

Siobhan stood, head bowed, apart from the others. They would not know who she was—probably thought she had no right to be there. None of them could know how much she had loved him. In her hand she held a rose—its petals, scarlet on the night he'd given it to her, now withered.

She watched as the flag was removed and folded. It was the standard of the people her dad and her uncle Davy called the enemy. How could a lovely man like Mike have been her enemy? How? She would have forgiven his deceit in his life, and as she had told her father when he had asked her not to go to the funeral, she would forgive Mike in his death.

She stared at the sky, black clouds layered like ragged slates on a decrepit roof, the rain pouring through, cold on her upturned face.

The movements of the soldiers caught her eye as they tailed onto the ropes to lower the coffin. She shuddered and hugged herself, arms across her chest, hands on her shoulders, fighting the day's rawness and the iciness within her very soul. She let her cheek fall onto the back of her gloved left hand, feeling it against her skin, the kid leather damp yet soft as his touch. Oh, Mike. Oh, Mike.

She glanced at the guard of honour and at a tall, bareheaded man wearing a dark raincoat. He stood rigidly, one hand holding a woman's hand as his other tried to keep an umbrella over her head. He had Mike's hazel eyes. Was he Mike's—no, she corrected herself, Marcus's—father, the weeping woman his mother?

Siobhan would not cry. She thought she had no tears left.

She flinched as the soldiers fired the feu de joie. The ragged volley scared a murder of crows from the elms. The black birds wheeled across the sky, their cawing and complaining a lament for the dead.

A bugler sounded "The Last Post," its liquid notes rising, falling, dying—their melancholy hers, their finality, Mike's. She could no longer hold back her tears, and her body shook to her sobbing. In her grief she barely noticed the shouted orders, the soldiers marching away, the departure of Marcus's father and mother.

When she was able to calm herself, able to see that, apart from a sexton, she was alone, she moved to the lip of the grave. The man withdrew, leaving his spade in the mound of earth. She could smell its damp mustiness. She looked down at a strip of polished wood, half hidden by brown soil.

"Good-bye, Mike," she whispered. "I love you."

She knelt, bowing her head and crossing herself, murmured, "Hail Mary, full of grace, the Lord is with thee. Blessed art Thou among women, and blessed is the fruit of Thy womb, Jesus." She let his rose fall. "Holy Mary, mother of God, pray for us sinners, now and at the hour of our death."

AUTHOR'S NOTE

This is a work of fiction. It is set in Belfast in 1974. Every effort has been made to ensure accuracy in the descriptions of the city, the political events of the time, and the organizational structure of both the Provisional IRA and the British Security Forces.

It is a matter of record that the Security Forces were in some disarray in 1974 and that interservice rivalries existed. Harold Wilson did visit Ulster on April 18. The Provisional IRA did use a flat in Myrtlefield Park and did have a direct telephone tap into the Thiepval switchboard. No senior member of the Royal Ulster Constabulary has been suspected of, or convicted of, treason.

The technical details of the explosive devices used in the story are authentic. I am deeply indebted to Special Constable Yves Pelletier, Police Explosives Technician, Royal Canadian Mounted Police. Yves has given generously of his expertise and, more importantly, has confirmed that there is nothing in these pages that is not already well known by the bomb makers of terrorist organizations.

It is not possible to create a work like this without referring to real people. Historical figures are named and the positions they held are identified. The fictional characters are mine, and any resemblance of theirs to anyone, living or dead, is purely coincidental.